Joy Redefined

by

Teresa Slack

© 2015 by Teresa Slack
Published by GraceArbor Press

All rights reserved. No part of this publication may be reproduced, stored in a retrieval system, or transmitted in any form or by any means without prior written permission of the publisher. The only exception is brief quotations in printed reviews.

This is a work of fiction. Names, characters, incidents, and dialogues are products of the author's imagination and are not to be construed as real. Any resemblance to actual persons, living or dead, is purely coincidental.

Also by Teresa Slack

Runaway Heart
The Ultimate Guide to Darcy Carter

Tender Blessings Series
Love Begins
A Little Goodbye

The Jenna's Creek Series
Streams of Mercy
Redemption's Song
Evidence of Grace
A Jenna's Creek Wedding *(A Christmas Novella)*
Legacy of Faith

Nine Brides for Cowboy Creek
Rennie
Eliza
Carrie
Bridget
Katie
Marianne
Scarlett
Rachael
Amelia

Willow Wood Brides Series
A Lawman for Lisette
A Love Letter for Jessa
A Dream for Harper
A Wedding for Felicity
A Hero for Ellie
A Cowboy for Meggan

Thoughts from Readers

"Nail-biting suspense told with humor and real-life honesty. Must read." *Reader Reviewer*

"I would best compare Teresa's writing style to Angela Hunt or Terry Blackstock." *Reader Reviewer*

"Slack outdid herself on this one!" *Reader Reviewer*

"A reluctant hero! Joy does not fit the mold." *Reader Reviewer*

"Five Stars! Stand up for what you believe in, or else live with what you don't." *Aryn the Libraryan*

"Hilarious and suspenseful at the same time! I wanted to slap sense into everyone in Joy's life." *Reviewer and Avid Reader*

"Teresa Slack has another winner on her hands. Joy Redefined is a great read…This book keeps you guessing until the end. This is another one of Teresa's books that is a keeper. I give it five stars." *Reader review*

"…The writer did a great job of laying the groundwork for a totally believable transformation in Joy. Good plot, realistic family issues and relationships and an exciting and captivating plot." *Reader review*

With love, to my very own Dorothea Westlake: Marjorie J. Reed who taught me about grace, gentleness, and how God really sees his children.

Chapter 1

I didn't have time to brace for impact. I didn't have time to do anything. One second, I was sitting in traffic waiting through a third light change for my turn to move through the intersection when the screeching of brakes and grinding of metal on metal brought my heart to a standstill.

The front end of my car jerked to the right, jerking my neck and shoulders with it. The airbag exploded against my chest as my hands tightened around the steering wheel in a futile attempt to hold the car in place. I learned later my car moved less than two feet from its original position, but at the moment of impact, it seemed like I had lost control of a runaway train.

My gaze flew to the backseat. Aidan's empty car seat filled the rearview mirror. Just to make sure my son wasn't with me but safe at my mother's where I left him two hours earlier, I fumbled with the seatbelt release and turned completely around to look over the headrest.

A list of errands a half a mile long had convinced me it was worth the trouble and inevitable lecture from Mom to call and beg for a few hours to finish them without my nearly-five-year-old son in tow. I never understood Mom's resistance the few times I asked her to babysit. She loved Aidan and always acquiesced in the end. I suppose it had something to do with her need to win an argument even when none was warranted.

Blood hammered in my ears as I sagged against the console and sobbed with relief.

Thank you, Jesus. Thank you. Thank you. Thank you.

After ascertaining Aidan was safe and the slamming of my heart returned to something resembling its usual rhythm, I did a quick physical survey of myself. My tongue hurt from biting down on it, and my hands smarted from having the steering wheel wrenched within my grasp. But nothing important was bleeding or pierced by an engine part. Even the white steam rising from under the hood looked benign enough.

My gaze came to rest on the sporty red car attached to my Toyota's left front quarter panel. The hood was buckled halfway to the windshield. Steam hissed from there as well, but it looked like my car had taken the brunt of the impact. I gulped. Now that I knew I would live through my first ever traffic accident I began to worry. Scott was going to have a fit.

I was okay. That's all that would matter to my husband of twenty-one years. Right?

I rested my forehead on the steering wheel and thanked God properly I hadn't been hurt. "Please let everyone in the other car be okay too," I finished. Anything else could be worked out among our insurance companies. If only my darling husband would see it the same way.

I could hear him now. "For crying out loud, Joy. Why'd you go and let yourself get hit?"

As if I gave other drivers permission to plow into the front of my car. But somehow the red Pontiac turning against the light would end up my fault. Everything that went wrong in the world—or at least in Scott's world—from dead batteries in the flashlight to Dylan's poor performance in school to rain on the first day of a scheduled vacation ended up my fault.

He meant well. He just didn't like disruptions in his well-ordered life. A traffic accident would rank right up there with emergency dental surgery or having my mother move in for an indeterminate length of time.

I wasn't particularly thrilled about this disruption myself. I was supposed to pick Aidan up by four if there was any hope of avoiding my mother's wrath. Thursday night was her Salsa dance class. She had something on her schedule nearly every night of the week. Dinner out with the girls on Tuesday. Midweek church service Wednesday. Pottery class Saturday afternoons. Now that Mom was semi-retired, she never spent a moment in her condo. For the life of me, I couldn't figure out how someone so busy had the energy to be so cranky.

The clock on the Toyota's dash blinked two-fifty-seven. I'd never hear the end of it if I didn't get the Pontiac's hood out of my car's front end in the next hour.

"I have things to do, Joy," Mom would say, her pert little nose wrinkled in frustration. "It isn't like I didn't sacrifice plenty after your father left us. I did the best I could to make sure you didn't suffer more than you already had. I forfeited my own needs without a word of complaint. Is it too much to ask for a little me-time after all I've done?"

It was an old song, and I knew every verse.

In the immortal words of Winnie the Pooh, *Oh bother.*

Over the grating sound of my mother's voice, Scott's disapproval, and my own thudding heartbeat, I became aware of voices to my left. For the first time, I looked beyond my crumpled fender and spotted a gathering crowd and a red-faced man advancing on my door. He didn't look happy.

My stomach took a nosedive. I was no good at confrontation. It was why my household subscribed to every magazine that called my cell. Why I bought Girl Scout cookies when I was trying to keep sweets out of the house. Why I supported every charity that didn't overtly clash with my Christian values. I couldn't say no, even to perfect strangers. What chance did I have with this goon?

Avoiding confrontation didn't look like an option, so I steeled what little nerve I possessed and reached for my purse.

The contents were scattered across the passenger's side floorboard. It took a moment to locate my cell phone. My shaking fingers closed around it. I straightened and put my hand on the door handle.

"You didn't do anything wrong. You didn't do anything wrong. You didn't do anything wrong," I chanted over and over for courage. I pushed against the door. Nothing happened except for a jolt of pain in my shoulder. I nearly dropped the phone. I winced, braced myself, and tried again, putting a little more force behind the shove. The door popped open with an angry squeal.

I'd never hear the end of this.

I set my feet on the pavement and climbed out on wobbly legs. I didn't have time to bang the door shut with my hip before the red-faced man was upon me.

"What were you thinking? I was in the intersection. Didn't you see me?"

My mouth went dry. This wasn't the way it was supposed to go. If anyone had the right to have her nose out of joint, it was me. "I....I didn't..."

"I know you didn't. You weren't paying attention."

I fortified myself with a deep breath. "I had the light."

My words lacked the conviction I had hoped for. This wasn't my fault. I wasn't a rule breaker. I didn't sample cherries at the grocery store and I always waited for the light. I even reported my correct weight on my drivers' license, for crying out loud.

He jutted his bristly chin in my face. His gut strained dangerously against the buttons of his shirt. I leaned away in case one of those buttons went flying. "Are you sure? Are you positive? If you had waited for the light, you wouldn't have pulled out while I was coming through the intersection."

My conviction turned to doubt. Had I waited? I remembered watching the bank clock across the street and comparing it to the one in the car as the seconds ticked away my afternoon.

"You were supposed to stop," Red-face repeated.

I had helped raise money for an anti-bullying campaign at my son's school a few years ago. I understood that bullies found their worth in tearing others down. Understanding it and steeling myself against it were two different things. If only Scott were here. He wouldn't let this guy talk to *him* this way. Why hadn't I insisted he come downtown to pay Dylan's court fees instead of making me do it? Or better yet, why hadn't Dylan done it? He was a licensed driver, and the court costs for a fender bender four months ago were his problem, not mine. They both knew I hated downtown traffic. They knew I hated parking in the dark narrow parking garage near the courthouse. They certainly knew I was helpless against anyone who pushed me around.

I tried to pull my trembling frame to all of its five feet, four and a half inches. I was a grown woman, perfectly capable of taking care of herself. I hadn't done anything wrong. I was in the right. I wouldn't take the blame for something I hadn't done.

"It was my turn," I said with stronger conviction. "I sat through three red lights. I had the light. You ran into me."

I didn't think it was possible, but his face turned even redder. "Are you kidding me?" He jerked his head around as if looking for a witness to share his incredulity. "Are you going to stand there and tell me you had the right of way and *I* ran into *you*? Why would I do that?" His head bobbed up and down the whole time he talked.

I leaned further away to avoid contact with his nose.

He drew closer. "Why would any sane person do that?"

I would've backed up if my legs weren't already pinned against the bruised Toyota. "I...I, uh, don't know..."

I couldn't let him rattle me. I wasn't wrong. After the light changed, I had let off the brake and eased into the intersection. There hadn't even been time to apply pressure to the gas pedal before he slammed into my car. I was a cautious driver without one point on my driving record. I wouldn't let his posturing make me second guess myself.

He arched his graying eyebrows and cocked his head as if reading my mind and not believing the words trying to formulate on my tangled tongue.

"The light changed," I said. "I had the light."

"If you say that again, I'm going to pop you in the mouth."

I gasped. My jaw went slack. I hadn't been threatened with bodily harm since sixth grade when my lab partner Janine Horowitz blamed me for the less than stellar grade we received for dissecting a frog. I was an adult now. Adult women who participated in prayer chains and baked cookies for bake sales and organized silent auctions for the ladies' ministry didn't get popped in the mouth.

Where were the police? Weren't they supposed to come to things like this and resolve matters peaceably?

Out of the corner of my eye I saw a man in a green polo shirt pushing his way through the crowd. His blond hair was cut in what we used to call a buzz cut so only stubble covered his head. I wondered if he kept his hair short so no one would notice a severely receding hairline.

"Back off, pal," he said to Red-face. "I saw the whole thing. She had the right of way and you know it."

My knees went weak with relief. I wasn't wrong or crazy. I had a witness.

Red-face swerved toward the newcomer. "You couldn't see from where you were."

His bluster had no affect on the other man. "You have no idea where I was."

Red-face glowered at him, then turned his anger back to me, the softer target. He whipped a cell phone from his pocket. "I'm calling the cops. I'm not paying for this. You weren't watching where you were going." He looked at Buzz Cut as he savagely punched numbers into his phone. "She shouldn't have a license. She's a moron and a nuisance."

Buzz Cut was unfazed. "There's no need for name calling. I'm sure the cops are already on their way. They'll figure out who's at fault."

"You better believe they will." Red-face stuck his phone to his ear and glared at me. "I hope you have good insurance."

"Why don't you shut up," Buzz Cut said. He took a protective step closer to me. I resisted the urge to hide behind him. He lowered his voice in compassion. "Are you okay, lady? You're not hurt, are you?"

I shook my head, mute as tears threatened.

He handed me a tissue from his jacket pocket. I hadn't realized how close I was to tears until I saw the tissue. I dropped my cell phone into my front pocket and blew my nose.

"I'm Steve Bruner," Buzz Cut said. "I saw everything. You don't need to worry."

I tried to smile. "Joy Kessler." I sagged against the car as the impact of what happened hit me full force. I thought I might be sick. The Wendy's cheeseburger I ate an hour ago threatened to end up all over Red-face's shoes—not that he wouldn't deserve it.

"I think I need to sit down."

Steve grasped my elbow. "Of course." He wrenched open the Toyota's door with his free hand and guided me into the seat.

The shaking in my legs subsided. I took a sip of my watered-down soft drink to settle my stomach.

Red-face pushed past Steve and practically climbed into the seat beside me.

"The cops are on their way. Don't even think about taking off."

"I wasn't."

"How can she go anywhere after what you did?" Steve said with a sweep of his arm over my front fender.

Red-face puffed out his chest like a territorial dog. "You'd do well to mind your own business, pal."

I held my breath. Red-face outweighed Steve by at least fifty pounds and was a good six inches taller. While he didn't look close to peak wrestling form, I figured he could do some damage to the smaller man if he chose to.

Steve narrowed his gaze and lifted his chin. "I suggest you back off. I'm not some weak woman you can bully around."

Other women would take offense at Steve's comment, but I was too busy fighting the bile rising again in my throat. Physical aggression always made me ill. I couldn't even watch fight scenes on TV. Now one was about to take place in front of me and might even include me. I cast my eyes around the crowd in a panic. Where were the police? Someone needed to diffuse the situation before it turned any uglier.

Red-face poked Steve in the chest with his finger. "You better get out of my face. This isn't your fight. It's between me and her."

Steve's face darkened, but he barked a humorless laugh. "Fight? You fight women?"

Several chuckles and a few catcalls sounded behind us. Red-face glanced around and seemed to realize he wasn't gaining support among the onlookers. He stepped back and his stance relaxed. "I just meant this isn't any of your business. You better not lie to the cops to protect your girlfriend."

"I'll only tell them what I saw."

"Aw, come on," someone called out from the crowd. "If you're not going to fight, get out of the middle of the street. I have to go to work."

Sounds of ascension came from every direction. I couldn't believe the only reason people were hanging around was in hopes of seeing a fight or something equally gruesome. They were probably disappointed there had been no injuries in the accident.

I finally realized I needed to call Scott. Though I dreaded his reaction, I needed his calming presence. I punched the preset number for his cell.

"Why don't you all shut up and get back in your cars," Red-face yelled at the crowd. "This doesn't concern you." He looked again at his car buried in the fender of my Toyota. Renewed fury shone in his eyes as his gaze found mine. "I'm going to miss work tomorrow thanks to you. I can't afford that. You could've killed somebody."

"Joy? Who is that? What's going on?"

I focused on the phone against my ear. "Scott? Oh, thank God."

"Where are you? What's all that noise?"

"I'm at an intersection downtown."

"I thought you were going to the courthouse."

"I am. I mean I did. I've been in an accident."

"An accident? What kind of accident?"

I sighed, suddenly weary of questions and the entire situation. "The usual kind. With the car."

"Very funny."

"You better be talking to your lawyer, lady," Red-face bellowed. "You're going to need a good one."

"Shut up and let the police sort it out," Steve yelled back at him.

"Joy," Scott practically screeched. "Are you listening to me?"

I winced. "Scott, please. There are enough people yelling at me already."

"Who's yelling at you?"

"The driver of the car that hit me."

Red-face leaned nearly inside the car. "I didn't hit you. I want to see your license. Where's your insurance information?"

"Joy, if no one's hurt, just exchange information and get out of there," Scott said. "That guy sounds unstable."

"I can't leave. I don't think the car is drivable."

I heard him suck air between his teeth. "Well, that's just great! As if I don't have enough to worry about today. I can't believe you let yourself get hit."

I nearly punched the end button and threw the phone into the gutter. I tried to remember why I had called my husband. I had known he would put all the blame on me before he even knew what happened, yet I had wanted to hear his comforting voice. I was a glutton for punishment!

17—Joy Redefined

"It was an accident, Scott. It wasn't my fault."

"Accidents don't just happen."

I looked around at the crowd, talking and pointing and shooting me dirty looks. Except for Steve, they looked like they agreed with Scott and I had purposely ruined their day. "I can't explain right now, Scott."

"Is Aidan with you?"

"No, I left him at Mom's."

"At least you did one thing right."

A siren split the air, cutting off my retort, not that I could've come up with one that adequately expressed my chagrin at his reaction.

The crowd turned in the direction of the siren. Red-face glared accusingly to me. "Now we'll get something accomplished."

"Give me your location," Scott yelled over the shriek of the siren. "I'm on my way."

I wanted nothing more than to let my husband take over, but I knew he would lose his temper and say things he'd later wish he hadn't. Besides, I was a big girl. I could talk to the police on my own. "Don't bother, Scott. You'll never get through. Traffic was backed up bad enough before the accident. No one's going anywhere now."

"Hey, lady," Red-face shouted. "Why don't you get off the phone and get over here. The cops will want to talk to you."

"Don't stand there and let that jerk talk to you like that," Scott said.

"It's nothing, Scott. Everyone's just upset."

"You should be upset, too, Joy. Just tell me where you are. I'll get through the traffic somehow."

"Scott, please. I can handle it."

"It doesn't sound like you're handling anything. Don't say a word, Joy. Do you hear me? Not a word until I get there."

"I have to answer the police when they ask what happened."

"Not a word, Joy," he repeated. "You open your mouth and I'll end up putting that guy's kids through college."

"It was a fender bender, Scott. You make it sound like I killed somebody."

"Not a word, Joy. I'll handle everything. Now where are you?"

Reluctantly, I gave him the street names. He ended the call. I exhaled in temporary relief. One less person to yell at me and tell me how the collapse of modern civilization was directly related to me getting out of bed this morning.

With a groan, I remembered I still needed to call my mother.

Clouds covered the sun, and a light rain began to fall. The crowd scattered to their cars. Red-face glared at me as if I were in charge of the weather as well. This day just kept getting better.

"I can't believe you stood there and let that creep put all the blame on you."

I removed the lid from the cookie jar and bit into a chocolate and vanilla sandwich cookie. I didn't particularly like this kind—I kept them on hand for Aidan, reasoning that if they weren't my favorite I wouldn't eat as many—but the conversation with Scott had been going on for twenty minutes and didn't look to be wrapping up anytime soon. I needed fortification.

"I didn't have much choice. I've found in my thirty-nine years of living it's really hard to control what comes out of another person's mouth."

"That doesn't mean you should let someone treat you like a piece of garbage. You should've taken up for yourself."

I chomped down on the cookie. "What did you want me to say? The cops could tell from the skid marks I wasn't to blame. Besides, I was nervous. Everything happened so fast."

Scott stood on the other side of our granite island countertop, his arms crossed over his chest, his face a mask of disapproval. We'd been married long enough for me to read his thoughts as he watched my mouth move around the cookie. My handsome, 38-regular husband had become a bit of a health nut after he realized we were among the older parents in Aidan's playgroup. Occasionally—and very subtly, of course—he tried to force his new lifestyle on me. I gave in a little. I stopped frying anything. I kept fresh fruit and veggies in the house to encourage healthy snacking from the boys. I even went out and bought cute workout clothes and thought of buying a gym membership. One glimpse of myself in the mirror was enough to convince me the world was already a scary enough place without seeing my thighs ensconced in spandex.

He glared at the cookie jar the way Red-face had looked at the wrinkled hood of his car. If Scott had his way, cookie jars would be banned from every home in America.

"It wasn't that fast," he said in response to my comment. "We sat there for hours."

I replaced the lid on the cookie jar and pushed away from the counter. Tears scalded the back of my eyes for the hundredth time that afternoon. Didn't he know I wished I'd handled myself better? The whole time I had watched them hook my beautiful Toyota to the back of a tow truck, and then all the way to Mom's to pick up Aidan in Scott's car while enduring the silence of his disapproval, I had thought of all the things I should've said in response to Red-face's tirades. Believe me, they were zingers. But with my car blocking the intersection and a hundred annoyed onlookers wishing they hadn't taken that street downtown, I couldn't manage a single coherent sentence. It had been God's providence alone that prevented me from turning into a sobbing mass in the middle of the intersection.

"I kept a cool head," I said firmly to keep the tears at bay. "Do you think Jesus would've blown his top?"

"Jesus blew his top all the time. Don't you remember how he talked to the Pharisees? Or the way he turned over the tables in the temple? When the other person needed a dose of the truth, Jesus was right there. In love, yes, but there all the same. Not you, Joy. You never stand up for yourself or what's right."

I exhaled in frustration. The cookie tasted like dust on my tongue. I couldn't win. "The guy was threatening and off balance. Did you really want me to go toe to toe with him?"

"Of course not. I would never suggest you put yourself in danger. But you can't let people push you around. The witnesses I talked to said he yelled and belittled you and you just stood there and took it. Don't you want people to respect you?"

"I'm too old to worry about whether total strangers respect me or not. What I want is respect from my own family."

He didn't seem to notice the dig. "If you want respect, you have to command it."

Tears threatened again. I willed them away. "Are you saying you don't respect me?"

He pushed off the opposite side of the island as if there wasn't enough space between him and his simpering wife. "I'm saying no one likes a mouse, Joy. This little stunt today is going to cause a lot of trouble. Who knows how long the car will be in the garage. Then we have to deal with the insurance company." He heaved a sigh strong enough to set the ceiling fan in motion. "I'm telling you right now, you can be the one on the phone arguing with them over settling the claim. I have enough on my plate already. I don't have time to fix this for you."

"I didn't ask you to."

"Good. This'll be your headache. Maybe next time you'll think twice before letting some ape sideswipe you."

"I didn't *let* anyone sideswipe me."

"All I know is I've driven in this city for twenty years and no one has ever crashed into me. If they did, I sure wouldn't stand there and take the blame for it. I've got to get on the phone and find you a rental car the insurance company will pay for."

I lunged for the cookie jar and extracted another cookie. "I told you I'd do it."

Scott was shaking his head before I even stopped talking. "No way. You'll have us puttering around town in some old beater they charge top dollar for. I'll handle it the way I have to handle everything around here."

I nearly spewed cookie crumbs all over his shirt. Was he kidding? He may have been driving around the city the last twenty years avoiding collisions, but I was the one who ran this house.

"I'll take care of it when I talk to the insurance company," I told him though the thought of spending all day tomorrow arguing with an insurance company and trying to figure out where to pick up my loaner car made me sick to my stomach.

I stomped around the edge of the counter and headed for the door. I couldn't be trusted one more minute in the same room with him…or the cookie jar.

Twin beams of headlights sliced across the bedroom wall. I had been listening to Scott snore and wishing I had taken a sleep aid two hours ago so I wouldn't be wide awake, pondering random unanswerable questions that plagued me whenever I was stressed and sleep alluded me. Like what year they started putting the warnings on rearview mirrors that objects were closer than they appeared, or the name of the actress who played Helen Keller's mother in the original version of *The Miracle Worker*.

I sat up slowly so not to disturb Scott and felt along the floor for my slippers. Dylan, our oldest son and the cause of every stress headache I ever had, was supposed to have worked tonight. I knew he hadn't. Even if he had, it was now two-fifteen in the morning and the fast food restaurant closed at ten.

Employees always had the grills scrubbed and floors mopped and were out of there no later than eleven.

Though I preferred to stay in bed and pretend I hadn't heard him come in, I owed it to my son and the prison system he would someday call home, to find out where he'd been all night.

By the time I reached the hallway he was at the foot of the stairs, one hand on the banister for support as he toed off one shoe and then the other. His shirt bore several assorted food stains and looked like he'd slept in it for three days, which he may very well have done. His jeans looked like they hadn't seen the inside of a washing machine for some time either, but the current style made it hard to differentiate between filth and fashion. Underneath the grunge and shaggy blond hair that obscured his face, he was a handsome kid. He had turned nineteen in January. He was now the age Scott had been when we met in college. When he smiled, which was seldom, he reminded me of that Scott from twenty years ago. Youthful, ambitious, passionate. Sadly, Dylan was none of those things. My heart ached at the sight of him. He was still a little boy underneath the bravado he displayed for the world. A scared little boy who needed his mother.

I stretched out my foot to the top step, then hesitated. Even from where I stood, I could hear his heavy nasal breathing. He was stoned again. A wiser woman would slip back to bed before she was noticed. Dylan would be irritable and surly and not receptive to criticism or correction. Still, this was my house. My rules. I was in charge. It was my responsibility to make him see the error of his ways before it was irrevocably too late.

Oh, bother.

With a deep breath to steel my nerves, I started down the stairs. "I thought I heard you come in," I said in a stage whisper. "Are you hungry?"

Dylan's bare foot dropped heavily to the floor as he straightened. His blond hair fell away from his face to reveal glassy blue eyes. If I tried hard enough, I could almost convince myself he was sleepy, but I'd seen that look too many times.

"I ate already." His voice was thick. "At work."

"Work? Josh called earlier to find out why you didn't come in."

One corner of his mouth pulled into a sneer, reminding me of when Scott yelled at me in the kitchen earlier tonight.

"If you already know everything, what do you want from me?" Dylan didn't bother to keep his voice down.

"I don't want anything Dylan. The truth might be nice, but I've lost hope of ever getting that out of you."

"Is that why you got out of bed? To yell at me?"

I descended the remaining stairs and reached for his arm. He jerked out of reach. I couldn't remember the last time he let me touch him.

"I got out of bed because I love you, honey, and I worry about you. You stay out until all hours. You don't go to work. You won't even talk about enrolling in a few college courses. I don't know where you go or who you're with. I don't want to think about what you do for money."

"Then don't think about it."

I inhaled sharply. "Dylan."

"Josh has no business calling here."

"He's your boss. He thought you were coming to work. So did your father and I. Why didn't you go in?"

He lifted a bony shoulder. "I didn't feel well."

"Yet you felt well enough to stay out until all hours of the night."

He leaned over and scooped up his shoes in one hand. He wobbled as he straightened. I reached out to steady him. "Get off my back, Mom. I'm a legal adult. I'm old enough to die for my country. I shouldn't have to clear every decision I make with you. I met Kyle at the park and we hung out a few hours. What's the big deal?"

"The big deal is your father and I are paying your way. The least you could do is go to work when Josh puts you on the schedule. And it wasn't a few hours. You've been out all night."

"Sorry I'm such a disappointment." He leaned forward and a drop of spittle splashed onto my neck. "I'm sure you're running a tab. I'll pay you back as soon as I can."

With what, I wanted to ask. You won't go to work.

Of course I didn't say that. I never questioned or challenged him. Dylan had been bullying me around since the day he fought his way out of my womb. It was easier to go along and put up as little resistance as possible. I imagined victims of the Holocaust had felt pretty much the same way in dealing with SS officers.

I exhaled. My shoulders slumped in defeat. "Dylan, sweetheart, I never meant to make you think I'm disappointed in you."

"Sure you did, Mom. It's what you've always wanted to say. You just don't have the nerve."

Hadn't Scott accused me of the same thing? I never had the nerve to say anything to anybody.

If you want respect, you have to command it.

Now was as good a time as any to try a little commanding.

"When you said you weren't ready for college you promised your dad and me you'd get a job and keep it. Neither of us liked the idea, but we agreed because you were going to keep your end of the bargain. You've already worked at three fast food places since graduation and it hasn't even been a year."

"Really, Mom? I don't have a calendar."

"There's no need to get sarcastic. You're the one who broke your promise."

"I'm still working."

"When, Dylan, when? You miss half the time. Josh says you have an attitude. He doesn't know how much more leeway he can give you."

"You and Josh are talking about me behind my back? I'm going to kill that little maggot."

"Don't say things like that."

"Why, Mom? Are you afraid to hear what's on my mind?"

More than he'd ever know.

"I don't appreciate talk like that in my house," I said instead.

"Isn't this my house too? Don't I have rights?"

"That's not what I said. You're twisting my words. I can't talk to you when you're like this."

He leaned closer. His foul breath made me draw back. "Like what, Mom? Repulsive?"

"No, Dylan. High. I can't talk to you when you're high. I can't and I won't. I am sick of you coming home like this. I'm sick of you not showing me respect. You won't talk to me anymore the way you have been lately, and you will no longer come into this house stoned where your little brother can see you."

"Who's going to stop me?"

The look he gave me chilled the blood in my veins. I didn't want him to see I was afraid, but I was. Standing here in my own house, not expecting anything more out of him than what any parent expected from her nearly grown son, and I was afraid for my safety like I had been earlier when Red-face threatened to pop me in the mouth.

At least Red-face was a stranger. I hadn't nursed him through childhood illnesses and sacrificed time, money, sleep, and personal dreams and desires to give him everything he needed.

Suddenly, the smile I cherished but seldom saw, spread across Dylan's face. The smile that could always convince me there was a heart of gold in there somewhere, and his chest pounding didn't mean anything, and I shouldn't take life so seriously. He draped an arm across my shoulders and leaned heavily against me. "I'm really sleepy. Can I go to bed now?"

I tried to push him away, but he turned into dead weight. "I fixed you a plate. You should eat something."

"Tomorrow, Mommy," he murmured drowsily.

I couldn't stay mad at him no matter what he did. That was my problem. He knew how to push my buttons. I shifted my weight under him and guided him onto the stairs. Balancing him between my body and the banister, we moved up the staircase. "I love you, Mom."

"I love you, too, Dylan."

"Are you still mad?"

"Yes, Dylan. You have to grow up and take responsibility for your actions."

"I will. Tomorrow. I promise."

"Oh, Dylan."

At the top of the stairs we turned, and I guided him into his room. The floor between the door and the bed was a minefield, strewn with clothes, shoes, and empty food containers. I tried to breathe through my mouth as the smell of sweat, dirty socks, and old pizza assaulted my nostrils. Dylan grew heavier with each step until I was practically carrying him by the time we reached the bed. He fell across the unmade mattress like an anvil. I turned him as best I could and tucked the pillow under his head and a blanket across his body.

"Good night, baby." I bent over and kissed the end of his nose the way I did when he was little. Razor stubble grazed my cheek, reminding me he wasn't little anymore. Someday I'd have to push my baby bird out of the nest.

Just not tonight.

Chapter 2

The next morning when I took Scott's first cup of coffee upstairs and set it on the sink as he was getting out of the shower, I knew he was still irritated. Instead of his usual, "Thank you, sweetheart. Did you sleep well?" I got a terse, "Don't forget to call the insurance company this morning. Talk to Howard. No one else. He's the only one who knows his ear from his elbow down there."

I knew better than to disagree even though I doubted the insurance company with whom we had entrusted everything we owned and held dear for as long as we'd been married employed only Howard and a pack of imbeciles.

Breakfast was the quietest on record since Aidan's birth. Even he picked up on the tension in the kitchen and spent most of the morning swirling his Cheerios around in his milk until he dumped the bowl on the countertop.

Scott merely scooped up the newspaper he'd been reading before the milk reached him and got to his feet. I grabbed a damp dishrag and sopped up the milk while Aidan demanded a fresh bowl of cereal.

"You weren't eating it anyway. That's why you made a mess."

"Pour the boy another bowl of cereal if he wants it." Scott didn't make eye contact. "I make enough money to give him all the cereal he can spill."

I didn't rise to the bait. We seldom argued over money. When I got pregnant with Dylan in college, we decided I would stay home and raise our baby while Scott continued his education and went to work. When the time was right, I'd go back for my degree. No one had to talk me into staying at home with Dylan and learning to run a household on one income. I wanted to do it. Sometimes I wondered if I had missed something by not pursuing a career. I'd see a woman in a business suit and carrying a briefcase, hurrying into an office building downtown and I'd wonder if I made the right choice. Then Dylan would call to me from the backseat and say something utterly adorable, and I'd pity that woman for missing out on what I took for granted.

Okay, so maybe Dylan seldom said anything adorable. He spent his preschool years grinding Cheetos into the upholstery and his pre-pubescent years terrorizing our neighbors' pets. Those days had been a walk in the park compared to his behavior after he hit thirteen. But I still loved being a stay-at-home mom. If Scott occasionally implied my contributions to the household weren't as important as his, it was because he was under a lot of stress. I didn't take it personally.

Or I tried not to. He was my husband, the head of our household, and I loved him with all my heart. That didn't mean I liked him all the time.

After Scott left for work Aidan played with his Hot Wheels cars and I dusted most of the living room with the phone clamped between my ear and shoulder while I was transferred from one department to the next within the insurance company. I usually avoided calling insurance companies even when I knew we had been overcharged on a premium or denied a claim for something our policy covered. Throughout the annals of time, I doubted anyone ever successfully appealed an insurance claim.

This claim wouldn't be denied. Red-face was at fault. Someone polite and cordial would deliver a loaner car here to the house sometime this afternoon without reminding me what a buffoon I was. Still, I couldn't rid myself of the knot in my stomach every time a new voice came on the other end of the line, and I had to begin my explanation of yesterday's events all over again.

Finally, Ashley—not Howard. I never got to speak to Howard—assured me everything was taken care of, and my Toyota would be as good as new in two shakes of a lamb's tail.

"But we want you to know, Mrs. Kessler, how terribly disappointed we are in you. We strongly suggest you take defensive driving lessons and grow something akin to a backbone before you get behind the wheel of a car again."

The last part was not spoken aloud, but we both knew it was what Ashley was thinking.

I needed to see a friendly face. I hung up the phone and turned to Aidan on the floor amidst a pile of metal cars. "Put your shoes on, Aidan. Let's go see Aunt Dorothea."

Aidan jumped up and pumped his fists. He was always ready for a trip out of the house. He especially liked crossing the street to visit our elderly neighbor. I think he loved Dorothea Westlake nearly as much as I did.

The rain that had fallen over an hour ago when I first got on the phone with the insurance company had abated. It didn't stop Aidan from grabbing the orange and black umbrella with the Cincinnati Bengals' logo emblazoned on every second panel my mother bought him last fall. If there was a hint of rain in the air, he wouldn't leave the house until we found the umbrella though he loved getting wet. Aidan loved our city's football team as much as Scott did. Even Dylan made the occasional appearance in the family room during football season. I learned to understand the intricacies of the game early in our marriage because Scott enjoyed it so much. With two sons, he no longer needed my support. These days I usually spent my free Sunday afternoons reading or playing around on the computer at the kitchen table while the guys alternately cheered and booed in the next room. Most seasons, there was more booing than cheering in the Kessler house.

Aidan twirled the umbrella as he jumped off the curb. I tightened my grip on his hand and followed. Dorothea Westlake wasn't really Aidan's aunt. She wasn't related to our family at all, but she was nearer and dearer to my heart than anyone on the planet, save the three men on my side of the street.

The day after Scott, Dylan, and I moved into our Cincinnati suburb home, Dorothea came across the street bearing a casserole and a platter of brownies. She told us her church was only a few blocks away and we were welcome to join her the following Sunday. The church I had attended since grade school and where Scott and I were married was nearly an hour's drive from our new neighborhood. While planning the move to Mason we had discussed finding a new one but weren't sure how or where to begin our search. An invitation from the sweet old lady across the street seemed like an answer to prayer.

The unlikely friendship with a woman fifteen years older than my mother and the acceptance of her invitation to church turned out to be two of the biggest blessings of my life.

"Aunt Dor'fea's got company," Aidan observed from under his umbrella.

I looked up in surprise. I had been so busy making sure Aidan avoided puddles before he walked into Dorothea's nice clean house, I hadn't noticed the silver two-door coupe with the Illinois license plate in her driveway. Dorothea seldom had company I didn't recognize. I knew her regular visitors and what days they came. Either the coupe's driver was an insurance salesman, someone taking a survey, a deranged killer Dorothea had invited in for coffee and a sermon on the perils of a life of crime, or a far flung relative, though I wasn't aware of any remaining family members on either side of the family.

I allowed Aidan to pick up the pace. After my mother's lecture last night about careless driving and Scott's repeated remonstrations about handling the insurance company and what an inconvenience my accident would surely turn out to be for him, I wasn't going to let a strange car in the driveway postpone my visit, even if it meant meeting distant relatives or disarming a killer. I needed a diversion.

More accurately, I needed Dorothea. I needed to talk to someone who didn't think I was the most incompetent individual the state of Ohio ever put behind the wheel of a car.

At the end of her driveway, I released Aidan's hand and watched as he ran up the sidewalk to the front porch. He stretched onto his toes to ring the bell. He always hung a little too long on the buzzer. I feared one of these days my ever-patient neighbor would snap and politely demand that I keep him at home. But Dorothea always answered the door laughing and saying how she knew it was Aidan on the other side.

I hastened up the walk, belatedly questioning my judgment about visiting while my friend was entertaining company. Just as I reached the porch and was nearly stabbed in the eye with the still unfurled Bengals' umbrella, the door swung open.

Dorothea Westlake hadn't started out half a head shorter than my five feet and four inches, but she was now. She often laughed that she had lost at least three inches of height during her seventy-five years of living but made up for them in memories and good friends.

"I wake up thankful and excited at the prospect of another day to enjoy my life," she often said. She claimed turning seventy had been the most exciting thing to ever happen to her, and she looked forward to eighty doubly so.

Dorothea had once worked for the Nixon administration and was a professor in the history department at the University of Cincinnati for many years. Her husband Albert had been Chief of Medicine at a hospital in the city after leaving a thriving private practice. They traveled extensively, including two trips to the Holy Land. Never having children was her only regret in life, especially now that Albert was gone. Having or not having them had been beyond her control so she didn't dwell on it. "I made up for it by collecting lovely friends," she would say fondly with a warm smile for me.

I always got tearful when she said things like that, which was silly since I was far from her only friend. I liked to think I was the best. Dorothea had that effect on people. You didn't feel stupid or bumbling or insignificant when she was around.

Dorothea clasped her gnarled hands together at the sight of us. Her pale blue eyes sparkled as she gazed down at Aidan. "I was hoping you'd come by today."

Aidan's eyes grew round. "You were?"

"I certainly was. There's someone here I want you to meet."

Aidan started across the threshold, but I held him in place and looked pointedly at the umbrella. He thumbed the button on the handle and handed it to Dorothea. She placed it in the stand under the coat rack in the foyer. Aidan leaped across the threshold, narrowly missing Dorothea's size six orthopedic sneakers with his Spiderman hikers. "We saw a car in your driveway, but Mommy said we could come over anyway."

I grinned sheepishly and laid a restraining hand on his shoulder. "We don't mean to be an inconvenience."

"Nonsense. Please come in. I want to introduce you to my nephew."

I was momentarily taken aback. I wasn't aware of any nephew. Dorothea had been the only child of parents who came from small families. Albert had a brother, but Dorothea seldom talked about him. No wonder she was so excited to show off a nephew.

Aidan scuttled around Dorothea and hurried into the living room as fast as he could without earning an admonition against running inside the house. By the time I caught up with him, my sanguine son—more like his father than me any day of the week—stood in front of a young man, somewhere in his mid to late twenties, lounging in an easy chair. A shadow of a beard darkened the young man's square jaw, and an unruly mop of dark hair obscured one eye.

"I'm Aidan," Aidan said, though the man didn't look like he cared. "I'm four. I'll be five on my next birthday. Who are you?"

"Aidan," I corrected. "This is Dorothea's house. You're supposed to give her a chance to introduce you properly."

Aidan swung his head around and looked at me over his shoulder. "Well, she wasn't saying nothing and I could tell he was wondering already. It would be ruder to stand here and not say nothing."

"I don't know if 'ruder' is a word."

"Sure it is. It means when you don't got no manners." He turned back to the visitor. "I know my manners. I say please and thank you and share my toys with other kids even though hardly no kids ever come to my house. You got kids? If you do, they can come to my house and see my room. Do you want to see my room?"

I stepped forward and pulled Aidan against me. I smiled apologetically. Dorothea's visitor couldn't have looked more bored at our appearance. The least he could do was muster some enthusiasm to humor a little kid.

"Okay, Aidan, that's enough. Let's use our manners and let Dorothea introduce us, shall we?"

He shrugged like it was too late to bother with formalities now.

The young man dropped his feet from the ottoman and stood up on a pair of long lanky legs. Dorothea stepped forward, her face aglow. "Gunner, this is my neighbor, Aidan."

The young man smoothed a lock of hair back from his face and leaned forward to extend a hand to Aidan. Aidan, well versed in the art of hand shaking from attending church three times a week since birth, solemnly took it and gave it two solid pumps.

"It's nice to meet you, Aidan," the man said in a clear, baritone voice that caused me to repent a little for judging him so harshly.

"This is Aidan's mother and my very good friend, Joy Kessler," Dorothea continued with true warmth in her voice. "Joy, Aidan, this is my nephew Gunnar Westlake. Actually, my great-nephew. Albert's brother Stephen was Gunnar's grandfather."

I relaxed my grip on Aidan's shoulders. "Nice to meet you, Gunnar."

Aidan's eyes widened. "Do you have a gun?"

Dorothea, Gunnar, and I stood in puzzled silence for a moment while I processed the meaning behind his question. "Oh. Because your name is Gunnar."

Dorothea chortled.

A shadow darkened Gunnar's hazel eyes. I wondered if he wasn't used to children or just didn't like them very much.

"He doesn't mean anything," I hastily explained. "He always asks a million questions."

Gunnar looked from Aidan to me, his gaze slowly softening. He directed a broad smile at Aidan. "No, I don't have a gun. At least not with me. I didn't want to scare Aunt Dorothea."

Aidan inhaled sharply, and his eyes grew round as saucers. "Oh, she wouldn't care." He looked over his shoulder for confirmation. "Would you, Aunt Dor'fea?" He turned back to Gunnar. "You can show me. I'm real careful."

Dorothea chuckled uncomfortably. "He's teasing you, Aidan. He doesn't have a gun." When she looked at me, her gaze lacked certainty. "Stephen was always more of a sportsman than Albert. He took Gunnar's father hunting every fall in Wisconsin. Someone on his wife's side of the family owned a large property there." She looked at Gunnar. "What was the name of that little town? I can't remember."

Gunnar lifted a shoulder. "Some place in the middle of nowhere. I don't remember either. We haven't been there in a long time."

Dorothea clicked her tongue. "That's a shame. Albert talked about how much those trips meant to your dad."

"He doesn't do that sort of thing anymore."

Her brow creased with concern. "Oh? Is he not well?"

"Just old."

"Gracious," she scoffed. "He can't be much more than fifty. That's not old."

Only good manners kept Gunnar from disagreeing though I could tell he wanted to.

"Oh, dear, where are my manners?" Dorothea motioned us to the sofa. "Everyone, sit. Would you care for anything to drink?"

"Apple juice," Aidan squealed.

"Aidan," I hissed.

"Well, she asked."

"He's right. I did ask." Dorothea ruffled his silky, white-blond hair. "One apple juice for Aidan. Joy? Gunnar?"

"Water's fine," I said.

"The same for me," Gunnar said with a congenial smile.

I watched him watch Dorothea leave the room. His designer jeans were torn and faded, indicating he had paid a lot for them. His shoes looked like they'd never walked across anything rougher than a carpeted floor. His haircut, though not to my taste, had been done at a salon. He didn't look like a bum. So what was he doing here? Did he have a job, and if so, why wasn't he there on a Friday morning? He was too old to be living off his parents. I thought of Dylan and wondered if he'd be doing the same thing at Gunnar's age. I shuddered at the thought.

When my gaze traveled back up to his carefully tousled locks, I found his eyes on me. A knowing smile curved his lips. Guilt colored my cheeks. What was I doing? Gunnar had given me no reason to judge him or compare him to Dylan. If my nearly grown son hadn't turned out the way I hoped, weren't my parenting skills at least partly to blame?

I cleared my throat. "Where are you from, Gunnar?"

"Chicago."

"Do you still live at home?"

"Sort of. I'm taking my postgraduate studies at Northwestern."

Impressive. "What are you studying?"

"Environmental Science."

"Um." I nodded like I knew what that meant. "How did you get away from school this time of year?" I hoped I didn't sound like I was prying even though it was exactly what I was doing.

"I'm working on my dissertation. I thought a change of scenery would do me good."

My nerves went taut. Dorothea didn't need a freeloading nephew sponging off her while he avoided school. "Are you planning to stay with Dorothea for a while?"

Dorothea breezed into the room carrying a tray of frosty glasses. Gunnar jumped to his feet. "Let me help you."

"Thank you, dear, but I've got it." Dorothea set the tray on a side table. She handed a plastic cup of apple juice to Aidan and glasses to Gunnar and me.

"What do you say?" I reminded Aidan just as he thanked Dorothea. I gave him a proud smile while inwardly kicking myself. Scott was always reminding me to give Aidan the chance to do the right thing before correcting him. I really wanted to. I was just so worried about repeating the same mistakes I obviously made with Dylan I couldn't relax with Aidan. If I didn't calm down, he would grow up with all sorts of neuroses.

Dorothea sat down in her usual chair. "I didn't see your car in the driveway this morning, Joy. Are you having it serviced?"

I groaned aloud. "I had an accident yesterday. They're supposed to bring me a loaner car sometime this afternoon."

Dorothea set her glass down with a thump and leaned forward in her chair, her face etched in concern. "What happened?"

"Nothing serious. I got sideswiped in an intersection downtown."

She came over to my chair and hugged me. Tears glistened in her eyes. "I'm so sorry. I wish now I had called last night when I noticed your car wasn't over there. Were you hurt?"

My heart swelled. Dorothea was the first person to ask about my well being first rather than what I'd done to cause the accident. "Thankfully, no."

"Praise the Lord for his protection. Was Aidan with you?"

"I was with Grandma," Aidan answered for me. "She said Mommy wasn't watching where she was going."

Blood rushed to my cheeks. "Aidan. You mustn't say things like that."

"I didn't. Grandma did."

"Well, it isn't true." I lowered my eyes. "I had the light."

"Of course, you did, dear," Dorothea said.

I could always count on Dorothea to accept my version of events at face value without challenging me on every point.

The older woman opened the door on the bottom of the side table and withdrew a stack of coloring books and a basket of crayons. She set them in front of Aidan, who promptly began leafing through his favorite one for the picture he'd left unfinished last time we were here. She smiled at her nephew over Aidan's head. "Gunnar is here to work on his dissertation. He's always been so smart. Just like his great uncle Albert." Her smile broadened as it always did when she mentioned her beloved Albert.

Albert died a few years after Scott and I moved to the neighborhood so I didn't know him very well. He was at least fifteen years older than Dorothea and in poor health by the time we met. It was obvious he adored and respected his wife. I remembered watching them together and wishing Scott would listen to me the way Albert listened to Dorothea, as though I had a working brain in my head capable of solving more complex problems than planning a dinner party or making the baby stop crying.

"How long has it been since you've seen each other?" I directed the question at Dorothea. I couldn't help but be curious about why Gunnar was here after all these years. A change of scenery seemed like a lame excuse to move in on an aunt he barely knew if there was nothing in it for him.

Dorothea went back to her chair and gazed adoringly at her nephew. "I haven't seen Gunnar since he was three. His dad's company moved him around a lot in those early years before they settled in Chicago."

That was a long time to go without seeing one's family though it wouldn't hurt my feelings if I didn't see Scott's brother or his pretentious wife for a year or two. I wanted to point out Chicago wasn't far enough away to prevent a visit for twenty years. I didn't. I had gathered from what little Dorothea said over the years that Albert hadn't gotten along with his brother, Gunnar's grandfather. I never asked Dorothea for details about the rift before. Now I wished I knew the whole story. It might help me feel better about what Gunnar was doing here now.

"I bet he's changed a lot since he was three," I said with a laugh.

Dorothea smiled at my joke. "I was getting ready to look for some old pictures when Aidan rang the bell. Gunnar's mother sent us a few over the years when he was in grade school. I guess time got away from all of us. We stopped getting pictures or phone calls." She sighed again, the pain of lost years evident on her face. "Albert wasn't usually stubborn, but he wouldn't talk about Stephen."

She looked apologetically at Gunnar. "He loved your grandfather. Unfortunately, both men thought they were right and weren't willing to listen to the other's point of view. Then your parents moved to Chicago and your grandfather passed away and Albert and I got old. It's a shame how much pride can rob from a person. I suppose that's why the Bible warns so much against it."

We sat in silence for a few moments with only the scratching of Aidan's crayons across the coloring page and the little sounds he made in his throat as he worked to keep us company. I couldn't stop wondering what happened between Albert and Stephen that was worth losing twenty years over. The only possible explanation was money. Albert and Dorothea weren't the type of people to talk about their financial situation though anyone could tell by looking they weren't hard up for cash.

Maybe Stephen had lost Dorothea to Albert. Love or money—the two usual things that could come between brothers.

Gunnar sat back in his chair and propped an ankle across his opposite knee. "Aunt Dorothea, you haven't changed at all." He flushed a little as if embarrassed by his confession. "Not that I really remember. We had a few pictures of you around the house too. Mom and Dad always thought the world of you."

Dorothea touched her hand to her cheek. "Oh, Gunnar, that's one of the nicest things anyone's said to me in a long time."

My nose tickled for Dorothea's sake. She never hurt for company with our close neighborhood and her church family and the girlfriends from her professional life. But nothing took the place of family.

"I always missed having a big extended family," Gunnar said. "Whenever my friends talked about aunts and cousins, I felt like a freak. It's high time we got to know each other again."

I slunk in my chair. I never should've questioned Gunnar's motives. I had no right to judge him so harshly because he reminded me of my own ne-er do well offspring still snoring in his room across the street.

I zipped my lips and sat back and smiled while Gunnar told us about growing up in a quiet northern Chicago suburb, the only child of over-achieving parents. I never got the chance to tell Dorothea how rotten Scott made me feel about Red-face smashing into my car. For the next hour I put the whole ugly incident out of my head, along with Mom's caustic remarks to Aidan about my incompetence as a driver and a human being. Even though nothing changed and no major problems were solved, by the time Aidan and I gathered our jackets and the Bengals' umbrella and prepared to leave, I felt better than I had in days.

"I met Dorothea's nephew today."

Scott stopped chewing and gaped at me. This was the first he'd looked at me since he got home from work.

"Nephew?" he said around his food. He finished chewing enough to swallow. He dabbed him mouth with his napkin. "I didn't know Dorothea had any family left."

"Neither did I, but apparently there's at least one. He's from Chicago and he's visiting for a while. He's Albert's brother's grandson...or something like that."

"He has a gun," Aidan piped up.

Scott swung his head around to look at him.

"No, he doesn't," I said quickly. "His name is Gunnar. Aidan just assumed..." I let the sentiment trail off.

"Mm." Scott lowered his head and went back to eating.

"He seems like a nice young man." I hoped to engage in some sort of conversation as long as it wasn't about how things went with the insurance company this morning. So far Scott hadn't asked, and I'd rather avoid the subject until they assured me a check was in the mail.

"Mm," Scott repeated.

I pressed on. "Dorothea was so happy to see him. His visit was unexpected, but she certainly didn't mind. She hasn't seen him in twenty years."

Scott raised his head, his eyes again alight with interest. "Twenty years? How old is this nephew?"

"Somewhere in his mid to late twenties from the looks of him. He's in his postgraduate studies at Northwestern. Environmental something or other."

"What's he doing here after twenty years?"

I was relieved Scott shared my initial reaction. "He said he needed a change of scenery. He's working on his dissertation. I think it's nice he bothered to visit at all. Dorothea gets lonely by herself."

"How can she get lonely with you running across the street every hour of the day?"

When Scott said things like that I could never tell if he was putting me down or making an honest observation. "Nothing takes the place of family," I said.

He looked unconvinced and went back to the meatloaf.

I wasn't going to let go of the conversation that easily. Even though Dorothea and Gunnar had seemed to share a real connection earlier today I couldn't stop stewing over Gunnar's sudden appearance. There was something unsettling about his expensive shoes and shifty eyes. Without giving Scott any preconceived notions, I wanted to see if he shared my unease.

"Maybe he's having trouble with his parents. Most people his age are out of school by now."

Scott shrugged and lifted his water glass. "Maybe a late bloomer."

I cringed inwardly, thinking again of Dylan. Would he still be living here at thirty, with lofty aspirations of earning a degree or looking for that one scheme that would make all his dreams a reality?

I took a sip from my own glass. "Or he figures Dorothea's getting along in years and has a little money socked away that he doesn't want to see her leave to the cat."

"Aunt Dor'fea don't got no cat."

I looked quickly at Aidan. I needed to watch what I said in front of little ears. I adjusted his plate so he wouldn't get his sleeve in the food while reaching for his mashed potatoes. "Of course she doesn't, Lima Bean."

"Then why'd you say she did?"

"I guess I wasn't thinking." I looked across the table at Scott. His expression seemed to say that happened a lot.

I silently repented for gossiping about my friend and her nephew. I was happy for Dorothea, and I didn't want to think Gunnar had ulterior motives for visiting her. I scooted my chair away from the table and stood. "I hope they have a nice visit. Dorothea's so excited about him being there." I reached for the casserole dish. "If everyone's had enough to eat, I'll clear the table."

"Don't forget to make Dylan a plate."

I swallowed an inward sigh. "I always do, don't I? Maybe if he came home for dinner once in a while, he could enjoy a hot dinner fresh out of the oven."

"Now, Mother, don't you remember what it was like to be young and free to come and go as you pleased?"

"Not really. When I was his age I had responsibilities. So did you."

Scott rolled his eyes. He nudged Aidan with his elbow. "Here we go, buddy. We're going to have to listen to Mommy talk again about how she had to walk ten miles uphill to school every day."

Aidan snickered behind his hand, though he clearly didn't get Scott's reference.

"Scott! I wish you wouldn't joke with him like that."

"He knows I'm kidding."

"That's not the point. He'll never take me seriously as long as you disparage every word I say."

Scott put down his fork and raised his hands in front of him. "Sorry. I wasn't aware I was undermining your authority. Aidan, always pay attention to your mother and take her seriously, even when she's making a mountain out of a molehill."

Aidan snickered again. "Mommy's making molehills. That's funny, Daddy."

I took a deep breath. Why was it so difficult to make the simplest point in this house? "I didn't mean to complain about the way I was raised. I appreciate every sacrifice my mother made for me. I was just pointing out when you and I were Dylan's age, certain things were expected of us. Like holding down a job. Or college."

"He has a job, Joy."

"This week. Until they get tired of having him call off every other weekend. He should be in school." I thought about telling him Dylan hadn't worked last night and had come home stoned again after hanging out till all hours with his loser friends. Scott knew Dylan dabbled in drugs, but like me, he liked to think it was nothing more than the occasional joint. We knew any amount of drug use was unacceptable, but fighting and lecturing hadn't worked in the past. Scott believed Dylan would outgrow his restlessness and grow up on his own. I prayed every night Scott was right and things would work out. We had brought Dylan up in church. We drew a firm line against drugs and other reckless behavior. But somehow we had missed it. Dylan didn't respect us. He didn't value our home or our rules. He ruled us, and our home turned on his whims.

Scott wouldn't want to hear any of this. We'd been having these discussions since Dylan was in the cradle. Somehow I always ended up looking like the hysterical parent while Scott remained cool and in control. Meanwhile Dylan drifted down the wrong path.

"He only graduated a few months ago," Scott said. "I wish you'd lighten up for once."

"Yeah, Mommy. Lighten up."

I turned an accusing eye to Scott, but he and Aidan were sharing another laugh at my expense. My teeth ground in frustration. Little wonder my children didn't take me seriously. No one on the planet took me seriously. No one except Dorothea.

I swallowed another sigh. Maybe Dylan's behavior wasn't so out of the ordinary. Things had changed since Scott and I were young. Not every young person went straight to college. At least Dylan was working. When he wanted to. I could only hope he grew up soon and decided what he was going to do with his life before he became the end of mine.

"I'll go make Dylan's plate." I turned to the kitchen.

Chapter 3

Every Saturday morning Scott woke at his usual six-thirty and went for a run. Most days he ran during his lunch hour at work too, but he looked forward to a couple extra miles on Saturdays. In the beginning he invited me along. Since I had no idea what I was getting into, I agreed. I couldn't think of a more fun and healthy way to get back into shape while bonding with my husband. We bought matching running shoes and shorts. Scott found heart rate monitors at a sporting goods store downtown. I read all the necessary articles to prepare me for the road ahead. A tortuous trip to the end of our street quickly dashed any illusions I had about bonding with my husband while pounding the cartilage out of my knees and ankles.

Scott wasn't upset the following weekend when I told him I'd rather stay in bed than run. He made a pretense of encouraging me to stick with it, but we both knew I slowed him down with my short legs and low center of gravity. He was all for me getting into shape as long as I didn't hold him back from achieving his own fitness goals.

After a fitful night trying not to over think the purpose of Gunnar Westlake's visit after a twenty-year hiatus and listening for Dylan to come in—hopefully sober this time—I feigned sleep as Scott got up and headed to the bathroom to brush his teeth. This was my only sleeping-in morning and I didn't want to waste it on a conversation about Dylan or the accident or anything else that made me look like a failure. I stretched out luxuriously as the bathroom door clicked shut behind Scott. Aidan wouldn't be up for another hour. Scott would be gone at least that long. A peaceful hour of dozing and daydreaming was a rare luxury in my house.

After Scott headed downstairs and out the front door, I snuggled deeper into the covers. I hadn't heard Dylan come in last night. According to Josh at McDonald's, he was on the schedule to work. He left here promptly at four carrying the smelly gym bag that contained his work clothes. Come to think of it, I hadn't seen the contents of that gym bag in weeks. I stopped doing Dylan's laundry when he was in the eleventh grade and told me to stop coming into his room and snooping around under the guise of gathering dirty laundry. I thought it was ridiculous—dangerous even—that any room in my house was off limits, but Scott thought Dylan was showing initiative by taking on a household chore. My maternal concerns were vetoed as Dylan became responsible for his own laundry and I was no longer allowed in his room. We learned to live with a lot of funky teenage boy smells over the next two years. I only did Dylan's laundry when he brought it downstairs and dumped it on the laundry room floor.

I rolled onto my back and stared at the ceiling. I couldn't remember the last time I'd seen a McDonald's uniform in the wash. A better mother would go into his room right now and demand to see the inside of that gym bag. Or at least find out what time he came in last night. He was supposed to be in by midnight, work or no work.

He stopped making curfew about two nights after we set one.

I rolled over and punched my pillow. Go to sleep, I ordered. Scott doesn't worry over what's in that gym bag. Why should you?

I worried just the same. The clock on the bedside table ticked away several minutes before I admitted defeat and got up. No sleeping in for me this morning. If I was going to be awake, I might as well do something productive. Thinking about laundry reminded me of the winter coats that needed taken to the drycleaners and rotated to the back of the closet for another year. I might even get ambitious and clean out the closets while I was at it. Aidan had outgrown quite a few things in the last few months. So had I, for that matter. I had kept my skinny clothes in the hope I would get back into them before they went hopelessly out of style. Who was I kidding? I had been a tight size ten before I got pregnant the last time. Now I was several sizes beyond that. Even if I took off a few pounds like I'd been telling myself I would, I probably wouldn't see a size ten again before Aidan was in middle school.

The pristine toe of a barely worn running shoe caught my eye from the closet floor. I grimaced when I thought of how much money we'd spent on those shoes. I grabbed the shoe and rotated it in my hand. It was a cute shoe. It deserved better than to dry rot in the bottom of my closet. I could find the mate and donate them along with my skinny clothes to a worthy organization for women who wanted to better their lives and their health.

After some serious digging I found the matching running shoe and threw the pair into the middle of the bedroom floor. I dragged a laundry basket out of the back of the closet and began to fill it with clothes that hadn't seen the light of days in longer than I cared to admit. I threw dresses into the basket, belts that barely reached around one thigh, let alone my stomach, blouses that no longer buttoned, and skirts that wouldn't zip. By the time the basket was full, I hadn't even gotten to my summer clothes. I was too depressed to delve further. I shoved the basket outside the closet door with my foot and set the gleaming, showroom-new running shoes of top of the pile. On Monday I'd take everything to the Salvation Army where they would have a chance at a better life.

I set my hands on my hips and looked down at the shoes on top of the laundry basket.

"These shoes were made for running." The sound of my voice startled me more than the ludicrousness of my words. I didn't want to give them away. Just like I didn't want to have wasted the money on the library of workout DVD's downstairs in the entertainment center. The shoes were running shoes, but that didn't mean I had to use them for running. I could wear hop and dance around the family room in them while streaming a workout video since no one used DVDs anymore. No one would see me panting and gasping and embarrassing myself on the sidewalk, and I might lose some on the baby weight from Aidan. From Dylan too, if I was completely honest with myself.

I set the shoes on the floor and went through the basket a second time. There were a few items I wasn't ready to let go. I held up a cute straight skirt from my thinner days. Wearing it had always made me feel leggy and confident, no mean feat for a woman of my height with a rear end too wide for her body. I folded the skirt and set it on top of the shoes. I'd keep the skirt for inspiration. Most of the time I felt tired and frumpy and a decade older than I really was instead of leggy and confident. Scott said it was from the extra weight. It's easy for people in great shape to point out flaws in the rest of us.

He was a wonderful husband, just disciplined and motivated and always showing me ways to improve. He had never been overweight or out of shape, yet he managed to lose twenty pounds since Aidan was born. He ate right and took multi-vitamins and exercised regularly. I knew women in his office flirted with him. They even did it in front of me. Even at church he got checked out by the young and newly divorced. I wasn't afraid he'd ever act on his opportunities. Scott had too much moral fiber to leave his frumpy, clumsy wife. But did he still find me attractive? We had a healthy enough sex life for people married twenty years, though I didn't have anything to judge it by. We hadn't experienced mad passion in a long time. Probably since I'd last been able to wear the skirt. I never worried my husband would leave me, but I did worry he might stay out of obligation rather than a desperate need to keep me in his life.

I clipped the skirt on a hanger with two clothespins and hung it on the outside of the closet door where I would see it every time I came into the bedroom. I set the shoes on the chest of drawers in a place of honor. I might not be ready for jogging, but surely I could modify a workout that wouldn't kill me.

In the kitchen I made a yogurt smoothie and added fresh fruit Scott sliced yesterday. I had barely taken the first drink when Aidan came downstairs with a hankering for waffles.

I put the smoothie in the fridge for Scott to drink later and dug into the cabinet for the waffle iron.

By the time Scott returned from his run, glistening and tangy and flat-stomached, Aidan and I had finished off the waffles.

Scott tousled Aidan's hair and pulled me into his arms. I guess he was over being mad about the car. "What are you doing up so early?" he asked after letting a kiss linger on my lips.

I breathed in the scent of him, relieved to see a little passion had survived twenty years. "The bed was too empty and cold without you."

He took a bottle of water out of the fridge, then reached into the pantry for a cereal bar. He tore the wrapper off the bar and bit half of it off. Guilt assaulted me as I thought of the skirt hanging on my closet door. My resolve to fit into it had only last until Aidan mentioned waffles.

"Any plans today?" Scott asked as he chewed.

What he really wanted to know was did I have plans that included him. Or rather, chores that needed his attention.

"I thought I'd clean out the flowerbeds before it rains again."

He nodded around his cereal bar. "It's a good day for it. I was thinking of texting Pete Hansford to see if he was up for a few holes of golf." He wadded up the cereal bar wrapper and tossed it into the trash.

I imagined him jogging around our neighborhood this morning trying to figure out a diplomatic way to ask if he could golf with Pete after giving me the cold shoulder for the last two days. He must really want to get out onto the course. He knew how much I looked forward to our weekends together as a family. I knew how seldom he got to do anything unrelated to Dad or Husband roles. He deserved a day to pursue his own interests, especially if it would get him one step closer to forgetting the accident and the loaner car in the driveway.

"You haven't seen Pete outside of work in months."

He nodded, hope evident on his face. He apparently expected more resistance. I thought about taking advantage of my position, but I wasn't devious enough to think of any favors he owed me that quickly.

"I haven't been on the course since that nice weekend in February."

I put my hand on his bristled cheek. He hadn't shaved or showered yet this morning. It only made him more handsome. "Enjoy your day with Pete and I'll catch up on some things I need to do around here."

He pulled me against him. "You're amazing, Joy. I love you." He kissed me again. Longer and deeper this time. I sank into his arms as familiar feelings of longing engulfed us both.

Aidan growled from his perch at the island. "I hate kissing."

Scott and I pulled apart, Scott grinning and me with heat flushing my cheeks.

I cleared my throat. "Finish your breakfast, Aidan."

"I did." He shoved an empty plate across the counter to me.

I took the plate and offered a guilty smile to Scott. He was already headed out of the kitchen. "I better get in the shower. I still need to call Pete and confirm. Have a good day with Mommy, Aidan."

Then he was gone, just like that.

I swallowed my disappointment. I had agreed to him playing golf this morning instead of helping me with some of the outside chores so I didn't have a right to get mad. Our playing around in the kitchen couldn't have led to anything anyway with Aidan right there. Still, it would've been nice to sneak back upstairs…

I didn't know what I expected from Scott. We hadn't made time for real intimacy in weeks. One of us was either too busy, or Aidan needed attention, or Dylan needed bailed out of trouble. There was always something more pressing that prevented us from enjoying each other as lovers instead of two stressed out parents hoping to keep one kid off the streets and the other from following the same path.

The first few years of our marriage were a blur. We never had a chance to get to know each other. We spent our first year convincing my mother and everyone else we weren't too young for such a big step. By our first anniversary I was pregnant with Dylan. He was a demanding baby, and I was a young, immature, tightly wound mother who wanted to do everything right. Consequently, I failed at all of it. Scott was determined to earn his degree in record time while keeping a roof over our heads. Proving ourselves to the world made it difficult to maintain the friendship we forged in college. Even now it seemed like I didn't know my husband, and he certainly didn't know me.

No sense wishing he'd realize he'd rather spend his Saturday at home with me than with Pete on the golf course. It was what it was.

An hour after Scott backed out of the driveway, grinning like a lunatic, I was dressed in a stained, stretched out pair of sweats and headed to the front yard pulling my garden buddy wagon behind me and warning Aidan to keep out of the street. A snowy winter, a wetter than usual March, and a propensity to avoid going out in the cold and damp had kept me from doing anything to prepare the yard or flowerbeds for the upcoming growing season. Spring was my favorite time of year. I loved seeing the earth come alive after a long winter. Tulips first, followed by daffodils and hyacinths. The streets lined with bright yellow forsythia bushes and the smell of the first neighborhood barbeque teasing my taste buds with the prospect of grilled meat.

I heaved an unopened bag of mulch off the garden buddy and dropped it with a thud in the middle of the flowerbed under the front room picture window. I straightened and wiped a line of perspiration from my forehead. I was tired already. I really needed to get into shape. Someday I would.

Maybe the weather would hold and I could put this off until next week. That way, Aidan and I could go to the park. I doubted a two-block walk to the park followed by an hour sitting on a bench while Aidan played would burn as many calories as cleaning out the flowerbeds. I loved colorful, well tended flowerbeds, but I wouldn't go as far to say I enjoyed puttering in the soil. If Scott and I ever got rich, the first person I'd hire was a landscaper.

I put a hand to the small of my back and arched until something popped. I needed to take care of this job while Scott was gone the way I said I would. Who knew? Next weekend he might want to surprise me with dinner in a nice restaurant or a night away from home. That would be nice. Just the two of us. Dylan could keep an eye on Aidan for us.

On second thought…

In the reflection of the picture window, I spotted movement across the street. I turned to see Dorothea kneeling on a square of carpeting she used to protect her knees while tending her own flowerbeds. Unlike mine, her flowerbeds were neat and tidy. Even the clusters of tulip and hyacinth stalks that had bloomed last month were drying in an orderly fashion. Her irises and anemones were several weeks from blooming but coming up nicely. Dorothea had a yardman who came every week, beginning the first of May. He did the heavy work; mowing, trimming, transplanting bushes, and replacing paving stones. Dorothea did everything else.

I stepped out of my garden. "Let's go say hi to Aunt Dorothea," I said to Aidan.

With his miniature garden shovel in hand, he started across the street ahead of me. I looked both ways for cars and hurried to catch up with him. Scott said I needed to relax and not sweat the small stuff. Getting hit by a car wasn't exactly small stuff, but there wasn't a car in sight as Aidan would point out if I yelled at him. No need to spoil a beautiful morning.

By the time I reached Dorothea's front walk, Aidan was already telling her about our morning. "Daddy's playing golf, but me and Mom's got work to do. Is that what you're doing? I can help if you want. I got my shovel. Mom lets me dig in our garden. I'm good at digging up bulbs. I can dig all kinds of things." He gazed hopefully down at her. "You got anything that needs dug?"

I smiled apologetically over the top of his blond head.

She sat back during his litany, ever patient, ever generous. "I was just thinking that patch of ground over there under my living room window could stand a little tilling before Martin plants a rhododendron there."

Aidan gasped with delight. I grimaced. "You don't have to do that, Dorothea. He might dig to China."

She waved away my concerns. "No harm will come if he does. The more pliable the ground, the easier the rhododendron will go in."

Aidan was already dragging his shovel in that direction. I followed him over and stomped out a border with the heel of my shoe. "Stay inside this circle. We don't want to ruin Dorothea's flowerbed."

Aidan rolled his eyes. "I know what I'm doing, Mom. This isn't the first time I helped in the garden."

I couldn't help but laugh. "Sorry. I forgot. I'll be right over here if you need me."

He gave me a look that said he wouldn't require my services anytime soon and began to dig. Satisfied Aidan had busy work that wouldn't lower Dorothea's property value, I went back to where she still knelt. "Thanks. "He loves to help."

"Of course he does. He's a gift from heaven."

I smiled at her words and crossed my arms over my chest. The sun was warming things up nicely, but there was still a nip in the air, especially for someone who wasn't exerting energy and burning off waffles.

"A beautiful day for gardening," I observed.

Dorothea kept her eyes on her work. "The best kind. I thought I'd take advantage of the morning and let Gunnar have some time to work on his dissertation without me hovering."

There was no need to point out Dorothea didn't hover. She was considerate to a fault. I watched her canvas gloves work the black soil. "It's not too wet, is it? We've had a lot of rain this year."

She shook her head and kept working. "We've had worse. I want to have everything ready for annuals by the end of the month."

It was only the first week of April. A lot could happen in Ohio in April. "I thought it was too early to think about annuals."

We had similar conversations every year. Dorothea knew everything about planting and pruning and harvesting, while I could barely retain enough knowledge to keep my marigolds alive throughout our hot dry summers.

"I won't plant my annuals until after Martin shows up the first of May. But there's plenty to do in the meantime. Anything might come up to prevent me from doing what I want when I want."

"You mean like an out of town relative?"

She smiled up at me. "At my age, I was thinking something health related."

"Or a handsome widower at church sweeping you off your feet."

She snorted and waved a dirty, gloved hand through the air. "Joy, you're terrible. The only handsome man who ever turned my head is already in Glory."

"You never can tell."

I sat down on the edge of her porch, mindful to keep my feet out of the dirt. I teased her every now and then about finding a new man, though we both knew it wasn't likely to happen. Dorothea's life was full enough with church and friends without adding romance to the mix, though if anyone could pull it off, it was she.

I glanced over my shoulder at her front door. All was quiet. "Speaking of houseguests, how is Gunnar enjoying his visit?"

A pleasant smile softened her etched face. "We're having a fine time. Gunnar is a very affable young man. I don't think he'd complain if he hated it."

I thought of Dylan, my resident complainer, still snoozing across the street. At least I thought he was in bed. I hadn't actually checked. I couldn't bear the thought of him breaking curfew again and not being there and what a sour note on which to start my weekend. Or worse, that he *was* in bed, and if I woke him, his surly attitude would ruin my day. Better not to rattle that cage.

My only hope was he'd outgrow his surliness and mean streak by the time he was Gunnar's age. Or maybe Gunnar was putting on an act for an overly trusting aunt.

"Do you have plenty to talk about?" I asked carefully, my initial suspicions stirring again.

Dorothea pushed a handful of mulch chips around a green shoot I couldn't identify. "We talk a lot about his childhood since there was so much Albert and I missed out on."

I wrapped my arms around my knees and leaned forward. "Why didn't you see more of Albert's family?" It didn't seem like prying when talking to Dorothea.

"Albert was five years older than Stephen. He was the one who followed in their father's footsteps. I'm not saying I approve, but I think their father favored Albert. Stephen paled in comparison. I'm not bragging. That's just the way it was. Albert was personable and successful in his field. He was a wonderful conversationalist and people were naturally drawn to him. Stephen, well, he just tried too hard."

She ran the back of her gloved hand across her brow and blew a wisp of hair away from her face as if giving herself time to think of how to graciously spill family secrets. "He had a hard time finding his place. He couldn't settle into one thing. He knew he didn't have Albert's brains or his father's respect. He was always trying to prove himself. That only made things worse."

She leaned to one side in order to move the piece of carpet she knelt on a little farther down the bed. She glanced at the house as she did so to make sure Gunnar wasn't within earshot. I followed her gaze. I hoped he didn't come outside until she had time to tell me the whole story.

After a few moments of softening the soil with her spade, she continued. "The distance between brothers widened as they became adults. Albert didn't talk about it much. He didn't like to paint someone in a bad light, and he didn't have many nice things to say about Stephen. He had just graduated medical school when Stephen and their father had a major falling out. I never knew the details, but it was over money. Stephen was practically disowned."

That confirmed my suspicions. I wondered anew if money had something to do with Gunnar's arrival.

Dorothea dug around the root of a dandelion shoot, careful to get as far down the root as possible before extracting it from the ground. She stuck her tongue out of the corner of her mouth in concentration. I hoped the weed wouldn't distract her from the story.

She laid the dandelion on a newspaper she'd brought with her for that purpose. While I waited for her to catch her breath, I looked at Aidan at the edge of the yard to make sure he was still digging inside the circle I made for him. Satisfied my little gardener wasn't hurting anything, I focused again on Dorothea.

"Stephen received only a small inheritance when their father died. By that time, we hadn't seen him in years. After the will was read, well, the whole situation went south. Albert said no inheritance was worth losing his brother over, but he respected his parents' wishes. They must've had reason to do what they did." She glanced at the house again and leaned imperceptibly toward me.

I scooted closer to her along the length of the porch. "Stephen ran through a small inheritance his wife received in pretty short order. Albert's father knew the same thing would happen with any money or family heirlooms as soon as he got his hands on them. I think Stephen knew it too. That made him all the more angry at Albert."

"You didn't see him after that?"

"Rarely, though we were invited to Geoffrey's wedding. That's Gunnar's dad. The whole time we sat in the banquet hall, like two islands in a sea with no one talking to us or looking at us, I wondered why they had gone to the trouble to invite us. I never told Albert, but I believe they just wanted to show off in front of us. Stephen's handsome son was marrying a beautiful girl in a wedding that would've made the Rockerfellers look like cheapskates. Far be it for me to speak ill of the dead, but it was like Stephen used the wedding to throw it in Albert's face that we never had children."

I knew her well enough to know she wouldn't make assumptions without the evidence to back up her claim.

"Cathy, Gunnar's mother, made a few overtures of friendship over the years. She didn't know any better than me what to do about the rift between Albert and Stephen. After Geoffrey's job transferred him to Chicago when Gunnar was little, they were either too busy or not interested enough to come home for a visit. Money might've been an issue. It always is when you're starting out. It wasn't completely their fault. The years got away from all of us. Eventually Cathy and I were only touching base at Christmastime. I hinted once or twice about going for a visit. Either my hints were too subtle or she was afraid of stirring up a hornet's nest by inviting us. The situation broke Albert's heart. In the end, I was the only family he had left."

I swallowed tears. At least Albert had Dorothea. Who did she have? Besides her church family and me, she was alone. No wonder she was so happy Gunnar had come to visit.

Apparently finished with her chores, Dorothea put her hands on the ground and pushed upward. I jumped off the edge of the porch and helped her the rest of the way to her feet. She leaned over to brush the dirt off the knees of her pants while I gathered her gardening tools. Dorothea grasped both handles of the wheelbarrow and grunted as she pushed it around the side of the house.

"How's Dylan?" she asked as I fell into step beside her.

I could tell by the tone of her voice she knew something. What had he done now? What could I have done to prevent it? How much would it cost to fix?

"He's fine."

We both knew that was a lie.

We reached the corner of the house. "Are you ready for a break, Aidan?" Dorothea asked my youngest. "We can make hot chocolate."

Even though the morning had warmed up several degrees more than when we started, Aidan was always on board for hot chocolate.

"Do you have little marshmallows or big ones?"

"Aidan," I scolded. "You don't ask something like that when someone offers you refreshments."

Aidan scrunched his forehead the way Scott did and gazed up at me. "She's not someone. She's Aunt Dor'fea."

"I don't care who she is. You apologize."

He blew out a puff of air that sent his blond bangs into the air. "I'm sorry," he directed at Dorothea. "I'd like some hot chocolate even if you don't got no marshmallows."

Dorothea set the wheelbarrow down and reached over to wipe a smudge of dirt from his cheek. "Thank you, Aidan. I'm pretty sure I have both sizes of marshmallows."

"See, Mom. It never hurts to check." He ran to get ahead of us on the narrow sidewalk.

"Don't go in until we get there," I called after him.

He didn't slow down to acknowledge my words. I looked at Dorothea. Her face wore a gentle smile. "He's such a sweet little boy."

I exhaled, much as Aidan had done a moment ago. "He's a handful."

"All children are, but worth every effort you put into them."

I thought again of how badly she and Albert must have missed children of their own. I couldn't imagine what women like Dorothea went through, wanting a family and slowly realizing it wasn't going to happen. I had gotten pregnant with Dylan practically on my honeymoon. I grew up an only child and dreamed of a big family. Scott wasn't of the same mindset. His biggest argument was the amount of money it cost to have children. We both knew it had more to do with producing another Dylan or subjecting a sibling to his unpredictability. There had been serious episodes of violence in his pre-teen years. Once he chipped one of my teeth during a temper tantrum. A fight over dirty socks on his bedroom floor resulted in four stitches to my left eyebrow. I finally learned to pick my battles.

It seemed irresponsible to bring a smaller, vulnerable child into our household. Still, I wanted another baby. Scott wouldn't give in. Just when we put the issue behind us, I became pregnant with Aidan. Scott accused me of intentionally forgetting my pills and every other ruse in a woman's arsenal to get what she wanted from a man. After about a month of listening to his displeasure, I'd had enough. I told him it was too late to lay blame. A baby was on the way, and there wasn't a thing he could do about it.

Five years had transpired since that argument, and I think he still suspected I went against his wishes and got pregnant on purpose.

Dorothea slowed our already sluggish pace. "You know I love both your boys, Joy."

I held my breath. Here it came.

"I would do anything for either of them."

This wasn't good. I already knew she was leading up to something with Dylan.

"If I saw one of them run into a burning building I'd do whatever I could to get him out, even if you or Scott tried to stop me."

Dorothea continued a few paces down the sidewalk before she spoke again. I wished she'd hurry up and get to the point. At the same time, I dreaded hearing what she would say.

"I saw Dylan leave your house last night, or rather, early this morning. I'm sure you and Scott didn't give him permission. He was being very careful to keep quiet."

I groaned aloud. I had tossed and turned most of the night, somewhere between dreams and wakefulness, comparing Dylan to Gunnar Westlake. One of the times I was jerked awake, it was probably the door closing behind Dylan.

Dorothea gave me a cautious look. "He got into a car parked a little down the street. I've seen that car pull in and out of this street many times." She stopped walking and set the wheelbarrow down. We were at the corner of the house and could see Aidan playing on the back porch. She touched my elbow and lowered her voice. "Those boys are doing drugs. It isn't just a rumor. I've seen them other places too. I know some of their parents. They're bad news and they're bad for Dylan."

I thought about crying, but I was too numb. I couldn't even pretend to be shocked. Not with Dorothea. "Oh, Dorothea. I'm afraid Dylan might be bad news for them. He came home stoned the other night. It wasn't the first time."

She looked past me to Aidan to make sure he was still occupied. "What did Scott say?"

I winced. "I haven't told him."

Her eyes widened.

"I couldn't," I said quickly. "He was so upset about the car."

She set her face in a hard line. "You think he would put the car over his son?"

"Well, no…"

How could I explain? Scott was a good father. He loved the boys, but part of him wanted to believe Dylan was simply discovering himself and sowing wild oats. Eventually he would find his niche and settle down. Unfortunately, we'd been waiting for that to happen for nineteen years.

"Are you protecting Dylan from Scott or Scott from Dylan?"

I opened my mouth to tell her I wasn't protecting anyone when I realized I didn't have an answer. Maybe I was trying to protect them both. Or myself. In truth, I didn't want to get in the middle. I didn't want the situation to see the light of day. If I named it, I was admitting it was a problem. My son was on drugs. He wasn't just smoking a little weed. Not that I approved of that either. He had a serious problem. A problem that wouldn't go away by ignoring it. What if it escalated to harder things? What if he overdosed on a bad batch of something? I saw it on the news all the time. What if he got mixed up with someone willing to kill over a drug deal? I'd heard or read that something like eighty percent of shootings in America were drug related. Was that what awaited my son? I shuddered in the April sunshine.

Dorothea must've read my fear. She leaned over the wheelbarrow handles and pulled me into an embrace. When she stepped back, tears shone in her eyes. "He's worth saving, Joy."

Tears sprang to my own eyes and spilled down my cheeks. "He's never listened to me. Ever. About anything. He certainly won't listen about this." I gave my head a helpless shake. "Neither will Scott. He'll say I'm making mountains out of molehills again."

Aidan laughed about something, and I thought of when he and Scott laughed at me the other night at dinner.

"I'm a joke in my own house." The pain of the realization tied my stomach in knots. "No one listens to me. I can barely control Aidan and he's only four. How can I make Scott wake up and see what's right in front of him? How can I make our grown son stop doing drugs?"

Dorothea laid her hand on my arm. "You don't have to do it alone, Joy. God is bigger than any problem we have. I know that sounds like a trite answer, but it's true. You're in the right. You have to make Scott see the problem is real, and you have to make Dylan listen. You need courage. You'll only get that by giving your problems to God."

I swiped the tears off my cheeks so Aidan wouldn't see. "I don't know how to do that. I've tried for years. I thought it would get better when we started going to church. I thought once Scott became a deacon he'd take his responsibilities at home more seriously. But nothing got better. Dylan has gotten progressively worse, and I've gotten progressively worse at controlling him."

"That's because he's not a robot you can program to do what you want. But you have to stand up to him. And to Scott. You have to let them know there are some things you aren't going to put up with any longer."

I tilted my nose into the air. "I've always strove to be a Proverbs Thirty-One wife. I can't usurp Scott's authority where the kids are concerned."

"But Scott is wrong." Dorothea took a deep breath and folded her skinny arms. "Joy, when is the last time you read Proverbs Thirty-One?"

I pursed my lips. I wasn't sure I'd ever read it, at least not in recent memory. "I just know I'm supposed to make my husband proud of me and my children will rise up and call me blessed."

She dropped her arms. "I suppose that's the end result. I think you need to read the entire chapter again. A Proverbs Thirty-One woman is courageous and strong and laughs at the thought of the future."

She watched me as I looked out over the yard. Aidan was digging at the cracks in Dorothea's patio floor with a stick. I started to tell him to stop, but I knew Dorothea would see it for what it was—a stalling tactic.

"A Proverbs Thirty One wife doesn't pass off the hard stuff to her husband."

I jerked my head around to stare at her. "That isn't what I'm doing."

She cocked her head. "Isn't it? You want Scott to be the heavy with Dylan. Since he hasn't done it, you let Dylan slide."

I wanted to protest, but I didn't have the right.

"Parenting won't make you popular, Joy. You make enemies of the ones you love most."

Fresh tears pushed at the backs of my eyes. Parenting was the thing I wanted to succeed at most. Consequently, it was my biggest failure. If I gave into the tears, Dorothea would give me a break and let the subject drop. She always knew what to say and how much of it. But she also knew what I needed to hear.

I pushed away the tears. "I'm not strong like you, Dorothea. I'm a marshmallow and everybody in the world knows it." I thought of Red-face who ran into my car and Ashley at the insurance company. "What if I stand up to Dylan and push him away? What if he hates me? What if I lose him forever?"

"Honey, if you don't do anything, you're definitely going to lose him. That's what's wrong with our society today. Parents are afraid of the children. Even in church. We're letting the kids run our homes, and the family is falling apart. I know what I'm telling you isn't easy, especially for someone with a meek personality like yours. But if you love your son, if you want to save him and your family from destruction, it's time you got tough."

I barked out a laugh. "Me? Marshmallows aren't tough. We're soft and gooey and inconsequential. This job is too much for me."

"Of course it's too much for you. That's why you need God in the fight. Believe me, you're in for the fight of your life. And Dylan's life. You have to do it, Joy. I just wish you had a little faith in yourself. If you only knew how much God respects and values you."

I didn't like to contradict Dorothea, but I couldn't let that comment pass unchallenged. "I doubt God has more faith in my abilities than I do."

"Joy, you mustn't say things like that, especially when they couldn't be further from the truth."

"Come on, Dorothea. I know God loves me, but he probably sees me the same as everyone else. An ineffective mother, a mediocre wife, and a disappointing daughter."

Dorothea's eyes hardened. I had never made her mad before. But she'd never made me dwell on my shortcomings before either.

"I wish you could see how important you are to so many people," she said. "Even to Scott and Dylan, though they may not act like it. Satan is going after your family like a lion after prey. You have to be a lion right back if you want to save your son."

A lion. Me? I liked the sound of it. I just didn't see it happening.

"Here's another proverb for you, Joy. *'The wicked flee when no man pursues: but the righteous are bold as a lion.'* Proverbs twenty-eight, verse one. You may not feel like a lion today, but she's in there," she tapped my chest, "waiting for you to set her free. If you really want to be a Proverbs Thirty-One woman you need to look after the ways of your household. That's going to require courage."

Perfect. Courage was the one thing in the world I lacked most.

Chapter 4

Back at home I walked past my untended flowerbeds and went inside to get my Bible. I needed to prove Dorothea wrong. She was right about most things, especially spiritual matters, but I was pretty sure I had her on this one. I agreed I needed to be stronger when dealing with drivers who plowed into my car. God never expected me to stand still while perfect strangers threatened and berated me. Nor was it in his perfect plan for my son to take drugs. But surely he would prefer that I continue my role as a dutiful and submissive wife who didn't start battles she had no hope of winning. Let Scott worry about what to do with Dylan while I took care of the laundry and the bill paying and had dinner on the table promptly at six.

I couldn't remember the last time I read Proverbs Thirty-One in its entirety. Apparently it had been long enough to forget the whole premise. I always thought a Proverbs Thirty-One wife was submissive, a good homemaker, wise with money, and a helpmeet to her husband. Her children worshiped the ground she walked on, and her husband thought she was the greatest thing since sliced bread. Apparently there was a lot more to this Proverbs Thirty-One business than I thought.

The Proverbs Thirty-One wife was also strong and wise and resourceful. She knew what she wanted and wasn't afraid to go after it. I was resourceful as far as clipping coupons and making crafts with Aidan out of toilet paper rolls and juice can lids. I was invaluable to Scott as a helpmeet whether he realized it or not. It was all that other stuff where I had basically dropped the ball. I thought submissiveness meant agreeing with him on financial matters and letting him call the shots as far as child rearing. Was I wrong there as well?

I grabbed the dictionary off the bookcase and looked up submission.

To yield to the authority of another.

Just as I thought. I was right. Dorothea was wrong. There was nothing wrong with submitting to my husband's authority. It was the way God wanted a marriage to operate.

I should've stopped reading while still in possession of a little dignity.

Yielding, obedient, docile.

I supposed those qualities could be considered admirable…if I were a Border Collie. I read further. *To give up; surrender.* My stomach clenched. That's exactly what I had done. I had given up on Dylan. He had always been a difficult child. Raising him was hard. Even loving him was hard, though I would never admit it to another living soul. Occasionally over the years I voiced my opinions to Scott when the psychologist said we should show Dylan we loved and respected him by giving him more of what he wanted. I believed we should take away some of his privileges when he misbehaved. The doctor—and Scott—looked at me like I was Evil Incarnate and reminded me Dylan had self esteem issues and was only secure and valued when doing things he liked. What sort of mother would deprive her child of value and security?

It sounded logical at the time so we kept paying for guitar lessons, though Dylan never pursued music. We let him go to an expensive baseball camp where he broke two teeth out of another boy's mouth over who was next in line at the soda machine. That was a costly summer. Apparently bullying anyone in his path and keeping his room a mess filled him with a sense of accomplishment and nurtured his self esteem.

Dylan wasn't my only blatant failure as a Proverbs Thirty-One woman. I wasn't a good wife either. I ranked barely above a paid servant. Scott said if I wanted respect, I needed to command it. That might be true with the rest of the world, but he was my husband. He was supposed to value and honor me, regardless of my shortcomings. I hadn't felt honored or valued since we first married. The Scott I fell in love with thought I was funny and smart and charming. I hadn't seen that Scott in a long time.

In all fairness, I couldn't remember the last time he'd seen the funny, smart, charming Joy who knocked his socks off in college.

So there was the rub. How could I change any of it? How could I make my family respect me and take me seriously when, according to the dictionary, I was supposed to be yielding and docile? Aidan still liked to spend time with me. He laughed at my jokes and seldom looked at me like I was an idiot. But every now and then I saw the same warning signs I'd seen with Dylan. The signs I conveniently ignored. One thing I knew, I didn't want to raise another Dylan. One was enough. But what could I do to prevent it?

The rest of the morning I prayed and repented and struggled against the sick feeling in my stomach. I couldn't quite muster the courage Dorothea said I needed to go upstairs and confront Dylan. I pictured breaking down his bedroom door and dragging him out of his nice comfy bed. While he cowered in the wake of my righteous indignation, I'd tear his room apart in search of contraband. If anything unlawful or ungodly turned up, I'd call the police without batting an eye.

Of course I didn't do any of that. I even went as far as to hold my breath and use as much stealth as someone of my girth and lack of natural grace would allow every time I passed his room to keep from awakening the beast.

Talking to Scott first would be a better tactic. Of the two, I stood a better chance of winning him over than my surly son. Still, the thought of discussing with Scott what was going on under our roof sent my stomach roiling.

Aidan and I ate green salads and macaroni and cheese for lunch while Dylan snoozed upstairs. I idly thought of what to fix for dinner, but I was too agitated to give it my full attention.

I made quick work of the lunch dishes, then Aidan and I headed back out front to the flowerbeds. He needed the fresh air now that the threat of rain was over, and I needed to work off the mac and cheese. The waistband of my jeans dug into my stomach as I squatted in the dirt. I tugged at the fabric and thought again of going on a diet and beginning a regular exercise routine. I thought of it nearly every day. I just didn't do anything about it. A Proverbs Thirty-One wife was probably fit and healthy in order to perform the tasks expected of her. I could barely climb to the top of the stairs with a loaded laundry basket.

Well, it ended today. I was getting into shape. I was going to stand up for myself. I was going to adopt a no-nonsense approach to parenting. No more kowtowing to my nineteen-year-old. This was my house and he could do things my way or he could…

Get out.

There, I said it. He could leave. He refused to talk to us about going to school. He wouldn't work steadily. We didn't know what he did with his paychecks or who his friends were or where he went after work every night. Things were going to change whether Scott agreed with me or not. I knew I had the Lord on my side. I didn't need Scott's consent.

I slapped last fall's dirt off my gardening gloves and peered inside for unwelcome guests. I'd read about recluse spiders and all sorts of other creepy things that liked to spend the winter in dark places. I always meant to stow my gloves in the house, but they somehow ended up in the shed with the shovels, gardening implements, and bags of leftover potting soil. Once Aidan was occupied on the porch with a pile of Legos and I had ascertained nothing had set up housekeeping inside my gloves, I set to work with the trowel and spade.

It had turned into a glorious day, the warmest since spring's arrival. I cherished the warmer temperatures and the respite from the cold, soggy days of March, but it wasn't long before I was sweating inside my sweatshirt. I should've finished this job immediately after my talk with Dorothea when it was still cool outside. I glanced at my wristwatch. Nearly one o'clock. Scott would be home anytime, refreshed, pink-cheeked, and feeling his oats from a day on the links. I would be hot and sweaty and grumpy. Physical exertion put me in a foul mood since I was so out of shape. No wonder my husband lacked passion for me. I thought of what Dorothea said about dividing her chores into manageable chunks. Maybe that was my problem. I tried to do too much, got overwhelmed, and gave up before the job was finished.

I started to work at the edge of the steps and worked my way down the sidewalk toward the street. Weeds had already sprouted through the soil among the dried stalks of tulips and daffodils. I never had as many blooms as Dorothea even though I did my best to mimic her gardening techniques. Every year she gave me more bulbs and explicit instructions on how to plant and care for them to maximize results. My gardens still managed to disappoint.

I blocked out all thoughts of Dylan and Scott and the battle ahead as I moved along the flowerbed. Several neighbors were also outside. Next door Ben Sanders was winding up the hose he had used to wash his silver BMW. Ben was a corporate attorney, and all his free time was spent outside pampering that car. I wondered if his obsession might've been part of the reason Wife Number Three moved out last fall. I prayed for Ben every time he crossed my mind. He had to be lonely somewhere deep inside though you'd never know it by looking at him. He was nice enough and waved every time he saw me in the yard, but we'd never had a real conversation. I always wondered how

I could share Jesus with him. Just looking at his car and expensive shoes intimidated me so much I could barely think of how to explain why he needed salvation should the opportunity arise.

The rich baritone of a masculine voice reached my ears. I looked up to see Ben disappear around the side of his house. Probably talking into his Blue Tooth. He did that a lot. No rest for the weary, I supposed.

The voice came again. Louder and more insistent this time, and in the opposite direction of where Ben had gone.

I jerked my head around to see if it was Dylan. I hadn't heard him leave his room all day, but maybe he was preparing to leave with a friend. He had another think coming if that's what he was planning. He wasn't leaving this house today unless he had to work. No better time to exert my newfound authority. I wanted to enjoy a nice family dinner with all three of my men around the table. Dylan had been gone enough lately doing God only knew what. Tonight he could stay home and at least pretend he was part of the family.

The only person on the porch was Aidan and his eight hundred Lego pieces. I wasn't ready to face Dylan yet. It was easy to lay the law down to Dylan in my head. The truth was, I didn't have confrontation in me.

Beyond the driveway on the other side of the street, I saw Gunnar Westlake pacing back and forth in front of Dorothea's house. His voice rose in volume again. His arms jerked in time to his punctuation. Though I was too far away to make out any words, I could tell whatever was going on had upset him. I went back to work on my weeds but angled my body so I could watch him while I worked. I shouldn't be suspicious of Gunnar. Dorothea was thrilled he was here. If he wanted to get into her good graces to insure an inheritance, it wasn't any of my business. Dorothea was nobody's fool. Even if she was, what she did with her money was up to her. I had no right to tense up every time I saw Gunnar. Still, I held my breath in hopes of overhearing a snippet of conversation. Aidan was making a tremendous racket with his Legos a few feet away. It took all my resolve not to yell at him to keep it down so I could eavesdrop on our new neighbor.

Gunnar continued to pace, clearly agitated with whoever was on the other end. As carefully and quietly as I could since the sound of my own heavy breathing drowned out his end of the conversation, I got to my feet and moved down the sidewalk. I pretended to examine the edge of the sidewalk for weeds or cracks in the concrete or anything else that wouldn't arouse suspicion while watching Gunnar out of the corner of my eye. He moved to the edge of the sidewalk as he paced. He stood on the curb with his heels hanging over and bounced up and down. Since no one parked on the street in front of Dorothea's house, he had plenty of room to pace. His voice grew louder, but I was still too far away to decipher anything. My curiosity mounted. I was usually generous and nonjudgmental. But I had to consider what was best for Dorothea. If Gunnar was a loose cannon or brought any dangerous baggage with him from Chicago, I wanted to know about it.

No better time to grab the mail. I moved carefully, hoping he wouldn't notice me, though technically I wasn't doing anything wrong. This was my house after all and my mail. But if Gunnar saw me skulking or realized I would soon be within earshot, he would end his conversation or go inside. I didn't want that to happen.

I eased open the mailbox, hoping the creak of metal wouldn't drown out anything important.

"I don't know what you want to hear."

My heart nearly stopped. Was he talking to me? I froze with my fingers inside the mailbox. I tilted my head to watch him under a fringe of light brown bangs in need of a trim. He continued to pace and glare as he talked. He definitely wasn't talking to me. Either he hadn't noticed anyone outside or was too agitated to care.

A lovers' quarrel would explain the agitation. It might also explain why he'd shown up to spend time with an aunt he barely knew when he could easily finish his dissertation at home. Maybe I should feel sorry for him instead of being so suspicious. Regardless of how I should feel, I took my sweet time leafing through a stack of junk mail as if it were of utmost importance.

Gunnar's pacing intensified. He growled something unintelligible into the phone. I took extra time closing the mailbox lid and looked around for something else to do to keep me close to the street. A spider's web stretched from the back of the mailbox to a budding lilac bush. I used a credit card application to brush off the web and then pulled a weed that was barely as tall as my thumb.

Gunnar still hadn't noticed me. He faced the street, though his gaze remained fixed on the ground at his feet. I headed up the sidewalk to the porch, moving slowly and keeping my eyes on my mail. I stepped behind a porch post though it would take a Grecian column to conceal me.

"I need more time, Maurice," Gunnar said. "I can't give you what I don't have."

So much for a lovers' quarrel. It sounded like he owed Maurice money. That figured.

He gave a nervous laugh. "That sounds like a threat." I peered out from behind the porch post. His smile remained in place, but his expression darkened across the expanse of green lawn.

"Mommy."

I gasped. I had forgotten all about Aidan. "Shhh," I hissed at the upturned face of my son.

His forehead puckered as he looked up at me. He opened his mouth to speak again, but I shushed him with a shake of my head and a cutting motion through the air with my hand. I peeked around the porch post in time to see Gunnar end his call and drop his arm to his side. He looked up, and ours eyes met across the sun dappled asphalt.

He didn't bother to smile or wave or give the illusion all was well. He did an about face and stalked toward the house. I reached down and grabbed for Aidan's hand. "Let's go inside and wait on Daddy."

Something about the look on Gunnar's face made me eager for the sanctuary of a locked door.

Dylan came downstairs before Scott got home and told me he had to work and would be spending the night with a friend afterward. He dismissed my reminder about church the next morning.

"Can't. Seth's mom picked up some flyers from a few local colleges. She wants to go over them with us."

He knew the prospect of researching colleges would get me off his back. I didn't really believe him, but I couldn't risk making him mad when he might actually be thinking of his future.

Scott was in such a good mood after his day golfing I didn't have the heart to rain on his parade by discussing Dylan or how I believed I deserved his respect, regardless of how worthy of it he thought I should or shouldn't be. Maybe our pastor would preach a message about letting children rule the roost and open the door for discussion later. I could only hope.

Instead I turned my thoughts to less troubling matters. "I'm worried about Dorothea," I confided as we got ready for bed.

"What about?" His eyes remained fixed on his phone.

I swallowed a sigh. Worry over Dorothea had never been necessary before. There was only one possible reason why I would worry now. "Gunnar." I hoped I didn't sound testy. "I think he has money problems. I'm afraid he might be expecting Dorothea to take care of them."

Scott tore his eyes away from the tiny screen, bored with the conversation already. "What makes you think that?"

"For one thing, he's here. Doesn't that seem odd when Dorothea hasn't seen or heard from him in twenty years? She's pretty comfortable. She and Albert didn't have children. There are no direct heirs to her estate that we know of."

Scott's attention was back on his phone almost as soon as I started talking. "What makes you think Gunnar has money problems?"

I swallowed my resentment at his implication. I wasn't crazy or given to melodrama. "I…um…overheard him on the phone today."

Scott gazed up at me from the edge of the bed, his phone forgotten for the moment. "You overheard him discussing his financial situation all the way from our yard? Where was he?"

"On the street in front of Dorothea's. I was getting the mail. I didn't exactly hear him talking about his financial situation."

He set the phone on the nightstand next to his wallet and car keys. "What, then? What made you assume he's a deadbeat after overhearing a little bit of conversation? You must've been paying awfully close attention."

No need to tell him that's exactly what I was trying to do. "He wasn't going to any lengths to keep the conversation private. I could tell he was upset by the way he kept pacing back and forth and raising his voice. I heard him say something to someone named Maurice about repaying a loan. It didn't sound like a friendly conversation. Yes, his behavior made me a little curious, but only because I want what's best for Dorothea."

"Who are you to say what's best for her? So what if her nephew's a deadbeat who owes people money? Who doesn't have one of those in the family these days? It's no reason to go skulking around the mailbox eavesdropping. I hope the neighbors didn't see you."

"I don't care what anyone thought. All I care about is Dorothea." I shouldn't have to remind Scott how much she meant to me. "It sounded like he was talking to a bookie or something."

"How many conversations with bookies have you been privy to?"

Why was he making this so hard? Scott loved Dorothea nearly as much as I did. He should share my concerns for her safety and well being. "It wouldn't be the first time a scheming relative moved in on a senior with the intent of tricking them out of their life's savings. Dorothea doesn't need that kind of heartache. She's too gentle a soul to have to deal with it. She'll probably believe any line he gives her."

Scott's expression softened. He stood up and put his hands on my shoulders. He brushed my hair away from my face. "Sweetheart, I wouldn't worry about Dorothea if I were you. I already told you she's nobody's patsy, even a smooth talking nephew she hasn't seen in years. Don't you think she's a little wary about why he's here after all these years? Trust me, Gunnar Westlake isn't going to get anything out of Dorothea she doesn't want to give up."

The tension slid out of my shoulders. Scott was right. Dorothea was a gentle compassionate soul. She was also shrewd and intelligent. I didn't know what Gunnar had in mind, but I knew Dorothea. Gunnar would know her soon enough as well. If he thought his elderly aunt was an easy mark, he was in for a rude awakening.

Scott pulled me against him and rubbed my cheek with the back of his hand. "Aidan's asleep and Dylan's out for the night. It'd be a shame to waste the whole night worrying about what's going on between Dorothea and Gunnar."

My conversation with Dorothea this morning flitted across my mind. I really needed to talk to him about Dylan and what Dorothea saw last night. Our son was hanging with the wrong crowd, and by all appearances, might be involved in illegal activity. Even if he wasn't, he wasn't showing us the proper respect by ignoring our rules and values. Somehow none of that seemed worth mentioning at the moment.

I leaned into Scott's embrace. Gunnar Westlake's possible financial problems were even farther down the list of reasons to waste a perfect opportunity to spend time with my husband.

CHAPTER 5

I lost the contented feeling I shared with Scott the next morning when Dorothea didn't show up for church. Scott suggested Gunnar had taken her to a nice restaurant for brunch. Or perhaps they'd stayed up late last night catching up on old times. They had a lot to catch up on, right?

Right. For some people. But Dorothea did not miss church because she hadn't seen someone is a couple of decades or she wanted to sleep in or have brunch at a trendy restaurant. Something was wrong. After a futile hour of trying to follow the pastor's sermon I scooped up my purse from under the pew in front of us and made a beeline for the door nearly before the altar service concluded. I wasn't the only one alarmed by Dorothea's absence. On the way to the door at least ten people stopped me to ask if we should put her on the prayer list. Dorothea was notoriously healthy, but she was seventy-five. Things happened, even to warhorses like her.

Warhorse was her word, not mine.

I barely heard Scott ask what I wanted to do for lunch. We usually went out to dinner after church, often with Dorothea in tow. For the first time in my life I wasn't interested in food. I didn't even notice Aidan's chants in favor of fried chicken until

Scott told him to settle down. All I could do was imagine Dorothea at the bottom of her stairs with a broken neck or stiff in her bed from a heart attack. Would Gunnar know to call me? Or worse, had his financial situation driven him to hurry along the process of nature?

I admonished my ludicrous thoughts just as Scott had admonished Aidan. Dorothea was fine. She hadn't come to church. People missed church every week, sometimes for decades.

Every time I tried to convince myself that's all there was to it, I got a sick feeling in my stomach. Something else must've happened. If Gunnar hadn't come to visit, I'd be the one notified by EMTs if she fell or slipped in the tub or had a heart attack. My number was plastered all over her house. I was her emergency contact at the doctor's office, hospital, and with the local firehouse. But with a relative in residence, EMTs would see no need to contact me.

I was pretty sure I would've seen or heard an ambulance drive through our neighborhood last night even in light of Scott's uncommon attention. If not, someone in the neighborhood would've seen something and called me to see what was up.

"Stop!" I shrieked as we drew abreast of Dorothea's house.

Scott slammed on the rental car's brakes and then gave me a disparaging look. "You can't barge in uninvited. Dorothea will think you lost your mind."

"No she won't. She'll tell me I shouldn't be such a worrywart, but she'll know I love her."

Scott exhaled as he put the car in park. "Don't be long. The chicken's getting cold."

"I won't. Start without me."

I didn't care about barging in unannounced or the colonel's chicken cooling in the backseat. I had to see for myself Dorothea was indeed enjoying a leisurely Sunday with Gunnar before I thought about eating. Considering how highly I regarded fried chicken, Scott should appreciate the testament to my degree of worry.

I jumped out of the car and hurried up the walk. Instantly I wished I'd left my purse in the car as it slipped off my shoulder. I hadn't run in years, but I was coming pretty close to doing so now. Gunnar's car occupied the same spot as it had the last few days. The garage door was down so I couldn't see if Dorothea's Crown Vic was inside, indicating they were enjoying a quiet Sunday at home or if Dorothea had driven him somewhere for lunch. She loved our southern Ohio countryside. Maybe she had driven him to the river for a tour.

I gave the heavy paneled door a hard rap and grabbed hold of the knob to let myself in. Dorothea and I had passed the stage of knocking on each other's doors before Aidan was born. I always insisted he ring the bell when he was with me to teach him courtesy and patience, but I never stopped to knock. Mindful of Scott putting the car in gear behind me and knowing he was probably shaking his head in disapproval, I let go of the knob and knocked again. Regardless of my friendship with Dorothea I was still a lowly neighbor. Gunnar was blood. I would respect that even though I wanted nothing more than to barge in and demand to know what was going on.

A few moments ticked by. I looked over my shoulder and watched as Scott pulled into our driveway. He climbed out and opened the back door for Aidan. Together they carried our take-home lunch and Bible supplies into the house. When the front door shut behind them I turned back and gave Dorothea's door another sound knock. I stepped to my right to look through the beveled glass in the window beside the door. My heart hammered faster. Dorothea never took this long to answer the door. Where was she? The side door to the garage didn't have a window so I couldn't look in to see if her car was gone. The fastest way to find out where they were was to open the door and walk inside. Ordinarily, that's exactly what I would've done, but I didn't feel comfortable doing so with Gunner visiting.

My fingers itched to try the latch. If it was locked, I would know they were out for the day. If not, they would surely hear me, and I would be busted for walking in like I owned the place.

I lifted my hand to knock again when I heard movement on the other side of the door. Relief surged through me. My mouth pulled into a grin as I prepared to give Dorothea a good-natured tongue lashing for making me worry. The door swung open and Gunnar's flushed face stared out at me. He slapped his hands together and a cloud of dust swirled through the air in front of him. "Yeah?"

I took in his disheveled appearance, and my grin changed to confusion. "Why didn't you answer the door? I was worried sick."

The distraction on his face was quickly replaced by irritation. "Excuse me."

My mouth went dry. I'd never spoken so abruptly to anyone in my life, especially a stranger standing in a doorway where he belonged and I did not.

I took a deep breath and began again. "I'm sorry. I'm just eaten alive with worry…about Dorothea. She wasn't at church this morning."

His stance relaxed but only marginally. "So?"

His annoyance calmed my nerves a little. If she had been in an accident or fallen sick, he wouldn't be so irritated. I gave him a tremulous smile. "Dorothea never misses church. Is she all right?"

He glanced over his shoulder as if I caught him doing something wrong. He grabbed the door and narrowed the space between him and the doorjamb. Instantly I wondered what he was hiding.

"Of course she's all right. Why wouldn't she be?"

"She never misses church," I repeated. Maybe he missed that part. "Everyone was worried about her. I couldn't go home without making sure she's okay."

He assumed a casual pose against the doorjamb, but I could tell it was to block my view into the house. "You should've called."

Calling hadn't occurred to me. "Dorothea and I don't call. We barge in. We're best friends." I gave a little laugh that sounded more hysterical than I was going for.

"You still should've called. She isn't here."

My mouth dropped open so far I thought I felt my jaw pop. "What do you mean she isn't here? She's always here."

"Not today."

While I waited for him to elaborate I wondered how much a nephew owed a neighbor who believed she was closer than flesh and bone family. I wasn't naturally a rude person. Nor was I nosy, but this demanded an explanation.

"Where is she?" I blurted when I couldn't take another moment of his blank face staring at me and his white knuckles clutching the door.

"Visiting family. I'll tell her she stopped by." The door began to swing shut in my face.

Instinctively I put out my hand. I didn't even have time to think about how I typically let life roll over me with no resistance on my part. The door smacked my palm, but thankfully it stopped. "Wait. What family? When will she get back?"

Gunnar's cheek twitched. He stared hard at me. For the briefest of moments I thought he might actually do something. I remembered how Red-face threatened to pop me in the mouth after the traffic accident. Twice in one week I witnessed a look that signified I was teetering on a fine line. I couldn't be sure what was going through Gunnar's head, but he definitely looked moments away from forcibly sending me across the street.

"I'll tell her you were here." The door swung closed in my face, forcing me to backpedal onto the porch. The distinctive sound of a latch sliding into place let me know no further explanation was forthcoming.

"I wish I knew what he was doing over there."

"Probably watering her plants and getting her mail and keeping an eye on things. Now will you get away from the window before someone sees you?"

I exhaled in frustration but stepped away from our picture window and faced my husband.

"None of this makes sense. Dorothea would've told me if she was going out of town? Just who is she visiting? Her own family is gone. She told me yesterday she hadn't seen Albert's family in years. Even then they weren't close. If this family wanted to see her so badly why didn't they invite her to visit before now?"

"Probably the same reason Gunnar never came before. You said it yourself. They're not that close. Lots of families are that way. I don't visit mine often enough."

We visited Scott's family plenty often enough to suit me, but I wouldn't be distracted by that right now.

"I know Dorothea. She never would've taken off without telling me. She knows I would worry while she was away, especially not knowing where she is."

"You shouldn't worry regardless. She has a right to visit family without clearing it with you first."

"That's not what I meant."

"Give it a rest, Joy. She'll be home in a day or two and tell you all about it."

"Then why didn't Gunnar say that? You should've seen him. He looked like I caught him with his hand in the cookie jar. He couldn't wait to get me off the front step."

"Maybe because you were being a pest."

"I'm not a pest. I love his aunt. He should appreciate that. He acted like he was hiding something. There's something about him I don't trust."

"You don't have anything to base your feelings on except he knows something about Dorothea that you don't. You almost sound like you're jealous of him."

"I'm not jealous."

Suspicious was a better word.

Scott leaned back into the sofa cushions and gazed up at me. "If you say so. You need to forget Gunnar Westlake and worry about your own family. With Dorothea gone for a few days, maybe you can get around to some of the chores you've been putting off around here."

I turned back to the window. I was worried about my neighbor's safety, and all he cared about was getting the utility room painted like I'd been saying I was going to do since last fall.

The discussion about Dorothea was shelved for the time being. Despite my best attempts not to, I made a hundred trips past the window before turning in for the night. Lights came on across the street as the night progressed. Dorothea's bedroom suite upstairs remained dark. At least Gunnar wasn't sleeping in her room. There wasn't anything I could do about it if he did, but I was happy he had the decency to stay in the guest room.

It wouldn't be so bad if I hadn't overheard his conversation yesterday. Was he a gambler? A drug dealer? A courier of illegal goods? Had he accrued debts from some dangerous types? What if he came here to hide out? Upon arrival, he would've realized Dorothea wasn't living on social security. She had antiques and a few valuables around the house. Albert had given her a few nice pieces of jewelry over the years. Some of them were real. With the price of gold, along with a few diamonds and gemstones, Gunnar might realize he could help himself to several thousand dollars worth of booty when Dorothea wasn't looking.

Most of her assets were tucked away in the bank or in stocks and bonds. I had no idea what she planned for her estate. We never talked about those things. I always figured she might leave a portion of her assets in trust to our church or her alumni scholarships or however people with more money than family disposed of their estate.

My stomach twisted. What if my friend was in physical danger? Would she see the danger before it was too late? Yes, she was shrewd and intelligent. She was also kind and good and unwilling to accept a person's faults without first looking deeper for virtue. Would a nephew's attention and flattery be enough to talk her into investing in a financial venture? If he gave her a sob story about his parents cutting him off or how he was drowning in student loans, would she forget her common sense and give over free rein of her checkbook? I didn't think so, but I knew how persuasive family could be. Especially to someone like Dorothea who had been missing one for so long.

There was a reason authorities always looked first to those closest to a person when one became a victim of crime.

I knew I should follow Scott's advice and focus on my own family issues while Dorothea was away. The Lord knew we had plenty. I still hadn't told Scott about Dylan sneaking out of the house the other night. Without Dorothea across the street to fortify my faltering nerve I couldn't muster the courage to bring it up. I was too worried about her and too worried about what Gunnar was doing in her house alone. I wouldn't be comfortable with Scott's brother and his ultra perfect wife staying at our house while we were out of town, and we were a lot closer to them than Dorothea was to Gunnar. The whole situation made absolutely no sense. I planned to get to the bottom of it. I didn't know Gunnar Westlake, and I had no right to make demands of him, but I was going to find out where Dorothea had gone and when she'd be back.

Chapter 6

The next morning I tried to pretend I had accepted Gunnar's version of events and wasn't obsessing over what really happened to Dorothea. All I could think about was getting over to Dorothea's and extracting some information. I didn't want Scott to try to talk me out of it. It was all I could do not to throw a protein bar at him along with his car keys and shoo him out the door. I wanted to leave the instant he did, but Gunnar probably wasn't as early a riser as his aunt and me. He might sleep till ten. I would have to wait. Breaking down the door and demanding an explanation wasn't an option though that's exactly what I wanted to do.

To kill time and take my mind off Gunnar Westlake, I opened the doors of the entertainment center and pulled out a stack of dusty workout DVDs I'd been collecting since Aidan was born. I cracked open the only one I'd ever tried and gave it a look. Was I really this desperate to kill an hour and burn off some nervous energy?

I was tired of the spare tire around my middle that hadn't changed much since I brought my Lima Bean home from the hospital. The weight had been much easier to lose after Dylan was born when I was barely twenty. My mother was quick to tell me I'd never get my weight back after having a baby at my age. I wanted to do it just to prove her wrong. Even if I never got into a size six, I'd like to feel better about myself and not get winded walking Aidan to the park.

Aidan came in and plopped down on the couch. "Are we watching a movie?"

I held out the DVD. "Let's work out instead."

His cherubic face turned from amazement to excitement in the span of an instant. It was a shame my son had never seen me interested in exercise. He jumped off the couch and began bouncing from one foot to the other. I should've included Aidan in my fitness plans earlier. With his four-year-old exuberance urging me onward, I might've stuck to a routine for more than one morning in a row.

While Aidan whooped and leaped around the room for the next thirty minutes, I followed the modified version of the workout and prayed it didn't launch me into cardiac arrest. I went left when everyone else went right. Working my upper and lower body at the same time was out of the question. I stopped apologizing for stepping on Aidan's feet or smacking him in the head during arm rotations. I figured it was his problem if he couldn't see me coming and get out of the way. The whole point was to get up and move.

"Even mistakes burn calories," the bubbly instructor squealed, making me wish she was in the room so I could sit on her.

"Can we go to the park?" Aidan asked as I ejected the DVD thirty minutes later and buried the case under the entertainment center where it couldn't hurt me again.

I groaned aloud. "Maybe later. I need a shower."

In actuality the park was the last place I wanted to go. The exercise had successfully taken my mind off Dorothea for half an hour. Struggling to catch my next breath and praying the elastic in my sports bra wouldn't give out kept me from worrying about where she was and whom she was with. Now that blood was returning to my brain, I needed to figure out how to get Gunnar to talk to me without making him think I was a pest or crazy or forcing him to shut down altogether.

I turned the TV to Aidan's favorite channel and hurried upstairs as quickly as my flabby, tired body would allow. Truth be told, the workout had energized me though my knees were wobbly and my arms fatigued. Everything I read assured me if I stuck with an exercise regimen, the light-headedness and double vision would pass. I paused at the top of the stairs to look across the street to Dorothea's house. In the daylight I couldn't see lights on in any of the houses up and down our street.

Gunnar's car sat where it had yesterday morning. I glared at the Illinois license plate. "Why are you here?" I asked under my breath. "What do you want?"

Since the car couldn't answer my questions and I couldn't leave Aidan downstairs unsupervised for long, I hurried to my room for an outfit before heading to the shower.

The first thing new mothers learn to do is shower and answer the call of nature in record time. Sailors and surgeons have nothing on us. Within fifteen minutes I had showered, moisturized, dressed, and was on my way downstairs.

I paused at the top of the stairs and looked at Dylan's door. It was after ten in the morning. Gunnar was surely up by now hard at work on his dissertation, or whatever it was he was doing over there. If he wasn't, he soon would be and I wouldn't feel guilty for disturbing him. I needed to talk to him, preferably without Aidan making me lose my train of thought. I looked again at Dylan's door. Why hurry through a shower and try to figure out how to get out of the house for a few minutes when I had a nineteen-year-old in residence perfectly capable of keeping an eye on his little brother?

Aidan wanted to go to the park. I needed to talk to Gunnar. I swallowed my trepidation and marched across the hall. Give me courage, I prayed as I squared my shoulders. Was Dorothea right? I was so afraid of confronting Dylan I gave him too much leeway in every matter? Neither Scott nor I put demands on him. We had absolutely no expectations. No wonder he continually under-whelmed us.

Before I could talk myself out of it or lose my nerve, I gave the door a solid knock. Though this was my house and I wasn't required to knock first, I did because I believed everyone was entitled to a degree of privacy. I even knocked on Aidan's door before entering.

Was it too much to ask the men in this house to grant me the same respect and courtesy I gave them?

I gave the door another quick rap before pushing my way in. The curtains were pulled tight over the dormer window directly ahead of me, and it took my eyes a moment to grow accustomed to the gloom. A blade of light shone from under the bathroom door. I needed to make my presence known before Dylan came out of the bathroom fresh from the shower and unprepared to greet me. My eyes turned toward the computer screen, the only other source of light. A screen saver picture of a scantily clad woman making suggestive movements on the screen was replaced with an even more exposed woman astride a horse. I swallowed my disgust as my heart wrenched for her poor mother somewhere, hopefully unaware of what her daughter did to pay her way through school.

"Dylan," I shrieked before I could check my voice. I kicked aside dirty laundry and debris as I stumbled across the room to the computer. I held down on the power button until it blinked off.

"Hey," Dylan said from the bathroom doorway. "You're not supposed to turn it off like that."

I straightened, breathless from the exertion and indignation. "You're lucky I don't throw it out the window. I won't have pornography in this house."

"Chill, Mom. That isn't pornography." Framed in the doorway in bare feet, wearing a cotton t-shirt and jeans, he reminded me of a cross between Aidan and Scott—innocent little boy and man. An image of the nearly nude young woman on his computer screen reminded me he hadn't been an innocent little boy in a long time.

A button down shirt was draped over his arm. His hair was still wet from the shower. At least he hadn't been on the computer recently. They were just screen saver pictures after all. He was a young man. I'd be more concerned if he wasn't enamored with images of beautiful women. No one had been completely nude. Even the Supreme Court refused to define pornography. But I was his mother. I knew pornography when I saw it. What if Aidan had come in and seen those disgusting pictures?

"Maybe it's not technically pornography, but if you don't delete them, I will. They're offensive and degrading to women."

He cocked his head and advanced protectively toward the computer. "The only women who think dressing like that is offensive and degrading are ones who wish they looked that good."

"That isn't true, Dylan. Those women are someone's sisters and daughters. Would you want someone ogling a sister of yours?"

"If she was hot I'd expect guys to look at her."

This conversation was pointless, and I didn't have all day to explain the error in his logic. "Aidan wants to go the park."

"He can go wherever he wants."

"You take him and I won't make a big deal over the pictures."

"Too late."

"I'll pay you thirty dollars for thirty minutes."

He paused, considering. "I was on my way out."

"To work?"

"Okay, fine. But I'm not pushing him on the swings."

I'd be happy as long as he didn't push him in front of a bus.

"He loves you, Dylan. You don't spend nearly enough time with him."

Dylan was already shrugging into his shirt. "Whatever. Thirty minutes." He went to the door. "Hey, munchkin," he called down the stairs, "you want to go to the park?" He stopped to look back at me. "Are you coming?"

I followed him into the hallway and pulled the door shut behind me. "I want you to take those filthy pictures off your computer when you get back, as well as anything else I might deem offensive and degrading."

"You're the boss."

Since when, I wondered, but I wasn't about to contradict his generosity.

Dylan and Aidan had barely disappeared around the corner when I buttoned my cardigan over a stretched out t-shirt and hurried out the front door. If Dylan had promised me thirty minutes, he would be back in twenty, claiming my watch must've stopped because he could swear he'd been gone at least an hour. It would've been easier and more efficient to call Dorothea's house to see if she was home, but I didn't want to warn Gunnar I was coming. Nothing would satisfy my curiosity until I saw her with my own eyes. With one hand holding the neck of my cardigan closed around my throat, I dashed across the street. I should've taken the time to grab a jacket. The wind had a bite to it even though the sun shone brightly through the new leaves on the trees. I hoped Aidan was dressed warmly enough, but it was too late to do anything about it. Dylan wouldn't keep him at the park long anyway.

I was breathless and the backs of my legs groaned in protest by the time I reached Dorothea's front door. This was why I never worked out. I didn't like discomfort. I would thank myself this summer when I didn't feel like a toad in my Capri pants. The activity would be good for Aidan too. I just hoped I wasn't kidding myself and those DVDs wouldn't see the light of day for another five years.

I smiled at my determination and leaned long and hard on Dorothea's doorbell.

Gunnar answered almost immediately. I wondered if he'd seen me crossing the street. He didn't bother with any kind of visual or verbal greeting.

"Hi," I said, feigning cheeriness. "Is Dorothea home?"

He exhaled as if I was the biggest idiot he'd ever encountered. I got that reaction a lot.

"I told you yesterday she isn't here. She's visiting family."

"I thought you meant for the afternoon. I didn't realize she was out of town."

"Well, she is." He started to close the door.

I pushed forward, anticipating his move. "When will she be back?"

If I hadn't been studying his face I wouldn't have noticed the tightening of his jaw or narrowing of his eyes. A sliver of fear wormed down my back. I clasped my cardigan tighter around my throat.

"Don't know," he said tightly. "She didn't say."

I cocked my head and smiled benignly up at him. All the while my heart hammered in my chest. "I wonder why she didn't tell me she was going out of town. She always lets me know these things."

"Probably because I'm here to keep an eye on things."

"So you're staying until she gets back?"

"Listen, if you don't mind…" He inched the door closed. "I was in the middle of something…"

"Of course." Inspiration struck. "Since you're all alone for the foreseeable future and don't know anyone, you might like to have dinner with me and my family. What about tonight?"

"Thanks, but I'm busy."

"Working on your dissertation?"

"What? Oh, that. Yeah, it's keeping me pretty busy."

The door closed more, forcing me off the stoop. "If there's anything you need, I'm right across the street," I said to the narrowing crack. "I'm always home."

I didn't expect a reply and didn't get one.

The first thing I noticed the next morning was Dorothea's garage door was up and her blue Crown Vic was missing. I had made a point on my way upstairs the night before to look across the street to her house. Now here it was, barely six o'clock in the morning, and Gunnar's car had been moved and the Crown Vic wasn't in the garage where Dorothea always kept it.

I unlocked the latch on the front door and stepped out on the porch. I didn't need to watch the weather forecast to know the temperature was near freezing. I hoped the cold snap wouldn't harm my budding flowering bushes and perennials. Dorothea always told me it took an extended hard frost to affect most of the bushes in our neighborhood. She was usually right about those things, but I fretted nonetheless.

I was dressed in sweats and a baggy sweatshirt, my usual morning attire for making breakfast and getting Scott out the door. I usually took my shower first to insure I had plenty of hot water and time to enjoy it. It wasn't until Scott was gone and the breakfast dishes were stowed in the dishwasher and Aidan stowed in front of his toys that I went back upstairs to dress properly, style my hair as it were, and add a touch of makeup if I felt so inclined. With my new determination to work out every morning—or at least twice in a row—I planned to shower after.

The neighbors seldom saw me outside in sweats. Sweats weren't an attractive mode of dress for most body types, especially ones like mine that were eight inches too short for the amount of weight I carried. My hips were too wide and my waistline nonexistent to attempt any type of athletic wear. It was the main reason I couldn't join a gym. Well, maybe not the main reason, but the easiest one to admit to myself.

I looked first one way and then the other before tiptoeing to the edge of the porch. No neighbors in sight. No one left for work this early. I took a deep breath for courage and darted off the porch and into the shrubbery. I ran down the sidewalk to the curb. I don't know what I hoped to find, but I had to know if Dorothea had returned home during the night. It wasn't likely that she would've moved her car between the time I went to bed and now. Even if she was back home, which I sincerely hoped was the case, there would've been no reason to move the car out of the garage. That could only mean Gunnar was driving

Dorothea's car. Most people would find nothing wrong in that. Dorothea was a generous person. But she was very particular about her car. Two years ago when Dorothea and I went to an overnight ladies' retreat in Columbus, Dorothea had left her car keys with Scott. Other than emergencies, I had never known her to allow anyone to drive her car.

"In case a water main breaks and you need to move it," she said.

I spotted a scrap of newspaper in the gutter and headed for it. If anyone saw me outside at this ridiculous hour looking the way I did, they would think I was cleaning up trash. In reality, I needed time to think. I knelt to pick up the paper and thought about the likelihood that Dorothea would let Gunnar drive her car late at night. Or at all.

There was always a chance she had lightened up about the car. Gunnar was family. People often allowed family to do things--even if it meant taking advantage--they would never allow others to get by with. Still, I didn't like it. I didn't like anything about the situation. Where would he go this early in the morning, and why go to the trouble of moving his own car to get hers out of the garage?

"Yoo hoo, Joy."

I groaned under my breath as I straightened. I'd been spotted. By Libby Patterson no less. She was a dear lady but could talk the arm off a politician. I didn't want to explain what I was doing out this early. I pasted on a happy face and met her halfway across the driveway. Her Pomeranian Sunny strained at the end of a leash.

"Hello, Libby." I hugged myself to keep warm. "You're out early."

"I think Sunny got into the trash during the night and now his tummy's upset. Isn't that right, precious?" She directed the last comment to the quivering bundle of overweight fur. Sunny was wearing a sweater in Cincinnati Bearcats black and red. Libby's son was a single and successful accountant who was also a huge college football fan. Spoiling his mother's dog was his only way to placate her for failing to give her a daughter-in-law and grandchildren.

Sunny looked up at Libby, leaped straight into the air, and let out a chorus of yips. I cringed at the decibel level.

"I'll let you get back to your walk then," I said. Sunny didn't look any the worse for wear after having gotten in the garbage, but if he was going to be sick somewhere, I didn't want it to be in my driveway.

"I never see you out this early, Joy," Libby went on. She looked as snug as a bug in a rug in her heavy quilted fleece and scarf. She had no need to hurry back inside.

I held up the scrap of newspaper. "Doing a little grounds keeping." I glanced toward Dorothea's. I figured the only other person on the block nosy enough to notice the strange events across the street was Libby. She lived on the first house on the left. Nothing happened around here that she didn't know about. "Dorothea's car's gone already this morning," I observed. "You didn't see her drive past your house, did you?"

Libby's gaze settled on Gunnar's car parked on the street. "I thought I saw her headlights go by last night just as I was turning off the news, but I couldn't be sure. I thought it was awfully late for traffic, especially for Dorothea."

"Could you tell if she was the one driving?"

Libby shook her head and pulled back on the leash. Sunny was getting impatient. It was okay by me. I was impatient to get back into the warmth of my cozy house. "I just saw the headlights, not the car. I figured it was Dorothea's since it's the biggest car on the block."

I nodded and shivered inside my sweatshirt. "Maybe Gunnar went to the airport to pick her up. I'm curious to hear how her trip went."

Libby's eyes grew round. "Oh? I didn't know she was out of town."

"Her nephew said she was visiting family. If he went to pick her up from the airport last night they've should be back by now."

"Maybe her flight was delayed."

That made sense. "Have you met Gunnar?" I asked Libby.

"I ran into him the other day when I was walking Sunny. Doesn't talk much."

In all fairness to Gunnar, it was difficult for even the most Chatty Cathy to get a word in around Libby.

"I'm sure Dorothea enjoys having him around," Libby continued.

If she enjoyed his company so much, why had she taken off to visit family practically the day he showed up? I pulled my arms in tighter against my body and looked across the street to Dorothea's house. Scott could say I was nosy and crazy all he wanted, but something was going on over there.

I brought my gaze back to Libby and forced a smile. Not an easy task with my lips nearly frozen to my teeth. "Thank you, Libby. I need to get back inside. Scott will wonder what happened to his breakfast."

She waved and turned on her heel. "Give everyone my love."

I waved back and hurried inside.

"What were you doing outside?" Scott asked as soon as I entered the kitchen.

I suppressed a shiver and went to the garbage can to throw away the newspaper. "I saw this fluttering in the gutter and didn't know what it was." He didn't look convinced, especially after I sidled into the warm spot on the floor where the sun shone through the window.

"It sure took you long enough to pick up one piece of trash."

"Libby Patterson was walking her dog."

He immediately lost interest in the conversation. Everyone on the street knew Libby. "Did you start the coffee?"

He asked the same question every morning. We'd had a pre-set coffeemaker since Dylan was little that I programmed for the same time every day. There hadn't been a coffee-less morning in this house since a huge power outage last winter.

Even then, Scott had braved the elements and risked life threatening personal injury to hike to the local coffeehouse for his morning fix. If we were marooned on a deserted island, he would wake up the first morning and ask if I'd started the coffee.

"You're usually not down this early," I said, ignoring the question.

"I heard you go out and wanted to see where you were off to. No breakfast for me. I don't feel well."

I went to him and cocked my head to study his face for signs of malady. "I hope you're not coming down with something."

"I'm sure it's nothing." He grabbed the oversized mug out of the cupboard he always drank from, removed the carafe, and stuck the mug in its place. "Did I tell you Chris called yesterday at work?" he asked while he waited for the mug to fill. "He and Valerie invited us up this weekend."

Everything became crystal clear. He didn't feel well because he dreaded telling me about his brother's call. My concern for his health vanished into the morning air. "Scott, I hate it when you do that."

"Do what?"

"Pretend you don't remember if you mentioned something or not when you know very well you didn't." I stepped into his line of vision. "You can stop hiding behind your coffee cup."

He tore his gaze away from the sputtering coffeemaker. "I already know how you'll react. You hate my sister-in-law and you don't want to spend the weekend with her and Chris."

"I don't hate Valerie," I said, though not completely convincing. "I just don't like…" I paused to give myself time to figure out the kindest way to tell him how I felt. Problem was, I didn't really know myself. I chose the easy, most obvious answer. "I don't like the way they invite us at the last minute as though we never have plans of our own. It's almost like they hope we can't make it."

"That's not true. They're very busy and can't plan things too far in advance."

"Unlike us who have completely blank schedules?"

Scott removed his mug from under the drip and replaced the carafe with a minimum of hissing drips on the plate. He was an expert. "I wish you weren't so sensitive when it comes to my family. If someone at church did the same thing, you wouldn't think twice about it. I don't know why you can't be as charitable to my brother and his family. "

No one at church made it their life's work to intimidate me and make me feel inferior. But Chris and Valerie were Scott's family. That meant they were my children's family too. My family. I shouldn't get my hackles up every time they called and invited us to their house. Fortunately, they were busy and it didn't happen often.

I braced myself. "What did you say?"

"I told him I'd talk it over with you."

"What's there to talk about? It's not like I have a choice in the matter."

He went to the fridge for his soymilk. He didn't respond until he finished adding a dollop to his cup and putting the carton back in the fridge. "You have a choice, Joy. That's why I'm talking it over with you."

"No," I insisted, hating the petulant tone in my voice but incapable of doing anything about it. "We don't have any other plans this weekend, and I can't stay home just because they make me feel like a bull in a china shop in their home."

"The way you feel in their home is your problem, not theirs."

"Maybe so, but isn't a good hostess supposed to make guests feel welcome and comfortable in her home? I never do. Neither do the boys."

Scott blew on his coffee. "I always have a great time."

"Of course you do. You spend the whole weekend joking and horsing around with Chris while I'm stuck in the kitchen pretending like I care while Valerie talks about all the important things she does."

Scott glanced at the clock on the wall and took another sip of coffee. He still hadn't gotten in the shower. "Maybe if you tried to care our visits wouldn't be such torture. Valerie has a lot of friends. She's very intelligent. Other people find her fascinating."

"Well, maybe they should go with you and I'll stay home."

He cocked an eyebrow. "Joy."

I sighed in defeat. "Okay, fine. You're right. They're family." I put my hand on his arm and guided him toward the door. "Go get ready for work and I'll start breakfast. Call your brother and tell him we can't wait to see him on Saturday."

He held the cup away from me and kissed my cheek. "Thanks, Joy. It won't be so bad. I promise to spend some time with you so you aren't marooned the entire time with Valerie."

I smiled and gave him another push toward the door. We both knew that wasn't going to happen, but it was nice of him to offer.

Chapter 7

I'm so happy you could make it," Valerie said as she handed me a heavy, color coordinated Phalzgraff plate to dry. "I know it was inconsiderate of us to wait until the last minute to invite you."

I wondered if Scott had told her how I felt. If he had, I'd wring his well toned neck. I took the offered plate and wiped it with a dishtowel that didn't look like it had been through the laundry five hundred times the way mine had. "We look forward to coming as often as we can."

"I hate it that Dylan couldn't get away," she continued in a sugarcoated voice. I tried not to cringe at the sound of it. She'd been nothing but congenial since our arrival. I thought of Scott's admonishment that if someone at church behaved like Valerie I would overlook it. He was right. I needed to be as gracious to Valerie as I was with everyone else.

"Where did you say he's working?"

"One of the fast food places in the mall. He was disappointed he couldn't make it."

I'd already lied about looking forward to her invitations. Might as well go all out. Dylan had been positively giddy when he found out Scott, Aidan, and I would be out of the house the whole weekend while he was stuck at home working. He was quick to remind me how important it was he keep his job. If we insisted he become a responsible member of our home and society at large, he couldn't very well run off to Indianapolis every weekend his aunt and uncle decided to hand out an invitation.

"Perhaps if we'd had more notice…"

"Of course. Of course." She motioned with a manicured hand. "I'll try harder next time. We're so busy all the time. If something fits into my schedule, Chris can't get away. You know how it is…" She let the sentiment trail off as if afraid she'd offended me, and went back to washing.

I resisted the urge to tell her I knew exactly how it was. Just because I was a stay at home mom didn't mean I didn't have schedules and to-do lists and meetings I couldn't get out of. Saying so would only sound juvenile and insecure. I wiped another dish and pretended I hadn't noticed.

My sister-in-law epitomized perfection in every way. Her hair was always in place, her makeup impeccable, even first thing in the morning the time they invited us to their timeshare in Key West. While I used my week at the Keys as an excuse to go without makeup and eat whatever I wanted and sit by the pool reading a book with no concern of whether or not my bag matched my flip flops, Valerie looked as gorgeous and accessorized as when having lunch at a trendy restaurant downtown.

Valerie was a legal advisor for a national bank. She made more money than Chris and Scott combined, though she was too big of a person to point it out. She always trilled with delight at the thought of being a stay at home mom, and wouldn't that be the life, and if only it were a possibility for her.

"How I envy you, Joy," she would say. It was always followed with a comment about how she needed the challenge of a real job that gave a person purpose and fulfillment. It never occurred to her she might find purpose and fulfillment at home with her family.

The only things more perfect in Valerie's life than Valerie herself were her two beautiful, clever, well-behaved children. Garrett was thirteen, that magical age when parents hid military school flyers in their underwear drawer and drooled over them while the kids were at school. The only thing wrong with Garrett was he hadn't yet gone through any awkward, neurotic, psychotic stages that faced most teens. He was respectful and funny and congenial and sincere. He rolled his eyes every time his parents opened their mouths but in a good-natured way that got a laugh out of all of us. When Dylan was Garrett's age I slept with one eye open. Everything within me wanted to hate Garrett. But he was too darned loveable.

Valerie pulled the stopper in the sink and swished the water around with the dishrag. She said she enjoyed puttering around in the kitchen, preparing a big meal, and cleaning up afterward when she had an evening away from the office. "It is so seldom I can enjoy my beautiful kitchen. Makes me feel like a regular person," she had explained with a laugh.

She dried out the sink and dropped the towel into a tiny hamper under the sink. "I don't know how you do it." She shook her head. Her blond hair was cut in a short bob that accentuated her long neck and the fact that she was nearly forty and showed no visible signs of aging. I suspected Botox. She could easily afford it but wouldn't admit it under oath. Her hair was tucked behind her ears, and even with her hands red from the dishwater and her makeup nearly gone from playing in the yard with the kids, she was still pretty and perky and flawlessly groomed.

"Do what?" I couldn't imagine anything I did that she wished she could do as well.

"How you let Dylan continue to coast along with no specific goals. I'd have gone off the deep end with him a long time ago."

Every time the family got together, someone invariably brought up Dylan's lack of motivation and direction, and it somehow came around to being a direct result of my poor parenting. You'd think I'd be good at deflecting the comments by now. I shouldn't be so sensitive about it, but I was.

I swallowed my inadequacies. "I can't very well hold his hand and make him go to class like I did when he was in the second grade."

"If memory serves me correctly, you couldn't do it then either." Her ensuing laugh sounded like a tiny bell.

I wanted to deny it, but that would've been pointless. "He's always been hard-headed. Like his father. Just try making either of them do something they don't want to do."

Valerie moved to the island and straightened a bowl of expensive potpourri. "Chris and I have always stressed the need for a good education to Garrett and Peyton. We believe the most important thing for a young person is that they achieve their potential. Without a solid education, they're so…limited." She gave a slight shudder.

"It's not as though Scott and I talked Dylan out of going to college."

"Of course not." She gave me a conciliatory smile. "Dylan is very smart. He always has been. I just hate to see his potential go to waste."

I wasn't exactly jumping for joy over it myself. "We've tried talking him into signing up for a few classes. Just something to see what might interest him."

"Community college," she said with a snort. "Wouldn't that be a hoot?"

"I'll take anything at this point."

"I suppose you would."

I searched my mind for a subject change. On the way here while Aidan napped in his car seat, I promised Scott I would make a concerted effort not to let little things get under my skin where they would fester and eat at me since I didn't have the nerve to speak up and defend myself. I didn't think Valerie intentionally tried to intimidate me. She was probably totally unaware of her effect on me. I was sure Scott was right, and the problem was with me and not anything she did. Still, it was getting harder and harder to smile at her comments, even if she didn't mean anything by them.

"A community college education works well for plenty of people."

"I suppose if you're in that situation, it's better than nothing."

I got the impression she likened it to eating grub worms if you were lost in the forest and only moments from succumbing to starvation.

"I could talk to Chris about it." She glanced toward the kitchen door before turning back to me. "We're more than willing to help in any way."

She lost me. "Help with what?"

She cocked her head. "You know. The money. If you and Scott are going through a rough patch…"

I gave my head a shake to clear the cobwebs. "Valerie, I—"

"The economic downturn has affected everyone. It's nothing to be ashamed of."

"We're not having money problems, if that's what you mean."

"Oh. I thought since you mentioned community college…"

"Dylan doesn't want to go to school. It's as simple as that. It's not because we're about to lose the house."

She exhaled a little too grandly. "That's good to hear. I just thought…"

"Well, don't." I checked my ire. She was only trying to be helpful. Wasn't she?

Thundering footsteps sounded on the stairs to our right. We turned our heads in that direction. I wondered if Valerie was as delighted by the interruption as I was. Peyton came into view first, followed by Aidan.

"Garrett's being mean to us," Peyton announced. She was nine. She had long, silky blond hair like her mother and big blue eyes that sparkled when she laughed. She was the smartest kid in her class and excelled at everything she tried. She was a swimming champ and loved the glee club. The poor kid had never done a thing to make me dislike her. Still, the sound of her voice was like a nail through my skull. I had secretly celebrated when Valerie called practically in tears seven years ago when Peyton relapsed in her potty training. Sadly, the lapse was short lived, but it was one of the happiest weekends of my life.

I realized I had been holding my breath. I exhaled gratefully that Aidan hadn't broken something or otherwise proven himself inferior to Valerie's offspring.

Valerie laid a hand on her daughter's flushed cheek. "I'm sure he isn't, sweetheart."

"Yes, he is. He called Aidan a pest and wouldn't let us play with his I-pad."

Aidan looked at me and nodded solemnly.

Ever patient, ever diplomatic, Valerie tilted her head. "Did you go into his room without asking?"

"He said we could. Then he told us to get out."

"You probably wore out your welcome. You don't need to play with his I-pad anyway." Valerie glanced at Aidan. I stiffened. I knew she was afraid my son would break their expensive electronics. Even though he probably would, I didn't want it pointed out.

"Why don't you and Aidan find something else to do?" I suggested.

"There isn't anything to do. Daddy said he'd take us for ice cream, but now he's talking to Uncle Scott and he's too busy."

"How about we play a game?" I clasped my hands and looked hopefully from one face to the other. I had never noticed how similar the children looked, but standing in front of me with lips pursed and faces flushed, it was hard to miss. Both had inherited their fathers' bright blue eyes and high foreheads. The only thing Aidan inherited from me was my upturned nose while Peyton had plenty of Valerie in her to guarantee true beauty was about three years out.

"I seem to remember you have an amazing collection of board games," I said to Peyton.

Their faces brightened, and the resemblance vanished as other traits rushed to the fore. They squealed with delight and turned as one toward the family room.

"Nothing electronic," I admonished as I started after them. I smiled apologetically over my shoulder at Valerie that our conversation had been put on hold until another time. I had no intention of allowing her to corner me again and force me to defend my oldest or my own lack of parental finesse.

"More coffee anyone?" Valerie held the carafe aloft and looked around the table. Scott held up his cup without stopping chewing on fresh bakery croissants. He had already commented on the taste and quality of the coffee and how he couldn't get anything remotely comparable at home without going into one of those overpriced coffeehouses.

The four of us sat at the oak table in the breakfast nook and watched Aidan and Peyton chasing the family's Golden Retriever around the backyard. Even their dog was picture perfect. So far I had seen no greater strife between the cousins than what one would expect when children with such a big age difference played together. Peyton was doing remarkably well entertaining her young cousin. I knew Aidan would tell me about it later if she wasn't. We hadn't seen much of Garrett except last night at dinner. As soon as he was excused, he dashed upstairs and was not seen or heard from again. Besides chasing the younger children out of his room and forbidding them to touch his things, he hadn't been unreasonable. I seemed to remember Dylan at that age hiding my crutches after I broke my foot and not giving them back until I promised to give in to whatever he wanted at the moment.

I drained the last of my cup. I wasn't much of a coffee drinker and could easily stop after one cup even if the brew in question was unrivaled in the tri-state area.

Chris popped the last of a croissant into his mouth and dabbed the corners of his mouth with a cloth napkin. He let out a contented sigh. "It doesn't get any better than this." He looked at Scott, and they laughed at the reference to an old beer commercial.

"You said it," Scott conceded. "Too bad we can't do this every weekend."

My ingrained graciousness caused me to chime in before I could stop myself. "You should come visit us next time."

The look Scott gave me was of pure shock. "No waiting until Thanksgiving this time," I went on. "Summer's only eight weeks away. I'm sure we can coordinate something by then."

Scott reached under the table and squeezed my hand in gratitude.

Chris and Valerie exchanged looks. "I don't know," Chris hedged.

"Peyton is going to soccer camp the first week of summer vacation," Valerie said. "Then she has 4-H and softball, not to mention dance that is nearly year-round."

"Garrett keeps a full plate all summer with pony league and College for Kids," Chris picked up when she stopped. "But you're always welcome to come here anytime you can get away. It would be much easier that way since Joy doesn't work. She can take off at the drop of a hat. I don't know how you do it," he directed at me. "Valerie would go out of her mind if she sat around the house all day."

Heat gathered in the middle of my back and worked its way around my shoulders and into my face and neck. "I don't exactly sit around all day." I looked at Scott for support. He slathered butter onto another croissant.

"Of course you don't," Valerie said with a laugh in her voice.

"Yeah," Chris said with a chuckle. "Throwing laundry into a washing machine, dishes into a dishwasher, and clicking the send button to pay your monthly bills must be exhausting."

"It takes a lot more than that to run a household." I shot Scott a desperate look. "It's why most professionals have assistants. Try getting along without us sometime."

Chris elbowed his brother. "Sounds like you forgot to buy a card for Secretary's Day, Scott."

Scott covered my hand with his. "I'll have you know Joy is invaluable. She's completely responsible for the boys' education and rearing. I'm too busy earning a living for much input there. If it weren't for her—"

"Dylan would probably be enrolled in a university somewhere," Valerie cut in with another laugh. The men joined in. "He needs a firmer hand, Scott," she said after she stopped laughing. "We all know what a pushover Joy is. She never could handle him."

Scott nodded in agreement. "It's an uphill battle. With Dylan sleeping till noon and his mother pampering him, I can't win. In Joy's defense though, she's so busy watching the neighbor's house all day I can't expect her to keep an eye on Dylan too."

I whirled in my chair to face him. "Scott."

Chris and Valerie propped their elbows on the table and leaned forward, rapt with attention.

He grinned at me before turning back to his audience. "Our neighbor's nephew is in for a visit. Joy is sure he's robbing the old woman blind or has already buried her in the backyard. She sits on the couch on her knees like an adolescent all day long and waits for the poor kid to come outside and do something suspicious."

"Scott," I said again, trying in vain to keep my voice light. "You know that isn't true. You also know Dorothea is my good friend. You'd feel terrible if something happened to her."

"She's seventy-five," Scott explained for Chris and Valerie's benefit. "The widow of a very successful vascular surgeon. If anyone needs looking after, Dorothea should be keeping an eye on Joy."

Chris and Valerie rocked with laughter.

Heat colored my face all the way down my throat.

"I keep telling Joy Dorothea's sharp as a tack. No nephew will talk her out of anything she doesn't want to give up. But our Joy…" He gave me an endearing look. "She's always looking for a conspiracy."

"I am not." I don't think anyone heard me. It was just as well. I sounded pitiful.

Always the helpful one, Valerie swung her head so her blond wedge fell across her face. "Too bad she can't redirect some of that energy to keeping Dylan out of trouble."

"That's what I keep trying to tell her," Scott said.

"I'm not the only one responsible for keeping Dylan out of trouble." This time my voice was forceful enough to get their attention.

Scott raised his hands in defense. "You're the one home with him all day."

"Why is that, Scott? He should be at school. Or work." I took a deep breath and made an effort to calm down. From the heat on my face I could only imagine how red my cheeks were. I hated for them to see they'd gotten to me, but I didn't like being cornered. Why did every conversation have to come back to what a mess I'd made of Dylan?

Through the window I saw Aidan shove Peyton out of the tire swing. I didn't want Peyton to be hurt but secretly congratulated Aidan on his timing. I jumped up and tore out the back door. Valerie tossed her napkin on the table and followed. Just as she shut the door behind us I heard Scott and Chris burst into fresh laughter.

Chapter 8

Tension began to lift from my shoulders the instant we backed out of Chris and Valerie's driveway. By the time we got onto I-74 the pounding at my temple had faded to a dull ache. Aidan slept nearly the whole way home. I was too tired and cranky to attempt conversation with Scott. He was better left alone when behind the wheel of the car anyway. He focused on the road and ball scores on the radio, and I watched out the window as we drove into the darkening sky.

We stopped once for gas and to stretch our legs. Aidan ran out of steam again after twenty minutes back in the car and went back to sleep. The gentle motion and quiet inside the car and the festering aggravation of the weekend's events lolled me into a semiconscious state.

"That went well."

I jerked my head around to glare at Scott.

"What?" he asked at my expression.

"What part went well, Scott? The part where you made fun of me for worrying about Dorothea? Or the part where they blamed me for how Dylan turned out. You didn't even defend me."

"I shouldn't have to, Joy. You're a grown woman. Defend yourself."

"You're my husband. You should take my side."

"Side? What side? We were kidding around. Didn't you hear Chris riding me about my golf game? Did I pout and go to my room or expect you to jump in and explain how busy I am and don't have as much time to hit the links as he does? No, because it was all in fun."

"Well, it wasn't fun for me. I don't know why you can't understand that. It was hurtful and demeaning. To know you agree with them makes it a hundred times worse."

He exhaled deeply enough that his shoulders moved up and down. "I don't agree with anything. We were having fun. I'm sorry you're so sensitive. Do you want me to call Chris when we get home and tell him not to tease my wife about not having a job because it hurts her feelings? Maybe you should make a list of things you don't want brought up in conversation. Like your weight. I know that bothers you. Or gray hair. Or how Aidan still sleeps in Pull-Ups."

"You don't even try to understand what I'm saying. I just want a little respect. I never hear the three of you tease each other. You always gang up on me."

"Maybe you're an easy target."

"What does that mean?

"It's easy to get a reaction out of you, Joy. Maybe it's juvenile of us, but you let every little thing rile you. It's your problem, not ours. Do you think I care that my hair's getting gray or I have to train twice as hard as the younger guys at work to keep up with them at racquetball? It doesn't bother me when they call me 'Old Man'. I'm secure enough not to let every idle comment from some knucklehead get under my skin."

"Well, bully for you. I'm not that strong, Scott. I care what people think. Right or wrong, I don't like anyone laughing at me about my weight or how I raise my kids or if I worry too much about things that don't necessitate worry."

"You can't blame the world for your insecurities, Joy. Instead of blaming everyone else, why not do something about it."

"Like what?"

"Like lose a few pounds if it bothers you so much. God knows it'd be a lot more peaceful around the house if you did."

"I can't believe you said that."

"You asked me. You talk about changing things, but you never follow through. Get a job outside the house if that's what you want. Go back to school. I've never stopped you and you know it. We'll work out something about Aidan."

"I don't want to go back to school and I don't want to leave Aidan in daycare."

"Then why are we having this conversation? If you're happy doing what you're doing, a few dumb jokes shouldn't shake your confidence. No one expects you to be like Valerie."

"I never said I want to be like Valerie." I practically screeched. I winced and looked at Aidan in the backseat, but he had barely moved in fifty miles.

Scott cocked his head at me. "If you aren't at least a little bit jealous of her, you wouldn't get so upset over everything she says and does. You don't need a career or a twenty-eight inch waist to feel significant. If you do, the problem is with you. That's all I'm saying."

I knew he was right, but it didn't make me ready to stop being mad at him. I turned my face toward the window even though it was too dark to see anything more than lights from the occasional community. I toyed with the phone in my pocket. I had called Dorothea's cell number several times over the weekend. Every time I dialed the call went straight to voice mail. Wherever she was and whatever she was doing, she couldn't be reached. I tried to remember where Gunnar said his family lived in Chicago. I couldn't imagine anywhere in the whole state of Illinois that didn't receive at least some cell service. Even if Dorothea had forgotten her phone at home while shopping and antiquing with Gunnar's mother, surely she'd received some of my desperate messages.

I wished I could talk to her now. Today marked eight days since I'd seen her last. She had never gone anywhere for a whole week before. I didn't care what Scott or Gunnar said. It didn't make sense that she would go to Chicago to visit Gunnar's parents practically the day Gunnar arrived from Chicago to visit her. Maybe the family decided he would study better without her in the house. But it was her house. It was illogical that she would leave the state, giving him free rein of her home when she barely knew him. I wanted some straight answers out of Gunnar, but I didn't dare ask the questions weighing on my mind.

It made even less sense that he would lie about her whereabouts. What would he gain by doing so? If he was lying--God forbid--the most likely reason was something terrible had happened to Dorothea that he didn't want me to know about.

I tried not to work myself into a worried lather. Let Dorothea be home, I prayed as we turned off the interstate. May she be safe and my last week's worth of worry is all for nothing.

I had nearly dozed off, but jerked awake at the sight of Dorothea's big Crown Vic parked in front of her house.

"Dorothea's home," I cried. As soon as the words were out of my mouth, I realized her car parked in the driveway in front of Gunnar's didn't mean she was home. It just meant Gunnar had probably used her car when his tank was low.

Scott's exhale filled the car. "Hallelujah. Maybe things'll get back to normal around here."

If I wasn't so excited about seeing Dorothea I would've gotten mad all over again at the condescension in his voice. I jumped out of the car as soon as he pulled to a stop in our driveway. I wanted to dash across the street and see Dorothea with my own eyes, but it was nearly midnight. Not to mention my sleeping preschooler in the backseat and a suitcase full of dirty clothes and who knew what disaster awaiting me inside the house.

I unhooked Aidan from the car seat and grunted aloud as I hefted him over my shoulder to carry him inside. It felt like he'd gained ten pounds since the last time I lifted him. Wouldn't Valerie be impressed to see me now? Cardio and resistance training at the same time. I lumbered up the sidewalk. The house was dark. I waited on the step for Scott to get the luggage out of the trunk. I didn't bother to ring the doorbell for Dylan. The restaurant closed at ten so he should've been home no later than eleven. We didn't like him to go out after work when we were due home, but neither of us were especially surprised to see his side of the driveway was empty.

"Looks like no one's home," Scott said as he set the bags on the porch next to me and fiddled with the key. He pushed the door open and stepped back for me to go in first.

I hit the light switch with my elbow and paused to survey the damage Dylan had left. The entryway showed no signs of wild partying. That didn't mean there had been no parties, just that Dylan had limited them to certain areas of the house. Scott raised an index finger to punch the burglary code into the alarm system but stopped before his fingers hit the keypad. The system wasn't armed. He heaved a defeated sigh.

I started up the stairs with Aidan while Scott moved toward the back of the house to satisfy himself that we hadn't been robbed or otherwise victimized. I was too relieved to have this weekend behind me to care much about what Dylan had or hadn't done. Everyone on our street had security alarms, and no one had ever been broken into in the nine years we'd lived here. It was a pretty safe neighborhood, with or without alarm systems. I could see why Dylan didn't bother with arming the system every time he stepped out the door even though we'd been reminding him to do so for years. I turned left at the top of the stairs without turning on a light and moved to Aidan's room. His door was open like it had been the day we left. Streetlights and a half moon shone through the bedroom window, illuminating the bed with the Spiderman comforter and Teenage Mutant Ninja Turtles lamp on the table. I shifted Aidan in my arms and leaned forward to fold back the blankets. I grunted again from the effort. Maybe during our next workout, I'd focus on more upper body work.

Who was I kidding? I needed to focus on all over body work. My jeans dug into my waist under Aidan's weight. I imagined deep gouge marks when I got undressed later tonight. Too much of me and not enough breathing room. I was even more aware of it after watching Valerie's size four body moving effortlessly around her house all weekend. Tomorrow I was going to start watching what I ate. I knew full fledged diets didn't work. Baby steps were the smart way to approach a lifestyle change, but I needed to do something, and fast. My already big girl jeans were getting tighter and more uncomfortable by the day. If I didn't figure out what worked for me, I was going to be wearing tracksuits and oversized men's t-shirts everywhere I went.

I flicked back the corner of covers and leaned forward to lay Aidan down. Feminine cologne wafted upward—the kind young girls bought at the mall when they were starting to play around with scents. I buried my nose in Aidan's hair. Peyton was a little young for perfume, but I didn't really know at what age girls started experimenting with stuff like that. I put my nose against Aidan's neck and inhaled. My nostrils filled with the familiar scent of tear-free shampoo and dog slobbers and little boy that I would bottle if I could.

I laid his pliant body on top of the covers and lowered my nose to the Spider Man pillow. This time my nose picked up a fainter smell of AXE cologne. There was no denying the obvious conclusion even though I desperately wanted to. Young women's perfume and AXE cologne could only mean one thing. A young couple had been lying on this bed. Rage, frustration, and dismay yanked a groan out of my throat.

What was Dylan doing bringing a girl into his little brother's room? Did he think I wouldn't figure it out? If he had invited a girlfriend over at the first opportunity, he wouldn't bring her into Aidan's room. Even if he was ashamed of the disgusting condition of his own room, I doubted he would hope to woo her on Spiderman sheets under the soft glow of a Ninja Turtle lamp.

That left one reasonable explanation. He had a sleepover and needed more than one bed for his friends to enjoy their trysts. I was suddenly very tired. I thought of flipping the pillow over, forgetting the whole thing, and putting an exhausted Aidan and myself to bed. But I couldn't put my innocent darling into a bed that had seen God only knew what over the weekend.

With a grunt of exertion, I hoisted Aidan back into my arms and laid him in the padded rocker where I used to rock him to sleep when he was a baby. Seemed like only yesterday.

I jerked open the bottom drawer of his dresser and took out a fresh sheet and pillowcase. While I made the bed, I grew madder and madder at Dylan. I hoped he realized how fortunate he was that he wasn't here right now. Who did he think he was turning our home into a bordello the minute our backs were turned? We trusted him. Well, not really, but we had left him alone in good faith, believing his story about having to work.

I rolled the soiled sheets into a ball and tossed them on the closet floor. I didn't want Scott to see them, and I sure didn't feel like trekking all the way downstairs to do a load of laundry. I moved Aidan back to his bed and removed his shoes and socks. Not for the first time, I was thankful he was a sound sleeper. I returned to the dresser for a fresh pair of pajamas. I pulled out a faded pair and turned back to the bed. My eyes were inexplicably drawn to Dorothea's house across the street. Her house was dark except for the hallway light at the top of the stairs. I paused for a moment to watch for signs of life. I wondered if Gunnar was still there. For Dorothea's sake, I should hope he was. It had meant so much to her to get to know him again.

I stepped to the window over Aidan's bed and pulled the curtain back for a better look. I wondered if Dorothea had gone to church tonight and left the car parked in the driveway. She was probably tucked safe in her bed unaware I had been worried about her the last week. She would laugh at me tomorrow and tell me how silly I was. She was a grown woman after all. Perfectly capable of taking care of herself. She would show me pictures and tell me what they'd done and the restaurants her family had insisted on taking her to during her visit.

I dropped the edge of the curtain and leaned over the bed to remove Aidan's clothes when movement caught my attention. I jerked back up and fumbled for the curtain. Dorothea's bedroom light was on. I knew the layout of her house as well as I knew my own. A large rectangle of light spilled into the hallway and reflected off the mirror hanging at the end of the hallway above the stairs. I couldn't see the mirror from my vantage point, but I knew it was there and recognized the bright light from her room shining directly onto it.

A shadow moved past the light. It was too tall to be Dorothea. Gunnar. What was he doing in Dorothea's room? Was she sick? Had something happened during the night, and she needed his care? Even if she was still out of town, she would never give him permission to sleep in her room. Why should she when the house was equipped with three other fully furnished bedrooms? How incredibly inconsiderate of him if that's what he was doing?

Or did the shadow belong to an intruder? Gunnar's car was still in the driveway behind Dorothea's, but that didn't mean he was home. Maybe he was out for the evening with friends. Perhaps Dorothea and Gunnar were both gone, and the intruder was going from room to room cleaning her out. Whatever was happening over there, I wouldn't rest thinking Dorothea was in danger or duress.

I hurriedly undressed Aidan using less care than I normally would and slipped his pajama top over his head. He made a few mewing sounds in his sleep but didn't awaken as I pulled the pajama bottoms up over his hips. I had just folded the covers back over him and straightened when I heard Scott go past the door toward our room. I tucked the covers around Aidan's sleeping form while inwardly imagining the thrashing I was going to give Dylan tomorrow for using this bed or letting his friends do the same.

I found Scott in the master bathroom leaning over the sink with a toothbrush in his mouth. "Hurry," I said in a stage whisper. "I need you to see something."

He nearly choked on the toothpaste. "What's wrong?"

"Something's going on over at Dorothea's."

He turned on the water and spit the toothpaste down the sink. He gave his chin a quick swipe with a towel and gave me a look through the mirror that said this better be good. Our room was at the back of the house and had no view of Dorothea's house from our window. I hurried out of the bathroom and through our room back to the hallway, listening the whole time to make sure he was behind me.

"What's going on?" he asked again outside Aidan's room.

"I don't know. I saw a man come out of Dorothea's bedroom."

I entered Aidan's room and hastened to the window.

"What do you mean you saw a man? It's as black as pitch over there."

He was right. Dorothea's bedroom light and the hallway light were now out. I pulled the curtain back to get a better look. "The hallway light was on. Then someone turned on her light. I saw a figure. It was too big for Dorothea."

Scott sighed heavily in the darkness. "Isn't Gunnar still over there?"

"Yes, but..."

"Doesn't it stand to reason he was the one in the room?"

"But why?" I hissed. Scott looked pointedly at Aidan to remind me to keep my voice down. "If it is Gunnar, what's he doing in Dorothea's room this late at night unless something's wrong? She must be sick. I'm calling over there."

I let go of the curtain and took a step toward the door. Scott grabbed my arm. He looked again at Aidan and ushered me into the hallway.

"You can't call a neighbor this late at night even if it is Dorothea. The light's off now. Whatever happened is over. They won't appreciate having to get up to answer the phone. If it isn't Dorothea in there sick, it's none of your business what Gunnar's doing in that room."

"He has no right to use his aunt's bedroom if she's out of town."

"Not your call, Joy."

"But what if she's sick. She may need me."

"She has Gunnar for that. I'm sure that's what you saw. She probably wasn't feeling well and he was getting her a 7up. It's probably indigestion and she'll be fine by morning."

It sounded like a logical explanation. Logical or not, I'd never get to sleep until I knew she was okay. "What if Gunnar's gone and someone broke into the house?"

"Do you really expect burglars to answer the phone?"

"Scott…" I began in a pleading voice.

He exhaled, louder and more tired this time. "I'll put my shoes back on and go over there. But I'm not ringing the bell or calling the cops. I'll look around and see if anyone's lurking somewhere."

"I'll go with you."

He was shaking his head before I finished. "Joy, please, just get ready for bed. If I need you, I'll send up a signal flair."

"That isn't funny."

He touched the end of my nose with his fingertip. "I'll be right back."

Through the front door pane, I watched him cross the street from one pool of streetlight to the next until he reached Dorothea's front porch. He put his hands against the glass on either side of his face and peered through the pane at the front door. I hoped no one else saw him. They would think he was a prowler. Then again, that might be the answer to my prayers. If one of them called in a prowler on Dorothea's front step, I would find out what was going on, and Scott couldn't blame me for sticking my nose where it didn't belong.

He dropped his hands and disappeared around the side of the house. With my heart in my throat I watched for what seemed like an eternity. My eyes flitted from the side of the house where Scott had gone to Dorothea's bedroom window. A good wife never would've sent her husband alone to check out a possible break in. I should've gone with him or at least reminded him to take his cell phone. What if he had been bashed in the head and was lying over there in the dark, alone and bleeding while I watched from the safety of my own front door? I should call the police. Dorothea would want me to, even if it turned out I was overreacting. She would've done the same for me.

"Better safe than sorry, Joy," I could hear her say.

I had just talked myself into dialing 911 when Scott appeared through the hedge and headed back across the street. I nearly burst into tears of relief. I opened the door and stepped onto the porch. "Well? Are you all right?"

He ushered me back inside. "It's as quiet as the grave over there. Just like I figured. It's a wonder I didn't get arrested for voyeurism or breaking and entering myself."

I didn't tell him I had thought the same thing. "Thank you, honey." I stretched onto my toes and kissed him. "I appreciate it and so would Dorothea."

"Can I go to bed now?" he asked, sounding irritable though he had a smile on his face. "Tomorrow's a workday."

"Of course. I'm sorry." I made sure the security alarm was armed and followed him upstairs. While he went into the bathroom to change into the old pair of running shorts he slept in, I yanked a clean set of sheets and pillowcases out of the drawer. I didn't smell any foreign perfume or other mysterious scents, but I wasn't taking any chances. I rolled the used sheets into a ball and stuffed them into the closet just as Scott came out of the bathroom. I turned away from the closet door, flushed and breathless.

He gave me an odd look. "What are you doing?"

"I thought I heard a mouse."

Scott threw back a corner of the fresh sheets and slid between them. "Ah, it's good to be home," he murmured as he settled in.

I couldn't agree more. I slid in next to him and curled my body against his. I was tired and emotionally exhausted from the weekend with Chris and Valerie, and distressed about what might be going on across the street with Dorothea, but it was a long time before sleep came. All I could think about was one of Dylan's moral-free friends using my bed as a wrestling mat with his girlfriend. I prayed Dylan would have a logical explanation for why his brother's bed smelled like a young woman's perfume, but I couldn't think of a thing.

Scott was cranky and irritable the next morning after not getting into bed until after one. When the alarm went off at 5:50, he pulled the covers over his head and rolled over. I climbed out of bed and hopped in the shower, forgetting my resolve to workout and ignoring the urge to look across the street at Dorothea's. Common courtesy dictated I didn't as much as call before nine no matter how close we were. Gunnar's car was still in the driveway. They deserved a leisurely breakfast together, especially if they'd been up late too, without interruptions from me.

Aidan crept down the stairs in time to kiss Daddy goodbye. I had hoped he would sleep in so I could talk to Dylan without him overhearing, but it wasn't to be. It was just as well. I was furious and indignant and in the right, but it didn't make confronting Dylan any easier. I almost wished I hadn't smelled the perfume on Aidan's sheets. I could go about my life in blissful ignorance. Scott and I knew Dylan had tried drugs in high school. Who hadn't in this generation? We had picked him up more than once from parties when he was too stoned to find his car in the driveway. We always told him we'd rather he wake us out of a sound sleep to bring him home than risk driving impaired. We promised never to lecture or punish him under those circumstances. We didn't want him to regret turning to the people he should trust more than anyone.

We had also lectured him on the perils of pre-marital, unprotected, casual sex. I wasn't surprised he hadn't listened to a word we said. But a girl in Aidan's bed! Possibly mine as well. What had gone on this weekend? I didn't want to know the details, but as a responsible mother I had to find out. Ugh! Times like this I wished I'd gone the childless route.

Aidan was cranky and fussy too. Out of all of us, I was the one who deserved to be in a bad mood, but moms weren't allowed mood swings. My job was to prop everyone else up and smile while doing so.

It was nine-thirty before Aidan was washed, fed, and acting more like his old self. "Let's go for a walk," I said cheerily. "Aunt Dorothea's home from her trip."

He bounced on the couch on his knees and pumped his fists in the air. At least something perked him up. I felt better too, just thinking of seeing my friend again. I couldn't wait to hear how she'd enjoyed her trip out of town. I wouldn't tell her how worried I'd been or how I hoped she wouldn't leave the house again without telling me first.

"Lord, help me be gracious and happy for what she has with Gunnar," I prayed as I helped Aidan into his jacket.

My heart lurched in my chest when I saw a strange car parked behind Gunnar's. Now what? Or should I say whom? I didn't think I could stand more family members descending onto our street.

We were halfway across the street before I made out the California license plate. Who did Dorothea know in California? She had said Gunnar's parents lived in various places before settling in Chicago when Gunnar was little. Maybe there was a distant cousin or step-something or other out west.

I thought about going back to my own house. I was, after all, just a neighbor as Scott readily pointed out every time the subject came up. Dorothea obviously wanted to get reacquainted with a much more extended family than either of us realized.

I looked down at my chattering, bouncing preschooler twirling a Bengals' umbrella over his head even though there wasn't a cloud in the sky. It wouldn't be fair to tell him we couldn't see Dorothea today. We'd stick our heads in the door and tell her how much we missed her. After a few days her out-of-state relatives would go back to wherever they came from, and life in my little corner of the tri-state would go back to normal. Aidan reached the door first, but he was so busy wrestling with his umbrella I was the one to knock on the heavy panel door. I pushed my shoulder length blond hair behind my ears as I examined my reflection in the glass window. I was overdue for a haircut. I usually let too much time go between cuts, and I never made time for manicures or facials. I didn't pay much attention to my appearance. A little mascara and blush and shoes that matched my bag and I was ready to go. The weekend in Valerie's shadow had me more aware of my crow's feet, faded hazel eyes, and limp hair.

But the weekend was over. All feelings of inadequacy and injustice had faded in light of what may have been wrong at Dorothea's house last night. After Scott's investigation, I was confident the only real danger had been in my imagination. I was still curious about why Gunnar had been in her room, but all that mattered was she was home where she belonged and hopefully feeling happy and refreshed after her vacation.

The door swung open. A tall slim woman in her early twenties stood framed in the doorway. Even standing above me on the threshold I could tell she was several inches taller than my five-feet, three-inch frame. Her heavy blond mane was pulled back in a ponytail. She hadn't bothered to apply makeup this early in the morning, though with her flawless complexion, she didn't need to. Her agate green eyes took in Aidan and me and dismissed us immediately. Her pretty mouth pulled into a pout.

"Where's Aunt Dor'fea?" Aidan demanded from the vicinity of my hip, having recovered before me.

The blonde looked down her straight nose at Aidan. My maternal hackles rose at her expression of distaste. "Excuse me," she said.

I squared my shoulders. "We're here to see Dorothea."

The blonde emitted a bored sigh and called over her shoulder. "Gunnar, it's for you." She gave us a parting impatient glance and went back inside without inviting us in. Gunnar appeared and mumbled something in her ear as she passed. From my vantage point it looked like she acknowledged whatever he said, but I couldn't be sure.

I was tired of standing on the stoop while my friend could be sick inside. This was her house and she would want to see me. I put my hand on Aidan's shoulder and pushed him inside ahead of me and closed the door behind us.

"Good morning, Gunnar," I sang out as though seeing him was the highlight of my day.

He came to a stop a few feet in front of us, effectively stopping our progress into the house. He didn't cross his arms over his chest, but he may as well have. "A little early for a visit, isn't it?" The corners of his mouth lifted in a half hearted attempt at a smile that didn't fool either of us.

"How's Dorothea?" I asked by way of an answer. "I saw her lights last night. I hope she isn't sick." I looked around him, my curiosity getting the better of me. What happened to the blonde? Where was Dorothea?

"What lights?"

I looked back at him. "In Dorothea's room. We got home late and I saw lights on in her room. I was afraid someone may have broken in so I sent Scott over to check things out."

He didn't bother to disguise his annoyance. "You did what?"

"We look out for each other in this neighborhood, Gunnar. I'm sure you're comforted in knowing your aunt has people watching out for her since she lives alone. I know her safety is your utmost concern."

"You needn't have bothered. She has me."

"And you have us."

Aidan tugged on the tail of my jacket. "Mommy, when are we gonna see Aunt Dor'fea? I have to tell her about riding a horse with Peyton."

I looked pointedly at Gunnar, waiting for him to field the question.

His shoulders rose almost imperceptibly in a resigned shrug. "She isn't here."

My heart lurched. "But her lights were on." It was an inane observation, but the only explanation that made sense.

"That was me."

What about the blonde? Did Dorothea know she was here?

"I thought Dorothea... Her car's been moved."

Gunnar's eyebrows went together. He looked as confused as I felt. Then he smoothed out the wrinkles in his face and smiled. "I hate to tell you but she won't be back for a couple more weeks, if then."

"Weeks? What are you talking about?"

"She decided to go on a cruise with my mother."

"A cruise? Dorothea?"

I remembered the trip the seniors' group at church planned a few years ago. Dorothea had been excited about the prospect of getting away until she learned the trip was a cruise. She confided she was terrified of water. "I'm not afraid of much, but I don't like the idea of being surrounded by water with no land in sight."

I tried to talk her into it. "You won't be alone. Jesus is with you. You'll have your friends from church. It'll be so much fun."

"I know you're right," she agreed. "Albert used to tell me the same thing. I should get over this silly fear, but I can't."

"Dorothea doesn't cruise," I told Gunnar.

He shrugged. "I guess Mom talked her into it."

"You don't understand. She's terrified. She would never take a cruise."

He cocked his head, and his gaze darkened. I realized I had basically called him a liar. I squared my shoulders. Would I have the nerve to stand up to him if he called me on it?

"I don't know what to tell you," he said finally. "Dorothea called Saturday and said she would be delayed a few weeks. She sounded excited about the whole thing."

"Why didn't she call me?" I cringed at the trembling in my voice. I wouldn't give into hysteria, though I was pretty close to doing so. "Dorothea always tells me when she's going out of town so I can look after things."

"She has Kimberly and me for that now."

I thought again of Dylan and his friends who had taken liberties in my house. Liberties of which they knew I didn't approve. I crossed my arms over my chest, my stance mirroring Gunnar's. "Who exactly is Kimberly?"

His eyes narrowed. "A friend, not that it's any of your business."

I knew I had overstepped my bounds. Gunnar owed me no explanations about what he was doing with a woman in the house, but my need to make sense of the situation took precedence over my usual meekness. "Does Dorothea know you have a guest?"

"Our arrangement doesn't affect you, does it?"

Of course, it affected me. I loved Dorothea. I didn't believe for one minute she was okay with Gunnar inviting a woman into her house, a woman who wasn't his wife and was probably sleeping in *her* bed. My face burned. If I was indignant about what Dylan and his friends did in my house this weekend, Dorothea would be downright scandalized. As her closest friend, it was my duty to do what she wasn't here to do herself.

"Dorothea would've called me, even if you are here to look after things. She knows I worry. I haven't seen her in nine days. Now you tell me she's on a cruise. She must be a nervous wreck, no matter how excited she sounded to you on the phone. I'm going to call her as soon as I get home."

"Good luck getting cell service in the middle of the Atlantic."

If she was indeed on a cruise, that would explain why my calls over the weekend had gone directly to voice mail.

"Where is she anyway?"

"Antiqua. Aruba. One of those tropical places. You don't need to give it another thought."

"Did you tell her to bring me a present?" Aidan piped up.

Gunnar looked down at him and smiled for the first time. "I didn't talk to her, sport. But I'm sure she'll remember."

He looked back at me and cocked an eyebrow. He was waiting for me to leave. I couldn't think of another reason to stay except I was convinced he was lying. Something wasn't right here. Dorothea talked to me before taking a shopping trip into the city. Two w-eeks on an island hopping cruise? I didn't buy it. She wasn't much of a traveler. She spent most of her time at home focused on her flowerbeds and church. She read, wrote letters to friends, and forwarded funny or inspirational quotes to her contact list online. She didn't drop everything to take a cruise to Aruba with a niece she hadn't seen in years.

Something was going on here, and I wouldn't rest until I found out what.

Chapter 9

As soon as Aidan and I got home I went straight to the phone. I wondered how hard it would be to hack into a cruise line's passenger manifesto so I could find out if Gunnar was lying. It was probably pretty difficult, especially for someone like me who had enlisted the help of her four-year-old to create a PayPal account. It wasn't likely I'd locate Dorothea anytime soon if she was in fact in the Caribbean. Instead I dialed Marge Kepinstall, one of Dorothea's dearest friends. They had known each other since college and remained in touch. Marge was also a widow, and she and her husband had been among the founding members of our church, just like Dorothea and Albert.

I identified myself and made a little small talk before getting to the point of my call. "Marge, I was out of town over the weekend so I'm a little out of the loop, but I wonder if you've heard from Dorothea."

"You know, Joy, I was thinking of calling and asking you the same thing. I can't remember the last time Dorothea missed a Sunday service. Now she's missed two and she didn't even call me. It's not like her."

Finally. Someone besides me who found the whole situation a little off. "That's what I was thinking," I said in lieu of bawling like a baby in relief. "Did you hear she's gone on a cruise with her nephew's wife?"

"A cruise?" Marge howled. "Dorothea? You must be mistaken."

"I just spoke with her great-nephew. He said she won't be back for a couple weeks."

"Huh," Marge said. "I guess you never know about a person. Maybe she's going through a late life crisis. You know, trying new things."

"I suppose." I was disappointed Marge was willing to accept Gunnar's explanation so easily. "If you hear from her, could you please tell her to call me?"

"Oh, sweetie, I'm sure you'll hear from her before I do. When you do, tell her I have a bone to pick with her that she took a cruise without me. I've been talking about one for years and she'd never give the idea a moment's consideration."

"I will."

I hung up, disheartened. I had suspicions, but what could I do to prove any of them.

Dylan's bedroom door was closed, as usual, when I got to the top of the stairs. I had been asleep by the time he got in last night, and he still hadn't made an appearance downstairs. At least not as far as I could tell. He probably sneaked down for something to eat when he knew I was across the street at Dorothea's.

I tapped on the door and listened a moment before pushing it open. The room smelled like it always did—dirty laundry, overheated gym shoes, used food wrappers, and somehow underneath all the teenage filth, a musky comforting scent that was utterly Dylan. I inhaled deeply, discarding the usual scents for evidence a girl had been in the room.

I tapped again as I entered. "Dylan, are you awake? I need to speak to you."

My eyes grew accustomed to the gloom, and I saw his shape slouched in front of the glow from his computer. "I'm up. It's almost noon."

I crossed the room carefully, avoiding potential hazards strewn across the floor. "I never know with you."

"Gimme a break, Mom."

I heard the playfulness in his voice. Maybe this wouldn't go so badly. I steeled myself nonetheless. I knew better than anyone how quickly he could go from benevolent to beast.

"Dylan, I need to talk to you about what happened here this weekend." I perched on the edge of the cedar chest at the foot of his bed. I could see his face now. He didn't flinch or turn his attention away from the screen. I was relieved to see no nearly nude women looking back at me. That was a plus.

"What happened?" he asked

I put on my stern Mom face, the one that had failed to intimidate him in the crib, yet I continued to rely on. "You know perfectly well what happened. This will go much smoother if you tell the truth now."

He finally tore his gaze away from the monitor. "You're going to have to tell me what you're talking about."

My patience snapped. "I know about the girls, Dylan." I intentionally chose the plural form of the word as I gazed at his face.

This time a germ of doubt crept over his face. He knew I knew something, but he wasn't dumb enough to admit anything that couldn't be proven. The chair squeaked as he drew in his legs and sat a little straighter. "Nothing happened, Mom."

"Save it, Dylan. I'm not stupid. I can't believe you'd have people over the minute our backs were turned. The only reason we didn't make you go with us was because we thought you were working."

"I did work."

"So you won't mind if I called Josh to check with him."

He hurled his weight back in the chair. "You would believe that jerk over your own son?"

"He has no reason to lie to me, Dylan."

"Neither do I."

"Then I suggest you tell me everything right now, and don't leave out the part about the girl in your brother's bed."

His shoulders slumped. For the first time in a long time I braced myself to hear the truth from my son. "It wasn't a party, Mom. Craig came home with me after work. I was there. You can call Josh if you want even though he was off that night. Anyway, Craig and I were hanging out and his girlfriend texted him, and the next thing I knew she and her friend were here."

He stopped as if no further explanation was necessary.

"And?" I prodded.

"And it got late and Craig and Bethany were getting a little warmed up and they wanted to be alone."

I shuddered. "So you sent them to your baby brother's room?"

"Come on, Mom. That would be disgusting."

"Then which one of the girls ended up in Aidan's bed?"

He leaned forward in his chair and studied his hands. "I didn't say it was okay for Craig and Bethany to use Aidan's bed." He brought his gaze up to meet mine. "That doesn't mean they didn't end up there."

"Dylan."

"You said you wanted the truth."

I took a deep breath to gain control of my temper. If I gave into emotions and jumped down his throat, he'd shut down and likely not open up to me again for who knew how long. "You're right. I want the whole story. I won't hold you responsible for what your friends do."

He visibly relaxed.

"What happened with Bethany's friend?"

He gave me a panicked glance before looking back at the monitor.

I grimaced and felt my breakfast sour in my stomach. "Dylan, in our house?"

"Mom, don't be naïve. Stuff happens."

"It shouldn't happen in my house. You're not married. You don't have a real job. What if she got pregnant?"

"She won't."

"That's what everyone says, but it happens all the time."

"Would you relax? I didn't get her pregnant, okay? It was just one time."

I covered my face with my hands. "That's supposed to make me feel better? That you had sex with a girl you barely know, *in my house*, as soon as your father and I were out of the way?"

"I told you I didn't plan it. It just happened. It won't happen again. At least not here."

I rubbed my fingertips against my eyes and willed myself not to cry...or scream. I took a few deep breaths so my voice wouldn't shake when I spoke again. "Dylan, sweetheart, the point is, what you did is a sin before man and God. You used a young woman."

"Maybe she was the one using me." His skinny chest expanded.

I shuddered. "You know how your father and I feel about premarital sex. You were raised in church. You participated in the True Love Waits seminars."

"I was a kid. I believed whatever you told me."

"You're still a kid," I shrieked. I instantly regretted my words. I swallowed again. My throat hurt from holding in my screams. "I'm sorry, Dylan. I know you don't appreciate being called a kid. But you are too young to engage in physical intimacy with a girl you barely know. Did I mention it's a sin?"

He sighed and threw his head back against the chair. He stared at the ceiling for a moment while I resisted the urge to say more. I wouldn't nag. He knew how I felt. I needed to give him time to speak. When he finally did, I felt even worse.

"Mom, you are so out of touch with reality. No one waits. Why should we? We're consenting and of legal age. I made sure she wouldn't get pregnant. So did Craig. You are making way too big a deal of this."

It took everything inside me not to jump up and slap his face. Why couldn't he see how skewed his logic was? "Dylan, you have missed the whole point. You waited until I was gone and then violated every belief I hold dear. You have shown an absolute disregard for your father and me. What does that say about how you feel about us? You don't care what we think. When you have your own home, you can do whatever you want. But as long as you're living here, you can at least pretend to respect us and our faith."

I stopped just short of telling him to pack his stuff and get out. If he couldn't control himself for one lousy weekend in the house his father and I paid for, he could leave. He was of legal age, all right. Old enough to engage in irresponsible activity and old enough to pay his own way if he didn't like my rules.

If he wanted reality, maybe I should exercise some tough love and let him see what the real world was like. He didn't have a clue. But I didn't have the guts to follow through. Where would he go? How would he pay his bills? Where would he live? With Craig? God only knew what kind of trouble the two of them would get into. He was my baby and I wanted to protect him, even if he only needed protection from his hormones. Not only that, Scott would kill me if I threw him out. He might even agree that I was a prude with too high expectations. I'd never been a teenage boy. What did I know about what they went through?

Dylan snorted. "I'll bet Grandma used that line of reasoning with you when you did something she didn't like."

"We're not talking about me, Dylan. We're talking about you bringing your friend and a couple of girls here and participating in behavior you know your father and I don't approve of."

"I bet there was plenty Grandma didn't approve of. You were barely twenty when I was born. Doesn't sound to me like you were much more responsible with your hormones than I am."

I thought of the hormone driven passion that had consumed Scott and I during those early years. But we behaved responsibly. We got married before we let ourselves be swept away. Not only was my husband the only man I'd ever slept with, he was the only one I ever *wanted* to sleep with. If I'd actually been tempted in the matter I might be more equipped to understanding Dylan now. What right did I have to tell him sex outside of marriage was unacceptable when I had never been in his shoes?

I leaped up and swiped at the tears sliding down my cheeks. I wasn't wrong. These weren't my rules. God had mapped them out well before Dylan or I came along. Where had I gone wrong? I tried to teach my son to value women. I wanted him see the honor in commitment. Obviously I had missed it by a mile.

Dylan pushed the chair away from his desk and stood up too, looking genuinely concerned. "Mom, don't freak out." He put his hand on my arm. "I shouldn't have let the girls come over when you and Dad were gone. I won't do it again."

I looked into his eyes and saw only sincerity and repentance. But all he admitted to doing wrong was having the girls over when we weren't home. He still couldn't see that he shouldn't have engaged in irresponsible behavior. If I couldn't make him see such a basic truth, what kind of mother was I? It was slipshod parenting like mine that had today's youth in such a state. I only had myself to thank for the mess under my own roof.

Unable to speak, I turned and started out of the room. "Mom, don't go away mad."

I stopped but didn't turn around. "I'm not mad, Dylan. My heart is broken." I continued out of the room. He didn't stop me.

About five minutes later Aidan tired of playing with his toys on the family room floor and demanded my undivided attention, thus depriving me of a few minutes to lie down with a warm cloth over my head to think about my failures as a mother, a Christian, and an overall human being. This was when I needed Dorothea most. I wished there was some way I could get in touch with her. It would be selfish of me to ruin her holiday with Gunnar's mother--if she was indeed on a cruise. The last thing she'd want was a phone call from me whining about my rude and careless son having reckless sex in our house while Scott and I were out of town. Hadn't she warned me this would happen?

Absently I opened the cabinet door and removed a bag of chocolate chip cookies, my go-to snack when I needed a sugar rush and hadn't baked anything fresh in a while. I unfolded the top of the cookie bag and pulled two out of the plastic liner.

I needed to talk to someone. I couldn't very well call my mother. She would make it all out to be my fault. If I had given Dylan a firmer hand growing up… If I provided a better example… If I did a better job teaching him responsible behavior… I wasn't even sure I felt like discussing the matter with Scott. I couldn't take it if he sided with Dylan and accused me of being too old fashioned.

I was right. Period. I had the Bible on my side. I just wanted to hear it from someone who loved me just as I was. I needed Dorothea.

My gaze traveled to the window where I had a partial view of the front of her house through the trees. Movement along the side of the house caught my attention. I moved closer to the window and pulled back the curtain. I ducked my head to see around the branches of the elm growing outside my window in time to see the business end of a ladder disappear around the side of Dorothea's house.

"Mommy, you aren't listening."

I tore my eyes away from the window and looked down at Aidan. The impatient scowl and firm set of his jaw reminded me so much of Dylan I almost drew back.

"I'm sorry, Lima Bean. What did you say?"

His narrow shoulders rose and fell as he exhaled dramatically. "I asked if you wanted to play with me."

I looked back out the window. "What do you want to play?" I asked, not really listening to the answer.

"Spiderman. You be the villain and I'll capture you and tie you to the wall with my web." He held out his hands and struck the classic Spiderman pose. This was one of his favorite games, but I didn't have the time or patience today to pretend to be stuck to the wall until he relented and cut me loose from my imaginary bonds.

"How about we do something outside? It's too pretty of a day to stay in."

"Where can we go?"

Inspiration struck. "Let's go for a walk around the block and look for the villain's hideout."

Aidan was immediately on board. It would give me an excuse to see if I could find out what Gunnar was into today and entertain Aidan at the same time. I still had a few hours before Scott was due home from work. Dinner was simmering in the crockpot so I had time to play detective. I could even burn off a few calories from the cookies. I was already regretting stuffing them into my mouth with only a vague awareness of doing so. If I couldn't eat more mindfully, the least I could do was walk around the block a few times.

I put an oversized L.L. Bean corduroy shirt over my fleece pullover and zipped Aidan's jacket up to his throat. The sun shone brightly against a blue sky, but the day was chilly. When we stepped off the front porch, I wondered if I shouldn't have gone ahead and grabbed a jacket for myself as well, but I figured I'd warm up soon enough.

Walk a little faster, sweat a little more, I told myself as I picked up my pace to keep up with Aidan who was already talking a mile a minute about bad guys and where they might be hiding. We walked to the corner and crossed over two houses down from Dorothea's. Instead of walking in front of her house, I led Aidan down the street where I could get a clear view of the side and back of her property. I didn't know what I expected to see, but with Aidan in tow, no one could accuse me of spying.

Across the backyards separating us, I could see Dorothea's house and the potting shed at the rear of her property. I crept closer to the edge of the neighbor's yard and craned my neck to see inside Dorothea's back door. Gunnar strode out of the potting shed with a crowbar clutched in one hand. I grabbed Aidan's shoulder and yanked him behind a maple tree.

"Ow. Mom."

"Sorry, sweetie." I smiled apologetically. "I thought I saw a bad guy."

I peered around the maple tree in time to see Gunnar disappear inside the house.

What did he need with a ladder and a crow bar? I couldn't imagine Dorothea asking him to paint or tend to some chore while she was gone. Maybe he had taken a project on himself, boredom or obligation driving him to put his strong young back to work while his aunt was sailing the high seas. Something told me there was more to it than that. I couldn't think up a valid excuse to cross the Potters' and the Smithfields' backyards to get close to Dorothea's potting shed so Aidan and I stayed on the sidewalk and circled the block. With Aidan distracted and still talking, it was some time before we circled back around until Dorothea's property came into view from the opposite side. The potting shed was concealed from my new vantage point, but I could see the back of the house clearly. The double French doors that led into the dining room were wide open. Why had Gunnar left the doors open? It wasn't freezing outside, but I could imagine Dorothea's huge furnace in the basement working overtime to heat the house. Somewhere on a cruise ship in the middle of the Caribbean, a shiver had probably just gone down Dorothea's spine.

A long driveway wrapped around the house of Dorothea's neighbors to the left. The driveway was empty since Mr. and Mrs. Wylie were at work. They were nice people like nearly everyone in the neighborhood. We lived in the kind of neighborhood where most people didn't mind if you cut through their backyard or parked in front of their house when you had a lot of company. I took Aidan's hand and led him up the paved driveway at the rear of the Wylie house. We followed it around until we were adjacent to Dorothea's dining room door, still standing open.

I stopped. Aidan looked up at me, expectant. Gunnar would not appreciate another visit. Truth be told, I was sticking my nose where it didn't belong, but I needed to know what he and Kimberly were doing in there.

Aidan reached out and took my hand. "Mommy, when's Aunt Dor'fea coming home?"

"Soon I hope."

We stood there, holding hands and looking across the Wylies' backyard to the open door for another moment. Aidan seemed to have forgotten to look for bad guys' hideouts. Just as I talked myself into going back across the street and putting Gunnar Westlake out of my mind until Dorothea returned from wherever it was she had gone, a terrible crash sounded from inside the house, followed immediately by a loud curse from a masculine voice.

Aidan and I exchanged glances. He was more fascinated by the curse word than any fear behind what had caused the crash. I tightened my grip on his hand and hurried across the Wylies' yard. Dorothea's patio had already taken on an unkempt, forgotten appearance in the nine days she'd been gone. Ordinarily April found her up to her elbows in mulch and potting soil. She planted countless bulbs from March through November. Her lilac bush had sprouted and the spent tulips needed trimmed back to make room for the irises. I couldn't believe she was off in the Atlantic while missing all this beauty around her. Yes, people took vacations. They were entitled to try something different, but not like this. If Gunnar had given me this story any other month of the year, I may have given it a little credence. But Dorothea wouldn't leave home of her own volition in April. I was sure of it.

Aidan and I hurried across the stone patio and up the two steps to the French doors that opened into Dorothea's dining room. I saw the feet of the ladder first. It was pulled against a bank of built-in cabinets that flanked the fireplace. Gunnar was climbing off the ladder as we came to the door. At his feet was a canvas painting. The picture frame was on the floor in a shower of splinters. A corner of the canvas had buckled. The painting was of a riverfront landscape painted by a local artist. While not a priceless family heirloom, it meant a lot to Dorothea. She and Albert loved to spend their weekends at a park on the river watching different artists at work. Albert had bought the painting a few years before he passed away. Dorothea told me once he paid two thousand dollars for it, but it meant more to her than any other artwork she owned.

I gasped as I stepped across the threshold. I was too shocked by his carelessness to care what he thought about my appearance. "What did you do?"

Gunnar jerked around to glare at me. "What do you want?" he practically growled, another curse word on the tip of his tongue.

I looked from the painting to him. "Dorothea loves that painting."

"I'll get her another one."

"You can't. It's an original."

"Obviously. It wasn't very good."

How dare he. I opened my mouth to tell him his aunt's taste in artwork was none of his business when I noticed the state of disarray in the room. The cabinets on either side of the fireplace had been emptied, their contents strewn haphazardly on the fireplace mantle, floor, and dining room table. Across the room Kimberly stood in the seat of a dining room chair Dorothea had spent a small fortune reupholstering last summer. Her ponytail was lopsided and fraying, and she wore a fine layer of dust and sweat despite the cool temperature in the room. She glanced guiltily at the framed picture in her hands. I looked from her to all the bare spots on the walls around the room.

"What are you doing?" I didn't bother to check the accusation my voice.

Gunnar stepped around the ladder. His feet crunched the splinters of wood from the broken frame. "I asked you what you wanted."

I resisted the urge to shrink away from him. I wouldn't let this man intimidate me. Well, okay, he scared the socks of me, but I wouldn't let him know it.

"Aidan and I were out for a walk when we heard something crash." I looked pointedly at the broken picture. "We wanted to make sure everyone was all right."

His lips pulled into a tight smile. "As you can see we're fine. I'm sorry about the painting."

Aidan slipped his hand out of mine and moved toward Kimberly. "Aunt Dor'fea's gonna be mad at you for standing on her chairs like that."

She stared at him for a moment before turning her gaze to Gunnar. She climbed down from the chair and added the picture to a pile on the dining room table before leaving the room without a word.

Gunnar took the crowbar looped over one of the rungs of the ladder and advanced toward us. An image of him coming after me with the crowbar made my blood stop in my veins. I straightened my spine. I wouldn't let him bully me. That's all he was doing. He was annoyed by my appearance, but he wasn't dangerous. Was he?

"You don't miss a thing, do you?" he said lightly. I didn't miss the threat in his eyes.

I glanced at Aidan. He stood several strides away from me, oblivious to any animosity we may have stirred up in Gunnar. I'd scare him if I lunged for him right now especially since it wasn't likely either of us were in any real danger. Still, the look on Gunnar's face and the set of his jaw made me wish I'd ignored the crash and gone home.

I edged closer to Aidan while trying to keep my face and stance casual. "You could call me a one-woman neighborhood watch," I barked out a laugh as I grabbed Aidan's shoulder and jerked him toward me.

"Ow," he cried.

I lightened my grip but kept hold of him. "Dorothea is a meticulous housekeeper. I can't imagine what you're doing when you have your dissertation to finish." I was amazed I could keep my voice so calm when inside I was quaking.

He swept the arm holding the crowbar around the room. "Just a little housekeeping. The trim in here needs a paint job. Kimberly and I decided to scrub down the walls before we get started."

I wasn't generally a judgmental person, but Gunnar Westlake was lying through his teeth. "There isn't as much as a chip in that paint. Dorothea takes great pride in her house."

"I know she does. That's why I want to spruce things up."

He stared at me, silently daring me to contradict him. I stared back, trying to see into that head of his. After a moment of neither of us wanting to back down, I looked toward the doorway where the blonde had disappeared. "Actually, I came over to invite you and Kimberly to dinner. There's a roast in the crock pot and my homemade rolls are rising on the counter. There's plenty if you'd like to come over."

He propped the crowbar on his shoulder. "No, thanks. We want to finish this today."

"I hope you cleared it with Dorothea first. She's very particular and she'll be heartsick when she finds out you broke her painting."

He tightened his grip on the crowbar and took a step toward me. "I wouldn't worry about Dorothea if I were you."

My insides puddled. What was that supposed to mean? I tightened my grip on Aidan's shoulder and drew him closer to me. I swallowed around a throat as dry as the desert and hoped the fear didn't show on my face. Gunnar reminded me of a big dog who could probably smell fear across the room.

"Are you sure you can't come to dinner? My husband would love to meet you."

"Mommy's a good cook," Aidan added, unaware of my trembling knees.

Gunnar looked at him and smiled his oily smile. "I'm sure she is, little fellow. I bet there's a lot of stuff she's good at." He brought his eyes back up to mine, full of malice.

I yanked Aidan tighter against me and put both my hands against his chest. "Well, um, if you change your mind, we eat at six. I bet you're overdue for a home cooked meal."

Gunnar angled his head and stared at me under hooded eyelids. I stood transfixed by his gaze until I caught movement out of the corner of my eye. Kimberly had reentered the room.

"That's really nice of you," she said. "We'll think about it." She shot Gunnar a warning glance.

"Yeah," he said, just as menacing. "We'll think about it."

"Um, okay." I backed out the door, my hands in a death grip around Aidan's jacket collar. "Six o'clock."

My knees nearly buckled under me when my feet hit the patio tiles. Someone shut the French doors behind us. I didn't turn around to see which one. I was afraid if I saw Gunnar's face again, I'd wet my pants. I wasn't as courageous as I wanted him and Kimberly to think.

By the time Scott got home I had whipped up a batch of homemade oatmeal butterscotch cookies and eaten half the dough before I could get them into the oven. My stomach was in knots. Not only because of the cookies and Gunnar's barely concealed threats, but also from the fear that he and Kimberly might actually show up for dinner. I didn't think I could sit across the table from him and pretend he hadn't freaked me out. What would we talk about? How could I play the role of hostess while all I wanted to know was why they were painting and undertaking a massive spring cleaning without Dorothea here to oversee? Come to think of it, there was a lot of moving and rearranging going on in that house. Almost as if they were searching for something.

But what? If Gunnar was looking for jewels or bonds or expensive collections, he need only go as far as Dorothea's jewelry box or find the keys to her safety deposit boxes. Maybe that's what he was looking for. Or passbooks to savings accounts. Even if Dorothea was the neurotic type who hid her passkeys and bankbooks within the walls, financial institutions didn't let anyone go in and clean out someone else's accounts, even when armed with a passbook.

Eating a pound of cookie dough and downing two Pepsis didn't get me any closer to finding the answers to my questions. Perhaps Gunnar and Kimberly really were painting and cleaning while Dorothea was gone. Some people used mindless chores to clear their minds when working on something as daunting as writing a dissertation. My own house would be a lot cleaner and spiffier and my waist a little narrower if I suffered from the same compulsion.

Scott motioned to the extra places set at the dining room table as he pulled out his chair. "Dylan having a friend over for dinner?"

I shook my head as I sat down across from him. "He left a while ago. He didn't say when he'd be back." I didn't bother to tell him about our conversation or the girls who spent the weekend at our house. Our failure as parents had slipped to the back of my mind in light of what was going on across the street.

"Then who's joining us?"

"It doesn't look like anyone. I invited Gunnar and his girlfriend over, but I told them six o'clock and they're not here yet."

"Gunnar?"

"Dorothea's nephew, remember?" I unfolded my napkin and set it on my lap and indicated to Aidan to do the same.

"How is Dorothea anyway?" Scott asked. "Is she feeling better since last night?"

"I have no idea. She isn't home. She went on a cruise."

"A cruise? I thought she was sick."

"Apparently not. The light we saw last night was Gunnar and his cute girlfriend getting cozy in Dorothea's room."

I didn't miss the corners of Scott's mouth turn up in a secret smile. Would he react the same way if I told him about our own son doing the same thing in our bed? My jaw tightened.

He, Aidan, and I stretched our arms across the table to join hands. After Scott gave thanks I stood up to ladle roast, potatoes, and baby carrots onto Aidan's plate.

"Is that why you invited them to dinner?" Scott asked, waiting his turn for the roast. "So you could pick their brains and report everything back to Dorothea?"

"No." I snatched his plate out of his hands. "Aidan and I were out enjoying the day when we heard a loud crash from inside Dorothea's house."

He didn't need to know I had taken Aidan out to enjoy the day for the specific purpose of getting a closer look in the back door.

"What crash?"

I opened my mouth to reply, but Aidan beat me to it. "He broke Aunt Dor'fea's picture of the boats. And that lady was standing on the chairs."

Scott raised his eyebrows in question as I handed over his plate.

"The picture Dorothea has over the fireplace. The one Albert gave her."

Scott set his plate down. "That's a shame. She loves that painting." He savored a bite of roast. "And the lady standing on the chairs?"

"Gunnar's girlfriend was standing on Dorothea's dining room chairs while she was cleaning."

"He had one of those metal bendy things," Aidan finished.

Scott looked back to me for clarification.

"A crowbar," I offered.

"Um," he nodded vaguely as he shoveled in another bite.

I wish he could muster a little more suspicion. Did I have to do everything around here? I lowered myself back into my seat. "They've taken every single thing off the shelves and out of the cabinets. All the pictures are off the wall and strewn around the room. Gunnar said they're painting, but I didn't see a single paint can or drop cloth. I got the impression they wished I hadn't walked in on them."

Scott chuckled around a bite of roast. "They're probably tired of you rushing over there every five minutes. Especially with Dorothea away. Maybe they want to play house for a day or two."

"Scott."

"It's none of our business, Joy."

I gritted my teeth. Why couldn't he see it was my business? Something strange was going on in Dorothea's house. As her friend, it was my duty to figure out what. I knew he wouldn't listen to that line of thinking. Scott was logical and analytical. He saw facts, not concepts like strange or suspicious.

"I think Gunnar is lying about the whole thing. You should've seen the dining room. The whole house, really. I can't believe a houseguest would decide to paint while their host was out of town. Who does that?"

Scott tore a piece of roast off and swirled it around in the juices on his plate. I had outdone myself with the roast. It was our favorite meal. But I didn't have much appetite with all the cookie dough sitting on my stomach and the concern about what was going on across the street clouding my mind. I put my elbows on the table on either side of my plate and leaned forward. "Think about it, Scott. Gunnar told me out of the blue Dorothea went to visit family. Don't you remember when he first got here? We didn't even know she had a nephew. Then she suddenly goes off to some unnamed city to visit relatives she's never talked about without telling me she was leaving.

Now she's on a cruise? Gunnar said she's with his mother, but he's very vague about the whole thing. He says he doesn't know the details. Who offers to housesit for someone without knowing when they'll be home? Don't even get me started on the fact that Dorothea would never go on a cruise. She told me so a dozen times. She's terrified of the open sea."

Scott waited patiently until I came up for air. "Let's pretend for a minute all your suspicions are valid. Why would Gunnar lie to you, except maybe for kicks? What is there to gain?"

"Dorothea isn't exactly destitute, and she doesn't have many heirs. There might be a lot to gain inside that house."

"Like what? She's too smart to leave piles of cash lying around. If Gunnar wanted to make some money, he'd ingratiate himself to her and hope she left him everything in her will."

"Not if he needs money right away. He's a graduate student. Maybe he's in debt or has a gambling problem. You said so yourself. There could be any number of reasons why he's hanging around."

"None of that explains why he's painting."

"Exactly." I sat back in my chair, triumphant. "That's how I know he's up to something and how I know Dorothea didn't go on a cruise of her own free will."

Scott barked a laugh. "Honey, even if Gunnar is after her money, he would have no reason to scheme to get her on a cruise ship. Unless he conspired with the captain to have the ship go down at sea."

He chewed on his bottom lip and tapped his temple. "The captain would go down, too, so why would he agree to go along with Gunnar's plan? Unless Gunnar was holding his family hostage and wasn't going to let them go until the cruise ship was resting on the bottom of the sea." He shook his head and looked back at me. "Sounds like a lot of trouble to go to to pay off some gambling debts."

I stirred my potatoes and carrots around on my plate. "That's great. Make fun of me because I'm worried about my friend."

Scott set down his fork. "Honey, I'm sorry. I'm just trying to make you see how bizarre this whole thing is. So Dorothea decided to combat her fears and take a cruise. Why is that so hard to believe? It sounds fun and spontaneous to me. Everything we know Dorothea to be. You know she isn't like most seventy-five-year-old women. She's just the type to pick up and take off without thinking about it should the opportunity arise."

"She might be fun and spontaneous, but she knows I'm not. She knows how much I would worry. She's too thoughtful to leave without talking to me about it and explaining how she figures it's time to face her fears."

"You were out of town," he reminded me, infernally patient. "She knew you would go by the house, and Gunnar could tell you everything."

"What about the girlfriend? Dorothea would never permit him to stay in her house with a woman he isn't married to. She would forego a vacation before she allowed blatant sin under her roof."

"I'm sure Gunnar knows that too. That's probably why he didn't tell her his girlfriend was coming over."

"Why lie to me about it? I'm not the one with a possible inheritance."

"He doesn't want you to tell Dorothea when she calls." He took a roll out of the basket and reached for the butter. "She'll call any day and tell you how much fun she's having and how she should've cruised years ago and you will feel like a louse for judging Gunnar so harshly."

I speared a carrot and popped it in my mouth. It wasn't as hot as I liked since I'd been stirring it around on my plate since I sat down.

"Dorothea's fine," Scott continued. "Gunnar may not be your favorite person, but he's fine too. Stop worrying about what your neighbors are doing and spend some time with your family. How did Dylan enjoy his weekend without Mom and Dad breathing down his neck?"

If he only knew. "Why don't you ask him yourself?"

"I wish he'd hang around for dinner once in a while. I'm going to talk to him about it. The whole family hasn't sat around the dinner table in months."

I didn't say a word. Let him deal with Dylan. I was exhausted.

Chapter 10

I tried to focus on other matters the next few days. Scott had a point. It was really none of my business if Gunnar invited his girlfriend to stay while he housesat for his aunt. It was Dorothea's problem, not mine. I couldn't even keep my own son under control, let alone someone else's. I began to wonder if what bothered me so much about Gunnar was that he reminded me of Dylan.

Besides the fact that he wasn't very friendly or hospitable, Gunnar hadn't given me any reason to compare him to Dylan. He was a graduate student. Not an easy feat. He seemed to have a bright future ahead of him. My son however couldn't be counted on to show up for work at the fast food restaurant in the mall. He wouldn't even talk about school unless it was to string his grandmother and Scott along. I had no right to be so hard on Gunnar. Once again, it was none of my business what went on in Dorothea's house. It broke my heart to think of the painting she loved so much lying in splinters on the dining room floor, but there was nothing I could do about that either.

I still hadn't decided if I was going to tell Scott about Dylan's weekend here at the house. It seemed sort of pointless. If he reacted the way he did upon finding out Gunnar's girlfriend had moved into Dorothea's bedroom as soon as she left for her cruise—or wherever she was—I would be furious. I really didn't feel like fighting with him about it. I hadn't gotten anywhere with Dylan. I didn't want to repeat the experience with Scott.

I replayed my last conversation with Dorothea in the flowerbeds. She would be so disappointed to hear the woman she believed was a lion didn't even have the courage to tell her husband their son had a sex party in the house while they were out of town. If I was a lion, I was more like the one in the Wizard of Oz who lacked courage. Dorothea would tell me I didn't need a wizard to give me courage. All I needed to do was open my Bible, which contained the answers I needed. She would also remind me I needed to decide what type of behavior I accepted in my home. If Jesus wouldn't allow it in his house, it was a pretty good indicator Scott and I shouldn't allow it in ours. I tried to muster a little righteous indignation about the situation. That only made my stomach hurt. I kept thinking I had been right, at least on one point. Dorothea might be a lion, but I was a marshmallow.

"Don't forget to call the garage today," Scott said on his way out the front door for work. "Your car is supposed to be ready. It's been two weeks."

"I thought you were going to take care of that."

"I don't have time. You're the one who wrecked it."

I wanted to remind him I hadn't wrecked the car. A careless, impatient driver had plowed into me. I didn't feel like getting into another argument I would invariably lose.

"Don't take any guff off them," he instructed. "Remind them they're the ones who created this schedule. We've been paying premiums to our insurance company long enough to be treated with respect."

I didn't know why he was telling me this when we both knew I didn't have the nerve to pick a fight with an auto body man.

The door barely shut behind him when the phone rang. I hurried to it, hoping it was either the garage telling me the car was ready so I wouldn't have to call them, or Dorothea telling me she was fine and getting some sun and wishing she had taken up cruising long ago.

My heart sank a notch when I saw my mother's name on the caller ID. "I need a ride to the eye doctor," she said in lieu of greeting.

I had enough on my mind already without having to deal with my mother. "Um, I have a lot of errands to run today."

"Then it will work out perfectly," she said. "You can pick me up on your way out. My appointment's at ten."

I resisted a groan as I looked at the clock. Aidan was still asleep. I had hoped to do some housecleaning before he woke up and got underfoot. "Can't you drive yourself?"

I hated to ask. She was my mother, and she seldom asked for favors. But why did she always wait until the last minute to call?

"I'm having my eyes dilated. They said I could drive myself, but I'd rather you take me."

"That doesn't give me much time to get ready and do the things I need to do."

"Then you better hustle." She hung up.

"Don't you have your car back yet?" Mom asked as she slid into the passenger side of the loaner car. I had pulled up in front of her condo with twenty minutes to spare before her appointment. We had plenty of time to get there, but she was waiting out front anyway. As I put the car in park she even pushed back the sleeve of her blouse to look disapprovingly at her watch.

I was prepared with my speech to defend myself for not getting here sooner when she threw me for a loop with the unexpected question. "It's still in the shop," I explained.

"Hopefully it'll be ready be Friday though it should've been done today. Scott's not going to be happy."

Mom fastened her seat belt across her Brooks Brothers pantsuit and set her Dooney and Burke handbag in her lap. "As well he shouldn't be. You can't let repairmen roll over you, Joy. They do that to women, you know? They think we're incompetent so they treat us like we don't have a brain in our heads. Not me. I don't put up with it. You should give me the number to the shop. I'll have your car sitting in your driveway like that." She snapped her fingers.

Aidan laughed from the backseat.

She turned around and smiled at him. Her face softened by a hundred degrees. I wondered if she ever looked at me like that when I was his age. "Good morning, Aidan. How are you this fine day?"

"I'm not Aidan, I'm Spiderman."

"Oh, excuse me, Spiderman. I didn't see your web there."

"It's okay, Grandma. Mommy never sees it either."

She turned to face forward. I stayed quiet, hoping she had forgotten about me and would spend the morning talking with Aidan. It would suit me just fine if I didn't have to say another word the rest of the day.

It was not to be.

"Has Dylan said anything more about those college brochures I brought over a few weeks ago?"

I wasn't in the mood to protect anyone, least of all Dylan. "I don't think he even looked at them."

She exhaled hard enough to stir the air freshener hanging from the rearview mirror. "Joy, he's been out of school for a year. How long are you going to let him hang around the house wasting his life?"

First Valerie, now Mom. How many times did I need to have this conversation? "I don't know what you expect me to do about it, Mom. He's practically a grown man and he doesn't listen to his mother."

She sighed again, though not as vehemently. "Tell me about it. I wanted you to get an education. But you had to marry the first boy who looked at you."

I looked pointedly at Aidan in the rearview mirror. "Mom."

She waved away my concern with a flip of her hand. "He doesn't know who we're talking about. I didn't want you to have things as hard as I did. My dream since the moment your father walked out on us was to give you a college education. I scrimped and saved and begged and borrowed for ten long years to make it happen. You wouldn't have any of it. Looks like Dylan is going to turn out the same way. Just sit back and watch his opportunities slip out the window."

"I think my life turned out pretty well. I'm happy. Isn't that what mothers want for their children?"

"You're happy *now*." She leaned toward me in her bucket seat and lowered her voice. "What happens if Scott decides to pull a vanishing act like your father did? Then where will you be? You won't be the first woman who thought she had a perfect marriage."

"Mom," I hissed.

"I never dreamed it would happen to me either. Now look at me. Sixty-six-years-old and still working at that office. I should be retired by now."

"You love your job."

"That's neither here nor there. The point is I wasn't prepared for what happened. That's my greatest fear for you, Joy. You've always had your head in the clouds. You only see the good in people. Scott could be running around on you right now and you wouldn't have a clue. That's what happened to me."

I looked in the rearview mirror. Aidan was drawing circles on the window with his finger, blissfully unaware of our conversation. "Mom, I don't know why you have to talk like this. Scott and I are fine. Nothing like that will happen to us."

Was I really so sure? I knew Scott loved me, but half the time I didn't know if he liked me. We seldom fought. Maybe that was because I rolled over and gave him his way. I thought of the look of disgust on his face every time the subject of the Toyota came up. He blamed me for the accident and the fact that the car wasn't ready yet. It was my fault Dylan wasn't in college and Aidan had been late with potty training. He wasn't always happy with his job. Did he blame me for that too?

Mom raised a hand in the air. "Every woman believes her marriage will be the one that lasts. Her husband will be the one who stays faithful. I've been around, Joy, and I know men. They're all the same." She leaned closer again as if speaking confidentially but didn't bother to lower her voice. "Scott seems to be one of the good ones, but you never know. You can't trust men. That's why I wanted you to get an education. Now look at you. Never even had a real job. What would you do if Scott walked out?" She sniffed and looked out the side window. "You'd come to me, that's what. I'd have to bail you out."

Over my dead body.

"Could we please talk about something else? There's nothing wrong with my marriage or my husband—"

"Knock wood," she chimed and pounded the armrest.

"—And we aren't the only ones in the car."

She glanced over her shoulder and gave Aidan another smile. "All I'm saying is I wish you would've stayed in school."

"We were having a baby," I reminded her. "It seemed like the thing to do at the time."

"Plenty of women go to school while they're expecting."

"Scott and I decided I should stay home with Dylan and go back to school later."

"You mean Scott decided."

"No," I reiterated, though she was partly right. I had suggested we take advantage of the university's daycare program so I could finish my second year of credits before I quit permanently, but Scott was against it. He didn't exactly forbid it, but I knew what he wanted. As usual, I put his happiness before my own fulfillment. I had no regrets. I made the right decision for our family. But still…

"I've thought about going back to school when Aidan's in school fulltime. I'm just not ready yet. It's my decision."

She didn't look convinced. "I hope so."

We turned into the office complex parking lot, and I let her out at the door. "I'll park and Aidan and I will catch up with you."

"Her office is on the third floor. Don't dawdle."

As if I ever did. I smiled in reply and pulled away. I was tempted to pull onto the street and keep driving. She'd figure out eventually I wasn't coming back and call a cab to get home. God knew I loved my mother, but spending any amount of time with her sucked the life right out of me.

"There was a spot, Mommy," Aidan said from his car seat. "You drove right past it."

I groaned inwardly. It looked like Aidan had been listening to Mom after all.

After fifteen minutes of waiting for someone to call Mom's name and getting kicked about two hundred times by Aidan who wouldn't stop swinging his legs on the chair, I told Mom I needed to get my restless son out of there. "You need to wait a while after they dilate your pupils anyway. I'll take Aidan across the street to investigate those shops we saw coming in. Call me after you're finished and we'll pick you up."

Mom didn't look thrilled about us leaving her to wait alone. The only reason she asked me to take her was so she'd have someone to listen to her trash the doctor, the staff, and most of the other patients littering the waiting room and taking up the doctor's valuable time. If she was the one who had to handle an overwound preschooler, she'd understand why it was better for everyone in the office if Aidan and I left for a while.

Aidan was as relieved as I was to get out of the sterile smelling waiting room. I let him skip ahead of me through the halls and down the three flights of stairs. Might as well burn some calories as well as some of his energy by avoiding the elevator. We hadn't worked out again with the DVDs after the third day. I really wanted to get into a routine, but it seemed like every morning there was something more urgent begging for my attention. I knew it was just an excuse. People made time for what was important. I needed to prioritize. Maybe Scott was right. If I wasn't so busy watching out the window to see what Gunnar was doing, I might have time to workout with Aidan, and read my Bible more as well. I still hadn't found the courage Dorothea said I needed to stand up to Scott and Dylan.

As soon as Aidan and I reached the lobby, I grasped his hand and led him outside. We crossed the parking lot and relatively quiet street to the line of shops on the other side. Most of them looked too upscale to risk taking Aidan inside. Near the end I spotted a Fuzziwigg's candy store and a novelty toy store. I had sworn off Fuzziwig's last Christmas when Dylan bought me a combination temptation sampler and I ate the whole thing by New Year's. I figured letting Aidan pick out a selection of Jelly Belly jellybeans would eat up a few minutes while we waited for Mom.

I made sure my phone was on and getting reception as we jingled our way into the brightly colored establishment. Aidan's eyes lit up at the selections. We made the circuit of the small shop. I proudly resisted the fudge counter and the brightly packaged gourmet cookies.

"Only jelly beans," I reminded Aidan after he insisted he needed every item we passed. "You can pick out ten kinds."

His eyes widened. "Ten. Sweet."

Yes, they are, I thought, as well as a low fat snack? Not like the gourmet cookies calling my name. The young woman behind the counter was most accommodating when Aidan had to try nearly every variety before making his choices. Allowing him to inject so much sugar on an empty stomach was a disaster waiting to happen, but it would be at least thirty minutes before Mom called for us to pick her up. Except for us, the shop was empty and the woman thought Aidan was darling. While she allowed him to put his sealed bag on the old fashioned scales to be weighed, I looked across the street to the doctor's office. Now would be the perfect time for my mother to call to say her appointment was over.

"That'll be $8.95," the clerk said loudly to me since she could tell my attention had drifted.

That must've been a lot of jellybeans. I turned toward the counter and reached for my purse as a young couple strolled past the window. I jerked my head in their direction. It was Gunnar and Kimberly walking arm and arm and chatting amiably. At least Kimberly was chatting while Gunnar looked slightly amused at something she'd just said.

I slid my debit card through the terminal and signed the screen. I grabbed the bag off the counter, took Aidan's hand, and practically dragged him out of the store.

"I want a jellybean," he whined before the door jangled shut behind us.

"Not until after lunch," I said in my mommy monotone without looking at him. "You've already had too many."

Gunnar and Kimberly were no longer on the street, but there were only so many shops they could've disappeared into. There was no way they could've made it to the end of the block or driven off in the length of time it took me to pay for the jellybeans and exit the store.

"Let's get Grandma and have lunch so I can eat my jellybeans?"

"She has to call us first, remember? After her appointment."

"I hate appointments."

He wasn't the only one, but I had bigger things on my mind at the moment. "Let's go for a walk while we wait." I grasped his hand as if he had a choice and took off in the direction Kimberly and Gunnar had gone. I hit pay dirt at the third door we passed. Gunnar and Kimberly were standing shoulder to shoulder at the counter of a jewelry store, immersed in conversation with a silver haired gentleman behind the counter. I slowed down as much as I could without Aidan protesting and tried to see what had captured their attention. Were they buying an engagement ring? I still didn't believe a couple should cohabitate before marriage, but at least they were doing something about it.

Then I saw what the jeweler held in his hand. He held out a gold pocket watch by the chain and examined it in the light. I gasped. Was it possible? Gunnar nodded in response to something the jeweler said. Aidan became engrossed in a display of sun catchers in the window. I stepped against the doorjamb so Gunnar and Kimberly would be less likely to see me spying on them, and pretended to look at the sun catchers. The jeweler made a few more comments and then opened a laptop on the counter. He laid the watch on a velvet cloth next to the laptop and seemed to be comparing it to something on the screen. Gunnar leaned toward Kimberly and whispered something to her. The jeweler did not look up. Either he didn't hear them or he knew the comment wasn't meant for his ears. Kimberly's eyebrows rose in response, but she didn't speak. The jeweler laid down his pen and picked up the watch again. A satisfied smile lit his features.

This time I got a better view of the watch. I couldn't be one hundred percent certain from where I was standing, but it sure looked like the watch that had been one of Albert Westlake's prized possessions. Dorothea had shown it to me once and told me the story of how his father had given it to him in the early years of their marriage not long before the old man died.

I grabbed Aidan's shoulder and gave him a push in the direction of the next store. My head was spinning. Dorothea would never sell that watch, even if she was destitute. The next store was a bookstore. I knew it was risky to take Aidan with his sticky, jellybean hands into such a place, but I had to get out of sight long enough to catch my breath and sort my thoughts. Was Gunnar selling off Dorothea and Albert's personal belongings while she was out of the house? How else had he gotten hold of the watch?

What would I tell Dorothea when she got home? She would be crushed to learn Gunnar had stolen anything from her, especially something with as much sentimental value as Albert's father's watch. Of course I didn't know for sure it was the same watch. Maybe Gunnar had been given a similar watch from his father who had received it as a gift from his grandfather. If that were the case, Gunnar was free to do whatever he wished with it.

Several customers wandered around the bookstore, but the manager focused his attention on Aidan. Who could blame the poor man? I kept my hands firmly on Aidan's shoulders and led him to a calendar display where we could watch out the front window. He looked at the calendars of puppies and sunrises and inspirational quotes while I watched for Gunnar and Kimberly to leave the jewelry store. Aidan tired quickly of the calendars and moved to a display of intricately painted scale carousels and carnival rides. My stomach clenched at the price tags.

"Don't touch anything," I said at least a hundred times before Gunnar and Kimberly finally walked past the store window, arm in arm, smiling and looking pleased. I gave them a few minutes to get out of sight before we left the store and went straight to the crosswalk to go back to the doctor's office.

My cell phone rang just as we entered the building. It was Mom. "We're on our way up," I told her as Aidan pushed the button for the elevator. "There's a nice little shopping center across the street. How about lunch? Aidan's starving."

My mother never turned down food, especially when I was paying. We found seats at a quiet little eatery that boasted a children's menu. I ordered the Chicken Cordon bleu and then asked Mom to keep an eye on Aidan for a few minutes. "I saw something in a little shop earlier that would be a wonderful gift for Scott."

"Isn't his birthday in October?"

"I was thinking Father's Day." I got up quickly and shouldered my purse before she had the chance to point out Father's Day was a month and a half away.

A well-dressed lady in low heels and a tweed wrapper was the only customer in the jewelry store when I walked in. I went directly to the men's watches while she talked with the jeweler about silver cigarette cases. I wondered if she gave her mother the same Father's Day excuse so she could get out of lunch. After a few moments, the jeweler left her alone to look further and came over to me.

His hands were clasped in front of him, and he spoke in a quiet, refined tone. "Good afternoon. Is there something I can help you with?"

"Yes. I'm looking for something special for my husband. He's always loved pocket watches. Antique." I felt a pang of guilt over the untruth. But I assuaged my guilt by telling myself this was for Dorothea. I knew God abhorred a lying tongue, but if Gunnar was doing what I thought he was doing, that was the bigger lie.

The jeweler's smile widened as he motioned to the display under the counter. "We have some lovely pieces here."

I stepped closer to the counter. "Actually I'm looking for a particular gold one. My friend has one my husband has always admired, and I happen to know he was planning on bringing it in today."

"Of course. I'll be right back." The jeweler stepped into the backroom and returned with the watch I saw Gunnar hand over. "This one came in a little while ago. I haven't had a chance to catalog it yet, but it's a marvelous piece." He laid a velvet mat on the counter and set the watch on top of it.

I couldn't breathe. It was Albert's watch.

"Is this the one you were thinking of?"

"Yes. It's beautiful."

"And only fifty-five hundred dollars. I'm sure you already know the story behind it. It's almost one hundred years old. Look at the craftsmanship. You can't get that in a contemporary piece. It's one of a kind."

I barely heard a word he said. My hands shook as I brushed a fingertip across the watch face. I wished I had nearly six thousand dollars lying around so I could buy it back. Poor Dorothea. I didn't want her to know what Gunnar had done. I could scarcely believe it myself.

"I'm sure there's an explanation, Joy."

My jaw dropped. I stared across the coffee table at my husband. I had bit my tongue and bided my time until Aidan was upstairs before relaying what I had seen in the jewelry store. I thought for sure this would make Scott see Gunnar Westlake was up to no good.

"What explanation would that be? Dorothea's out of town and Gunnar is hocking the family jewelry. She would never give him permission to sell that watch."

He lifted a shoulder and turned another page of the Wall Street Journal. "Isn't he her last heir? Doesn't it make sense for her to give him the watch? It's a shame he sold it. I'll give you that. But it's his property to do with what he wants."

"I don't think it is. I think he stole it."

Scott lowered the paper and looked at me over the top of his reading glasses. "Making accusations like that is a good way to lose a friend. It's a family matter, Joy. It's best to stay out of it."

"Is that what you'd say to someone who caught Aidan or Dylan selling something that meant the world to you?"

He grinned. "We don't have anything that valuable."

"I'm serious, Scott."

"I know you are, Joy. That's the problem. You need to stop obsessing about that young man across the street. Did you talk to the body shop man today?"

I exhaled. How could he worry about a stupid car while our dear friend's house was plundered? "The guy said hopefully it will be ready by Friday."

He rattled the paper and buried his nose in it. "Friday. You want to talk about a bunch of crooks. You should worry about the ones holding your car hostage."

I sat back in the chair and reached for the novel that had been waiting for me on the end table for two weeks. It was due back at the library tomorrow, and I barely could remember any of the characters. My life had become a novel. Too bad nobody was rooting for the heroine.

Chapter 11

I closed the front door behind me with barely an audible click. Scott was in the living room with his laptop. He'd be engrossed in the news and ball scores for the next hour. Aidan was sound asleep. Dylan had left hours ago wearing his work uniform. He might actually be going to the mall this time. For once I was thankful my family generally ignored me.

I leaned around the porch post and waited for the count of ten. Nothing moved across the street. No sound came from the house. I was beginning to think I had built this whole thing with Gunnar into something much bigger and more sinister than it really was. Scott was right. My mother was right. I'd been stuck in the house too long. I needed to get out more. I needed to think about going back to school. Not that I knew what I'd take. I'd be forty on my next birthday. I was twenty pounds overweight and hadn't used my brain for anything more complicated than creating crafts out of Popsicle sticks in twenty years. I didn't have any interests beyond trying out new recipes, getting the stains out of Aidan's play clothes, church, Scott, and Dorothea. Not necessarily in that order.

What could I learn in school that I really wanted to know?

A light came on at the back of Dorothea's house. It was the one over the dining room table. I watched as a shadow moved across the room. Gunnar. The shape moved back and forth. It looked like he was going from the kitchen to the dining room and back. Probably setting the table for him and Kimberly. Eating my best friend's food. I should barge over there right now and demand to know why he was really there. Where was Dorothea? What had he done to her? Maybe everyone else believed she was on a cruise, but I didn't. I knew my friend. She wouldn't take a cruise. She wouldn't go anywhere without making plans and lists and letting me know. Not that she owed me an explanation for every move. She was just considerate that way. She knew I would worry, and she would worry that I was worried.

She wasn't on a cruise, and she wasn't visiting family. She was in danger. I knew it. I had to prove it. I couldn't confront Gunnar. He'd only lie again and then he'd know I was onto him. I had to find out for myself. Get proof before I confronted him. I wasn't sure what sort of proof that would be, but I figured I'd recognize it when I saw it.

I crept across the yard until I got to the privacy fence in the corner of the Ben Sanders' yard. I ducked between the fence and the hydrangea hedge—a rather tight squeeze. The branches plucked at the fibers of my sweater. Next time I went sneaking through the neighbors' bushes, I'd wear something that didn't snag. I glanced back at my house. At this point I was more concerned about Scott seeing me than anyone else. I could imagine him yelling from the front door for me to get back in the house and stop acting like an amateur sleuth.

With a deep breath for courage, and to still the pounding of my heart, I hurried across the street. This was my most vulnerable point. I kept listening for Scott's voice. I made it across the street without detection. I leaped into the shadows at the tail end of Kimberly's car. I was careful to keep my hands off it in case she had some kind of car alarm. I didn't think most compact economy cars were equipped with alarms, but what did

I know about things like that? Just as I neared the side of the house, Gunnar passed in front of the window. My heart nearly stopped in my chest. Before I could pee my pants, he moved into the kitchen. I realized this was good for me. As long as he left lights on through the house I could see in, but he couldn't see out.

I waited for a moment but didn't see further movement. It was eerie knowing he was just on the other side of the wall. I edged along the sidewalk to the back corner of the house, making sure to stay in the shadows.

At the back corner of the house I calculated the distance from the planter boxes to the patio. Twenty feet? Six running paces and I'd be there. The patio offered several hiding places to choose from. Behind the chaise lounge or the ornamental trees would work for a smaller woman, but I doubted they'd provide me with adequate cover. What if Gunnar came outside for something? I wouldn't be able to get back to the corner of the house without him seeing me, and the thought of being so close to him was a little unnerving. I couldn't think of a plausible excuse that would bring me out this late at night. Borrowing a cup of sugar was a flimsy excuse, even for me. I could say I heard a prowler. I was a terrible liar, and Gunnar would know what I was really up to.

I would just have to pray he didn't come out and catch me.

I looked at the window one last time. I fixed my gaze on the potted topiary between the back door and the small window over the kitchen sink and took off. I ran without thinking about someone looking out the window and seeing me. It was too late to worry about that. I was more concerned with reaching the topiary before my lungs burst from the exertion. I really needed to start working out with Aidan again in the mornings.

I reached my destination with no one yelling at me or hurling something out the window on top of me. I sagged against the brick wall to catch my breath. Above me the kitchen window cast a square of light onto the patio floor. I could climb on the edge of the patio wall and take a peek, but my face would be too close to the glass. Anyone on the other side would see me. I needed to get to the dining room window for a better look into the house. I wouldn't need to climb on anything or stand too close to the window in order to see into the room. I edged in that direction. I didn't notice the empty watering can until I kicked it halfway across the stone patio.

I froze as it clattered against the flagstones. I leaped against the wall, my heart hammering in my chest until I realized I was standing right next to the back door. Footsteps sounded inside the house. I dove for the cover of the patio table. I didn't climb under it for fear I'd knock over one of the chairs. Instead I huddled between the table and the side of the house and hoped whoever came to the door wouldn't look in my direction. I squeezed my eyes shut as the light over the back door came on. Too late, I realized closing my eye did not make me invisible. I shrank against the side of the house and prayed I was far enough in the shadows I wouldn't be detected.

I heard the familiar creak of Dorothea's back door. I opened my eyes a slit. Under the edge of the door, a Doc Marten clad shoe stepped over the threshold. I didn't dare lift my head to look at the body leaning around the edge of the door to find the source of the disturbance. I knew those shoes belonged to Gunnar. I wondered if he suspected I might be lurking around. If he saw me crouching here he would know I hadn't seen a prowler. If he had indeed done something to Dorothea, she would be in more serious danger.

My heart froze in my chest. It was the first time I'd admitted to myself something could be seriously wrong inside Dorothea's house. Until now it had almost been pretending or scaring myself like I used to do on Halloween when I was a kid. This wasn't pretend. It was real life. Had Gunnar actually done something to Dorothea? Was she hurt? Or was she simply on a cruise having a wonderful time with Gunnar's mother?

I stared at the foot poking over the threshold and willed it to stay where it was. Please, God, don't let him come off the step, I begged. I know I'm spying on my neighbor, but it's for Dorothea. Let me stay hidden.

After a painful few seconds, the foot backed into the house, and the storm door swung shut behind it. Another moment passed, and the light went off. I exhaled. Thank you, Jesus. I stayed rooted in my spot, waiting for Gunnar to close the interior door. I needed to go to the bathroom really bad, but that would have to wait. I'd sneaked out of my own house and come all the way over here. I wasn't leaving until I learned something.

Through the large window over the breakfast nook I saw Gunnar's shadow as he took a seat at the table. I groaned. Leaving the door open would make it easier for me to see what they were doing inside the house. It would also make it easier for them to see or hear me on the porch. After a few more moments of holding my breath I carefully straightened and came out of my hiding place. I edged along the wall toward the dining room window, keeping my eye opened for stray watering cans or other objects that would alert Gunnar to my presence. More and more of the dining area came into view as I moved toward the window.

Gunnar sat alone at the table, his head bent over Dorothea's laptop. The table was strewn with papers. From where I stood I couldn't tell what they were, but they looked like important documents. I edged closer, scooting my feet across the patio floor to avoid making noise. Occasionally Gunnar would pick up a paper for a closer look and compare it with something on the computer screen.

He set down the paper and turned his head toward the stairwell. I heard a woman's voice a moment before Kimberly came into view.

Her narrow oval face was darkened in anger. "Don't you think you've wasted enough time on this?"

"Let me worry about that."

"I've been here over a week and nothing." She moved closer to the window so Gunnar had to turn in my direction to talk to her. I stepped nearer to the side of the house and into the shadows. I didn't want him looking at Kimberly and seeing me behind her.

"There's more here. There has to be."

I frowned. What were they talking about? Had he gotten rid of Dorothea so he could search for whatever treasure he thought the house held? I held my breath, wishing for a better look into the room but terrified they would see me.

"Maybe she got rid of it," Kimberly countered. I could tell by the sound of her voice she had moved closer to the table, but I maintained my spot. Gunnar would still have his head turned in my general direction to talk to her. "Maybe it was sold years ago. Maybe it never existed."

"Then where's the money? There's no indication she sold anything of that value."

I heard a chair scoot away from the table. I assumed Kimberly sat down. I edged a tiny step toward the window. She was sitting at the table adjacent to Gunnar with her back to the window. He was looking at her and the computer, not the window. I risked another step closer.

Kimberly folded her hands on the table and leaned back in the chair. She looked irritated and impatient. "People spend money, you know. Or they lose it in the stock market."

Gunnar didn't bother to look up from the papers on the table. "Not people like Dorothea Westlake. She and Albert are too smart to let something like that happen."

Kimberly slumped in the chair. "This is turning into a colossal waste of time."

Gunnar set his jaw in a hard line. "I'm not giving up."

"Well, I don't like the risks. The longer it takes, the more likely we'll be detected. The woman across the street already suspects something. It won't be long before she convinces someone else she's right."

"She's a joke. No one takes her seriously. We could pile bodies in the street and no one would believe a word she said."

It didn't take a rocket scientist to figure out what neighbor they were talking about. Sadly, he was dead on right.

"We could stay here another two weeks and find nothing," Kimberly said.

"It won't take two weeks."

"What about the old woman?"

I stiffened. Dorothea. What about her?

"That's taken care of."

Kimberly scooted her chair out and got hastily to her feet. I ducked out of sight. She moved toward the window and into my field of vision. She flicked back the curtain and gazed into the backyard. I knew she couldn't see anything but the reflection of the room thrown back at her, but it was unnerving to have her face just a foot or two above mine. I was afraid to exhale.

"It's too big of a chance," she said more adamantly. "I can't wait around any longer."

"What do you mean?"

"I mean I'm out of here."

Gunnar got up too. "You're not going anywhere."

"Try to stop me. I got my things together earlier."

"You can't leave. I need your help."

"You don't need anything."

"Kimberly."

"Don't call me that. Kimberly's dead. I'm outta here." The back door flung open. I nearly cried out in surprise. How had she crossed the room so quickly without me hearing her? I supposed agile women could do stuff like that. She had a duffel bag slung over one shoulder and a purse over the other. I ducked into the narrow space between the patio table and the wall. The wrought iron legs of the table offered little camouflage. Maybe Kimberly would change her mind and leave through the front door. If she continued this way, she would have to go right past me to get to her car. I knelt down and tried to make as small of an object as possible. Even if she didn't see me, she might still hear my heart hammering against my ribs.

Fortunately for me, Gunnar was too busy yelling after Kimberly to hear the blood pounding in my ears.

"Don't go. I need you."

"You don't need anyone," Kimberly shouted back. "You've got it all figured out."

Gunnar joined her on the back step and grabbed her wrist. "How do I know you didn't find something on your own and you're going to double cross me?" He snatched the duffel bag off her shoulder.

"Give that back, you jerk. How dare you accuse me of anything? You know me better than that."

"Apparently not. I didn't think you'd leave."

"You better stay out of my bag."

"Or what?"

"It's mine," she shrieked.

"You're being awfully protective."

"Why shouldn't I? I'm the only one who knows what you're capable of."

I could only see the back half of Kimberly's body holding open the storm door and only part of Gunnar. I wished they would take their fight back inside so they wouldn't find me hiding. If Gunnar found me now, with his anger at Kimberly bubbling over, I didn't even want to think about what he might do. I glanced at the corner of the house. With them occupied with each other, I could probably make a break for it, but I needed to hear the rest of the conversation. My usual timidity was losing out to my curiosity.

When Gunnar spoke, his voice was low and menacing. "Are you threatening me?"

"I have no reason to threaten you." Kimberly's voice was just as menacing.

That she wasn't afraid of him should have given me hope. Instead, it made me that much more fearful.

She took a deep breath. Her next words lost their venom. "You're wasting your time here. Your greed is going to cause you to mess up and ruin everything. I'm not hanging around to watch."

"Where are you going?"

"Home, where I can hopefully forget I ever knew you."

"If I find out you double crossed me—"

"Ow."

The pain in Kimberly's voice made me flinch.

"Let go of me," she said between clench teeth. The storm door slammed shut as she jerked away from him.

I heard mumbled voices and scuffling. What was going on in there? Would he forcibly keep her in the house? What would I do if he did? I didn't have any reason to like or empathize with Kimberly, except she was a woman, and I couldn't bear the thought of anyone suffering in the hands of someone bigger and stronger. But if I called the police on a domestic disturbance, Gunnar would immediately suspect me. Would I be safe? What about Dorothea?

The scuffling stopped. I didn't hear anything. Had they moved toward the front of the house? I wanted to sneak a peek in the window but feared they were still on the other side. My knees screamed in agony from my crouched position. If I didn't move soon, my body might lock up and I'd never get home. I edged around the corner of the table and tried to straighten. My right knee popped, and I emitted a pained cry like an animal caught in a trap. My gaze shot to the back door. It didn't open, and no lights came on. I braced my hands behind me and walked them up the wall as I straightened to my full five feet, three inches. I listened for another moment. The house remained quiet. I needed to get back across the street before one of them came out the back door or Scott realized I was gone and opened our front door and yelled for me. Gunnar would know in a minute where I was.

I kept one hand and shoulder against the wall of Dorothea's house as I moved across the patio to the walk. As I reached the corner of the house I heard the front door open. I shrank against the house. A car door opened and closed, and headlights illuminated the night. If I had been a few steps faster, the lights would have pinned me against Dorothea's garage door. The headlights made a wide arc as the car backed onto the street and drove away. I turned the corner of the house and slunk along the darkness. By all accounts, Gunnar was alone in the house. And angry. If he had threatened Kimberly, and possibly hurt her, what would he do to me, someone he openly despised?

The thought of his wrath made me pick up my pace. I looked through the bare rose bush arbor at Dorothea's front door. It was closed against the night, and the porch light was off. I took a deep breath and stooped my shoulders as if that would make me less noticeable and hurried as fast as I dared across the street. The running shoes that had less than a block's worth of running on them felt like clouds beneath my feet, yet each step across the asphalt sounded like gunfire in my ears. I set my sights on Ben Sanders' privacy fence and hoped the sound was more fear and adrenaline than actual noise.

I leaped onto the curb just as a sweep of headlights turned onto our street. I dove behind the fence. Had Kimberly returned? It was probably someone in the neighborhood coming home. Regardless, if it had come along a moment sooner Gunnar would've seen me if he had been at the window watching Kimberly's exit.

The car slowed. I held my breath and waited for Gunnar to turn on the front porch light. I was fairly certain he couldn't see me concealed behind the privacy fence, but if the light hit it just right, or if he had seen me crossing the street a moment ago…

I didn't want to think about that. The car stopped in the middle of the street a few feet away from me. A rear door opened. Music and two young people spilled out. Spilled being the operative word since both struggled to remain standing as they staggered, laughing and lurching, toward my house. It was Dylan, in a very drunken state, and a young woman I'd never seen before.

"See you later, baby," Dylan said after a long sloppy kiss that soured my stomach.

She sagged against him, and he backpedaled on unsteady legs. "Aren't you going to invite me in?"

I ground my teeth in anticipation of his answer.

"Why don't you invite us all in," a masculine voice called from inside the car. "We can party some more."

"Would you shut up," Dylan yelled. "You're going to wake the whole neighborhood."

"Yeah," someone else shouted. "You'll wake everyone up."

Someone cranked up the stereo even louder inside the car and laid on the horn. Everyone started laughing, Dylan included. He obviously wasn't too concerned about disturbing his neighbors' sleep. I wondered what he'd do if I popped out of the bushes. I envisioned them cowering at the righteous indignation on my face, falling over themselves to apologize and repenting of their evil deeds. Reality hit me over the head like a mallet. Even Aidan didn't cower in my presence. Or the man who sideswiped me with his car. A group of drunken teens would not be impressed.

"Are you going to call me tomorrow?" the girl hanging all over my son asked.

Dylan held her at arm's length. "I don't got your number, baby. I can't even remember your name."

She gave him a playful smack on the chest. "It's Emily, you pig. After everything we did tonight, I can't believe you don't remember my name." She threw her arms around his neck. "I bet you'll remember me after this." Her mouth found his, and she ground her body against him. I averted my eyes as Dylan's hands traveled around, up, and over her body. What was going on with my son? Where had he learned such behavior? My face burned with shame. Shame for the young woman cheapening herself on my sidewalk. Shame for my son who obviously thought Emily had been put on earth for nothing more than his physical pleasure. And shame for me that I had to watch this display. If it was on TV I could at least change the channel. This wasn't TV. This was my life. A life I'd made a huge mess of.

I waited until the car pulled away before I sneaked inside. As usual Dylan didn't bother to lock the door or set the alarm so no one heard me come in. I thought of going into the living room and asking Scott if he had heard our son and his drunken friends playing their music on the street. He would say no. To his defense, he probably hadn't heard a thing. My husband had an uncanny ability to tune out anything unpleasant or objectionable.

Upstairs I dropped into bed and squeezed my eyes shut against the image of my son pawing that girl on our sidewalk. How had I made so many mistakes in raising him? Worse, how would I ever undo them?

Chapter 12

Tuesday dawned gray and rainy, a typical late April morning. When I crawled out of bed fifteen minutes past my usual time I had pretty much forgotten the exchange between Gunnar and Kimberly. My sleep had been fitful and restless at best, and I was a little hazy on the details. My heart had resumed its natural rhythm after nearly being discovered on Dorothea's patio. I couldn't imagine what would've happened if they'd seen me. Would Gunnar have called the police and had me arrested for harassment? I was coming pretty close to stalking the guy. The only solid proof I had on him was he was a terrible boyfriend, not a very responsible house sitter, and a less than respectful nephew.

I was pretty sure he had stolen Albert's watch, though Scott could be right as well. Dorothea didn't have anyone else to leave her late husband's watches to. It made sense she would want Gunnar to have them. I thought it was pretty rotten to sell off Albert's property at the first opportunity, but would I expect anything less from my own son?

Gunnar didn't have a job. If he was truly a student working on a dissertation on the migratory patterns of honeybees, or whatever it was he told me the morning we met, he was probably broke. Five thousand dollars in his hand had to hold more appeal than an antique watch passed down from an uncle he never knew. Why keep it when he could certainly have an immediate use for the money? Dylan would probably sell one of my kidneys if someone offered him five thousand dollars.

Dylan.

I couldn't even think about Gunnar and his problems with Kimberly after seeing my darling son hanging all over a young woman and making intimate innuendoes about how they'd spent the evening. All this could've happened after the restaurant closed last night, but I didn't think so. Adding insult to injury, Dylan was carousing and engaging in behavior his father and I found deplorable and debase, and lying to us on top of it. I had protected him the night we came home from Chris and Valerie's by never mentioning the episode to Scott. I couldn't keep covering for him or making excuses for his behavior. Like Dorothea told me, I needed to grow a spine and stand up to my son before I lost him forever.

When Aidan trudged downstairs for breakfast an hour later I could tell his mood matched the weather outside. After twenty minutes of arguing with him to eat his breakfast and finally mopping up most of it off the countertop after he knocked the spoon out of the bowl, I whisked the bowl away and dumped the rest of the contents down the sink.

I didn't have the time or energy to deal with his mood swings this morning. I needed to talk to Dylan, and I was going to do it before my Tuesday morning Bible Study, the second one Dorothea had missed. Probably the second one she'd missed in her life. I had no intention of waiting until Dylan's usual wake up time of eleven or twelve. I was tired and cranky and almost itching to pick a fight with someone. If he had the energy to stay out late every night, his habit of sleeping till noon was about to be broken.

"Time to get moving," I told Aidan. "It's Bible Study Day. We can't be late."

He shook his head, still grumpy. "We can't go. Aunt Dor'fea's not home yet."

"Looks like we'll have to go without her this morning and tell her about it when she gets home."

"It's not the same."

"I know, but she wouldn't want us staying home just because she isn't here to go with us."

Reluctantly he slid off the stool and took my hand. "Mom?" he asked as we started down the hall.

"Hmm?"

"When's Aunt Dor'fea coming home? I miss her."

"I do too, buddy."

I left him in his room to choose an outfit for the day and headed across the hall to Dylan's room. It was barely nine o'clock. My oldest hadn't seen nine o'clock in the morning since he got out of high school. I was sure he wouldn't be happy to see it today.

I banged on his closed door before turning the knob and letting myself in. As suspected, he was sound asleep in a tangle of blankets and long legs. I stumbled through the debris and went straight to the window. I snapped up the shade with a quick, noisy jerk. "Rise and shine, sleepy head. The day's wasting."

My action would've been more dramatic if a bright morning sun could've seen fit to break through the clouds at that moment and illuminate the bed in a blaze of indignant glory. But the sun had chosen this morning to hide behind low-hanging clouds. With the shades up, the room was only marginally brighter than before.

"Get up, get up, get up," I said again, louder and maddeningly cheerful. "There are places to go and people to see."

"Mom," a voice mumbled from beneath the covers. "I'm asleep."

"Not anymore." I jerked back the blankets, but only halfway in case he wasn't properly clothed.

His hands clawed for the covers like a blinded animal yanked out of hibernation. "What're you doing?" One eye opened, and he raised his head a few inches off the pillow to look at the clock. "It's not time to get up yet. Leave me alone."

I plopped on the edge of the bed, the playfulness gone from my face. "I'll leave you alone after you answer a few questions. First, what time did you get in last night? Where were you and who were you with?"

"Huh? What is this? You can't wake me up out of a dead sleep and interrogate me."

"Want to bet?" I had used up all my patience and restraint with Aidan. I was tired and headachy, and my jeans were too tight. Someone was going to get hurt this morning.

"You better answer me, and don't waste your time lying. I know all about Emily."

"Who?" His face was a mask of confusion.

"Your date last night," I snapped. "The one who seemed to think the world of you, but you couldn't remember her name."

He sat up further, his eyes still glazed and clouded with sleep. "Were you spying on me?"

"Don't pull that load of garbage, Dylan. I won't allow you to turn this around to be my fault. As long as you live under my roof and come stumbling in at all hours with your friends playing their music loud enough to wake the entire neighborhood, I'll spy all I want."

His expression turned contrite, but I knew the drill. He would feign remorse to get me to end the lecture that much sooner.

"Mom, I didn't realize how late it was until we got here. Then Craig had the music up really loud. They were all clowning around. I told them to knock it off, but they weren't listening."

At least he was telling the truth so far. "Why weren't they listening? Had they been drinking?"

"Come on, Mom. What do you want to hear?"

"I want the truth, Dylan."

He flopped back onto the pillow and rubbed his hands over his face. He was beginning to wake up with razor stubble. It wouldn't be long before he couldn't avoid shaving every morning. Where had I been while this transformation happened to my son?

"No, Mom, I don't think you do. You can't handle the truth," he said in a deep, though not well played, Jack Nicholson impression.

I didn't laugh.

"Okay, okay," he began again. "It was after midnight before I got in. Craig and Seth and me were driving around and we ran into a couple of girls Seth knew. They wanted to hang out…" Long pregnant pause. "So we did. It was no big deal."

"Didn't you go to work last night?"

He exhaled and rubbed a hand over his face again. "I don't work there anymore."

I came off the bed. "What? You were wearing your uniform when you left the house."

"I didn't turn them all in."

"What does that mean?"

"It means I quit last week."

"You haven't had a job for a week?" Then something more grave occurred to me. "Did you quit or were you fired?"

"I was fired, okay. What's the difference?"

"There's a huge difference. What did you do?"

"I got in a fight."

I put my hand over my heart. "Oh, Dylan, no. With whom?"

"Don't worry, you're not going to get sued or anything."

Fantastic. He just gave me something else to worry about.

"Who did you fight with?" I repeated. Please don't say Josh, I silently begged.

"Some jerk you don't know. Lyle McFarland. He works with me during the closing shift. He always puts the worse of the work on me and I got sick of taking his crap."

I didn't ask for further details. It didn't really matter.

"You can't go around picking fights with people who don't pull their load at work. You are going to run into them for the rest of your life. Deal with it."

He sat all the way up in the bed, his face red with indignation. "Don't you even care what he said to me?"

"No." Heat filled my face. "I don't care. What you did is inexcusable. Is he over eighteen? He could file charges. If he's a minor, his parents may file charges. Don't you care about going to jail? What about his parents suing us? Would it be worth proving your point if we lost our house?"

He slumped against the headboard. "That's why I didn't say anything. You're always so dramatic. I told you they're not filing charges under the condition that I walked out with no intention of ever going back. As if."

I couldn't let him see how relieved I was that no one was suing us or that a lawsuit was my greatest concern at the moment. "What if you had hurt him, Dylan? Or he hurt you? These situations can easily escalate. What if he had a knife? Or worse?"

"Calm down, Mom. It's over and nothing like that happened. You look for the worst in every situation."

"No, I don't. I look for reality. It might not have ended badly this time, but you have to learn to control your temper. The world doesn't revolve around you." Even as I spoke the words, I knew his father and I had given him every reason to believe it did.

He jerked up in the bed, nearly propelling me onto the floor. "You don't even care what he did to me. It wasn't my fault. I got canned because they were looking for a reason. If it had happened to anyone else, we both would've been fired."

"I can't exactly believe that, Dylan. If they thought you were at fault, it's probably because of all the trouble you've gotten into before."

He leaped off the bed. I jumped up too. He pushed past me on his way to the bathroom that separated his and Aidan's rooms. "I don't want to talk about this anymore."

I stared after him, not sure how to proceed. I didn't want to talk about it either. I saw the look on his face. I had seen it before, and it usually ended badly for me. I'd never forget the time he threw a Hot Wheels car at me and left a gash on my eyebrow that required four stitches. Or the time he picked up the crystal rabbit my aunt Josephine had given me when I graduated from high school and smashed it on the kitchen floor.

While I swept up the pieces and Scott reminded me Dylan was a child and I should've known better than to push his buttons, I thought of the look of pure rage on his face. Had I pushed him too far? How much had been my fault? I was his mother. I shouldn't have to worry about pushing his buttons by reminding him to hang up his backpack. There was a similar look on his face now. I didn't know if I was up to following him to the bathroom and risking getting a taste of what Lyle got at work for annoying my volatile son.

"I want you downstairs as soon as you get out of the shower," I said through the closed door. "You can keep an eye on Aidan while I get ready for my Bible study." I figured he'd be back in bed before we pulled out of the driveway, but that wasn't the point. If he wanted to lay around the house, unemployed with no thoughts of his future, I was through making it easy on him.

He said something I didn't quite catch, which was probably just as well. I hurried out of the bedroom and down the stairs before he could yell or cuss or throw something at my retreating head.

Aidan was uncharacteristically quiet all the way to the church. He looked forward to our Tuesday morning Bible studies almost more than Dorothea and I. It was one of his few weekly opportunities to socialize with kids his own age. The ride to church was usually filled with animated chatter and speculation over who would be there and who would play with him. Not this morning. I didn't know if it was the weather or overhearing the exchange between Dylan and me or the fact that Dorothea hadn't joined us this morning. Whatever it was rubbed off on me. If not for the conviction that I desperately needed my weekly dose of fellowship and instruction from my sisters in Christ, I would've crawled back between the covers and stayed home myself.

By the time I left Aidan at playgroup and got to the fellowship hall where class was held, the seats I usually occupied with Dorothea were filled. I scooted into the fourth row as unobtrusively as possible and dropped into the first empty seat. I might as well have dropped my Bible, knocked over a chair, and smacked the woman in front of me on the back of the head. Conversation came to a halt and all heads swiveled in my direction. Even Joanie Delong at the podium stopped thumbing through her notes to look at me.

"Where's Dorothea?" Rita Lambert loudly demanded. She was dreadfully hard of hearing and said everything at top volume. A person who didn't know her well would assume she was abrupt and rude. She told anyone who would listen she was eighty-nine years old and didn't have time to waste on idle chit chat.

I cleared my throat and scanned the sea of inquiring faces before fastening my gaze on Rita. "She's on a cruise."

"What'd she say?" Rita asked her daughter-in-law, Vicki, seated beside her.

"She's on a cruise," Vicki hissed against Rita's ear.

"A cruise?" Rita cried. "Dorothea? Impossible. Not in a million years."

The rest of the women were nodding and whispering among themselves and pretty much agreeing with Rita as they fixed their eyes on me as though I was keeping something from them. I hastened to explain. "Her nephew says she went to Aruba or somewhere with his mother. She should be back next week."

I didn't really know that part. I was just hoping.

"Well, good for Dorothea," Joanie said from the front of the room.

Murmurs of ascension and approval made their way around the room. I exhaled in relief, glad my role as bearer of unlikely news was over, though I wished I could accept the news as easily as they had.

"That's the craziest thing I ever heard," Rita nearly shouted from her position two rows ahead of me. She craned her neck to see around the women separating us. "If Dorothea's on a cruise, I'm going to enter the Miss Teen Ohio pageant next month."

Several ladies hid smiles and giggles behind their hands. Beside me, Sonya Daulton laughed outright. "I have to agree with Rita," she said. "I won't believe Dorothea's on a cruise until she shows up with pictures and a tan."

Finally. Someone who shared my doubts. I couldn't wait to tell Scott.

"Joy wouldn't say she was on a cruise if she wasn't," Anna Brewer piped up. "Would you, Joy?" I hated being in the hot seat. I wanted to set their minds at ease. No use worrying everyone if Gunnar was telling the truth. Why wouldn't he be?

I wanted nothing more than to share my doubts about Gunnar and Kimberly and make them understand why I thought Dorothea wasn't on a cruise. She could actually be in danger. Of course they'd think I was crazy. If I couldn't make my own husband give my concerns a little credence, how could I burden these sweet sisters in Christ?

"I...um..." I didn't want to lie. I believed Dorothea was on a cruise about as much as Rita and Sonya did. But I couldn't very well tell them I thought Gunnar was lying and I had seen him sell Albert's gold watch downtown yesterday. They would want to know what would possess Gunnar to lie, and more importantly, where I believed Dorothea was if she wasn't on a cruise ship somewhere off the Mexican coast. I hadn't been able to bring myself to think that far.

"Her nephew said she is on a cruise with his mother. I can't think of a reason why he would lie about it."

There. The truth as it had been revealed to me.

"Well then," Joanie said from the podium. "Good for her. I'm sure we all hope Dorothea is having a wonderful time and will pray for her safe return. Speaking of which, Anna, would you like to open our meeting with prayer?"

There was much shuffling as everyone turned to the front and bowed their heads. I barely heard Anna's prayer. I was too busy petitioning God to watch over Dorothea, wherever she was, and to bring her home safely as soon as possible.

After the Bible study we all moved as one toward the fellowship hall for cookies, punch, and coffee, Marge Kepinstall took hold of my elbow. I slowed my pace so the older woman could keep up though I suspected she was in better shape than I was. "You haven't heard a peep from Dorothea?" she murmured.

I shook my head and kept my voice down so we wouldn't worry anyone else. "Her nephew isn't very forthcoming with information though I've given him every opportunity."

"Have you talked to Scott about it?" she asked.

I rolled my eyes. "He says I have too much time on my hands."

"No, dear, that isn't it." She pursed her lips again and went back to processing her thoughts. I wanted to prod her into talking, but I knew it wouldn't do any good. She'd talk when she was ready. I waited patiently. We were nearly at the front of the line when she tightened her grip on my arm and pulled me out of line. "We need to petition the Lord, honey."

She led me over to the wall and bowed her head. "Lord, we have a problem here. You know all about it and you already know the outcome, but I'm going to bring it before you anyway. Our good friend and your servant, Dorothea Westlake, is missing."

My heart lurched at Marge's choice of words. Missing. Someone else had said it first. I wasn't crazy. I wasn't the only one worrying. It took every bit of resolve not to burst into tears.

"She might not be missing in the true sense of the word," Marge continued, and my heart sank a bit. "But we don't know where she is and we're worried for her safety. Wherever she is right now and whatever she's doing, we need you to watch over her and keep her safe. Let her feel our prayers and your shelter at this time, whether she's in need or just having a great time without us.

"Lord, I sure don't want to spoil Dorothea's fun, but it would be nice if she called one of us to let us know she's okay. That would give Joy and me and everyone here at church a great peace. We give her completely over to you and will stop worrying about her and trying to figure out what's going on. We know you have everything under control. We just ask that you watch over her and let her know we love her. Thank you, Heavenly Father, for your love and mercy. We ask it all in our Savior's precious name. Amen."

I knew she added the last part for my benefit since I was the one doing most of the worrying. Though it wasn't likely I'd stop anytime soon, I needed to hand my concerns and doubts over to God. There was nothing else tangible to do. If only I had Marge's peace.

Chapter 13

Marge's prayer ran through my head the rest of the afternoon. I felt a little better knowing someone with a much stronger faith than mine was also praying for Dorothea's safe return, but nothing would satisfy me completely until I knew where Dorothea was. Every time I passed the telephone, I stopped to look at it and will Dorothea to call me. I wasn't sure how cell phones worked onboard cruise ships since I'd never been on one, and I doubted Dorothea had an international calling plan, but I figured Gunnar was probably right. Service might be practically nonexistent. But didn't boats ever dock? I'd heard that phone calls from the islands to the mainland were outrageously expensive. Dorothea was frugal to the core, but surely she would call at least once. She was too thoughtful and considerate not to let me know where she was and when to expect her home.

She would also want updates on our church family, no matter how much fun she was having on vacation. Caroline and Pete Reagan were expecting a multiple birth any day. Rose Waterman had undergone bone marrow surgery the week before Gunnar arrived. Several couples in the church were having either financial or marital difficulties. Dorothea was a dedicated prayer warrior and would want to know how everyone was doing.

"Come on, Dorothea," I said aloud to the phone more than once. "Just one little phone call. Then I'll back off and leave Gunnar alone."

The flowerbeds. I glanced out the front window at Dorothea's house across the street. Her lilac bushes were budding and the tulips needed trimmed back. Maybe later I'd grab my clippers and head over there. Gunnar would run me off, but I knew Dorothea wouldn't want to come home to unkempt beds.

Aidan had outgrown his need for a nap. Tuesday afternoons were the exception. After playing hard with his friends all morning at playgroup while I was in Bible Study, he usually conked right out after lunch. This Tuesday afternoon I decided to take advantage of the free afternoon. I supervised while he changed into a pair of play shorts and an old t-shirt. Then he crawled under the sheet and blew me a kiss on my way out the door. I went straight downstairs to my laptop and logged on.

I typed Gunnar Westlake and Chicago into the search engine and waited. Immediately I was rewarded with several thousand results to choose from, most of which were probably useless. I clicked on every link on the first page that looked remotely like the same Gunnar Westlake. He had applied for a driver's license, helped organize a campaign for a local politician, and participated in a book drive for a local library. Except for the driver's license, I couldn't imagine the Gunnar Westlake across the street doing any of these things. But it had to be the same Gunnar. I even found an old P.O. Box number from when he was living in the dorms at Northwestern.

I typed his name into several social media sites where I had accounts. There weren't many Gunnar Westlakes online. Only one of the accounts used a personal picture as an avatar. I saw a few pictures of friends having fun at clubs, and one of a guy with his back to the camera piloting a boat on a lake. I was pretty sure Dorothea had mentioned a family cabin on a lake in

Wisconsin. But Gunnar had said they didn't go there anymore. He couldn't even remember the name of the town where it had been.

After nearly forty-five minutes of following links and reading everything I could find that might lead me to a phone number or street address for his parents in Chicago, I was tired of looking. If only I knew something more about him. A work history, the name of his neighborhood, friends or other family members. I couldn't even remember his parents' names.

The only one I remembered was Stephen, Albert's brother and Gunnar's grandfather. For lack of something more productive to do and not yet willing to admit defeat, I typed in Stephen Westlake. According to Dorothea he was a successful attorney, but I didn't know where he had practiced. It turned out it didn't really matter because I came up with less about Stephen than I had Gunnar.

This was getting me nothing but a headache and the waste of a rare free afternoon. I needed something more to go on than Albert's brother's name if I wanted to know what was going on across the street. But what?

I wasn't a detective. I left the computer and went out front to play around in my flowerbeds. It was still early in the season. I stepped onto the front porch and looked across the street to Dorothea's. Her house was the most beautiful on the block. Not only was it obviously the most expensive, it was also the most architecturally appealing. As long as I'd known her, she put hours and hours into her gardening and landscaping. This time of year was when she was busiest. The last few years, she had talked about turning more of her maintenance chores over to Martin her yardman since the job was getting too hard on her seventy-five-year-old back and knees. So far she hadn't taken that step. I helped pull weeds every few weeks without making it look like I was helping. Her yard was her pride and joy, if you could call it that, and she hated to say farewell to that independence.

Dread filled my stomach as my eyes traveled up the front of her house to the second story. The windows where I had seen light and movement the week before faced the street. I had been in that suite many times. Years ago, Albert had knocked out a wall or two to double the size of the bedroom. A walk-through closet separated the sleeping area from a massive master bath more impressive than my kitchen. A small sitting room off the bedroom looked over Ben Sanders' immaculate front yard. Coveting was a sin I stayed away from, but if ever a woman could be tempted, I would covet Dorothea's bedroom suite.

Was it possible Gunnar was holding her hostage in her own bedroom?

I gave myself a mental head slap. Where had that ridiculous notion come from? That only happened in made for TV movies. Not in my neighborhood, and not to my friends.

Still I couldn't squelch the sense of discomfort rising in my stomach. Stranger things had happened. Weren't neighbors always the last to realize a crime was being committed under their noses? It hadn't been that many years ago when two children were discovered chained to their beds in a seemingly nice neighborhood in the city. Just a few months ago a college student went missing from our quiet town and was later found beaten to death in a park. It was discovered she had been held hostage and repeatedly raped and tortured in some freak's apartment.

I wondered if the freak's neighbors had noticed anything strange or reported strange noises from that apartment during the three days the poor girl was held there.

The knot in my stomach rose to my throat. Was that what was happening to Dorothea? Gunnar was definitely looking for something, something he couldn't look for with Dorothea underfoot. I remembered what Kimberly said last night.

"Kimberly is dead," she told Gunnar.

At the time I thought she was being dramatic and expressing the time wasted on a loser like Gunnar. Could she have meant something more sinister?

I had to get into that house.

I thought of all the detective shows on television any night of the week. I'd watched enough of them over the last few years I should know how to think like a detective, or at least Hollywood's version of one. The one thing I could count on them doing in every episode was to act. They wouldn't sit across the street and peer between the drapes like a scared rabbit waiting for something to happen. They would make an opportunity come to them.

Aidan was still asleep in his room. Dylan had been moving around upstairs when we got back from the church. If Aidan woke up while I was gone, Dylan could keep an eye on him for a few minutes. I hurried around the side of the house to the tiny potting shed in our backyard. I slid the aluminum doors apart and stepped inside. I took a gardening trowel, a pair of gloves, and a hand rake and retraced my steps along the short brick walk to my front porch. Before my fledgling courage could fade, I crossed the street and walked up the walk to Dorothea's stoop the way I'd done nearly every day of the past ten years of my life. Without knocking or warning Gunnar about what I was doing should he look out the window and see me, I knelt down at the edge of the stoop and went to work.

I seldom helped with this job so early in the season. The early perennials had already bloomed and faded a few weeks ago. Martin usually showed up in time to clean out the perennials and prepare the beds for the annuals Dorothea would pick out and plant herself. He trimmed bushes, resituated rocks and edgings that shifted over the winter, and hauled away dead limbs or debris that had blown in over the harsh Ohio winter. Before his visits began, Dorothea always surveyed the yard so she could give him specific instructions if something other than usual maintenance was required. Martin had worked for Dorothea for twenty years and knew her yard backward and forward, but she was a hands-on employer. They understood each other. Since she was allegedly in Aruba or the south of France or whatever lie Gunnar was telling this week, as a good neighbor, I would take it upon myself to see what was in store for Martin when he showed up the first Monday of May which happened to be next week.

I kicked rocks, adjusted stepping stones with my foot, took note of a broken paving rock under the picture window, and hacked away at embedded roots with my trowel as I made my way around the side of the house.

I almost hoped Gunnar would see me and barrel outside to run me off. At the same time, my heart was in my throat at the thought of a confrontation. I rehearsed and went over things I would say and the explanation I would give, which sounded pretty reasonable in my head. If what he had told me last week was true, Dorothea wouldn't be home from her cruise for another week. She had apparently forgotten about Martin's scheduled visit. As her friend, I was taking care of a chore Gunnar couldn't do in Dorothea's place.

I didn't expect him to know about Martin or what to look for in the garden. I was the only one who knew Dorothea's preferences better than Martin. Still, my heart hammered in my chest every time I thought I might actually have to tell him as much. Gunnar's car was parked alone in the driveway so that meant Kimberly was probably gone for good like she said. I imagined Gunnar was still in a snit and would be none too pleased to find me nosing around the yard.

I glanced across the street to my own house. Aidan wouldn't sleep much longer. Dylan didn't even know I was gone. I picked up my pace, moving to the bushes at the corner of the garage. I wouldn't go around back. That was too personal to do without Dorothea in residence. In truth I wasn't as brave as I pretended. The issues I found in the front of the house would be enough to tell Martin when he showed up next week. Unless Dorothea really was on a cruise and had called Martin to tell him to come the week after next when she returned.

I had nearly lost my nerve and was doubting my right to be here by the time I reached the corner of the garage. Desperate for a valid reason for pulling weeds from Dorothea's flowerbeds while my own were still in shambles, I stepped carefully between two arboretum bushes and jiggled the pipe coming down from the eaves. Just above eye level, I saw a screw had worked its way out of the metal bracket holding it against the wall. It was something Martin wouldn't miss in a million years, but my confidence boosted at the prospect of something legitimate to report when he got here.

I looked down at my feet as I backed out of the flowerbed, mindful of crushing a faded hyacinth or tripping over the exposed root of a bush, and came up against the unmoving form of a human body. I gave a little cry of surprise and whirled around to stare into the eyes of Gunnar Westlake.

His eyes were flinty and unyielding. His mouth was set in a grim line, and his jaw twitched at the sight of me. "Isn't there a law against trespassing in this neighborhood?"

The story I had rehearsed as I moved around the flowerbeds flew out of my head. "I…uh…" I mumbled around my dry throat. "Er…"

His gaze hardened even further. His eyes narrowed. He didn't move. He stood barely ten inches in front of me and gave no indication of stepping aside for me to get the rest of the way out of the flowerbed. I had never been good at handling intimidating people. I remembered a girl in my Girl Scout troop who bullied me the entire year. When we went away to camp, her bullying escalated. She snatched my snacks out of my hand on two occasions, knocked me down in the gravel while we were going to the lake, and always took the seat I was headed to during outdoor lectures. My friends told me to stand up to her. She could tell I was intimidated and only bullied me as a way to have control over me. She never attempted such behavior with the other girls.

"She'll never stop, Joy, until you make her stop," they told me over and over again.

I didn't make her stop. When she took my seat, I found another. When she "accidentally" knocked my lunch tray out of my hands, or stepped on my open suntan lotion bottle and emptied the entire bottle into the grass so that I didn't have any for the duration of camp, I suffered through sunburn and bought another lunch. It was easier to ignore her than to stand up to her. I would be going home in a few weeks and our paths would never cross again so why make things unpleasant?

Every time I thought of that girl at camp, I got angry with myself all over again and a little ashamed that I never stood up to her. Here was my chance at redemption, to vilify myself, and let the world know Joy Kessler wasn't going to be pushed around anymore.

With Gunnar glaring at me, a dangerous gleam in his eyes, I realized it was easier said than done. I thought of the girl from summer camp and how I had so desperately wanted to stand up to her but never found the nerve. I thought about Emily hanging all over Dylan last night and how he lied about her to my face. I thought about my mother and how she always made me feel like I didn't measure up to her standards. I thought about how I paled in comparison to my beautiful and sophisticated sister-in-law and how it was my own fault she intimidated the socks off me. My insecurities and failings were my problem and no one else's. Most of all, I thought of Dorothea and how I knew as well as I was standing here with my knees knocking and my mouth as dry as chalk dust that Gunnar was lying about her being on a cruise.

"Saturday is May 1st," I blurted without a hint of the terror I felt in my voice.

His brows twitched, easing the intimidation in his stance enough to let me know I caught him off guard.

"Dorothea's yardman always comes the first of May to prepare her gardens for planting. I'm sure she forgot to cancel in the excitement of preparing for her cruise. I came over to see what I would need to tell Martin when he comes."

I squared my shoulders, proud of my ingenuity and prouder still that I had been able to say all of it without wetting my pants.

"I appreciate your help," he lied through his teeth, "but I'm perfectly capable of handling landscapers."

"You don't know the way Dorothea likes things," I pointed out.

"I'm sure the landscaper does."

I shook my head. "Dorothea is very particular. She'll be disappointed to come home and see this downspout loose." I whacked it with the heel of my hand to prove my point.

He knew I had him, and there was nothing he could do about it. "I'll point it out to him."

"His name is Martin. You can expect him on Monday. That is, if Dorothea isn't home by then," I added pointedly.

"Thank you."

His gratitude didn't quite match his gaze.

I straightened further, not nearly as unnerved by him as I was two minutes ago. "I'm sure all either of us care about is Dorothea's happiness."

I waited a moment to see if he'd agree with me. When he didn't, I stepped around him. "I've got to be going," I said as if we were having a lovely chat. "If there's anything you need, don't hesitate to call. You know where to find me."

He turned to watch my progress as I headed to the sidewalk. I could feel his eyes boring into my back. At the curb I spun around to find him still staring at me. "The invitation to dinner still stands. You and your friend are welcome any evening."

He didn't tell me Kimberly was no longer staying with him. I didn't think he would. I gave him another chance to respond. When he didn't, I waved lightly and tripped across the street, very pleased and feeling like I'd stood up to someone for the first time in my life.

Aidan and Dylan were sprawled in front of the TV when I got home. Dylan dropped his feet to the carpet and sat forward.

"'Bout time you got back. It'd be nice if you asked before you disappeared leaving me to baby sit."

"Excuse me."

He stood up. "I got places to go, Mom. I don't have time to sit around here all day and do your job."

I was still flying high from my altercation with Gunnar, and I wasn't ready to let the feeling go. "It won't kill you to keep an eye on your little brother for five minutes while I do a favor for a friend."

"You still could've asked."

I stared at him a moment, his green eyes flashing, arms akimbo, and shoulders slouched, and tried to figure out how I knew this person. Dylan had never been the most accommodating of individuals. He always thought more of himself than anyone else. Sadly, Scott and I had been grievously lacking in setting him straight.

"Dylan, you just got fired from your job for fighting. I caught you coming in last night with a girl whose name you don't even know. You're living here rent free and obligation free, and you have the nerve to tell me I need to ask you to keep an eye on your brother. Well, that isn't going to happen, young man. And you aren't going anywhere today so sit back down."

I'm not sure which one of us was more startled. Even Aidan stopped playing on his Ninja Turtle tablet to give us his full attention. So this was what power felt like. I sort of liked it.

In the span of two seconds, Dylan's expression went from disbelief to defiance, a look with which I was all too familiar. He sniffed dismissively. "I'm outta here."

He started around me. I snagged his elbow and held on tight. "Dylan." The warning in my voice was unfamiliar to my ears. Dylan froze and looked down at me like he'd never seen me before. Aidan tensed on the sofa, his blue eyes sparkling with unshed tears. "You're staying home today."

For a split second, neither of us knew what would happen next. Then the scene played out exactly as I suspected it would. Dylan jerked out of my grasp and stormed out of the room.

I followed as far as the doorway. I was aware of Aidan watching the drama unfold from his seat on the sofa. If I blew this, I'd be cementing an image in his mind that would take more than dynamite to blast out. An image of his ineffectual mother trying to make a rebellious child do what she wanted him to do.

"I'm not through talking to you, young man," I called after Dylan.

"Well, I'm through talking to you," he called back.

"Dylan. Dylan," I yelled, not sure if I was angrier at him for not seeing the validity of my argument or angrier at myself that I couldn't talk my son into doing me a simple favor without turning it into World War III.

I took a deep breath to fortify my resolve and hurried after him. He had reached the top of the stairs by the time I got to the foyer. "You are not leaving this house."

"Try and stop me," he yelled back before slamming his bedroom door in finality.

I stood at the foot of the stairs with my hand on the newel post and wondered how to handle the situation. What would Dorothea do? I squeezed my eyes shut and tried to summon a prayer that wouldn't sound like I was whining. God had heard enough of those from me over the years. A better mother would never put up with a fresh-mouth son who wouldn't go to college or work for more than a month at the same place. A stronger mother would go upstairs and yank his door off the hinges and make him listen to her. A better mother never would've let her son become so insolent and rude in the first place. He hadn't become this way overnight. Dorothea was right. I couldn't keep waiting for Scott to turn Dylan into the young man I wanted him to be.

What could I do about it now? Today? I couldn't exactly go up there and force him to stay in his room. I could sit on him for five or ten seconds until he shrugged me off, or barricade the door, but he was smart. He would figure a way out. How important was it for me to prove this particular point? Did I want to ruin what was left of my day over a battle I was destined to lose?

No other woman I knew would stand at the bottom of the stairs feeling sorry for herself or yelling empty threats. They would make something happen like I had done earlier with Gunnar. But Gunnar wasn't my son. At this moment I didn't like Dylan very much. I was ashamed I felt that way, but only a little. Being his parent was hard. I wondered if he was too damaged for redemption. At this moment it would be pretty easy to admit defeat and let him go. Toss it up as a lesson learned and focus my energy on Aidan.

Tired tears stung my eyes. I had read books about the bonds between mothers and sons. How she was a successful role model and he would fight giants to defend her. Defeated and weary, I trudged back to the family room and flopped down on the couch beside Aidan. I wanted to put on a brave face to make him think all was well and his mother wasn't a total failure. What was the point? He had seen and heard the whole thing. He was no dummy. This song had been playing his whole life.

I put an arm around his shoulders and pulled him against me. I nestled my nose in his hair and breathed in the scent of him. We sat like that for a moment until we heard Dylan's feet thunder down the stairs. We both jumped when the front door slammed behind him.

I kissed the top of Aidan's hair and blinked away tears. He pulled away and looked up at me. "Don't cry, Mommy. I still love you."

I gave him a trembling smile and pulled him against me again. My tears flowed faster. I didn't know how or what, but something in this house had to change.

I didn't broach the subject of Dylan with Scott until after Aidan was sleeping snug in his bed. I hadn't wanted to think about it, much less discuss it, but if things were going to change around here, it was going to take a team effort between the two of us.

I took extra care with my nighttime beauty regimen, delaying the inevitable. When I came out of the bedroom, Scott was already in bed, his reading glasses perched across his nose. He looked so cute sitting there I almost lost my nerve. We had so few moments together without talking about bills or the car or the kids, or lately, Gunnar and Dorothea. I'd like nothing better than to throw back the covers and crawl in beside him. I imagined snuggling against him while he read scripture out loud before one of us turned out the light.

It had been a long time.

But what I had to say couldn't be put off another minute.

I remained standing. I didn't want to fight in bed. "Dylan and I got into an argument today because I stepped out for a few minutes and left him in charge of Aidan without asking his permission."

"Where'd you go?"

Was he kidding?

"That's not the point, Scott. All I expected from him was a little courtesy. The same I would expect from anyone. He's our son, but he runs this place. We have no rights except to provide him with a comfortable life and ask nothing in return."

Scott leaned into the pillows and opened the Bible across his legs. "He's a teenager, Joy. They're supposed to be selfish."

"Selfish I get, but openly defiant? I told him not to go out. He told me to try and stop him."

Scott smirked, his eyes still on the Bible. "He's always been a handful."

I swallowed the scream welling up in my throat. "This isn't funny. We're not talking about a precocious preschooler. He cannot think he is free to come and go in this house, talk to me however he chooses, and reap no consequences."

Scott sighed heavily and brought his gaze up to mine over the top of his glasses. "Honey, I really think you're overreacting. Dylan has always had a temper. You have always resisted him, and that's made the situation worse. You have to pick your battles."

"Pick my battles?" I leaned forward and snatched the Bible off his lap and gestured at him with it. "Does it say anything in here about honoring your mother and father? I seem to recall a proverb about sparing the rod and spoiling the child."

Scott seldom lost him temper, and his ability to hold onto it tonight only added fuel to my fervor. "I don't believe it meant literally," he said in a reasonable, controlled voice that made me want to sling the heavy volume across the room. "Could I please have my Bible back? I have to study for Sunday morning's lesson."

"Are you hearing a word I'm saying?"

When he raised his eyebrows in question to his Bible in my hands, I relinquished my hold on it. "Scott, you're a leader in our church," I pointed out in a level voice. "How do you think it looks that our son never attends with us? Everyone knows he's always in trouble. The Bible also says something about a deacon who can't control his own household."

This got a reaction as I knew it would. He sat forward on the bed and glared at me. "Don't you dare throw scripture at me. I know it backward and forward. The Bible also says a wife is to reverence her husband. I am the spiritual leader of this house and I have everything under control. There isn't a parent alive who doesn't have some trouble with their children, especially teens, so no one should cast stones at me."

Common sense told me to back down. Scott was a good husband. He was a good provider, and he loved his children. I had it a lot better than many women I knew. But he was wrong. He was blind to Dylan's faults, and I needed to do something to yank those blinders off before we lost Dylan forever.

"You don't have everything under control, Scott. Not by a mile. Dylan is doing drugs. Under this very roof, as far as I can tell. He uses girls with no regard to the consequences of his actions. He doesn't care about anyone but himself. He openly defied me this afternoon in front of his little brother. He got fired from his job. Did you know that? For fighting with another employee. He isn't a rebellious teen, Scott. He's been rebellious and insolent and belligerent since the day he was born. We sat here on our thumbs and let him get away with it. So don't tell me you have everything under control. We're losing him."

By the time I reached the end of my tirade, I was screeching. My cheeks blazed, and the back of my throat felt like I'd swallowed sandpaper.

I could see the anger in Scott's eyes, and I feared I had gone too far. Like I told Dorothea, I wanted nothing more than to be a submissive wife, but not at the expense of our son and our family. It might be too late to undo the damage done to Dylan, but what kind of parent would I be if I didn't try? I thought of the courage Dorothea said I would need. In the last few weeks I'd learned courage came with a price. It wasn't easy, and it wasn't comfortable. When I first started studying the Proverbs Thirty-One woman I thought I would need that strength to face giants like Gunnar Westlake. Now I realized the hardest battles to fight were in my own house.

Scott closed the Bible and looked up at me. "Would you listen to yourself? You're hysterical. You let a harmless argument get you all out of shape. Dylan will be home in a little while, just like always. He'll be sweet and contrite tomorrow and go out of his way to make it up to you." He reached out and caught my hand. "You'll see. He may not show it, but he loves you. I'm sorry he defied you. There was no excuse for that. I'll talk to him tomorrow." He pulled me down next to him. He stroked the side of my flaming cheek. "Everything will be fine. Now please, leave the worrying to me."

He pulled me against him and guided my head onto his chest. I felt the rumble of his gentle laugh through his pajama top. "Sometimes you get too worked up about little things. Haven't you heard not to sweat the small stuff?"

I stiffened and sat up.

"Joy..."

I stood and walked around the edge of the bed.

"Joy, where are you going? I'll handle everything. I always do, don't I?"

I resisted the urge to remind him he hadn't handled anything with Dylan, and he never had. I closed the bathroom door and leaned heavily against the sink. How was I supposed to discipline our son when Scott couldn't admit there was a problem? I had always been the dumb one, the ineffective one, the one who swung at windmills with Dylan. Sometimes I wished I were more like Scott and couldn't see the writing on the wall than try so hard to turn Dylan into a responsible member of society. But I couldn't—I wouldn't—continue to turn a blind eye to his behavior. No matter what it took, I'd make Scott see the truth and make Dylan shape up.

I examined my face in the mirror. Who was I kidding? I couldn't talk a church bell into ringing.

Chapter 14

As I carried a bag of trash out of the boys' bathroom the next morning, Scott ducked out of Dylan's room and pulled the door shut behind him. He gave me an encouraging smile and followed me downstairs. I didn't say anything. I was still annoyed about last night, and I didn't have much confidence in my husband's parenting skills. He put his hand on my back as we hit the bottom of the stairs and headed for the kitchen.

"Dylan and I had a nice long talk this morning. Everything will be fine from here on out."

I jerked away from him. "It'd better be. I'm not putting up with much more around here. From anybody."

His eyebrows shot into his hairline. He looked about to say something but thought better of it. "I'll see you later. Have a good day."

I nodded and returned his kiss. I wondered if I was being too hard on him and Dylan. Then I remembered what Dylan said yesterday, and I shoved aside the doubts. I was right. Dylan was out of line. Scott had his head so far in the sand he didn't know what was happening under his own roof. I watched Scott back out of the driveway and pull onto the street. I backed into the house and started to swing the door shut behind me when I saw Gunnar step out of Dorothea's front door. I closed the door to barely a crack and watched.

He turned at the front door and checked the locks, then dropped Dorothea's house keys into his jacket pocket. He glanced up and down the street before looking pointedly at our house. I gasped and ducked further into the house, my heart hammering. He paused long enough to nearly send me into cardiac arrest before leaving the porch and heading to his car. I hadn't seen Dorothea's car in days. While Kimberly had been here, they had driven her car everywhere. Now that she was gone, he had gone back to driving his own. I supposed filling Dorothea's gas tank was too much for him, even though he was working his way through her jewelry box.

I couldn't tell for sure from the distance, but it looked like Gunnar was staring right at me in the rearview mirror. I shut the door the rest of the way and hurried to the living room window to watch him turn the corner. I practically ran down the hall to stuff the bag from the upstairs bathroom into the big trashcan in the utility room and then went back to the front of the house without even bothering to wash my hands. I threw open the front door and stepped onto the porch. My eyes darted to the street corner and back to Dorothea's house. My mind whirled. I had no way of knowing how long Gunnar would be gone. He might have run down to the store for milk. Or he could be gone all day.

What to do. What to do.

One thing was certain, I couldn't waste an opportunity dropped into my lap.

Without allowing enough time to talk myself out of what I was about to do, I ran to the kitchen and tore open the junk drawer. My fingers clawed frantically through pizza coupons, matchbooks, spare batteries, and stray toothpicks until they closed around a key ring holding the keys to Dorothea's front and back doors. Dorothea had a set of keys to our house so she could water the plants and collect our mail when we were out of town, or in case of emergency should she ever see smoke pouring out our windows. As Dorothea aged, she became more aware of all the accidents that could happen in a person's home. "If I ever slip and fall in the bathtub," she told me the day she gave me the keys, "you better come over and help me into my robe before the EMTs get here. I'll never forgive you if you let them see me in my ratty old-lady underwear."

I dropped the keys into the pocket of my sweatpants and ran as fast as my out of shape legs could carry me to the staircase. By the time I got to the top of the stairs, a trickle of perspiration was running down my spine, and my breath was coming in short gasps. Heat pricked my cheeks. I stopped on the landing to catch my breath. I really needed to resume my workouts. This was ridiculous. I wasn't even forty, but I felt like I'd run a 5K. If I wanted things to change around this house I needed to look no further than the reflection in the mirror.

I took another deep breath to still my heart's pounding as much as to catch my breath and then headed for Dylan's room. I paused long enough to give it a good rap before I threw open the door. "Dylan, get up."

"Chill, Mom, I'm right here," he said from the corner where he sat with his laptop open across his legs.

"I'm going out for a few minutes. Keep an eye on Aidan. He's still in bed, but he'll be up any minute."

His eyes remained fixed in his computer. "No problem. When I hear him moving around, I'll fix him a bowl of cereal."

My doubts that I had overreacted yesterday came rushing forward. Scott had assured me everything would work out, and so far, it looked like it would. I gave him a quick smile and a hurried 'thanks' before backing out of the room.

I ran into my bedroom and yanked a pair of socks out of the drawer. I danced into them and laced up my nearly showroom new cross trainers. I patted my pocket to make sure the key ring was still there as I bounced down the stairs. I grabbed the first jacket out of the front closet, which turned out to be a windbreaker of Dylan's, and pulled it on as I hurried out the front door.

I checked both ways as I crossed the street. My heart was in my mouth. If I ran into one of the neighbors I probably wouldn't even be able to speak to them. I'm sure I looked wild-eyed and slightly deranged. They would probably call Scott at work and tell him I had finally done what they all expected me to do someday and gone off the deep end.

Fortunately I encountered no one on the street. I ducked between Dorothea's garage and the hydrangea hedge. I prayed aloud at the back door as I fumbled to get the keys out of my pocket and to shove the right one into the hole. I wiped my sweaty hands on my rear after the key kept slipping between my fingers and the knob. "Please, God. Don't let Gunnar come home too soon. I'm doing this for Dorothea. I hope I'm wrong and she's having a blast on her cruise. If I am wrong, forgive me for being suspicious."

The key finally slid home, and the lock clicked open. I exhaled with relief and dried a sheen of perspiration off my forehead with the sleeve of Dylan's windbreaker. I didn't have time to consider his change of heart from yesterday. Had Scott made him see the light this morning? Was he truly repentant? Or was he in a generous mood today and willing to do his hysterical mother a favor? Now that he was out of work, he probably planned to hit me up for spending money. He knew a kind word, or if I was being a particularly tough sell, a hug and an 'I love you, Mom' would do the trick.

I hated to tell him it was going to take a lot more than that this time. Mom was tired of being everyone's patsy. There was a new wind blowing, and Mom was through letting the world knock her down.

I pushed open the kitchen door and peered around the lintel to make sure the kitchen was empty even though I knew it was. I had not seen Kimberly since the other night, and the garage was only big enough to house one car at a time.

I tiptoed into the kitchen and looked around. I sniffed and curled my lip in distaste. Dorothea's kitchen always smelled lemony fresh. Now a stale air pervaded every surface. If she was indeed on a cruise and due home in a week, Gunnar had barely enough time to get everything in shape if he worked from now until her ship docked. The countertops were strewn with carryout containers, prepackaged food wrappers, crumbs, and candy wrappers. The small table in the breakfast nook was nearly buried under newspapers and references books. I never would've pegged Gunnar as a heavy reader, but it looked like I was wrong. He was supposed to be working on his dissertation. My brow furrowed as I read a few spines. Pop culture. Autograph facsimiles. The twentieth century. What did any of that have to do with environmental science?

Whatever Gunnar had been doing in the dining room had overflowed into the kitchen. Not a picture remained on the walls. Cabinet doors stood open, and nearly every item had been shoved aside as if he was looking for something. Cabinet drawers were pulled open, and much of their previous contents had spilled onto the floor.

I stepped carefully over everything so I wouldn't disturb the state of disarray. I glanced at the refrigerator. A snapshot of Aidan, partially obscured by a recipe card, smiled out at me. The bunny rabbit magnet he made for Dorothea a few weeks before Easter, complete with a cotton ball tail and ears, was in its usual spot. He was always making projects, and like me, Dorothea kept every one. My nose stung with unshed tears as I pictured him at our kitchen counter, his tongue poking out of the side of his mouth and the counter strewn with cotton balls, construction paper, glitter flecks, and glue droplets hardening on the granite surface.

I sniffed away my tears. No time for sentimentality. I was on a mission. I had to find out where Dorothea was and if she was okay before Gunnar came back.

I made my way up the staircase as quickly and quietly as I could, all the while brainstorming possible excuses should

Gunnar come back and catch me. I would tell him I heard the smoke alarm. Or saw a mysterious figure in the backyard and feared for Kimberly's safety. Or the Wylie's dog chased a rabbit through the doggy door. The only problem was Dorothea's house had no doggy door. My best defense was not getting caught.

As I hurried through Dorothea's second floor, I stared forlornly at the blank spots on the walls where photographs and artwork had hung. I stepped carefully around an armoire standing askew about a foot from the wall. Though it truly looked like someone was preparing to paint, I saw no paint cans, drop clothes, or taped off doorways and molding. What in the world was Gunnar up to? He was looking for something. I just couldn't figure out what.

Surely he knew someone like Dorothea wouldn't leave stocks or bonds hidden under loose floorboards if he was hoping for an easy payday. Any amount of money laying around would be trivial and not worth his efforts. Even selling Albert's gold watch had probably only netted a few thousand dollars. Was that worth all the time and work he'd put into the job, not to mention possible jail time if he got caught?

I thought about calling the police. What would I tell them? Being a terrible painter wasn't a crime. Nor was selling a gift, though it was tacky enough it should be illegal.

I headed down the hall to Dorothea's bedroom. Her door was open. That was a good sign. Gunnar would've locked the door if he was holding her hostage inside. Still, when I peeked into the room, cast in shadows from the pulled shades, I called out in a stage whisper. "Yoo hoo, Dorothea? Are you here?"

I waited a fraction of a second for a reply before heading to the closet. The room reminded me of Dylan's. I passed the unmade bed and several piles of discarded clothing. Dorothea's duvet had slipped off the edge of the bed. I could tell Gunnar had stepped on it several times since it landed on the floor. Every part of me wanted to change the sheets and make the bed and replace the decorative pillows piled on a chair in the corner. Of course I couldn't do that.

I shivered in sympathy for Dorothea as I entered the cavernous closet. As far as I could tell, most of Dorothea's clothes hung in their usual places. In the back corner I found her expensive luggage. How was she on a cruise if most of her clothes and her luggage were still in the closet? I was pretty sure Gunnar would have a perfectly logical explanation should I ask, but it made me that much more certain she hadn't went to visit Gunnar's mother.

"Dorothea?" I hissed again as I jerked more hangers aside. I went as far as tapping on the walls in the back of the closet in search of a secret passage. I felt a little stupid, but I'd feel even worse if I later discovered she was mere inches from my groping fingers.

I didn't find my friend or anyone else. I couldn't decide if I was thankful she wasn't a hostage or disappointed I hadn't found her.

Back in the bedroom I put my hands on my hips and surveyed the room. The corners of the sheets were peeled back exposing the bare mattress. Papers and envelopes were scattered on the bedside table and every flat surface. I fingered through a pile of papers, careful not to disturb the order or make my presence known. Subterfuge and sneakery didn't come naturally to me. I couldn't even tell a decent joke since my listener always deduced where I was headed long before I reached the punch line.

I carefully picked up a stack of letters, receipts, and scraps of paper and leafed through them. After it was too late, I wondered if Gunnar had a fingerprint kit hidden somewhere in the house and could tell I had been here. It wasn't likely, but just to be safe I rubbed my hands across each piece I touched, knowing from the detective shows I watched that smeared or incomplete prints were virtually useless.

Besides a Lowe's receipt for a hundred-foot heavy duty extension cord, I found nothing to explain what Gunnar was doing. I put the stack of papers back on the dresser and shuffled them, hoping he wouldn't notice anything amiss and went back to the purpose of my mission. I didn't have much time. Not only did I not want Gunnar to know I was here, I didn't want Dylan or Aidan to see me coming away from Dorothea's house when I left. I didn't want them asking questions, and I definitely didn't want them blabbing to Scott about my morning rendezvous.

I went to Dorothea's vanity in front of the window that faced my house. She had a nice roll top desk downstairs that had been Albert's, but she used this vanity to address Christmas cards and write occasionally in a journal she kept. The drawers were askew. I opened the top one with a heavy heart. Just as I figured, the contents had been stirred and rifled through with no concern about damage done. Several sheets of stationary had been wrinkled or shoved out of the drawer where they lay trampled on the carpet. It wasn't even my vanity, but I felt violated for Dorothea. She would be so hurt when she got home. I only hoped Gunnar found whatever he was looking for and was long gone by then. His presence and his lying explanations would only add insult to injury.

At the back of the drawer, I finally found what I was looking for. I took the leather bound address book I had given Dorothea for Christmas five years ago and flipped to the back. There were only two Westlake addresses listed. The first was Stephen and his wife Ardith. Dorothea was old fashioned and held tradition in high regard. Even though Stephen had been gone for at least ten years, she had written his name next to his wife's. Ardith had passed away as well a few years ago so she had no need to keep their names in the book. Yet here they were. The remaining Westlakes were Stephen's son and daughter-in-law and their son, Gunnar. Geoffrey and Cathy Westlake. Trying to memorize the Chicago address would take too long. I couldn't trust my memory if I got spooked or Gunnar came home before I was safely across the street.

"Sorry, Dorothea," I said aloud in the quiet room. I carefully tore the page out of the address book, careful not to leave any hanging scraps in the binding.

I folded the page into a tiny square and shoved it into the pocket of Dylan's jacket. I replaced the address book where I found it and stood up. Through the window over the vanity I saw Gunnar's car turn the corner of our street.

I let out a terrified shriek. I jumped away from the window, knocking the chair over in my haste. I righted it as quickly as I could and fled from the room as fast as my short legs could carry me. I tried to remember if I had moved the door when I came in. It had been open but not all the way. I pulled it shut a few inches behind me and hoped it was close enough that Gunnar wouldn't notice. As I raced down the stairs, I wracked my panic stricken brain to remember if I had left anything undone. As far as I could recall I had replaced everything exactly as I found it.

I hit the bottom of the stairs at practically a dead run. As I rounded the end of the banister, a flash of chrome turned into the driveway. I'd been in the house less than ten minutes. Where in the world had Gunnar gone in that length of time? Perhaps he had forgotten something and came back to get it. I couldn't take the chance of hiding and slipping out later. I had to get out of here now. The house wasn't as tidy as it had been when Dorothea was here. I didn't notice the heavy ottoman pulled away from a chair until I whacked it with the toe of my shoe. I grunted in pain but kept going. It moved an inch or two, but I didn't stop to put it back in place. Surely as careless of a housekeeper as he was, he wouldn't remember the exact position of an ottoman.

I ran through the house and into the kitchen in bad need of a bathroom and an EKG machine. I couldn't die in Dorothea's house. How would I explain it to Scott and the boys? I thought I heard the key in the front door's lock as I rounded the island in the center of her newly renovated, state of the art kitchen. I had nearly reached the back door when I saw movement out of the corner of my eye. I had stirred up enough of a headwind in my haste that a page of the calendar on the wall fluttered down to show the following month. May was still three days away. Gunnar would certainly notice if the calendar had been changed, and he wasn't the one who had done it.

The front door opened, and I very clearly heard Gunnar step inside. Go upstairs. Go upstairs, I silently begged. My trembling fingers would barely cooperate as I fumbled to turn the page of the calendar back to April. I nearly pulled the nail out of the wall in my haste. "Calm down, Joy," I hissed under my breath.

I couldn't draw a deep breath no matter how hard I tried. A set of car keys hit the table in the foyer, and a man's footfalls headed in my direction. My shoulder banged soundly against the refrigerator as I turned away from the calendar and toward the back door. Thankfully none of Dorothea's magnets hit the floor. Gunnar would've surely heard me then. My hand was sweating so badly it took two tries before I was able to grip the doorknob enough to let myself out. The calendar was swinging gently against the wall as I quietly closed the door behind me. I turned left toward the Smithfields' house and away from any windows that might afford Gunnar a glimpse of me as I beat my retreat through their yard. As expected, their little dog began yapping madly from the back of the house. Enid locked the little thing in a kennel in the laundry room while she and Joe were at work. A dog walker came by every afternoon at one to walk him around the neighborhood. From the fuss he was kicking up, the terrier was in ten times better shape than I was. I didn't take the time to look back to see if Gunnar heard the dog barking and stepped out the back door to investigate. I didn't stop running until I reached Pence Street, which ran perpendicular to ours. I collapsed against someone's garage and clutched my side until my breathing slowed and my vision cleared. What had I been thinking? I wasn't cut out for sleuthing.

In a panic I touched the folded paper in my sweatpants pocket. It was still there, along with the keys to Dorothea's house. I nearly collapsed in relief. It wouldn't have done for me to risk my life only to lose my cache as I fled the scene of the crime. Another ten minutes elapsed before I was confident color had returned to my face and I didn't look like I had been fleeing Al Quedi operatives. I crossed to the other side of the street and walked home as though I'd been out for a morning stroll. Maybe I didn't do it every day, but it wasn't like I'd never thought about it. When I came in sight of Dorothea's house, I held my shoulders stiff and straight and prayed Gunnar wouldn't barge out the front door and interrogate me. He hadn't actually caught me so I would tell him he was mistaken, and Mrs. Wylie said she thought she saw someone prowling around the neighborhood earlier, and that was probably who he saw running from his yard. He couldn't prove it was me. I was home free. That knowledge did not go far in stilling the wild beating of my heart.

Chapter 15

I nearly collapsed from an anxiety attack the instant I closed and locked the door behind me. I couldn't believe how close I'd come to getting caught breaking into someone's house. Okay, so I may not have actually broken in since I had a key, but I had definitely not been invited. I tucked the folded page from the address book into the junk drawer in the kitchen and hung Dylan's jacket back in the closet. After insuring Dylan hadn't sold his little brother to gypsies while I was out, I got busy mopping the kitchen floor and cleaning out the refrigerator. Anything to disguise the wild shaking of my hands. I also stayed away from the front of the house. I half expected Gunnar to pound on the front door at any minute, demanding to know what I'd been doing in Dorothea's house while he was out. If he caught a glimpse of my face he would surely recognize my guilt.

After a thrown together lunch of grilled cheese sandwiches and tomato soup, I sat Aidan in front of the TV and went to the phone. I didn't grill Dylan when he disappeared upstairs for several hours and then said he was going out. I had too much else on my mind.

With Aidan occupied and Dylan out of earshot, I huddled in a corner of the kitchen with the phone and the page I tore out of the address book to make my call to Chicago.

I didn't know how to start the conversation.

"Hello, you don't know me," I imagined myself saying. "My name is Joy Kessler and I'm your Aunt Dorothea's neighbor. Anyway, Gunnar's here and he says Dorothea's on a cruise with your wife, but I think he's lying because I saw him sell Albert's watch and now he's wrecking Dorothea's house."

Of course if Gunnar's mother answered the phone, that would blow holes in the whole cruise story since she was the person who was supposed to be on the high seas with Dorothea.

The dilemma of what I'd say when Cathy Westlake picked up the phone was taken care of when a computer generated voice told me the number I was trying to reach was no longer in service. I stared at the phone in my hand, relieved and disappointed at the same time. I wouldn't have to explain to a stranger that I suspected her son may have done something to my friend. Nor would I find out today if the two women were actually on a cruise like Gunnar said.

I redialed and got the same message. Short of driving to Chicago and asking point blank where Dorothea was, my sneaking into the house the moment Gunnar turned his back had scared five years off my life for nothing.

Or maybe not. I had the Westlakes' address and access to the World Wide Web. I wasn't exactly computer savvy, but there should be ways to track down the family without going all the way to Chicago. I went into the family room and grabbed the laptop.

"What're you doing?" Aidan asked, giving me a little attention during a commercial break.

"Surfing the net," I answered simply. "What're you doing?"

"Watching Phineas and Ferb. Do you need help?" He got off the couch and came over to stand next to my chair.

"More than you realize." I pushed the chair out from the desk and motioned him into my lap. He was probably better at this than I was, and how many more opportunities would I have to hold my son in my lap? "Do you know how to use Google Maps?"

"You mean to look down on our house from space?"

"Sort of."

He put his hand over mine on the mouse and guided the cursor to where he wanted. After he clicked the proper box, I began to type.

We watched the screen in fascination as the camera panned over a neighborhood past trees, a fire hydrant, wrought iron fences, and stop signs. It took only a few moments to find the right street and the right house in the center of the block. "Are we making a treasure map?" he breathed.

"Something like that."

"Cool."

We worked together, Aidan guiding the mouse while I swallowed my impatience and let him play around a little. The program was cool. It was like being a bird swooping over rooftops and treetops until we found the address we wanted. Aidan watched while I copied addresses and phone numbers for our treasure map. He even took a post-it notepad and wrote names and numbers in his oversized, childish script.

After playing around a little longer than necessary with Google maps, I searched the Cook County auditor's office and online white pages for phone numbers to go with the addresses I found. Since it took me longer than the average bear to figure out the program, and my spelling stinks on the best of days, most of the afternoon had passed by the time I finished a task most people would've completed in twenty minutes. I figured with the price of gas and the distance between here and Chicago, I was way ahead of the game by the time I created a list of possible neighbors.

Armed with my list of names and phone numbers, I zipped Aidan into a jacket, and the two of us went outside to the sandbox. While he scraped around in the hardened sand and made roads for his dump trucks and earthmovers, I sat down on the picnic table and started punching in numbers. I didn't think my job would be easy, and it wasn't.

After telling the third answering machine I had reached the wrong number, I thought it might be a good idea to call later in the day when everyone was home from work. But most people who worked all day wouldn't appreciate me butting into their evenings to ask if they knew the Westlake family at 5560 Bradenton. Nor were those people likely to know much about their neighbors. I needed someone who spent her day looking out the window to see what her neighbors were up to. Someone like me.

Calls four through seven, I reached residents who didn't know their neighbors, or they didn't know what I was talking about, and didn't I have better things to do with my time than pester busy people. I was a little bruised and weary by the time I hit pay dirt on the eighth call.

A genteel, matronly sounding lady answered the phone. I imagined snow white hair, a purring cat winding around her ankles, and the smell of baking bread wafting from the kitchen. She was probably the exact type of elderly person often scammed by smooth talking telemarketers who made her think she was talking to a friend while they sold her death and dismemberment insurance she didn't need.

After identifying myself I got straight to the point. "I don't know if you can help me, but I'm looking for Geoffrey or Cathy Westlake. I'm not a bill collector or anything. I'm just a friend of their aunt. I think they still live in your neighborhood."

I nearly wept with relief when she said she knew Geoffrey and Cathy. "My name is Myrtle Kinnamon, and I know nearly everyone in the neighborhood."

"Oh, Mrs. Kinnamon. I'm so pleased to hear that. I was hoping to find out how to reach Geoffrey and Cathy. I can't get them by phone."

"That may be because they moved away last summer."

My heart sank. I held the phone away from my mouth so she wouldn't hear my audible groan.

"They sold their house," she went on, unaware of my dismay. "Didn't get as much for is as what they would've liked. But you know how it is."

I did sort of know what it was like, but I hoped she wouldn't get derailed. I needed information I figured only she knew.

"Do you know where they are now?"

"I'm afraid not. It was just too hard on them to keep living here, the poor dears. Especially after all that trouble with their son."

"Gunnar?" I squeaked.

I could hear the smile in her voice. "You know Gunnar?"

"Oh, yes," I said as if we were the best of friends.

"So then, you know about his problems."

"Well," I hedged, feeling dishonest for the first time. "Not really."

"It was tragic." I heard the springs of her chair shift as she settled against the cushions. I wondered how long it had been since she had someone to listen while she talked. "Geoff and Cathy lived here for years, since Gunnar was a little thing. He was such a sweet boy. Rowdy, of course. All boy, but with a heart of gold."

"Um," I murmured in agreement. I was having a hard time picturing the boy she described with the man across the street pillaging Dorothea's house.

"He was fine until he got mixed up with those drugs." She clicked her tongue. "It breaks my heart when I hear of a young person throwing his life away like that. I can't understand it myself. All that potential, all that promise, bam, down the drain."

I made another murmur of agreement when she paused. I was sure she thought I knew more than I did. I wasn't about to interrupt her train of thought to set her straight.

"I blame it on that crowd of boys he started hanging around. They were trouble. I knew it from the first time I saw them."

I chewed my bottom lip. It almost sounded like the conversation I'd had with Dorothea the day before she disappeared. Only she had been talking about Dylan and the boys he was hanging out with. I thought of the endless supply of excuses I kept on the tip of my tongue. It was always the other boys' fault. Never Dylan's. Not my angel. He couldn't dream up such mischief without input from someone else. Oh, the naiveté of parenthood.

Mrs. Kinnamon shifted again in her chair. "It broke poor Cathy's heart. She and Geoff put everything they had into that boy. They couldn't accept what Gunnar was doing, though it was pretty obvious to the rest of the world."

I tried to focus on her words, but thoughts of Dylan invaded. I had accused Scott of refusing to see what Dylan was doing. Scott wasn't the only one. Neither of us wanted to face the facts right in front of us. How Dylan always had money even though he missed work more often than he showed up. How he was irritable and moody for no apparent reason. Why he slept all the time and never brought his friends home to visit. If Scott and I didn't wake up and face what our son was doing, we would lose him forever like Dorothea warned.

I tuned back in on Mrs. Kinnamon's words just in time. "I think the straw that broke the camel's back was when Gunnar dropped out of school."

"What?" I broke in. "When was this?"

"Um, let me see. Four years ago. Yes, that's about right. I think he was in his second year." She sighed heavily.

"It was my understanding Gunnar is taking his post graduate studies," I said.

"Oh, dear, no. He never even earned his Associate's Degree. It was always Geoff's dream that he go to law school. Geoffrey is an attorney. Did you know that?"

"Yes," I replied, distracted. If Gunnar wasn't here to work on a dissertation, what was he doing? Had Dorothea seen through his lies? Is that why she suddenly went…on a cruise? I was more convinced than ever something terrible had happened. But what? And how could I prove it?

I looked across the yard at Aidan. He was still in the sandbox and had barely looked at me. Sand lined his upper lip and hairline. I would have to give him a good scrubbing before he had a chance to sit on any of the furniture inside.

It sounded like Mrs. Kinnamon took a drink of something before continuing. "I think Gunnar started dabbling in drugs in high school. It wasn't until after he started college the situation truly worsened. He lived at home so it was easy to see he was going downhill fast. Cathy and Geoffrey kept making excuses for him. They couldn't see." She clicked her tongue again. "I suppose parents never do."

I cringed. Wasn't that the truth?

"He hung around a while after he dropped out, but Geoffrey made it pretty tough on him. Said if he didn't want to go to school, he could get a job and pay his own way."

The similarities between Gunnar and Dylan were giving me a stomachache.

"Gunnar moved out. I heard he moved around a lot after that. It was never the same between Geoff and Cathy. Cathy blamed Geoff. Gunnar called less and less until eventually they didn't know where he was." She lowered her voice, and I had to cover my other ear to hear her over the sound of Aidan talking to his toys. "I think it was hard on their marriage. You know, all the tension. They had to mortgage the house after the last time Gunnar got in trouble. I think that's why they sold everything and moved out."

I hugged the phone closer to my ear. "What kind of trouble was it?"

"I don't know all the details. Cathy wasn't talking much to me by that time. Too embarrassed, I suppose. From what I gather, he had been embezzling money from his job. It was just a small operation, and the owner said he would let it go if Gunnar paid back the money. Cathy and Geoff paid it, along with the court costs and whatever else goes with something like that. Then Gunnar never called them again."

That sounded like the Gunnar I knew. "Those poor people," I said with all the anguish of a mother who understood.

"I'm sorry I couldn't be more helpful to you," Mrs. Kinnamon said.

"Oh, no, you've been most helpful."

She brightened. "Thank you."

"Do you know if Cathy and Geoffrey stayed in Chicago?"

"I'm sorry. I'm afraid I don't know one way or the other. Did you say you know Cathy's aunt?"

"Actually it's Geoffrey's aunt, Dorothea Westlake." I figured I owed her at least a partial truth after all her help. "She hadn't seen Gunnar since he was little, and I was trying to find out as much as I can for her."

"I hate for you to have to give her a bad report because of me," she said with regret in her voice.

"Don't apologize. She'll appreciate any information I can give her."

"You tell her to remember the little boy she used to know," Mrs. Kinnamon advised. "That's how I remember him. I'll never forget the day they came home from a trip to Florida and Gunnar was wearing a pair of those Mickey Mouse ears. He was ten or eleven at the time. He was grinning from ear to ear. He usually didn't grin that big because he was so embarrassed about his braces. But with those Mickey Mouse ears, he seemed to forget about them. He talked about that trip the rest of the year." She sighed into the phone. "That's how I'll always remember Gunnar. Standing on my front porch in those Mickey Mouse ears."

"Thank you very much, Mrs. Kinnamon," I told her.

Aidan stood up and clapped his hands to get rid of the sand. "I'm hungry," he announced.

"It sounds like you have one of your own," she said.

"Yes, it's my son Aidan. He's getting hungry and he's covered with sand so I better clean him up before he goes inside without me."

She laughed, a musical, somewhat rusty sound. "You better or you'll have a mess on your hands. What did you say your name was, dearie?"

"Joy Kessler. Could I give you my phone number, and if you think of anything else, you could give me a call? Or you could call to chat anytime you like," I added, sensing her loneliness through the phone lines.

"Oh, certainly. I would like that."

I wondered if I had made a mistake as I repeated the number slowly twice so she had time to write it down. What if Gunnar found out I had talked to her about him? Then I thought of Mrs. Kinnamon and how she sounded like she didn't have many people in her life. What harm could come from talking to her? Gunnar hadn't been in the old neighborhood for years. Now that his parents moved, he would have no reason to talk to an elderly neighbor he probably didn't even remember.

I said goodbye and hung up and went to clean up Aidan. Heaviness pressed my chest. I knew more about Gunnar, chiefly that he had lied about working on his dissertation. Was he in financial trouble again, and he knew his parents were tapped out? What if there were loan sharks or a bad element looking for him? This was the ideal neighborhood in which to hide. If that was the case, was he hidden well enough? How much danger was Dorothea in? How much danger were all of us in? I pictured our neighborhood cordoned off with yellow police tape and a S.W.A.T. team hiding in Dorothea's shrubs while a news chopper hovered overhead.

For all my searching and phone calls today, I still didn't know the thing that tormented me most. Where was Dorothea?

Chapter 16

I hated to say anything about Dylan after he worked so hard at being pleasant all evening. An hour before Scott got home from work, he came back from wherever he'd been. Even more amazing, he was in a good mood. He bounced into the kitchen and offered to peel potatoes for dinner. I was so shocked by the offer he was already perched on a stool in front of a pile of potatoes and a wire basket with a knife in hand before I could respond. Aidan climbed up beside him and scraped carrots with a play knife from a toy kitchen set. The two of them kept me in stitches the rest of the afternoon. I watched Dylan out of the corner of my eye as I finished the rest of the dinner preparations and wondered if he ever wished we could have more days like this the way I did. At the same time my cynical side couldn't keep from searching for signs of drug abuse.

I kept rehashing my conversation with Myrtle Kinnamon. The similarities between Gunnar's parents and Scott and me were too glaring to ignore. Like them, we had kept our heads buried in the sand since the day Dylan wailed his first protest from the crib. He had been a cranky and belligerent child, and Scott and I were young inexperienced parents. We believed it was better to express our love through tolerance and understanding, not by placing limits. We thought if we made our desires known in a reasonable fashion, Dylan would respond in kind. I began to realize we were missing a key point in his development when friends began to pull away.

I thought our friends weren't getting together as often as they had in the past until I ran into two girlfriends on a shopping trip. They also had small children who were with them that day, dressed in cute outfits, their eyes free of tears and cheeks clear of the telltale signs of recent temper tantrums. The friends apologized for not inviting me to join them. "We just didn't think about it," one said, her eyes unable to meet mine.

"You're always so busy," said the other.

Reality smacked me in the face as they eyed Dylan as though observing a wild animal. They didn't want to be around my son. Frankly, neither did I. He was destructive and loud and a bully other children feared. He embarrassed us in public places to get his way, which I always hurriedly gave him to avoid a scene. Even though I understood my friends' motives, I went home in tears.

"We're doing something wrong, Scott," I blubbered with a struggling Dylan under one arm. He had just broken the rearview mirror off the windshield for the second time because I wouldn't stop for ice cream on the way home. "Our friends are still hanging out. Just not with us."

I dropped Dylan into Scott's lap and dug into my handbag for the rearview mirror. "They don't want our son contaminating their children."

Scott bounced Dylan into the air. "Who needs them? Right, buddy." Dylan's tears dried, ice cream forgotten.

"I need them," I insisted. I waved the rearview mirror in his face. "This doesn't happen to other people. He tried to hit me with it after kicking my purse off the front seat because I wouldn't give him what he wanted."

Scott lifted Dylan's shirt and blew a raspberry on his bare belly. "Then I suggest you give him what he wants."

"Scott, this isn't funny. His behavior is sometimes dangerous. We need to use a firmer hand with him."

"Dangerous? Don't tell me you're afraid of him."

I ground my teeth in frustration. "Of course I'm not afraid. I'm just saying his behavior is unacceptable. He's unruly and unpredictable. No one wants to be around him, and no one invites us anywhere because they know we'll bring him along."

Scott's eyes flashed. "Too bad. We're a package deal."

"I'm not suggesting otherwise. I'm just saying we need to rein in his behavior before it gets totally out of hand. He's still small enough I can manhandle him into behaving. The day will come that I can't. Then where will we be? He needs to learn boundaries."

Scott sighed and put Dylan on the couch next to him. He took hold of my wrists and pulled me down on the other side of him. "Joy, honey, Dylan's just impulsive. Boys are supposed to be that way. I'll fix the mirror. It's no big deal. If your friends—"

"Our friends," I corrected.

"—If our friends can't handle a rambunctious two-year-old, it's their loss."

I hadn't totally agreed with him that night, but he made it sound so logical. That was the thing about Scott. He could make me see logic in just about anything. Sometimes I wondered if he ever heard my concerns or if he manipulated me the same as Dylan, only in a different way.

Tonight, like many others around our house over the years, Dylan remained funny and charming throughout dinner. Scott was equally charmed and pleased. He gave me several 'I told you so' glances, and I dared hope things could stay this way. After dinner, Dylan and Aidan loaded the dishwasher and then Dylan asked Scott for twenty bucks. It was my turn for the 'I told you so', but what was twenty bucks between father and son? Borrowing money that would never be paid back was the name of the game in parenting.

I wanted to hope things would stay the way they were tonight. Dylan would come home and tell us he decided to go back to school. We'd dig out the brochures he'd collected during his senior year and the ones Mom brought over now and then and go through them, laughing and brainstorming and teasing him about how in the world we would pay for everything since he wasn't exactly an exemplary student who had amassed a pile of scholarships. Even more, I wanted to wake up in the morning and find my son at the table telling me he had decided to go back to church. He was sorry for desecrating our home with parties while we were out of town. He realized his behavior was irresponsible and reckless, and he had turned over a new leaf.

Most of all I wanted Scott to take my side and accept we had failed Dylan by not setting boundaries and demanding acceptable behavior from him. I didn't want him to end up like Gunnar Westlake; lying to people about writing dissertations and falling into a deeper and deeper pit of drug use. There was not really anything I could do about Dylan's choices. But there was something I could do about mine. I just wasn't sure I was up to doing it tonight.

When Scott came downstairs from putting Aidan to bed I scooted over on the couch and motioned for him to join me. He eased down beside me and guided my head to his shoulder. I sank against him, suddenly not so eager to talk about Dylan. Scott was always busy, and we didn't have much time together as a couple. When we did I hated to waste it rehashing our failings as parents.

Scott gave a contented sigh and rested his chin on top of my head. "How was your day?" he asked.

I sat up so I could look at him. "I learned a few interesting things about Gunnar."

He dropped his head into the couch cushions. "Joy…"

"Listen to me, Scott. Gunnar isn't here to work on his dissertation. He dropped out of college."

"Why are you telling me this?"

I sat up on my knees and looked down at him, excited to finally have an audience. "Because he's lying. He said he came here to work on his postgraduate studies. He doesn't even live with his parents."

"How do you know all this?"

I paused, considering if I should tell him the lengths I went to to learn the truth. "I talked to one of his neighbors from where he grew up in Chicago."

Scott sat up and leveled his gaze at me. "How do you know he grew up in Chicago?"

This part I could answer without hedging. "Dorothea's mentioned it the day she introduced us. As for the neighbor's address…" I glanced away. "I found it lying around somewhere."

He cocked his head. "Joy, what are you up to?"

"If you mean, am I trying to figure out where Dorothea is and why Gunnar lied about being a student when he dropped out of college in his second year, then yes, I'm up to something."

He ran his hand through his sandy hair, still thick and luxurious with no discernible receding hairline even though he turned forty on his last birthday. "Did you ever think he might've made up the story about a dissertation to impress his aunt? As for finding Dorothea, she's in the Caribbean with her niece. Frankly, you're the one I'm worried about. All you talk about is Gunnar Westlake. You're obsessed with the guy. You're going to feel like an idiot next week when Dorothea comes home happy and rested and tanned and you have to tell her you thought her nephew had pushed her over a bridge abutment."

I stood. "I really hope that's how I feel next week. I hope I'm wrong. But he sold Albert's watch. He's destroying her house, and he's lied about everything from the moment we met him. Maybe he is nothing more than a mooch and habitual liar, but I'd like to think someone would care if they saw me being taken advantage of. I'm going to bed."

"Joy, don't get bent out of shape. I'm worried about you."

I spun around. "Don't be. Worry about Dorothea. Worry about your son and why he won't hold a job. But don't worry about me. I'm the only one around here with my head on straight."

I went upstairs forgetting our brief moment on the couch. When I slid between the covers fifteen minutes later, I stared at the ceiling and thought about Dorothea. I clasped my hands and tucked them under my chin like Aidan when he prayed.

"Lord, I pray Scott's right and I'm wrong. I want nothing more than to see Dorothea happy and rested next week. But if she needs me, help me know what to do."

I was asleep by the time Scott came to bed.

I was tired of being mad at my husband. Like I told Dorothea, I really did want to be a submissive Proverbs Thirty-One wife. I wanted to make his life easier, to make his home a pleasant refuge at the end of the day. I tried not to greet him at the door with problems that required immediate attention. Sometimes it was unavoidable. Thursday was Mom's day off from work since she was semi-retired and her usual day to join us for lunch. She'd missed last week because of her doctor's appointment, but she called early to tell me she'd be over as planned.

I tried to muster a little enthusiasm. It wasn't easy. I had things on my mind and wasn't looking forward to having her remind me all day long of my shortcomings. I still hadn't decided how to handle Dylan or get Scott behind me in the matter. I hadn't even convinced him there was a matter to get behind. Dylan stumbled downstairs around ten, bleary eyed, unshaven, and wearing a ratty pair of gym shorts and a stretched out t-shirt about four days overdue for the wash.

"Good morning, Dylan," I said cheerily, hoping the new and improved Dylan from yesterday was somewhere under those scraggly whiskers.

He grunted in reply without looking at me and headed for the fridge. So much for Scott's promise he'd work on Dylan's attitude.

"Are you hungry?" In this house if you missed breakfast the first time you were out of luck. But I had cooked bacon and eggs for Aidan and Scott, and I was in a generous mood.

His grunt was barely audible this time. He took an orange juice carton out of the fridge and put it to his lips.

"Dylan," I cried, too late to stop him. His Adam's apple bobbed up and down without missing a beat. "Someone else might want some of that."

He stopped gulping, wiped his mouth with the back of his hand, and held the carton out to me. "Go ahead."

I grimaced and waved it away. "No one's going to want it now."

He shrugged and put it back in the fridge.

I bit back the retort he'd heard and ignored a thousand times.

Note to self: Don't drink the orange juice or give any to Aidan.

Since he wasn't going out of his way to be civil to me, I figured no harm could come from asking what I was itching to know. "What time did you get in last night?"

"You mean you weren't watching out the window? Or you were and you hope to catch me in a lie?"

"I don't appreciate your implications."

"I don't appreciate being treated like a kid."

"Then stop acting like one."

He lowered his head and glared at me. I was taken aback by the loathing on his face. Ah, yes, there was the son I knew so well.

"Sure, Mom. That's all I am, a worthless, pitiful kid. I'm surprised you kept me around as long as you did considering how disappointed you've always been in me."

My shoulders slumped. "Dylan, that's not it. You've never been a disappointment…"

I could be pretty thick, but it slowly dawned on me what he was doing. We'd played this game so long over the years we both knew our parts. He would distract me from whatever had made me mad, and I'd stop yelling. The corners of my mouth twitched.

"What?" he said, his scowl still solidly in place.

"Not this time."

At least he had the decency to look puzzled. "Not this time, what?"

I crossed my arms over my chest and leaned a hip against the counter. "I asked what time you got home."

He exhaled loudly in defeat. His shoulders drooped this time. "I wasn't watching the clock."

"Then you're grounded. You can stay home through the weekend until you learn to keep an eye on the clock. Or you find gainful employment, whichever comes first."

He exploded, just as I knew he would. The explosion didn't intimidate me as much as it once had. "This blows. You can't ground me because I don't know what time I got in last night."

"That isn't the only reason I'm grounding you."

I could see the shock on his face at the even tone in my voice. It even surprised me. Where was my normal trepidation when dealing with my nearly grown son? "As your mother," I continued, my confidence growing with each word, "I don't need a reason to ground you. But I have several in case you're interested."

He didn't ask, but I ticked them off on my fingers anyway. "I'm sick of your attitude. I'm sick of your bullying. Most of all, I'm sick of your entitlement attitude. You're almost nineteen. You've been out of school for nearly a year. You can either get a job—a real one you go to on a regular basis—you can enroll in some classes, or you can move out. The choice is yours. Since you won't be going anywhere this weekend, you'll have plenty of time to make your decision."

It took him a full five seconds to process what he'd just heard. His jaw dropped and his arms hung loose at his sides. Then he pushed away from the refrigerator and assumed the threatening stance he'd been using on me for fifteen years. The one that always made me back down. I didn't budge, though inside I was already second guessing my hasty pronouncement.

"Does Dad know about this?"

"He will soon enough, I expect."

"You can count on it," he practically screamed.

"Mommy?" Aidan said from behind him.

I stepped away from the counter toward my youngest son. Dylan spun around to face him. "Get out of here, twerp. This doesn't concern you."

Aidan's lower lip began to tremble. Dylan took a step toward him. I pushed between them and blocked his path. "Don't even think about it," I growled through clenched teeth.

Dylan paused, feeling me out. Aidan pressed his trembling body against my hips. It made me even angrier that Dylan had this entire household quaking before him. Scott and I had created this mess. Aidan was innocent. The fact that he had to pay for our failings made me madder than I'd ever been.

I reached behind me and stroked Aidan's silken hair. "Go to your room, Dylan. Don't come down until you can be civil."

He barked out a one syllable laugh. "Who's going to make me?"

"Hello? Anyone home?"

Mom's greeting from the front of the house broke the spell. "Grandma," Aidan squealed and raced through the kitchen door. Dylan and I continued to glare at each other.

A moment later Mom entered the kitchen with Aidan in her arms. "What's got my grandson all upset?" she demanded. Neither Dylan nor I moved.

"Joy? Dylan?"

Reluctantly I turned away from Dylan. "Everything's fine, Mom." I held my arms out to Aidan. He looked warily at Dylan before sliding out of Mom's arms and running to me. I got down on my knees and hugged him close. "It's okay, Lima Bean. I'm sorry I scared you."

Mom set her hands on her hips. "What is going on here?" Her eyes flitted from Dylan to me.

"Nothing, Mom," I said gently for Aidan's benefit. "I'm handling it."

"Yeah, she's handling it," Dylan snapped behind me. "She just kicked me out of the house."

Mom inhaled sharply. "Joy? Is that true?"

I swallowed another wave of anger. Did Dylan have to involve Mom of all people? I straightened. "I didn't kick you out. I gave you a decision to make."

"Yeah. Straighten up and do things your way or get out."

"Joy," Mom exclaimed.

I ignored her. "This is my house," I said to Dylan. "Why shouldn't I have things my way?"

Dylan leaned past me to look at his grandmother. "See what I mean? Just because I got in late last night, she's tripping."

"This doesn't concern anyone else, Dylan. I asked you to go to your room."

"Why? Are you ashamed of how unfair you're being?"

"I'm not ashamed of anything." My voice shook with barely concealed anger. "You were rude to your brother and me and I want you to go to your room."

"I'm surprised you even let me sleep there since this is your house." He pushed past me, banging roughly into me with his shoulder. I staggered back a step. "Next thing you know, you'll start charging me rent."

"Don't tempt me," I called after him.

Mom and Aidan watched him go and then turned back to me. I shot Mom a warning look that begged to let it go, at least for now. As usual, she ignored what I obviously wanted.

"What is this about? Surely you didn't kick your own son into the street."

"He's still here, isn't he?" I went to the coffeemaker and poured the remainder of this morning's coffee down the drain. In dismay, I realized my hands were shaking. "Let's not talk about it now, okay, Mom? Would you like some coffee?"

"I want to talk about it," she said, ignoring the offer. "What did you do to get him so upset?"

I whirled around, away from the rush of water into the carafe. "What makes you think I upset him? Has it never occurred to you he might be wrong?"

"He's a child. You're the adult. You're supposed to control yourself and not make empty threats when he doesn't do something exactly the way you want it done. You can't control people."

Was she kidding? She'd been controlling my strings as long as I could remember. When I married Scott, he took up where she left off. I had never made a decision in my life based on what I thought was right, but instead on what everyone expected from me.

I shut off the water and clanked the carafe down hard on the coffeemaker's hot plate. "I didn't make an empty threat. I'm tired of being bullied in my own home."

She tossed her auburn highlighted locks. "Bullied? Really, Joy."

"Yes, Mom, and I'm tired of it."

"He said you kicked him out because he came in late last night."

"Does that sound like something I'd do, Mom?"

"I don't know, Joy. You haven't been yourself lately."

"You mean the woman everyone in this house can bend to their will."

"What does that even mean?"

"It means I've never stood up for what I think I deserve, but I'm starting now. Dylan has to learn responsibility. There's no reason why he can't get a job he'll keep or go to school. I told him the choice was his."

"Don't you think you're being a little hard, blindsiding him like this out of the blue?"

"I think I should've done it a long time ago. If he's going to live here, he can do it my way."

She shook her head. "I don't even recognize you anymore."

I opened my mouth to apologize and then swelled out my chest instead. "Neither do I."

CHAPTER 17

I couldn't remember the last time I had a more enjoyable time with my mother. Either she was being outwardly polite to avoid my possible wrath, or I was flying too high to notice her usual digs. She didn't complain the deviled eggs I served for lunch were too runny or the potato salad too salty. Had I commanded her respect without even trying?

The only sore spot was Dylan didn't make an appearance downstairs the rest of the afternoon. I braced myself for when Scott came in from work. Dylan had probably called already to tattle on me. Scott wouldn't be happy I'd threatened our son without consulting him first, which made my decision feel all the more right. I'm been consulting and pleading with Scott for years that we do something about Dylan. My concerns had been disregarded and pushed aside. Well, not today. I'd drawn a line in the sand, and I dared anyone to cross it. I felt light, free, powerful.

After Mom left I told Aidan we were going for a walk to the park. He had been watching too much television lately with me so distracted over Dorothea and Gunnar. Our morning workouts had only lasted a couple of days before the DVDs went back into the depths of the entertainment center. Demanding respect from Dylan and Mom had made me want physical respect as well, starting with myself. I was tired of the way my clothes fit. I was tired of the new, barely worn workout clothes hanging alongside the stretched out, faded daily togs in my closet. Every time I looked in the mirror I wondered how much longer I would let my weight dictate how I felt about myself. I wanted to get to the top of a flight of stairs without getting winded. Today was as good a time as any to start.

We stepped outside into a brilliant spring day. There wasn't a cloud in sight to mar the bright sun hanging high in a pale blue sky. It had been a rainy April. If Dorothea actually was in the Caribbean she had missed a dreary couple of weeks. Tomorrow was the first day of May. I thought of her flowerbeds and Martin coming at the first of the week to prepare them for planting. Mine had been neglected as well, and I hadn't even been out of town. This weekend I'd clean out my own beds and yard, and then make a list for Martin. If Gunnar saw it as meddling, well, that was his problem. I was tired of tiptoeing around those who didn't want me doing what I believed needed done.

I took a deep breath of crisp clean air and lengthened my strides. Aidan giggled and picked up his pace beside me. At least my new attitude was having a positive effect on one of the men in my life.

The park was seldom crowded this time of day. I usually planned our visits when it wasn't so crowded that Aidan couldn't get near the swings. At the same time I preferred another kid or two around for him to play with. Even though he didn't know the kids that had commandeered the jungle gym, he ran ahead and climbed aboard. Two moms at least a decade younger than me sat on the bench closest to the jungle gym, engrossed in conversation. If I had some of Aidan's boldness I'd walk right over there and plunk down beside them. They looked nice. We had mutual interests and concerns obviously.

They might appreciate the wisdom of a mom who had already dealt with whatever they were facing today.

Who was I kidding? Except for Dorothea I hadn't had any close friends since motherhood. I wouldn't know what to say unless they wanted to know how to get crayon marks out of carpeting. I was a pro at that, but pretty inept at everything else.

Stop it, Joy, I scolded. This wasn't a day for degrading myself. Scott and Dylan would do enough of that tonight. For now I would concentrate on what I came to the park for.

I made sure Aidan was having fun and not in need of anything for a while, then started walking, keeping the jungle gym in my peripheral vision. I took some deep breaths as I walked, which I read somewhere people didn't do often enough, and relished the warmth of the sun on my face. It didn't seem natural that I was in such a good mood after a fight with Dylan. Or spending the day with my mother, for that matter. Ordinarily such encounters left me exhausted and depressed and in need of fried food, especially knowing how Scott would react when Dylan told him what I said.

But no reaction from Scott could dim the euphoria I felt at standing up to Dylan. Had I known it would feel this good, I might have tried it years ago.

"Forgive Scott and me, Lord," I mumbled softly so the two young mothers wouldn't think I was crazy if they overheard me talking. "Help us do the hard part of parenting."

I picked up my pace and let my arms swing loose at my sides. I walked the playground perimeter farther from the jungle gym than I'd ever been. The grass hadn't been mown out here yet, and tiny nettles scratched at my ankles and latched onto my socks. I smiled as I drew abreast of the moms. They smiled back and called out greetings as I sailed past. This was better than sitting on a bench though a stitch clutched my side and the smile on my face became a little forced. No sense in overdoing it. I slowed my pace a degree and focused on breathing in and out and ignoring the flashes of light dancing before my eyes. I was really out of shape. I couldn't do anything about being older than most of the mothers I ran into in the park, but I sure could do something about outweighing them.

Aidan waved to get my attention as he jumped off the jungle gym and headed for the slide. The moms gathered their youngsters and prepared to leave. No one else was in sight. We should probably head home too. I circled the pavilion and a sea of picnic tables, my view of the playground momentarily obscured. When I got to the other side I looked toward the slides, expecting to see Aidan at the top waiting for me to watch him go down. He loved to perch at the top and call for me until he had my undivided attention before going down at breakneck speed. I lost count of how many times he hit the ground at full speed and my breath would catch in my throat until he jumped off and scampered around for another trip up the rungs. He had been fearless from the moment he was born. I had gotten used to the way my stomach would drop when he attempted something I deemed unsafe, and had learned to overlook it when the situation wasn't truly dangerous. I wondered if daughters gave their mothers heart palpitations the way Aidan did me.

On second thought, maybe the heart palpitations were from too many dollars handed over to the guy who drove the ice cream truck.

The slide came into view, but Aidan wasn't waiting at the top. I clutched my side and picked up my pace, my eyes flitting from the jungle gym to the swings to the sandbox. I craned my neck to see around the playground equipment sure he was on his way up the ladder and temporarily out of my line of sight. He wasn't there. Had he followed the other kids to their minivan? Had he gone into the street? The walk back to the playground was on a slight downhill slope so my pace quickened as the ground dropped away from me. The panic in my throat obscured the stitch in my side. I stopped at the slide and stood in the empty playground. My head swiveled in every direction.

"Aidan. Aidan." I looked where the minivan had been parked. Had it really belonged to the mothers? Had they walked off down the street while some freak in an inconspicuous minivan drove off with my baby? How had I let this happen? A scream threatened behind my clenched teeth.

Aidan's white blond head popped out from behind a tree. "Did you see it, Mommy? Did you see it?"

I exhaled from exertion and fear and stomped over to him. "Aidan," I gasped, my face hot and sides heaving, "don't ever do that again. I couldn't see you."

Indignation colored his cheeks. "I was right here."

I took another deep breath and put my hand over my pounding heart. Don't overreact, Joy. Don't make him afraid of every little thing the way you are.

"Of course you were," I said. "What did you want me to show me?"

"The snake."

"Ewww." I made an appropriately horrified face. "I hope you didn't touch it."

He laughed. "I tried, but it got away."

"Good." My heart rate had returned to normal, and the pain in my side subsided to a dull ache. It was too early in the season for the ice cream truck or I would've been tempted to undo the benefits of my walk. God didn't tempt me above what I was able to bear. Apparently I couldn't bear much. I needed to work on that.

I reached for Aidan's hand. "Your friends are gone. We need to go home too."

"Already?" he said with a groan.

"We need to start dinner for Daddy."

"And Dylan?"

"Yes, and Dylan."

"Is he still mad at you?"

"I hope not."

He twisted his mouth in thought. "I bet he is."

That was a bet I wasn't willing to take.

Aidan chattered all the way home. At least one son loved me. At this stage in his development, his tantrums only lasted a short time. If Scott and I didn't make some changes, it wouldn't be long before that changed. The only problem was I wasn't sure what changes to make. I didn't want to start smacking him around when he got fresh or using fear and intimidation to get him to behave the way I wanted. There had to be a better way. I wondered if Scott would be open to signing up for some parenting classes based on scripture. Maybe I'd stop by the Christian bookstore tomorrow and see what they had in stock. If I started exhibiting some constructive parenting methods, he might follow suit.

I repeated my earlier prayer in my head while Aidan gave names to the clouds in the sky and asked for what must've been the thousandth time why we wouldn't get a dog. "Can we have a Popsicle?" he asked as we rounded the corner and our house came into view.

"Isn't it a little cold for Popsicles?" I asked, thinking of the ice cream I had dreamed of earlier. A Popsicle was a much better snack choice. With Aidan around to keep me motivated, I might lose a pound or two.

"It's never too cold for Popsicles," he said gleefully.

"What color do you want?" I asked, already knowing the answer.

"Blue."

"I'll see if we have any. You go clean the leaves off the picnic table." It had always been my experience Popsicles were best eaten outside where the drips couldn't do any damage.

With a whoop of delight, Aidan took off around the house. I followed him and let myself in the back door. We were the kind of family that kept ice cream and frozen treats in the house year round. I agreed with Aidan; it was never too cold for Popsicles. Only one blue raspberry Popsicle remained in the box in the freezer so I chose an orange one for myself. I unwrapped them and ran cold water from the tap over them to wash away the ice crystals and headed back outside.

My heart stopped in my chest. Gunnar sat on the picnic table next to Aidan. "Did you bring a Popsicle for Gunnar?" Aidan called out.

Gunnar raised his head. The smile he gave me over Aidan's head froze the blood in my veins as hard as the Popsicles. My tongue was suddenly glued to the roof of my mouth. I forced one foot off the back stoop and then the other. I moved woodenly across the yard, my eyes locked with Gunnar's.

"What…" I smacked my lips together for moisture and started over. "What are you doing here?"

"Thought I'd stop by for a neighborly visit."

"Where have you been?" Aidan asked him as he plucked the blue Popsicle from my hand. He took the orange one and handed it to Gunnar. Gunnar bit off the end.

"Ask your mother," he said to Aidan, his eyes never leaving mine. "She knows all about me."

My heart dropped to my shoes. I wondered how I could calmly extract Aidan from the picnic table without scaring him or making Gunnar mad.

Aidan didn't notice the tension. "Is Aunt Dor'fea home yet? I miss her."

Gunnar smiled at him and tousled his hair. "Not yet. I'll tell her you were asking about her."

Aidan," I said, my voice amazingly calm. He concentrated on slurping the Popsicle. I stepped over to him and clamped my hand on his shoulder.

"Ow!"

"Aidan, sweetie, why don't you go in the house? I think it's time for your show."

Gunnar reached out and caught hold of his sleeve. "I don't think so. I want to spend some time with my buddy Aidan."

Aidan beamed up at him and continued eating.

"Aidan, now." It took all my resolve not to yank my son off the picnic table.

Gunnar put his arms around Aidan's shoulders and hugged him close. "He can watch TV anytime. We haven't seen each other in a long time."

Aidan looked from Gunnar to me, his forehead furrowed in confusion. He didn't stop licking his Popsicle. Nor did he get off the table.

I edged closer to Aidan. "We're busy, Gunnar. I think it's best if you go."

Gunnar dropped the hand holding the Popsicle to his side and managed to look wounded. "So you don't have time for your old friend Gunnar anymore, is that it? I was just being neighborly. You know how it is, no locked doors between friends. Right, Aidan?"

Aidan nodded around the Popsicle.

My heart froze in my chest. He couldn't possibly know I was in Dorothea's house yesterday.

"I thought you understood, too, Joy. You let yourself into my house while I'm out, and I come over here whenever I want. Isn't that the way it works?"

I blinked, trying to form a word of defense. He knew. Somehow he knew.

He held up a key ring and jangled it at me. It was the keys to our house, keys I'd given Dorothea years ago. While searching for the keys to her house, I'd forgotten Gunnar had access to keys to my house as well.

I don't know how he figured out I was at Dorothea's yesterday, but he knew and I wouldn't insult him by denying I'd been there. Worse, I wouldn't put Aidan in danger by denying it. "It's not your house. It's Dorothea's."

"Speaking of Dorothea, I have something you might be interested in." He shifted away from Aidan and reached into his back pocket. I took the opportunity to tighten my grip on Aidan. Gunnar pulled out the address book I had torn the page out of yesterday. "Is this what you were looking for?"

I gasped and nearly choked on an intake of air. "I...uh...have no idea what you're talking about."

That slow, maniacal smile was back on his face. He climbed off the picnic table and stood a few inches in front of me. I resisted the urge to step back. "The way I see it, Joy, is as long as you respect my privacy, I'll respect yours. Just like today at the park. I was about to step in and help when I saw you couldn't find Aidan."

Heat rushed to my face.

"I could've gotten my hands on him any time I wanted. But I didn't. I realized you might not want my help." He leaned closer, his icy green eyes boring into mine. "I thought you might appreciate it if I kept my distance. So that's what I did."

His gaze had me mesmerized like the snake charmer's in old cartoons, though in this case, Gunnar was the snake.

"I'm sure you appreciate that," he finished.

I tried to speak but no words would come.

"I know you'll return the favor and give me my space."

He waited, but I still couldn't find my voice.

Finally he exhaled and straightened as though satisfied he'd gotten through to me. "You can be confident in knowing I'm here when you need me, Joy. I hear everything and know everything that goes on in this neighborhood. You don't have to worry about anything happening to Aidan as long as I'm around."

He reached out to tousle Aidan's hair again. I jerked Aidan out of reach. "Don't touch him."

"Mom." Aidan gave me a dirty look.

Gunnar held up his hands in affront "Is that any way to talk to a neighbor? Like I said, I'm only being neighborly. Looking out for my friend. Aidan, if you ever want to go to the park and your mom is too busy, you just walk on over to my house and I'll be happy to go with you. You don't even have to ask."

"Get out of here, Gunnar. And don't talk to my son."

"Mom!"

Gunnar chuckled. He gave me a sly look before turning his attention to Aidan. "You listen to your mother, Aidan. She's only trying to protect you from all the crazies around here." He looked at me through hooded eyes, though his words were directed at Aidan. "There are a lot of bad people in the world."

I wrapped my arms around Aidan and jerked him off the picnic table. The Popsicle flew out of his hand and landed with a plop in the grass. "Mom!" he shrieked. "Look what you did."

I grabbed his arm and dragged him toward the house. "Go away, Gunnar," I said over my shoulder, my voice trembling with fear and rage.

Gunnar held up the address book that had fallen in the grass. "Joy, wait. You dropped your book."

I dragged a struggling Aidan into the house and locked the door behind us. While he protested and bemoaned the loss of what he soon found out was the last blue Popsicle I tried in vain to stop shaking. I watched out the front window as Gunnar ambled back across the street. He stopped just outside of Dorothea's door and looked back at our house. Though I didn't think he could see me behind the curtain, he made a gun with his hand and pointed it right at me. He took careful aim and fired, mouthing the word 'Bang' before going inside.

Chapter 18

I did something that night I hadn't done in months, perhaps years. I ordered pizza for dinner without a special occasion warranting it. Aidan thought it was his birthday already. The look Dylan shot me when the doorbell rang said he thought I was feeling guilty for yelling at him earlier. Even Scott raised his eyebrows when he walked in the door and sniffed the air. He probably thought I was too distraught over my altercation with Dylan to cook dinner. If he only knew.

I couldn't very well tell him I'd sneaked into Dorothea's house and ultimately put our preschooler's life in danger. I already knew what he'd say to that.

"Gunnar didn't actually threaten you, Joy. What were you doing snooping around Dorothea's house when no one was home anyway? You're the one who said he was a loose cannon. Do you want to go and get yourself killed? Or arrested? Don't you know there are laws that protect homeowners from uninvited guests?"

I kept my mouth shut. I tried to put the whole episode out of my head. It wasn't easy. I couldn't stop thinking how he followed Aidan and me to the park. He had apparently been close enough he could've grabbed Aidan during that short moment when I was on the other side of the pavilion. I shuddered in the steam coming off the pizza box. What had I gotten myself into with this guy? His behavior only confirmed my beliefs that he had done something to Dorothea. I couldn't let him bully me into doing nothing about it. I wasn't kidding when I told Mom I was through being pushed around and manipulated. But we'd been talking about Dylan's insolence and disrespect, not a crazy man who threatened Aidan.

What was I going to do?

Dylan glared at me over his pizza and made a point of not speaking directly to me. I knew his presence at the table was merely to remind me of the injustice shown him. If he knew how little his childish behavior mattered at the moment, he wouldn't bother.

With a final scathing look he disappeared upstairs. Scott played on the floor with Aidan while I cleared the table and set the dishwasher. When I turned around from filling the coffee filter for the next morning, Scott was in the doorway, his shoulder against the frame and his hands deep in his front pockets. The scowl on his face let me know he was prepared for battle.

I wasn't in the mood, but it couldn't be avoided.

"Dylan called me at work today," he started.

I looked around him to Aidan on the floor engrossed in play with a pile of trucks and motorcycles. "I figured as much."

"He said you kicked him out of the house."

I swallowed the desire to defend myself. I had nothing to defend myself against. "What did you say?"

His jaw hardened. "I told him I make the final decisions around here."

I really wasn't in the mood for this. "Oh, is that right?"

Scott's eyes widened for a split second, unaccustomed to me displaying anything resembling a backbone. Had I always been such a patsy? I thought of Gunnar's threats this afternoon.

It was bad enough being bullied by a stranger. I was through putting up with it in my own home?

Scott pushed away from the door and came over to me. "I thought we agreed the other day I had everything with Dylan under control."

"No, Scott, you agreed. I didn't say anything. Like always."

"What's wrong with that? I'm the head of the household. I thought that's how we wanted our home to run. It wasn't like I forced you into anything."

"No, you didn't. I have always wanted a Biblical household. But that's not what we have. The Bible warns over and over about the perils of putting the child in charge. We're proof of how well that works."

"What are you talking about, Joy? There's nothing wrong with this family. At least there wasn't until you decided to kick our teenage son out of the house because he didn't come home the moment you expected him to."

I left the counter to get a clear view of Aidan. I didn't want him to pick up on the tension in the kitchen. We'd made enough mistakes with Dylan. It might be too late to redeem him, but I wasn't going to repeat them with Aidan.

"I didn't kick Dylan out of the house. I simply presented him with some choices. I told him he could get a job, enroll in some classes, or move out. I don't think that's unreasonable."

Scott leaned his hips against the counter and stared as if he didn't recognize me. "I don't understand why you're in such a rush for him to grow up. He's going to be buried under responsibilities soon enough. Why can't he enjoy being a kid?"

"I have no problem with him having fun while he has the chance. What I have a problem with is him drifting with no plans for his future. He hasn't given a moment's thought to a career, going to school, or even to what he'll do next week. I don't expect him to know what he wants to do with the rest of his life. But it's not healthy that he has no clue of what interests him."

"So you're trying to force him to conform to what you think he should be."

My jaw dropped. "Of course not. That's ridiculous. I don't understand how you are so willing to let him keep floating along with no consequences for his actions."

"What actions? What has he done that's so terrible?"

Regardless of how badly I wanted to wrap my fingers around my husband's neck and squeeze until his eyes bugged out, I knew blowing up or losing my patience would get us nowhere. Scott reacted to every situation with logic and reason. He didn't lose his patience or act impulsively, and he didn't take seriously people who did. "Honey, don't tell me you haven't noticed the mood changes, his lack of friends, the late hours, and sleeping all day."

He snorted. "You just described every teenager who ever walked the earth."

"Possibly, but there's more to it. He flaunts his disrespect for our beliefs in our face. I for one, am tired of it. Maybe because I'm here all day and I take the brunt of his attitude, but also because most of it is directed at me."

"That's because you have always been so judgmental where he's concerned. He's been a disappointment to you since the day he was born and you don't even try to hide it."

Dylan had said the same thing this morning. I couldn't help wondering if Scott believed it or if he was simply repeating Dylan's words. "Scott, I love Dylan. I have never been disappointed in him. I just know he's capable of more than he's ever displayed. You're the one who doesn't have faith in him. When nothing is expected of him, that's exactly what he gives."

"When did you become an expert in human behavior? You have no right to talk about a young person's lack of ambition. The only thing you ever wanted was to sit at home and raise kids. You weren't even very good at it."

He couldn't have hurt me more if he had slapped me. I took great pride in my role as a stay at home mom. I believed it was the most important job in the world, and I did everything in my power to do it right. Yes, I had apparently missed the mark with Dylan, but I still believed my decision to stay home with the boys full time was the right one for us. I thought Scott believed it too.

"My decision not to go back to school was not from a lack of ambition. I wanted to do the best thing for our family."

"You always used that as an excuse not to apply yourself. You'd be done raising kids if you hadn't kept nagging me about another baby."

My eyes shot to Aidan in the other room. Hot tears filled my eyes. "I thought we both wanted to have Aidan," I said under my breath.

He shook his head in disgust. "Don't get hysterical. I'm not suggesting I don't love Aidan. All I'm saying is I didn't want another baby and you knew it. We had our hands full with Dylan. Maybe if you hadn't been so consumed with a baby, you could've put more effort into raising the one we had."

"Oh, is that right? I messed up all by myself, did I?"

"You were the one here with him day in and day out. You said so yourself. If any mistakes were made, they must've been made by you."

I hadn't wanted to turn this into a blame game, but I couldn't see how to avoid it now. "You never let me do what I wanted. I tried to warn you when he was little he was out of control. Our friends wouldn't visit us at gunpoint. Even our families didn't want him around. You said the problem was mine. Everything he did was my fault. Perhaps if you had done your job better as head of the household, we never would've lost control."

His dark eyes flashed. I had hit a nerve. I wondered if I'd gone too far. Then I recognized the same look in Gunnar's eyes today—the look designed to manipulate me into shutting up and playing nice the way the old Joy so willingly did.

"He's not out of control," Scott said through clenched teeth. "If anyone's out of control, Joy, it's you. I don't even know who you are anymore. Ever since Dorothea left town, you've become a different person. I'll be glad when she gets back and things around here go back to normal."

"You mean when I go back to being manageable?"

He threw his hands into the air. "Where do you come up with this stuff?"

"I get it from you and Dylan and everyone else who wants me to keep quiet and agree with whatever decisions are made for me."

"You are so emotional. I can't talk to you when you're like this."

"I'm through keeping my opinions to myself because they conflict with yours?"

He snorted again. His hand came down hard on the countertop. "I'm not arguing about this anymore, Joy. I'll tell you what I told Dylan when he called me at work. I'm not forcing him to make any serious life choices before he's ready. Your threat to kick him out has been rescinded."

I gasped. "Shouldn't you have talked this over with me first?"

"You mean the way you discussed it with me?"

"That was different, Scott. He disrespected me in front of Aidan. I wanted him to see—I wanted both of them to see--such behavior is no longer going to fly in this house. Do you want him living here when he's thirty with no signs of becoming an adult?"

"That isn't going to happen."

"Why not? We certainly are making it easy for him."

"Why shouldn't we? We're his parents. Parents are supposed to want their children's lives to be easier than theirs."

"I'm not trying to make his life difficult. I just want him to see the consequences of his actions."

"And I want you to lighten up. Stop trying to turn him into someone he's not."

It was my turn to drop my hand onto the countertop. "Fine, Scott. You're in charge. I hand it all over to you. You can handle him from now on out. You deal with it when he smokes dope in his room. You deal with the pornography on his computer. You handle it when he brings girls over for all night orgies when we're out of town."

His face turned red. "What girls?"

"Ask your son. I'm done." I pushed away from the counter and kicked a stool across the tile floor in my haste. I stormed out of the room, aware of Aidan's surprised gaze watching my exit.

I didn't know what Scott was doing. I didn't particularly care.

Chapter 19

I stayed upstairs the rest of the night. I wished I'd thought to bring the package of Macadamia nut cookies I'd bought at Kroger's with me. For my hips' sake, it was just as well they were downstairs with Scott. I wasn't going down there unless the house caught fire. Even then…well, I hadn't made up my mind about that yet.

Aidan brought a storybook into the bedroom and climbed up beside me. My only regret in blowing up at Scott was that it had upset Aidan. He wasn't used to arguing in our house. Like everyone else, he was accustomed to a meek, obedient mother who never made waves. He snuggled against me and lay perfectly still while I read the story three times through. Sometime during the second read-through I heard Dylan go downstairs and out the front door. Aidan and I lay still and listened as his car fired up and backed out of the driveway. When the sounds faded into the night, I went back to reading.

Scott came to bed a little after ten. I didn't want to go to sleep with this between us. I wanted to sink into his arms and confide my worries about Gunnar. I was worried about Dorothea even more than before. I didn't know what Gunnar was up to, but I knew after his reaction today he was capable of anything. He had threatened Aidan. But I couldn't tell Scott. He would accuse me of overreacting and sticking my nose in where it didn't belong, thus endangering our family. He would probably say he understood why Gunnar was outraged that a nosy neighbor sneaked into his house, and he would probably do the same thing if someone sneaked into our house uninvited.

Maybe he was right. Maybe I had no right to go into Dorothea's house. After she was found safe and sound, I would apologize to her for how I treated Gunnar. In my gut I knew we'd probably never have that conversation. I only hoped if something ever happened to me, someone would know me well enough to realize something was wrong. They would know if I would go on a cruise or to a mountain retreat or that I would never leave my plants to die untended on the windowsills or leave my good shoes on the back porch to get ruined by the rain. I was beginning to wonder if anyone knew me at all.

The next morning Scott and I didn't speak. No one had ever accused me of pettiness. I was always the one to bury the hatchet and take the first step toward peace. This time I didn't have it in me. As far as I was concerned what happened last night wasn't an argument. It was an epiphany. For the first time in our marriage I finally caught a glimpse of how Scott really saw me, and it broke my heart.

I still believed Scott loved me. I believed our marriage was strong. But he didn't respect me anymore than he did one of the boys' teachers or an elected official. I was doing a job I'd taken on when we married. I wasn't fabulous at it, but he knew no one else would want it so he had to make the best of my less that stellar capabilities.

Strangely I wasn't even sad about the realization. I was angry. More angry with myself than with him. He told me weeks ago if I wanted respect I needed to command it. I hadn't done it with the girl at camp who stole my canteen money. I hadn't done it with my own son who wrapped me around his little finger with every tantrum. I hadn't even done it with the man who stood before God and our loved ones and vowed to cherish me and love me every day of his life.

If I couldn't make that guy respect me, well, then I doubted there was much hope for me.

I didn't want to live the rest of my life like this. I didn't think for a minute God expected me to. I was supposed to be courageous. A lioness didn't ask before she roared if she would disturb the peace of the jungle. She roared and made her presence known. I wasn't a lion. I was a lamb. Less than a lamb. I was the annoying little squealer that made noise but only enough to annoy the hearer.

Well, no more.

I poured coffee into Scott's favorite mug and set it next to a blueberry cereal bar on the counter because I wasn't petty. Then I made myself scarce. I didn't want a goodbye kiss. I didn't even want an apology. If he tried to apologize when we both knew he didn't think he'd done anything wrong, I might have smacked him.

I went upstairs and dressed in a pair of jeans and a pretty blouse instead of my usual sweats and baggy tee shirt. In front of the mirror, I ran my fingers through my thick, dull blond hair and held it out away from my head. At its peak it was the color of sun-kissed wheat just before harvest. This time of year after being denied sunshine for six straight months, it was mousy and depressing. Every couple of years I got tired of looking at it and bought a box of hair color at Target. I turned my face from side to side and smoothed out the wrinkles around my mouth with my fingers. I couldn't do much about the toll of gravity on my face, but the color of my hair was an easy fix. I might even go to a salon this time. Scott liked to remind me he could afford to take care of this family. He could start with my hair.

I spotted Aidan watching me in the mirror. I grinned at his reflection. He didn't grin back. He was still traumatized by the way his father and I had rocked his secure little world last night.

I wouldn't apologize. I was through apologizing for having feelings and thoughts independent of my husband.

"Where are we going?" he asked in a tired voice.

"Nowhere."

"Then why are you putting on clothes?"

Good question. I laughed and squatted in front of him. "I just thought I'd put a little effort into myself today." I batted my mascara covered lashes at him. "How do I look?"

He giggled. "Beautiful. Just like church day."

I pulled him into my arms. "Thanks, Lima Bean. I really needed to hear that."

I never got around to calling a salon. Aidan and I spent the day in the family room putting together puzzles and watching nearly every movie we had saved on the DVR. We had popcorn and a fresh fruit platter for lunch. The Toyota was supposed to be ready tomorrow. If I still wanted to color my hair by evening, I'd hire one of the young moms from our church to watch Aidan and make an appointment for when I was out of the house to pick up the car.

I fixed oven fried chicken for dinner--a perennial favorite--along with a green salad and cheddar biscuits, to prove I was above throwing a can of chicken noodle soup down in front of Scott when he got home like a spiteful wife would do. I supposed proving I wasn't petty was the definition of true pettiness. I didn't care.

Scott came in the back door and set his briefcase on the counter. I knew something was up by the way he loosened his tie and wordlessly watched me take the chicken out of the oven. He never came into the kitchen while I was cooking. He knew I could handle it. I didn't ask what was on his mind. He'd tell me as much as I needed to know.

"Chris called me at work today."

I set the baking dish on the stovetop and slid the pan of biscuits into the oven. "Uh huh. Dinner will be on the table in five minutes."

He shed his jacket and draped it over his arm. "They want us to come up. Tomorrow. Dylan too."

The news didn't annoy me the way it usually did. "Guess it works out now that Dylan isn't working."

Scott looked slightly puzzled at my reaction but heartened I hadn't blown my top. "An internship at Chris's firm is opening up the end of May. He can get Dylan in if he wants it. They're hoping we can be there by mid-morning. That way Dylan can shadow Chris and see if it's something that interests him."

He paused, waiting for some kind of response. I moved to the refrigerator to get the salad.

"Funny how Chris calls out of the blue after we were talking last night about Dylan's future," he added with a cautious smile.

Is that what we'd been talking about? I thought I was talking about Dylan's future and Scott was ordering me to calm down and get off the boy's back.

Scott looked more relieved by the moment. I hadn't yet screamed or insulted his brother or burned his dinner. Things were looking up. "What do you think?" he asked. "It's a great opportunity."

"Sounds like it."

I didn't bother to remind Scott he had been trying to get Dylan interested in a business career since we took the training wheels off his bicycle. Dylan made it clear he'd rather pull latrine duty on Guantanamo Bay than do what Scott did every day for the rest of his life.

"If nothing else, it'll get Dylan out of the house for the summer. It's definitely too far for him to commute. He'll have to stay with Chris and Valerie."

Even I didn't dislike Valerie that much.

I could see what Scott was doing. This was his olive branch. He didn't agree with me, but he was willing to push our little bird out of the nest, at least as far as Indianapolis.

"I was going to call from work to clear it with you first, but I went ahead and took tomorrow off. I know it's hard for you to get Aidan up that early, but if we leave by eight, we'll be there in plenty of time to get Dylan downtown so he won't miss much of the morning."

I took salad bowls out of the cabinet and carried them, along with the salad, to the dining room table. "Why not leave tonight? It's only a two-hour drive. That way Dylan could be with Chris the whole day and no one will have to get up so early."

He beamed. "Babe, you're the best. I was afraid you wouldn't want to go."

"Oh, I don't want to go. And I'm not." I set the four salad bowls around the table and turned to face him. "But you go and have a great time."

"Joy." His voice was stern. "Don't be childish."

"If I was childish, I'd stomp my feet and throw a fit. I'm a grown woman and I don't want to go, so I'm not going."

"You expect me to take Dylan myself. What will I tell Chris and Valerie? They'll think we're fighting."

"Don't forget Aidan. He's going with you."

His knuckles whitened around his suit jacket. I'd press out the wrinkles later. "You're just mad about last night. That's why you're not going."

I shook my head. "Last night has nothing to do with it. I'm not going because I don't want to. I have things planned around here, and I'll get a lot more accomplished without Aidan under my feet. I need to pick up the car at the garage, and Martin is coming to check out Dorothea's yard. I need to make sure he does things the way she likes."

"Martin's been her yardman for years. He knows more about what Dorothea likes than you do."

"No one knows more about Dorothea than I do," I said just as stern. I exhaled and smiled benignly. "It's the least I can do for her. You take the boys and have a nice weekend with your family."

The more I thought about the idea, the more I liked it. Especially about having Aidan out of the neighborhood for a few days. Gunnar's threats still sent chills down my spine every time I thought of them. I didn't think he would actually use the keys to our house, not as long as I stayed over here out of his way. But I would sleep better tonight knowing Aidan was safely tucked away in Indianapolis.

I couldn't remember the last time I'd had the house to myself for a whole weekend. Probably the weekend before Dylan was born. It was tough saying goodbye to Aidan. I'd never spent a night without him under the same roof. Truth be told, it was even a little hard saying goodbye to Scott and Dylan. I hugged and kissed them both and told them I loved them. But when the car turned the corner, I felt almost giddy with the sense of freedom. I didn't know what to do with myself. My excitement dimmed a little after waiting at the body shop nearly an hour before my car was ready. I expected them to realize they were dealing with a new and improved Joy Kessler and speed up the process. Apparently they hadn't gotten the memo since I sat in the drafty waiting room with all the other peons. Finally the forms were filled out and I was once again behind the wheel of my beloved Toyota. I couldn't tell it had been in an accident, though I supposed after three and a half weeks in the shop they could've built me three new cars instead of just fixing the one.

At Target I bought a box of Beach Blonde Number Ten. As soon as I found out the salon charged seventy-five dollars for color and highlights I lost my determination to teach my husband a lesson. I wanted him to know I was serious about things changing around the house. I just wasn't willing to spend so much money to do it. The new color was within the range of my natural color but a few shades lighter than anything I'd tried before. I wanted to look like myself, just a fresher and hopefully thinner version. I wondered if Scott would like it. I wondered if he'd notice. I reminded myself all that mattered was I liked it.

I felt so good about saving seventy-five dollars on the hair color I decided to treat myself to takeout from my favorite Chinese restaurant. Aidan didn't like Chinese food, so I never brought it home. On the rare occasions Scott and I were out together, we would go someplace special like the Montgomery Inn. Something as simple as ordering whatever I wanted from Chinese takeout was a treat for me.

I arrived home a little after one, hungry and ready to devour my lunch. Exercising incredible restraint, which wasn't that hard since I'd snitched an egg roll and wonton on the way home, I set the carryout bags aside and began putting away groceries. I had bought several healthy food options at the grocery. The new Joy didn't want to keep wearing frumpy Mom clothes that caught in all the wrong places. I wanted to look attractive for my husband. That was going to take more than a bottle of hair color. Not only did I want to lose a few pounds, I wanted to bend over to pick up toys without getting light headed. I might even work out this weekend. If Scott was determined to live to be a hundred, I needed to make sure I was around to keep an eye on him. My anger and frustration toward him had cooled while I waited for the car. He was a good husband and loving father. Every parent wanted to give their children more chances than they deserved. He had been listening last night or he wouldn't have taken Dylan and Aidan to Indianapolis for the weekend by himself.

I wondered idly what they were doing. If Dylan was at the firm with Chris, Aidan had Scott all to himself. I don't think that had ever happened before. Aidan was a great kid, as Scott would soon figure out. Hopefully he'd learn more about Dylan, too, and Dylan would realize Scott and I only wanted the best for him. I hoped he liked working with Chris. Not only would it get him out of the house for the summer, it would get him away from his friends and give him a chance to figure out what he wanted to do with his future. Even if he decided not to go into business like Scott and Chris, he might still find his niche.

By the time the groceries were put away, I could no longer resist the siren's song of my takeout. I fixed a small plate with some veggies from the fridge and lowfat dressing for dipping. The best part about Chinese food was leftovers so I'd savor this meal the rest of the day. I thought of Aidan and Scott probably eating cheeseburgers in a downtown restaurant while Chris showed Dylan the life of a working man. I missed them already. I wondered if Scott was having the same feelings of regret that haunted me. I couldn't stay mad at him no matter what he did. I hated that we'd barely spoken last night. I thought of calling him but resisted. He and Aidan needed some serious bonding time. I wouldn't interrupt, even if it was to tell Scott I loved him and couldn't wait till he got home Sunday night.

I wondered how things were going for Dylan. I hoped a little of Chris's drive and ambition rubbed off on him over the weekend. He could certainly stand a fire lit under him. If anyone could motivate him without trying it would be Chris.

I ate the bigger half of my lunch and washed the few dishes from my breakfast of juice and bagels. I noticed a ring of grime around the canister while drying the counter so I took everything off and gave it a good scrubbing. That led to taking a bucket and sponge from under the sink and washing down the cabinet fronts. I couldn't remember the last time I'd done it. The refrigerator and stove looked dingy next to the gleaming cabinets so I emptied the contents of the fridge down the sink, then cleaned the stove and oven.

Upstairs I changed into my workout clothes and laced up my cross trainers. I hurried downstairs, avoiding the mirror and any other shiny surface that might throw my reflection back at me. Before I could talk myself out of it or get lured back into the kitchen with my Chinese food, I rooted around in the entertainment center until I found the workout DVD I had done a couple of times with Aidan. With the stereo blasting to drown out the annoying shrieks from the crew in the studio, I jumped and cavorted around the family room. I found Scott's dumbbells behind the recliner and slung them around a few times. I wasn't very graceful, and I went left when everyone else went right, but I felt like I was doing something good for myself, something just for me.

The workout left me energetic instead of tired and frustrated like it usually did. I wondered if this was the runner's high I heard so much about. No wonder Scott was into it.

I carried the weights into the front room we seldom used and switched on the TV in there. Another perk of having the house to myself was watching whatever I wanted on TV. I could only hope one of the classic movie channels was playing Gone With the Wind or a Jane Austen marathon. Living in a house of men meant chick flicks were seldom seen on my TV. I did a few bicep curls and overhead presses while scrolling through the guide. No guilty pleasures until after I ran the sweeper and took a shower. Then I could relax with no more chores hanging over my head. I switched to the local news, then hauled the vacuum out of the closet. As I straightened from plugging it in, I saw movement across the street at Dorothea's.

I dropped onto my knees on the couch and peered out. It was only late afternoon so I was confident Gunnar couldn't see me watching if he happened to look over. Despite knowing how light and shadows worked, I lowered my head to peer over the back of the couch just in case. I was glad Scott wasn't here to see me. Without a glance in my direction, Gunnar climbed into his little car and backed out of the driveway. I watched his progress until he turned at the intersection and drove out of sight.

I chewed my bottom lip as I switched the vacuum on. I pushed the machine back and forth across the carpet and thought about Gunnar and why he left such a bad taste in my mouth. It wasn't out of the realm of possibility that Dorothea had gone to visit her nephew and his family. Maybe Cathy,

Gunnar's mother, had already scheduled a cruise. She might've shown Dorothea the brochures and her wardrobe for the trip and talked Dorothea into joining her.

Who knew? Stranger things had happened. I'd lived long enough to know people were capable of surprising me. Dorothea was a spontaneous, adventurous person. Why wouldn't she take a cruise? Maybe spontaneity was what it took to get her onto the open water.

I put an attachment onto the sweeper hose and began cleaning between the couch cushions. While I worked I prayed to God. Last night I told Scott he could have all our problems with Dylan. I was through. Extracting oneself from motherhood was not that simple. I couldn't give Scott my burdens if I wanted to. The only one who could handle them was God. But I couldn't turn them over in the heat of anger and frustration like I had with Scott. This needed to be a sincere parting of my own ways and letting God take the reins in my life. I couldn't control Dylan. I couldn't turn him into a responsible young man who revered women and wanted to work. He had a say in it. I had done my job with him as a mother. I had made some serious mistakes, and there were no do-overs. The damage was done. All I could do now was stop making the same mistakes and pray God would show him grace and mercy and teach him to make the right choices.

I wanted him in church again. Scott and I needed to stop making it easy for him to miss Sunday morning services. They wouldn't be back home for church this weekend, but starting next week, Dylan was going to join his family for worship. That was just the beginning. He could start pulling his weight in chores around the house until he found a job. I prayed Scott would support me, and Dylan wouldn't give me too much headache about it.

I couldn't change my son. I needed to accept that. He was his own person. Even parents who did everything right sometimes ended up with kids who wouldn't listen to a thing they said. All I could do was stand on my principals and my faith and pray I didn't lose my son to the world.

I also prayed for my marriage. Scott loved me, and I loved him. I didn't agree with my mother and think all men were waiting for an opportunity to cheat on their wives. There were other things that could drive a couple apart. Like not respecting and honoring each other. Now that I thought about it, it had been a long time since I showed honor to Scott. As Dylan grew more and more out of control, I began to lose my respect for Scott as a father and a man of God. He hadn't taken his obligations seriously so I stopped taking him seriously. That was wrong.

I toed off the sweeper and sank onto the couch cushions I had pushed onto the floor while vacuuming. I muted the TV and prayed for a long time, seeking the Lord for forgiveness, compassion for my family, and strength to handle the struggles ahead. I prayed Dorothea would be home soon and she was all right. I even prayed for Gunnar. I believed he was up to no good, but according to Mrs. Kinnamon, he had serious problems. Like Dylan, he might not realize it. He could use a little compassion from me.

After my prayers I put the couch cushions back into place and plumped the throw pillows. I dropped onto the sofa, emotionally and spiritually tired, but feeling better than I had in weeks. I stared at the TV screen for a moment, still lost in thought until I realized what I was looking at. I grabbed the remote and hit the mute button. The announcer's voice filled the room.

"Now to the story we've been covering all afternoon," began the blond anchorwoman with the oversized smile whose name I could never remember. "Authorities have recovered the body of a young woman in a car taken from the river near the bridge spanning Highway 18 near Florence, Kentucky early this morning. The car, discovered by a passing motorist, was thought to be abandoned until rescuers were able to reach it. The young woman inside the car has not yet been identified.

Tanner Willamette has been on the scene all afternoon. We'll go there now for the latest. Tanner?"

A handsome thirtyish field reporter with a piercing gaze and obligatory scowl stood across the road from the scene where authorities encircled a tow truck and muddy sports car.

"Officials believe the car has been in the water south of the Fields Ertel Bridge just across the river in Kentucky for several days," Tanner told the viewing audience. "It is believed the young woman was put behind the wheel of the car post mortem and the car pushed off the road. Police are searching databanks for missing women who fit the description, but so far they do not know her identity. Officials have set up a special hotline for any tips concerning this crime. Authorities assure us the tip line does not have caller ID and callers will remain anonymous."

As Tanner talked I got off the couch like a woman in a trance and approached the television. The LED screen of the TV I had been against Scott purchasing emitted a crystal clear picture. I could make out every detail, including the slight cleft in Tanner's chin and the color of the sheriff's eyes as he oversaw the operation. The camera cut back to Tanner, but not before giving me a close view of the backend of the car where the license plate had been pried off before plunging into the water. I pointed the remote at the TV and froze the picture.

I covered my mouth to stifle a scream.

It was Kimberly's car.

Chapter 20

I replayed the segment three times, even going back to the part I had missed while I was praying. The car had been forced off the road. There were no suspects or motives at this point, mostly because the woman in the car remained unknown. But not for long.

I needed to call the police. I was nearly to the phone when I began to second guess myself. What if it wasn't Kimberly's car? There were plenty of little red cars in the city driven by young women. If I called with nothing more to go on than I didn't like my neighbor and I had heard him fighting with his girlfriend a few nights ago when I sneaked over to spy on them, I would sound like a kook or a nosy neighbor with an ax to grind. Kimberly would be found safe and sound wherever she belonged, and Scott would never leave me home alone again.

I went back to the couch and looked over at Dorothea's empty driveway. I wished I had Kimberly's phone number, or even her last name. I could call her family and find out if they knew where she was. Not liking Gunnar was not enough of a reason to suspect him of killing her and pushing her car into the river.

I stared at the driveway for several minutes, something nagging at the edge of my mind. My stomach finally began to growl, and I remembered the rest of my Chinese takeout in the kitchen alongside my Beach Blond Number Ten hair color. I would think better on a full stomach.

I took a heavy bowl out of the cabinet and the leftovers out of the fridge. I prayed the girl in the car wasn't Kimberly. It was certainly a selfish prayer because someone's daughter, someone's sister, had died in that river. I prayed for the young woman's family. I prayed for authorities and that she would be identified soon.

I thought of Gunnar as he spun out of Dorothea's driveway in his little car. Where was he going? Had he seen the same segment I had? Was he on his way to identify the body? Was he running away? Was he disposing of evidence?

I tried to recall everything Kimberly said to Gunnar the night she left. She told him they had wasted enough time looking for something that probably wasn't inside the house. Kimberly knew what Gunnar was looking for. Had he feared she would go to the police? Or did he think she might've found the cache on her own and was going to sell it and keep the money for herself? I remembered how he told her she better not double cross him. It sure sounded like a threat to me, and it had sounded like one to Kimberly.

I didn't like the path my mind had taken. If Gunnar was capable of doing something to his girlfriend, he was certainly capable of hurting an old woman who stood between him and whatever it was he was hoping to find in Dorothea's house. He wouldn't think twice about getting me out of his way either. Or anyone I held dear.

My heart thudded in my chest. I stared at the Chinese food I had just spooned into the bowl. Suddenly I realized what had been bothering me since Gunnar pulled out of the driveway. He had been driving Dorothea's car since she left for her alleged vacation. Since Monday--the last time I'd seen Kimberly--he was back in his own car.

Why? Where was Dorothea's car and why wasn't he driving it?

The first splatters of rain hit the sidewalk in front of me as I stepped off my porch. I ducked my head and hunched my shoulders inside Dylan's windbreaker. I looked up and down the street, almost hoping a neighbor would be out walking, preferably a sane person with whom I could share my suspicions so they could tell me I was overreacting…again. They had seen Kimberly just today and she was fine and Dorothea had called and would be home this evening.

It was nearly dark on another rainy night, the last day of a soggy April. Dorothea certainly hadn't missed much while she was away, except for her flowerbeds going to seed and me slowly going out of my mind.

I looked in the direction Gunnar had taken then hurried across the street. I headed straight for the garage. I was confident as long as I didn't go inside, I would hear if Gunnar came home and I could take off through the neighbors' backyards and circle the block to my house. He'd never know I was here.

I'd only take a moment. I just needed to see Dorothea's car to put my mind to rest that Gunnar had nothing to do with the sports car they fished out of the river. I looked again toward the intersection before hurrying up the short driveway to the house. I wondered what the rest of the neighbors would think if they saw me skulking about. Like Scott, they had probably stopped paying attention years ago to the crazy stuff I did.

I headed around the side of the garage. My foot nearly went out from under me. I looked down at a trail of green liquid coming from under Dorothea's garage door. I took another step and came to a dead stop.

A sticky sweet, metallic smell rushed up at me. An image of Red-face's car buried in the front of my Toyota came back to me in a flash. The sound of metal grinding against metal and the steering wheel wrenched from my grasp. I had smelled the same odor when the tow truck driver hooked the winch to the front of Red-face's car and saw a similar green puddle on the asphalt as he towed the car away.

Antifreeze. A telltale sign of a front end collision.

I knelt closer to the trail of fluid under the door and inhaled. My stomach hurled.

I straightened and stormed around the garage to the side door. As expected the door was locked. I stretched on the tips of my toes and felt along the ledge above the door. Either Gunnar didn't know about the hidden key, or he hadn't thought to hide it from his nosy neighbor. Score one for the nosy neighbor.

I let myself into the garage and waited a moment for my eyes to adjust to the gloom. Dorothea's Crown Vic took up most of the space. There was only a narrow path all the way around it in which to walk. I edged along the length of the car and circled the front end. The open side door threw a rectangle of light across the hood of the car. I could barely see the front. I wished I'd thought to bring a flashlight with me. I couldn't risk turning on the overhead light. I leaned in close and stretched out my hand. My fingers felt the damage before my eyes saw it.

The grill was cracked. The center half of the front fender was pushed in as if something had punched the Crown Vic in the nose. As my eyes grew accustomed to the dim light, I noticed gouges of paint in the smashed-in chrome. Just to be sure I saw what I thought I was seeing, I scratched the gouges with my fingernail and held them out to the light.

Red paint that matched the car they'd pulled from the river flaked under my nails. Kimberly's car.

I leaned over and took a few deep breaths. If I had anything on my stomach, I would have lost it in Dorothea's garage.

I ran to the door of the utility room that entered into the kitchen. It opened easily in my hand. Gunnar must've thought since the garage was locked, he needn't lock the interior door. Big mistake.

Something else had been bugging me since I sneaked into the house the other day. I remembered the picture of Aidan on the refrigerator in the frame he had made a few months ago during arts and crafts time at playgroup. *For someone I love* had been stenciled in cheery letters. When Dorothea expressed pleasure at the crooked row of Popsicle sticks, he proudly presented it to her.

I remembered my disappointment. I had thought the frame was meant for me.

Dorothea read my expression. "I'm sure your mommy would love to have this," she told Aidan.

"But I want you to have it. Mommy's got plenty of stuff I make."

So that was that. Dorothea promptly put a picture of Aidan in the frame and hung it on her refrigerator. I remembered seeing the frame the day I sneaked into the house while I was adjusting the calendar. I had been in such a hurry and so worried about getting caught I barely noticed it. Something had been nagging me about it. I hadn't connected the dots at the time, but now I was pretty sure why that little detail had lodged in my brain.

I hurried to the refrigerator. Just as I thought, the clue Dorothea had left behind was staring back at me from my son's picture frame. Aidan's picture had been replaced with one of me. The picture currently in the crooked, handmade frame was taken last year during the neighborhood Christmas party Dorothea always hosted. Someone had snapped a not-so-attractive shot of me bent over the buffet table pouring eggnog into a jewel toned plastic cup. There I was on Dorothea's fridge in all my glory, looking over my shoulder straight into the camera with my mouth half open, lights from the Christmas tree illuminating my double chin, and my rear end looking larger than life—as if any part of my body needed enlargement.

The first time I saw the picture I wanted to rip it to shreds. I couldn't believe Dorothea had paid money to print it. She wouldn't let me tear it up but promised it would never see the light of day. Now here it was on her refrigerator in Aidan's frame. Gunnar never would've hung a picture of me on the fridge. Maybe on a dartboard but never in a frame that read *For Someone I Love*.

I cast my eyes around the room. Gunnar had killed Kimberly after the fight I overheard Monday night. She had argued with him about selling Albert's watch. For some reason, Gunnar had seen her departure as a threat to whatever he was doing in Dorothea's house.

I stood in the center of the kitchen as the pieces fell into place. I knew now what he had done and chastised myself for not realizing it sooner. I headed back to the utility room and threw open the door on the other side of the washer and dryer.

A light was on in the basement, just as I suspected it would be. I clattered down the stairs nearly losing my balance. I grabbed the banister at the bottom of the stairs and swung to the left. Dorothea looked up at me from an old rocking chair she didn't use anymore.

"Dorothea," I shrieked, my knees weak from adrenaline and relief at seeing her in one piece.

She looked a little pale, but none the worse for wear. She was dressed in a pale yellow pants suit and held a crocheting project in her lap. Her hook came to a stop when she looked up at me.

She sat back in her chair and put her hand over her heart. "Thank the Lord. I knew you'd come."

Then her gaze traveled beyond me. Her expression hardened. Something foul smelling and cloying clamped over my mouth. The basement went dark.

Chapter 21

My eyes felt like someone had put sand under my eyelids and glued them shut. After what seemed like several minutes of concentrating on nothing else, I opened one and then the other. I blinked and tried to lift a hand to my face. My limbs felt like lead. I shifted, and the familiar smell of my own house rose like a cloud around me. The room was so dark I could barely see, but I recognized the seldom used sofa in our front room I had cleaned earlier.

How had I gotten here? Where was Gunnar or whoever had put the rag over my face? With great effort, I waited until my eyes grew accustomed to the dark before I shifted as gingerly as I could.

A piercing pain shot through the right side of my head and out my right eye. My first thought was residual pain from whatever he had used to drug me. I realized I had a knot behind my ear. My hand moved toward the knot, the effects of the drugs wearing off enough that I could move in what felt like slow motion.

I needn't have gone to such lengths to be quiet. "You're awake." I recognized Gunnar's voice in the darkness.

I turned my head in the direction of his voice. The drapes were drawn over the picture window that faced the street. Through the cracks I saw the streetlights had come on, but it wasn't completely dark outside. I must not have been out too long.

"You hit me."

"No, I dropped you. You don't skip many meals, do you?"

"I'm working out." I bit my tongue. No need to explain to this jerk why I wasn't a size four.

I heard him shift on the occasional chair my mother passed on to us when she redecorated her condo two years ago. "After you lost consciousness I carried you upstairs. I lost my grip about halfway up and banged your head on the banister."

It sounded like something that might happen to Lucy and Ethel if they were ever kidnapped. I bit back a laugh as pain once again shot out my right eye. The whole situation was so ludicrous I couldn't believe it had happened. "How did you get me across the street?"

"It wasn't easy. I didn't want the neighbors to see me putting you in and out of my car. I just put my arm around you and half walked, half carried you across. Thankfully, this infernal rain has kept everyone indoors."

I snorted. "Yeah, lucky for me."

I heard rather than saw him stand and approach the couch. I tensed. My mind whirled with escape scenarios. There was no way I could overpower or outrun him. I'd have to rely on cunning and dumb luck to get away. I didn't believe in dumb luck, and I was fresh out of cunning. I'd have to think of something else.

Gunnar sat down on the edge of the couch. Fear gripped my insides, and my bladder loosened. *Dear God, thank you Scott and the boys aren't here right now.* I hated being alone with this monster, but I didn't want to put them in danger because I had followed Gunnar around like a bloodhound for the last three weeks.

I braced myself against the couch cushions and prepared to launch across the room. It wasn't far to the front door. If I could get a running start, I could maneuver through the downstairs in the darkness and possibly get away. He grabbed my forearm and held on tight. "Don't try it."

I inhaled, filling my lungs to blast out a scream that would bring my neighbors out of their dry, cozy houses. His other hand clamped over my mouth, jamming my lips against my teeth. "I'd keep quiet if I were you. You might remember I still have your friend next door. By the time the police got here, you and she would both be dead."

Relief surged through me at his threat. Dorothea was still alive. I didn't know how, but I needed to make sure she and I stayed that way.

Gunnar slowly lowered his hand from my mouth. He leaned toward me. I held my breath until I realized he was just resituating himself. Something solid and metallic whacked against his leg. My heart sank. I'd never held a gun in my hands, but I definitely recognized the sound. I took a deep breath and willed my heart to stop pounding.

I unstuck my tongue from the roof of my mouth and managed a painful swallow.

"Who are you?" I croaked.

The white of his teeth gleamed in the darkness. He loosened his grip on my arm but didn't let go. "Who do you think I am?"

"I know you're not Gunnar Westlake."

He let go of my arm and stood up. I sank against the cushions in relief. Even though he was still in control, I felt better with a little distance between us. Keeping an eye on me, he moved across the room. At the window he flicked back the curtain and glanced out. The window faced the Townsends' house. They were probably sitting down to dinner in their great room right now. From that window I could throw something against the side of their house. They might hear and come to see what was wrong. The only problem was Gunnar, or whoever he was, was at the window. Even if he wasn't, the window stuck, and I could never get it up on my own.

He turned back to look at me. "What gave me away?"

"Your teeth."

"Pardon?"

"Your right canine overlaps the one behind it." I licked my lips to put a little moisture in my mouth. My head was pounding. I wanted to lie back and bury my head in the sofa cushions, but I had to keep my wits about me. Now wasn't the time to give in to panic or self-pity. I sat up a little straighter. "It's barely noticeable, but orthodontia would've corrected it. Mrs. Kinnamon remembered you…I mean Gunnar, wearing braces all through middle school."

His smile widened. "Mrs. Kinnamon?"

"The woman who lived next to the Westlakes in Chicago while Gunnar was growing up. I found her address on the Internet when I tore the page out of the address book."

The corners of his mouth twitched as he dropped the curtain. "Sounds like I should've talked to Mrs. Kinnamon before coming here."

"Maybe you should have."

The phone rang, sending my heart into warp speed. I shrieked and covered my heart with my hand. Both our heads swiveled toward the phone on the side table. "That's Scott. He'll know something's wrong if I don't answer."

"He'll figure out what as soon as he gets home."

I didn't want to consider the implications in that statement. "If he doesn't get me here, he'll try my cell. He probably wants to make sure everything went okay with the car at the body shop. He'll keep calling until I answer."

Gunnar shook his head. "No, he won't. He'll figure you're running errands and forgot your phone or let the battery go dead. You're the type to do that. Or he'll figure you're still pouting over your fight two nights ago and are not answering to prove a point."

"How did you know we were fighting?" Before he could answer I waved my hand. "Never mind. I don't want to know."

The phone rang a fourth time. The answering machine picked up in the kitchen. We sat in the darkness for a moment but couldn't hear well enough from this end of the house to tell who was on the line. I didn't want to think I might never hear my husband's voice again.

"He'll send one of the neighbors to check on me."

He shook his head again. "He won't want to inconvenience anyone. I imagine he's having too much fun without you bringing down the party to give you more than a passing thought."

I clenched my teeth. Right again. How tragic that I was so transparent a complete stranger knew more about my marriage than I did.

I needed to stall for time while I figured out how to get Dorothea and me out of this mess. "Since you're not Gunnar Westlake, would you at least tell me who you really are?"

"What difference does it make?"

A slash of light from between the curtains illuminated his face. A five o'clock shadow roughened his narrow jaw line. Crow's feet had just begun to form at the corners of his eyes. I should've noticed earlier how much older he was than Gunnar Westlake. Dorothea told me she hadn't seen Gunnar in twenty years when he was only three. This guy was easily close to thirty.

"After all we've been through together I have a right to know your real name."

He lifted a shoulder. "I suppose it doesn't matter now. It's not like you'll have the chance to do anything with the information."

I refused to acknowledge what he meant by that.

"My name is Brian Russell."

Brian Russell. What a benign name. With a start I realized much of my fear had dissipated. Peace flooded me as if Jesus were sitting beside me telling me everything would be okay. I supposed he was. Either I had resigned myself to death and what awaited me on the other side was glorious and worth every trial I'd been through in life. Or God was letting me know Dorothea and I would get out of this alive and I didn't need to be afraid. In the meantime I needed to stay calm and learn as much about the Gunnar imposter as I could.

I pulled myself into a sitting position and gingerly touched the sore spot on the back of my head. The goose's egg knot pushed out through my hair. My fingers didn't feel any moisture so at least I wasn't bleeding. That was a good sign. I wondered if the medical examiner would notice the spot during my autopsy. Would it raise suspicion if Brian tried to make my death look accidental? Did real M.E.'s even notice stuff like that?

I dropped my hand and tried to stop thinking about autopsies and unexplained household accidents. "Since the day Dorothea introduced us, I've been trying to figure out what you were after. Now that I know you're not Gunnar Westlake, I'm even more confused. Dorothea isn't rich. The real Gunnar must've told you that."

He grunted. "Gunnar had a big mouth. He was the most boring individual you'd ever want to meet. If it weren't for his propensity to blab his business to the world without discretion, you and I wouldn't be in this situation."

"Is that why you killed him?"

He arched an eyebrow. "What makes you think he's dead?"

"He was a loose end. Like Kimberly. He hadn't been in touch with his family in years. You couldn't take the chance he'd call home or his mother might call Dorothea's house while you were here doing whatever it is you're doing."

He smiled appreciatively and relaxed a little. His right hand hung loosely against his leg. I couldn't see it in the dark, but I knew that's where he held the gun. There was no way I could wrestle it away from him, but if I could get him to lower his guard enough to put it down, I'd have a tiny window of opportunity in which to escape.

He leaned a shoulder against the window frame. "I thought about making Gunnar part of the plan. It didn't take long to realize he didn't have it in him. He couldn't stop whining for two minutes about the rotten hand life had dealt him. Not to mention he didn't know how to keep his big mouth shut. I knew he'd tell someone what we were doing before we finished the job."

"And Kimberly? Wouldn't she let you finish the job?" I already knew the answer, but I wanted to keep him talking.

"She was in on it from the beginning. I wish I never involved her. I had no way of knowing she'd turn on me."

"Because you stole Albert's watch."

"Should I ask how you know that?"

"The same way you know Scott and I have been fighting. The only thing I don't know is why you came here in the first place."

"I suppose it doesn't matter now if I tell you or not."

My chest tightened. Coming clean with me meant I had become a loose end like Gunnar and Kimberly. He planned to take care of me the same way he had them.

"I met Gunnar Westlake in Ventura Beach, California where he'd been bumming around for a few years. I don't know if anyone told you this, but the guy was a loser. Talk about entitlement issues." Brian exhaled and shook his head in disgust. "According to him, his great-grandfather was the team doctor for the Brooklyn Dodgers. You know, the ones who moved to Los Angeles. He only worked there a few years but long enough to build an incredibly valuable collection."

I swung my legs off the side of the couch and leaned forward. My head swam. I blinked away the black dots in front of my eyes. "I think I knew that. Dorothea has some baseballs and stuff in a display case in her living room."

The pseudo-Gunnar smirked. "Yeah. Baseballs and stuff. Somewhere in the neighborhood of several million dollars."

I nearly fell off the couch. "No way. There isn't that much. An autographed ball and maybe some rookie cards. But nothing worth millions of dollars."

He exhaled as though he couldn't imagine anyone being so dense. "An autographed team ball from the 1955 World Series. Jackie Robinson. Babe Ruth. Those names ring a bell? According to Gunnar, the doctor had an amazing collection, a lot more than Dorothea has in her display case. Mint condition. The autographed special edition Robinson rookie card alone is worth a quarter of a mil."

My eyes bulged. "That's why you were taking Dorothea's house apart."

"The old man left the entire collection to Albert, the older brother." He smirked again. "After getting to know Gunnar it wasn't hard to figure out why. If Stephen was anything like Gunnar, no wonder his dad didn't trust him with something so valuable. Stephen probably would've sold the whole collection for a handful of magic beans."

Dorothea had pretty much told me the same thing the day before she disappeared.

"I'm sure you've realized by now there's no collection like that in Dorothea's house. If there ever had been, she and Albert would've put it in a safety deposit box at the bank."

Brian shook his head. "That shows how much you know. Gunnar insisted Albert had a safe built into the house. He wanted the collection close to him. Sentimental to a fault."

That sounded like Dorothea. "What makes you think she didn't sell part of it or give it to a museum years ago?"

"I did my research before I wasted the gas to get here. Those cards and memorabilia aren't on any database in the country. They're unaccounted for, which means they're part of a private collection. They've been stashed across the street for decades."

"You could've just asked her. She either would've told you or said it was none of your business."

"Or she didn't tell me because they're all she has left of Albert, and she doesn't want to lose them."

"No," I said, feeling confident for the first time since coming to. "She wouldn't lie to you. She couldn't. Whatever she told you was the truth."

His lips curved again in approval. "I've come to realize that much is true."

I watched Brian's face. Why was Dorothea still alive when he killed Gunnar and Kimberly the instant they became liabilities? Brian was a murderer and a thief, but he had kept Dorothea relatively comfortable in her basement for three weeks. God had surely shown her grace and favor in this situation. Would he show the same to me? I wasn't nearly as good a person as Dorothea. I wasn't wise and discerning and compassionate like her. I yelled at my husband and kicked my own son out of the house. I wasn't a very good mother, and my skills as a wife were obviously suspect. Dare I even ask him to show me the same favor he had shown Dorothea?

I forced my train of thought to a halt. There were no degrees of righteousness. I was just as saved as Dorothea even though it didn't look that way most of the time. Jesus would've hung on the cross if I'd been the only sinner. He'd have done it if Brian were the only one.

This was not God's plan for my life. I still had things to do. I had two children to finish raising. Aidan would turn five in August. He needed me. Dylan needed me, too, though he only realized it when he was hungry or out of clean underwear.

Even Scott needed me. My eyes misted. I couldn't let our last words said to each other be thrown in anger. I didn't want him to live with the fact that he never got to tell me he loved me one last time. I wanted to tell him again I still loved him even though he sometimes drove me crazy. I was sorry I hadn't been honest with him over the years about what I wanted. I had let him take the lead with the boys because it was easier than standing up to him. Though I told myself I wanted to be a submissive wife, I was really a coward. Following his lazy parenting had been easier than standing up to him or alienating the boys.

It wasn't too late. I could still claim victory over this situation. I was alive. Gunnar or Brian or whoever he was, hadn't killed me yet. I wasn't ready to leave my husband to another woman. I didn't want Aidan to grow up without me. I certainly didn't intend to lose Dylan to a world bent on destroying him.

Think, Joy, think. This is your house. You know it better than some thug who plans to steal your life from you. You can't overpower him or outrun a bullet. But you have your brains. You figured everything else out. You can figure this out too.

I closed my eyes in the darkness and prayed for God's help. I needed him more than I ever had before. I knew he didn't want me to die in this house. Nor did he want me to give into fear. I'd done that my whole life. Not anymore. I needed to fight. I needed to fight for Dylan. For my marriage. For Dorothea. I needed to fight for myself.

For the first time in my life I had absolutely no one to rely on but God. I couldn't ask Dorothea for advice. Scott couldn't pay my way out of the situation. My mother couldn't berate me into becoming a better decision maker. I was totally dependent on God and the wisdom he'd given me over the years. It was a terrifying position. It was also absolutely exhilarating.

Chapter 22

"I need to use the bathroom."

"Huh uh."

"Please. You can't let me sit here and wet my pants."

"In a little while it won't matter, I guarantee it."

"What does that mean?"

"Don't worry about it."

I wanted to tell him to just go ahead then and do whatever he was planning. I couldn't stand the waiting. Despite my fledgling courage, I wasn't ready to sign my death warrant just yet. "There's a bathroom right there in the hallway." I pointed through the door.

He exhaled and pushed off the wall. He motioned me up with the hand holding the gun. The light glinted off of it. It was a lot bigger than I first realized. It looked huge and ominous and capable of stamping the life out of me. And Dorothea. Is that what he planned to do? I took a shuddering breath and sent another prayer heavenward.

Brian put the gun barrel against my back and ushered me across the floor. He flipped on the bathroom light. Both of us blinked in response. If I hadn't been temporarily blinded, I might've made a run for the door. By the time the thought occurred to me, both of us could see again and my opportunity had passed. He glanced around the tiny half bath I'd decorated myself using ideas from Pinterest. Apparently satisfied I couldn't get out of the bathroom without going through him, he gestured with the gun.

I scooted past him. "Well…"

"Well, what? Go ahead."

"You can't just stand there."

He exhaled and backed out of the bathroom. "You are one difficult woman."

He pulled the door halfway closed behind him. I went to the commode and put my hands to the snap of my jeans. I looked back at the door. He was still there with his back to me, his hand holding onto the knob. "Could I have a little privacy please? You know I'm not going anywhere."

He exhaled again, louder this time, and pulled the door a few inches toward him. "All the way, please," I called out in my Mom voice. As soon as the words were out of my mouth, I wondered what kept him from leaning in and blowing my brains out.

As the door clicked shut behind him, I thought of the woman who couldn't even stand up to the driver who had plowed into her Toyota. What would Red-face think of me now? He had stopped fighting the citation only after my insurance company threatened to sue him. Even though I was in the right and his negligence had caused the accident, I had been sick with dread at the thought of facing him in court. Now here I was telling an armed home invader who had murdered two people to close the door so I could use the bathroom. What a difference a few weeks made.

I prayed again for peace and comfort until Brian tapped on the door with the butt of the gun. "'Bout done in there?"

I flushed the toilet and went to the sink to wash my hands. He opened the door to make sure I wasn't carving a weapon out of a bar of soap. "Thank you," I said to his reflection in the mirror. Maybe he would find it difficult to shoot a woman with such impeccable manners.

"Now get back in here," he growled.

He didn't move out of the doorway. I squeezed past him and went back to the front room. He motioned to the couch, but I stood my ground. "How exactly is this going to work?"

"You talk too much."

"Actually I don't say enough. I think you bring out the best in me, Gunnar…er, I mean Brian."

The confidence in my voice startled me. My knees and shoulders trembled so hard from fear I could barely stand. I wanted nothing more than to sink to the floor in a blubbering blob and wait for Scott or one of the neighbors to rescue me. That wasn't going to happen. I needed to learn as much as I could about this guy if I wanted to get out of here alive.

"Where are you from? My guess is the Midwest. Milwaukee? St. Louis?"

"We're not becoming friends here, Joy."

"I'm not trying to become friends. I just want to get the whole story straight. Like Dorothea did. How long did it take her to figure out you weren't her nephew?"

He chuckled. "Two days. What is it with the women in this neighborhood?"

My chest swelled a little in spite of my fear. Brian saw me as strong and smart just like Dorothea. I needed to survive so I could tell Scott and my mother.

"Is she all right?" I asked Brian. "You know she's in her seventies."

Lecturing him probably wasn't a good idea, but I couldn't stop myself.

He cocked his head at me the same way Dylan did when I was getting on his nerves. "Don't worry. She's fine. At least for now."

I swallowed hard. I had to know what he meant even though every part of me screamed to remain clueless. "Why didn't you...you know? Do what you did to Gunnar and Kimberly when Dorothea got in your way?"

He chuckled. "Getting rid of you and her will take a little more thought. Gunnar was living a vagabond life in California. No one knew where he was or cared enough to ask questions when he disappeared."

"His parents cared. They loved him. It broke their hearts when he disappeared from their lives."

"Maybe, but don't you figure they were probably a little relieved when he left and didn't come back? Out of the house and out of their hair. Someone else's problem."

The sad part was he was right. With Gunnar gone they could convince themselves he was building a life somewhere—working, in a stable relationship, maybe even starting a family. If they learned of his death, they could find comfort in a belief that he was finally at peace. I wondered if it was the same for Kimberly's family...or whoever she was. I wouldn't ask for details. I already knew too much. I couldn't take knowing she had parents, grandparents, maybe a sister or a friend who would learn today she had been murdered. Whatever life she lived before she got mixed up with Brian Russell was over. A few days ago I hadn't liked her. I thought she was one more person taking advantage of my friend. Now I saw her for what she was, a young woman who had made a few poor choices and paid with her life.

What a waste. Anger at the injustice welled up inside me. Anger at Brian. Anger at the greed and envy and hatred in the world that tempted people to lie, cheat, steal, and kill with no thought of how their actions hurt others and destroyed lives.

I stiffened my aching shoulders. "Scott and the boys will be home any time."

"Nice try. They're visiting your husband's brother in Indianapolis." He smiled at the confusion on my face. "You're not the only one who listens in on other people's conversations. By the time they find your body, I'll be a thousand miles from here."

I suppressed a shudder.

"It should bring you comfort to know they'll finally see you were right. I'm not like them, Joy. I respect you. I knew you were a threat from the word go. I would never take you for granted the way they do. In another life I could've liked you. I know what you're capable of, even if no one else does."

"Do you expect me to thank you?"

"It was a compliment."

"I realize that, but it's little comfort if I never see my husband or my sons again."

He chuckled. "At least you won't have to visit his family anymore."

"That isn't funny."

"Sorry. Just trying to lighten the moment. I am sorry, Joy. I know you don't believe me, but I'm not a sociopath. I don't take pleasure in the suffering of others. I just can't let you stand in my way. Just like I couldn't let Dorothea."

"What are you going to do?"

"You've been upset lately. When you discovered your friend had a heart attack in her home, you couldn't take it the pain. You shot yourself."

I struggled to keep my voice calm. I needed to keep him talking long enough to come up with a plan. "We don't own a gun."

"No, but Dorothea had this old revolver of Albert's." He brandished the gun. "After you found her body, you took the gun and came home."

"No one will believe that. I would call 9-1-1 the instant I found her."

"It was too late. Her body was already cold."

"But her body isn't cold. She's still alive."

"She won't be by the time your family gets home and finds your body. She will have had a day or two for rigor to set in."

"It will never work. I'm a Christian. I have a family. I get mad when the boys leave greasy fingerprints on the furniture. I would never shoot myself. Too messy. I've got a Jane Austen scheduled to record on the DVR. I have Chinese take-out in the kitchen. Scott will never believe I killed myself with General Tso chicken in the house."

"There won't be any left by the time he gets home."

"You're going to eat my chicken?"

He laughed at my indignation. "Of course. I've been smelling it from the moment I walked in the front door."

The nerve of this guy. "Even if I did shoot myself, the authorities will know I died before Dorothea."

He shook his head patiently. "Joy, you watch too many crime dramas on TV. Dorothea's death will be ruled natural causes and yours will be a suicide. Detectives are busy in this city solving real crimes. Scott will tell them how you haven't been yourself lately. You've been paranoid and suspicious of the simplest overtures of kindness. The people at church will back him up. As for Dorothea, seventy-five-year-old women have heart attacks all the time."

I shuddered as a macabre thought occurred to me. "Aidan. What if he finds me?"

"Scott's not a complete imbecile, though I've had my doubts over the last few weeks. He'll realize something's wrong when you aren't at the door to greet them like the loyal spaniel you are. He'll discover your body. Don't fret. He'll come up with something to tell Aidan."

"Is that supposed to make me feel better? You'll never get away with it. They'll know it was you."

He shook his head. "No, if they do think a crime was committed, they'll believe it was Gunnar Westlake. I'm an enigma. I don't exist. And we both know they'll never find Gunnar."

My knees buckled. I dropped into the nearest chair. "What about Dorothea's cruise? I told Scott and everyone at church about your lie to explain her prolonged absence. They'll wonder how she got home. There are no plane tickets on record. She hasn't flown or been away from home. Your alibi has too many holes in it."

He grinned the way he had when he sat next to Aidan on the picnic table—the grin that let me know he was capable of anything. "You're the only one who heard mention of a cruise. There's no evidence of a trip over there. No souvenirs. No luggage in the hallway. They'll assume it was another of your delusions. You haven't been yourself, remember?"

"I'm not the only one who saw your car parked in her driveway. Other neighbors have seen you coming and going for the last three weeks with no sign of Dorothea."

He waved away my arguments. "Again, they'll be looking for Gunnar. They'll probably call his parents to ask about him and tell them about Dorothea. They'll say they have no idea where he is. Believe me, they'll be more excited to hear Dorothea has gone to her eternal reward, leaving them a boat load of money than to worry over Gunnar. They'll be spending their inheritance by the time they get off the phone. They'll be disappointed when they find out the Dodgers' collection is gone, but they'll figure Gunnar has it and wish him well."

My heart sank. I didn't think the people at church would take my and Dorothea's passing in stride as he assumed, but I wondered how much of an investigation would be launched. Scott wasn't the only one who said he didn't recognize me. Mom would probably tell investigators she knew it was a matter of time before I went off the deep end. She was only thankful I did it when everyone was out of town.

Brian had it all figured out. If I didn't think of something I was going to die in this house. I looked around the room. My gaze settled on the fireplace we only used on Christmas and whenever there was a power outage. When we moved into the house, Scott and I talked about romantic evenings in front of a roaring fire. Those only happened a few times that first year. I studied the decorative metal poker in the stand along with a tiny black broom and shovel. A poker was the weapon of choice among movie heroines. It wouldn't do me any good since I didn't have the upper body strength to hurl a kitten across the room.

Brian grabbed my arm and jerked me to my feet. "Time to go. We've wasted enough time talking." He shoved me through the doorway. My shin slammed against the heavy ottoman I had pulled out while I was vacuuming. I staggered and gritted my teeth against the pain. I couldn't let him take me upstairs. I might as well sign my death warrant if that happened.

I twisted my body to relieve the pressure of his hand on my arm. "You put one mark on me and your suicide angle will be hard to prove."

"I don't care anymore. They'll be looking for Gunnar, not me." He gave me another shove toward the stairwell.

I started forward, trying to focus through the pain in my shin and the terror rising up within me. I knew I should pray, but I couldn't form a thought. I was going to die. Aidan would never know the comfort and acceptance of a mother's love. He and Dylan would feel abandoned and not trust another woman as long as they lived. Scott would never forgive himself for going to Indianapolis before we resolved our big fight. I couldn't do that to them. I had to survive.

We moved slowly through the front room and toward the stairs. The front door loomed ahead of me like a beacon of safety. How could I get to it before Brian stopped me? The couch was pulled a little away from the wall where I hadn't completely pushed it into place after cleaning behind it. Could I somehow make him trip over it or something? But we weren't going near the sofa. There was no escape. My only hope was the bruises left by his handprint would alert the medical examiner I hadn't killed myself. Fat lot of good justice would do me in the grave.

I hadn't even got to watch my Jane Austen movie.

I thought of Dorothea across the street, probably worrying and praying for me right now. After Brian got rid of me, he was going over there to finish off my good friend. I had to do something. God wasn't through with either of us. We still had things to do, purposes to fulfill. We were spiritual giants. Our lives couldn't end this way.

Think, Joy, think. Pray.

Movement caught my eye. I nearly wept with relief. Through the narrow vertical window next to the front door, Libby Patterson came into view, propelled along by her annoying little dog. I stared at her and willed her to look toward the house. Dogs were supposed to have some sort of sixth sense in dangerous situations. Maybe Sunny would smell my fear and start barking and alert Libby to what was going on inside my house.

Brian must've seen her too. He tightened his grip on my upper arm until tears came to my eyes. He held me back in the shadows. He put the gun to the side of my head. "Keep your big mouth shut," he hissed in my ear.

I cast my eyes around me. Nothing was close enough to grab in hopes of causing a crash Libby would hear from the street. Even if there was, she'd be little protection compared to Brian and Albert's old gun.

Libby shuffled along the sidewalk. Sunny came to a stop at the edge of our driveway and sniffed my arboretum bushes. Libby glanced around as the little dog made two circles before hiking his leg. I ground my teeth. I knew that little fleabag was the one hiking his leg on my bushes. He walked a little farther into the yard and dropped a package right in the middle of my Black Hills mulch. Libby looked at the window as if expecting me to charge out and accuse her. If Brian and I had been a few feet closer, she could've seen us looking back at her. I tensed, waiting for her to take a baggie out of her pocket to clean up the mess.

Come on, Libby. Be a responsible pet owner and pick up after your dog.

She looked once more at the door. She cocked her head slightly and appeared to fix her gaze on me. Was it possible she could see well enough into the darkened house? The light in the kitchen was on. Did it cast enough light down the hallway to illuminate Brian and me? I held my breath, willing her to see me. Then she called for Sunny and pulled him out of the flowerbed. I watched despairingly as the two of them moved past the door and out of sight.

Brian pushed the barrel of the gun into my back. "Hurry up. Let's get this over with."

I turned toward him so he could see the pleading in my eyes. "You found the baseball collection, didn't you? Take it and go. Dorothea and I won't say anything. No one but Gunnar and his family knew she had it. Geoffrey and Cathy probably think she sold it already for her retirement."

"You do-gooders will never be able to keep your mouths shut."

He shoved me again, harder than before. I staggered off balance and hooked my toe in the carpet runner in front of the door. I thrust out my hands to catch myself. My left wrist twisted painfully as I landed on the floor. Brian grabbed hold of the waistband of my pants. I don't know what he did with the gun, but both hands were grappling to get me back to my feet. I twisted out of his grasp and rolled toward the sofa table. Over his shoulder I saw the vase teetering on the edge of the table. It wasn't heavy enough to hurt him, but I had to try something if I wanted to save Dorothea and my own hide.

Brian was faster and stronger than I anticipated. Before I could get to my hands and knees he grabbed my hips and yanked me toward him. I scrambled for traction on the freshly waxed floor. My hand hit something hard and unforgiving under the table. One of Brian's hands loosened its hold on me. He was probably taking aim with the gun. I lunged under the table and then jumped to my feet. I swung the five-pound dumbbell as hard as I could. It made contact with the side of his head just as he raised the gun.

The dumbbell must've made a noise when it hit him, but I didn't hear anything over the explosion of the gun. Black, deafening pain threw me against the door. In the sudden silence I stared at Brian on the floor and wondered how he got there. The dumbbell lay beside his prone body. Drops of dark liquid spotted the floor.

I killed him. I would go to prison, and the boys would grow up without me after all.

A drop of blood splashed onto the floor. My right hand hung limp at my side. I watched as another drop fattened and dripped off the end of my finger and landed in a tiny puddle on the floor. The blood wasn't coming from Brian. It was coming from me.

Nausea roiled in my stomach. I pushed off the door. Too fast. I froze and waited for the blackness to clear. I spotted the gun in the doorway of the front room. I shouldn't leave it there in case Brian was still alive. But I didn't have the nerve to step over him to get it. He could grab my ankle the way the bad guys always did in movies.

Courage, Joy. You are a woman of courage.

My head swam. I took one giant step around him and kicked the gun as hard as I could. It disappeared under the couch. That would slow him down if he regained consciousness. I threw myself against the front door and fought with slippery fingers to disengage the dead bolt. At shoulder level I saw a ding in the steel door and a surprisingly small circle of blood surrounding it.

My stomach heaved and vision blurred. My blood—my tissue—buried forever in the door I'd painted Carriage Door Red three summers ago.

I had to focus. I couldn't lose consciousness. I heard the wondrous metallic click of the locks turning free. I threw open the door and leaped across the threshold.

"Help!" I screamed for all I was worth. I took a deep breath and bellowed. "9-1-1." I fell to my hands and knees. Pain and blind terror propelled me back to my feet.

"9-1-1!" I repeated over and over as I staggered and lurched across the yard in the direction Mrs. Livingston had gone. I couldn't tell if I was saying it out loud or not. I ran out of steam as I crossed Ben Sanders' driveway. I wasn't sure if his porch light blinked on or if I was looking into the welcoming lights of heaven.

At least the boys won't think I killed myself, I thought as I crumpled in his yard. Darkness overtook me.

CHAPTER 23

Scott and the boys didn't get home until long after the excitement was over. Thankfully Mrs. Livingston had not run blindly back to help when she heard the gun go off but whipped her phone out of the pocket of her running togs and dialed 911. Ben Sanders reached his porch already dialing. Of course I was unaware of any of this until I awoke to paramedics maneuvering my arm into an uncomfortable position.

"Appears to be a superficial gunshot wound," one of them said.

I didn't understand a lot of the words used in emergency situations, and the pain medication made it difficult to concentrate, but I clung to superficial and thanked God through gritted teeth. Superficial, though, I quickly learned is not synonymous with pain free.

Dylan ran his hand gently down the length of my bandage. "This is so cool. None of the other guys' moms have ever been shot. You rock."

"I'm glad I finally did something to impress you."

He leaned over my hospital bed and carefully encircled me with his arms. "Aw, Mom, I've always been proud of you. When you get home, can I bring Craig and Seth over to look at your wound? Do we have to lance it or anything?" His gray eyes sparkled.

"Dylan!"

Scott stepped forward and took hold of Dylan's shoulders. "Okay, son. I think your mom's had enough excitement for one day."

"Make that for a lifetime," I corrected.

Dylan leaned forward and kissed me. I couldn't remember the last time that had happened. I wrapped my left arm around him and held him in place for a moment. Ordinarily he would pull away and tell me to get a life. This time he turned his head and rested his cheek against mine.

"I love you, Mom. I'm sorry I've been such a spaz lately."

I turned my face and kissed his bristled cheek. "I love you, too, Dylan."

Scott cleared his throat. I think he just wanted to rid the tears in his own throat before he spoke. "Dylan, why don't you go out and talk to your grandma and Uncle Chris? I'd like to have some time alone with your mother."

"Gross." Dylan turned up his nose, but he was smiling.

I waved and blew him a kiss with my left hand and then turned to Scott. "Where's Aidan?"

He eased down on the edge of the bed on my uninjured side and took my hand. "He's with Valerie and Peyton at our house. They followed us here from Indy. They were almost as worried about you as Dylan and me. You were asleep when we got here. That was a couple of hours ago. Some people from church have been in and out too. The waiting room's full of your entourage."

Tears stung my eyes. "Really?"

He nodded. "I told them you won't be ready for visitors for a few days, but nobody will go home."

I couldn't hold the tears in check. "That's so sweet."

He squeezed my hand. "Your mom has been the best. She beat the ambulance here. She talked with the doctors and got the details straight for me when I got here. Do you remember seeing her?"

"I don't remember anything after I ran out of our house."

He gave my hand another squeeze before putting it to his lips. Tears spilled down his cheeks. I couldn't remember the last time I saw him cry. I squeezed his hand in return. He stroked my cheek with his free hand while we looked into each other's eyes. I still couldn't believe it was over.

"What did you tell Aidan?" I finally said.

"Just that you had a little accident and we needed to come home. He wasn't that disappointed to leave early." Scott kissed the back of my hand again. "Neither was I. It wasn't any fun without you."

I pointedly rolled my eyes. "Oh, please. You and Chris probably didn't even notice I wasn't there."

Genuine hurt creased his brow. "Don't say that, Joy. I mean it. The ride was no fun. The boys played on their tablets the whole way. No one laughed at my tired jokes about passing landmarks the way you always do."

"You have it pretty good, don't you?"

He stood up and leaned over the bed. He brought his forehead to within an inch of mine. I braced myself for the pain of impact against my shoulder, but he was careful not to lean into me. Tears shone in his eyes. I never doubted my husband loved me, even when he was distant and Mom kept insisting all men cheated. Until this moment I couldn't remember seeing it etched so clearly in his expression.

"I'm so sorry, Joy-bell. I'm sorry for everything. I've been a colossal jerk. I don't deserve you. None of us deserve you. When your mom called last night…" He straightened and took a shuddering breath.

"It was the scariest moment of my life. If something would've happened to you…" He didn't finish the sentiment.

"But it didn't."

He gazed at my shoulder as if wanting to transfer the injury from me to him.

"I should've listened to you. You warned me over and over that something wasn't right at Dorothea's. As usual, I didn't give your concerns any credence. You know Dorothea well enough to know something was wrong. I shouldn't have argued with you about Dylan. You were right about that too. You were right about everything. If we'd have come home and found you…"

"Scott, stop. Stop blaming yourself and stop talking so much. You're making my head hurt."

"Oh. I, uh, I'm sorry."

I squeezed his hand and pulled him back onto the bed. "Honey, please, it's all right. None of this was your fault."

"I talked to the police when I first got here. They said you were amazing, figuring out who Brian was. A reporter tried to come in, but the nurses ran him off. After they positively identify Kimberly's body and tie her back to Brian, every reporter in town will want to talk to you."

I put my hand to the side of my head. The slightest movement around my head and shoulders sent my pain meter through the roof. "I don't want to talk to anyone. I just want to go home."

Scott pushed my hair away from my face. "You will as soon as the doctor says you're able. You had a busy day yesterday. From what I hear, you gave Brian a pretty good wallop with that dumbbell." He smiled admiringly.

I smiled back. "It was the toughest workout I've had in a long time."

He shook his head in disbelief. "Brian Russell. I'm still amazed you figured out he wasn't Gunnar."

"Dorothea figured it out first. That's why he locked her in the basement. He needed to search the house without her in his way."

"Poor guy didn't know what he was up against when he came into our neighborhood."

I smiled at his praise. Brian had said pretty much the same thing, but I wouldn't tell Scott. Not yet. Someday I'd give him the entire blow-by-blow account. I didn't think he was ready for it at the moment. I didn't feel like talking about it either.

"Have you seen Dorothea?"

He nodded and gestured toward the ceiling. "She's one floor above us. I went up to see her after I looked in on you."

"How's she doing?"

He shook his head again in admiration. "She's a trooper. She's a little perturbed they made her stay last night. Since Albert was Chief of Surgery here, they're treating her like royalty. You know there's a wing named after her. No way were they going to let her go home."

"Good. I hope she lets them do their jobs."

"I'm sure she will. She's Dorothea Westlake. Gracious to the core."

I closed my eyes and leaned against the pillows. The only other times I'd been in a hospital were when the boys were born, and those were joyous occasions. This wasn't much of a celebration. I was happy to be alive, but I wanted this day to be over.

I felt Scott lean in close. "Are you all right? Do you need me to call the nurse?"

I opened my eyes and smiled softly at the concern on his face. I reached out and clasped his hand. "I'm okay. Just tired. And sore and headachy and a little freaked out about everything."

Scott stroked my cheek again. I couldn't remember the last time he couldn't stop touching me. It was nice. "I'm so thankful you're okay." His voice was hoarse as if moments away from breaking down. "I love you, Joy. You're my world."

"Do you mean that?"

"Of course."

"Good." I took a deep breath. I needed to get some things out in the open. Now was the time to take advantage of his generosity. "I've been lying here in and out of consciousness thinking about Gunnar. The real Gunnar, and what his family went through for him. I keep drawing the same conclusion."

"What's that?"

"Dylan has to move out." I braced myself for the reaction that came every time I tried to talk about where we'd gone wrong with our son.

Scott lowered his head and nodded. "I've been thinking the same thing."

I nearly fell off the bed. "You have?"

"He's had it too easy for too long. Valerie and Chris and I talked about it for a long time."

I groaned. I would've rolled my eyes if it didn't hurt so much.

"It isn't what you think," he said quickly. "We weren't blaming you. It's all on Dylan. He needs direction. If he wants to keep living under our roof, some things are going to change, starting now."

My head was beginning to pound. I wasn't sure if the medication had worn off or if my husband's revelation was too much to handle. "Are you giving in to me because I could've been killed?"

He squeezed my hand. "No. We talked about it even before we got the phone call from your mom. After spending the whole day with him, Chris saw firsthand what you've been saying all along. He said Dylan acts more like a high school freshman than a kid who should be in college. I guess I saw it too. I just didn't want to face it. I shirked my responsibility as Dylan's dad and spiritual leader of this family. It was easier to hope the situation would work itself out than try to do something to make it right."

I pulled my hand out from under his. I liked what I was hearing, but it wouldn't work without a plan of action. Dylan was going to feel sorry for me and treat my nicely for about fifteen minutes. Then life would go right back to the way it always was unless Scott and I didn't allow it to happen. I wasn't going to bear the load on my own. Nor would I put it completely on Scott's shoulders like I threatened the other night.

"What exactly are we going to do to make it right?"

For a moment he looked uncertain. My heart sank. More talk. More rhetoric that wouldn't change a thing.

He took a deep breath and looked me in the eye.

"The first thing I'm going to do when I get home is take his laptop, as well as his phone, Ipad, and any other device that allows him to go online."

I sucked air around my teeth. "That isn't going to earn you very many points for Dad of the Year."

He didn't smile. "It can't be helped. I had no idea he had pornography on that computer. That's no excuse though. I should've checked periodically. I completely dropped the ball on that too. After the computer's gone, he and I are going to sit down and have a nice long talk. I'm going to take care of everything before you come home. This won't be your headache, Joy, I promise you that. Chris thought Dylan really liked the work at his office, even if he spent most of the day fooling around. We both believe spending the summer up there, going to work every day and not having you to push around, will go a long way in helping him grow up. If he doesn't want to do that he'll either get a full time job here in the city or become a full time student. No more playing around. Aidan has more responsibilities than he does."

We looked into each other's eyes for a long moment before he leaned forward to kiss my forehead. "I'm sorry it took me so long to see it, Joy."

I felt a huge weight lift off my shoulders. Scott had taken responsibility. Our son wasn't "fixed". We had a long road ahead of us, but at least the burden was no longer mine to bear alone. I exhaled audibly in relief.

"The boys and I are going to church tomorrow," Scott said. "As long as they live under our roof they'll be expected to join us for church every Sunday. Dylan will be excused for work, should he ever get another job, but that's it." He sliced through the air with his hand and sat back on the bed looking like he'd closed a major account.

My heart puddled. There was the Scott I remembered.

"I'm so glad to hear you say that, honey," I told him. "We have to follow through no matter how hard Dylan makes it. I don't want to lose him the way the Westlakes lost Gunnar. You should've heard Mrs. Kinnamon talk about him. She could've been saying the same things about Dylan. It's too late for the Westlakes. They've lost Gunnar forever."

I blinked away tears. I wondered if they knew yet.

"I don't want to lose Dylan. I'm ready to do whatever it takes, become as unpopular with him as we need to be in order to save him. I have a confession to make. A couple days ago I thought he was beyond redemption. I was ready to give up on him."

I glanced past Scott to the door. Scott followed my gaze and then looked back at me. I lowered my voice and leaned toward him. "Sometimes I don't like him."

Scott chuckled. "You want to know something? Neither do I. Does that make us bad parents?"

"No, just lazy ones. We let this happen. It took his whole life, but we let him think the world revolved around him. It's going to be hard to change that mindset. It'll be even tougher not to repeat the same mistakes with Aidan."

"It won't be hard now that we know what we're doing and we're in it together."

I laughed at the seriousness on his face. "We're only about nineteen years late on figuring it out."

He laughed back. "You know what they say; it's never too late."

He reclined onto the bed and settled his chest against me. I snuggled against him as much as my bandages and stiffness would allow. It felt nice being in my husband's arms, transferring the stress and frustration of the last nineteen years onto him. It wasn't fair to expect he fix everything, just like it wasn't fair of him to expect me to be the bad guy all the time. If our family was going to work the way God designed, we both needed to accept our responsibilities.

I wanted to maintain our position, but my shoulder was getting sore. "If we're going to be a team, there are a few other things we need to figure out."

We carefully disengaged. I leaned back into the pillows, exhausted from the simple embrace. Scott sat up and looked down at me, confusion on his face. "Whatever you want, sweetheart."

For a while there at the house, I didn't know if I was going to get away from Brian."

Scott set his mouth in a firm line. "I don't want to talk about it, Joy."

"We have to, Scott. It's important. I've learned a lot about myself in the last few weeks. I've learned a lot about us, about our marriage."

"What about us?"

"My biggest fear was the boys would think I killed myself. That was Brian's plan. He said everyone thought I wasn't being myself lately and they'd believe I committed suicide. The sad part was he was right. For the most part, I don't think anyone really knows me."

Scott looked about to interrupt. I hurried on. "The only person I feel like who knows and accepts me the way I am is Dorothea. If Brian had his way, he was going to kill her too."

"Joy, I—"

I gave my head a hard shake. "No, Scott. You don't know me. You think you know me, but you don't. Not really. I'm not the Joy you married. I was a kid back then. I didn't know what I wanted. I didn't know who I was, and I let you and my mother define me."

He opened his mouth to interrupt again, but I kept going, determined to get it out. "Not anymore, Scott. The only one who will define me from now on is Jesus and who I am in him. I'm tired of being weak and ineffectual and taken for granted."

"When have I ever taken you for granted?" he exclaimed, forgetting for a moment he was thankful I was alive.

My jaw dropped. "Are you kidding? You take me for granted every day of my life. You never take me seriously. You don't respect my opinions. You don't realize I might have something of value to say."

"Maybe I don't take you seriously because you've never stood up for yourself. Not with the kids, with your mom, at church. Not even with me. How do you expect anyone else to take you seriously when you don't do it yourself?"

"You don't see me as a thinking, intelligent adult."

"No. We don't see you as an adversary. Before the other night I don't think you and I ever had a toe-to-toe fight in all our years together. You would give me your opinion, and as soon as I shot it down, you backed off and agreed with whatever I wanted. If my business partner did that I wouldn't take him seriously either. I probably never would have become partners with someone so insecure in the first place. People disregard what you have to say because you don't believe in it yourself."

I wanted to defend myself. That wasn't true anymore. I possessed a new confidence, not in myself, but who I was in Christ. The last few weeks had proven I could do anything as long as I fully trusted God to bring me through it. Brian could've killed Dorothea and me. That bullet could've gone through my neck instead of my shoulder. If it had, I would still have victory in knowing Jesus loved me and would use me for a greater purpose if I had the courage to stand up and say, "Here I am, Lord. Send me."

I studied my husband for a moment. I could tell he was worried he'd said too much. He was trying to be nice because I was hurt, but this was probably the most important conversation we'd ever had. I wouldn't end it just because it was getting difficult to hear. "You're right, Scott. I sat back and allowed everyone to dismiss me. But I won't let it happen anymore. Our marriage should be a partnership. That doesn't mean we need to come to blows every time we plan a vacation."

He snuggled closer and put his hand on my neck under my hair. "I wouldn't want it like that either. I don't want to fight and scratch and turn everything into a battle. I don't want you to try to earn my respect by screaming and clawing for it. You get it by respecting yourself. By acting like what you say is of worth."

"Maybe I never thought it was before."

He kneaded the muscles on the back of my neck. I couldn't remember the last time he'd done that, if ever. A stirring warmed deep in my belly, something I hadn't experienced in a long time. "I'm so sorry I made you feel that way, Joy-bell." He leaned closer again. The scent of shaving foam and mouthwash that was distinctly Scott filled my nose.

I shifted under his hand. "I need more from you than to be treated like your wife," I said quietly.

He pulled back. "You are my wife."

"I want more than that. I want you to think of me as more than someone who washes your shorts and has a meal on the table every day at six."

"What's wrong with that? I thought it's what we both wanted."

"It is what I want. I have no problem being at home with the boys while you go to work."

He exhaled in frustration. "Then what are we talking about?"

This wasn't coming out the way I wanted. I didn't mean to complain about the laundry and cooking dinner. I didn't mind doing those things. I wanted to do them for my family, but not because it was expected of me. Still, none of that mattered right now. I just wanted Scott to see me as more than a housekeeper and babysitter.

I pulled away from him and stared at the ceiling for a moment. I could feel Scott's gaze on my face. He was probably wondering if I had taken a blow to the head after I was shot. I wasn't making sense, not to him and not even to me.

Lord, help me make him understand.

I brought my gaze back to his. "I want you to get passionate with me once in a while. I know you're capable of passion. I've seen it when you watch sports or talk about work or argue with your brother."

"Passion? Is that what this is all about? You want to go on a second honeymoon?"

I fought down the urge to scream out loud. "I'm not talking about sex, Scott. Well, not entirely. I want you to get passionate about us. I've never seen the passion, the zeal, you display toward everything else in your life directed at me. With me, you're like a dead fish."

He dropped his hands and moved away from me. "Way to boost a guy's ego, Joy."

The distance between us seemed like a gulf I'd never bridge. "You still don't get it. Everything in our house is 'Yes, Joy.' 'No, Joy.' 'We can't afford it, Joy.' 'Why did you let that happen, Joy?' You treat me more like a well-liked housekeeper than a wife."

Pain and confusion dropped onto his face like a mask. "That's insulting. I treat you like a queen. Don't I give you whatever you want? I never say a word about the Macy's bill or the clothes you buy and never wear. Don't we always go where you want for vacation?"

"Only because you don't want to deal with planning something else. But that's not what I'm talking about." Blood pounded against my temples. My stomach churned. I probably shouldn't have gotten into this conversation right now, but I couldn't stop with only half of what I wanted said. If things were going to change they needed to start with me. I couldn't back off from making my point when things got tough. I needed to get everything out in the open.

Scott was staring at me as if the medication was doing the talking, not his sweet demure wife who never raised her voice or caused a stir. This wasn't Joy. Brian had done something to the real Joy, and things would be just peachy as soon as she came back where she belonged. I hated to tell him that Joy

299—Joy Redefined

wasn't coming back. Not the Joy everyone remembered. This was the new and improved Joy. I had redefined myself, and my family was going to have to get used to it.

I put my hand to the side of my head and took a steadying breath. "This isn't about money, Scott. It's about respect. It's about you treating me like the woman you want to spend the rest of your life with. Not because I'm a decent assistant who would be hard to replace, but because you need me. Because you can't imagine the void in your life if I were gone. Because your heart would burst open with grief if something happened to me."

His shoulders slumped, and tears filled his eyes again. "Joy, that's exactly how I felt when I heard what happened with Brian."

"It shouldn't take a crazy person holding me at gunpoint to get your attention. What is it going to be like next month or next year when you know I'll be there when you get home from work with dinner on the table and the bills paid."

"That's not why I love you."

I started to give him a pat answer I knew he wanted to hear. The answer that deep down he probably did feel though he hadn't shown me in twenty-one years. "Maybe not, but you've gotten used to the way things are, and I think you like it. I was so busy wanting to be a Proverbs Thirty-One woman I didn't tell you what I needed. I thought meekness meant being your doormat."

He stiffened.

I held out my hand to stop his interruption. "I'm not saying you've treated me like a doormat. But when I was in the house with Brian, I realized if something happened to me, you'd miss me for all the wrong reasons. You'd miss me for the readjustments you'd have to go through and you'd miss me for the boys' sake. But I don't think you'd toss in our bed and stain our pillows with your tears. Not because you don't love me. But because you aren't passionate about me the way you are everything else in your life."

Scott dropped his head to his hands. His shoulders slumped, and I thought he was crying. I resisted the urge to apologize. I'd been doing that for too long. He needed to hear how I truly felt. I couldn't blame him for not understanding what I needed if I never told him what it was.

When he looked up, his eyes were glassy. "Joy, I would miss you. Not for those things you said, but because I love you. I thought you knew that."

"I know you love me, Scott, and I love you. But there are a lot of things missing in our marriage. Things other couples have that I want. I want more than to cohabitate and raise our kids in peace. I want passion, friendship. You know your suits are going to be in the closet facing due west and your dinner will be on the table at six and reservations will be made before we check into a hotel. I know you won't complain about the bills or an unexpected expense. But that makes a good boss, not a good husband."

He still looked confused. "I thought that's what a good husband was. A good provider. A loving, caring, generous man who puts his family's needs before his own. My father did all that, and my mother never complained."

"That's what your father did when he was on your side of the bedroom door. That's what you saw. But I'm sure there was more to it than that. I'm sure your dad respected and cherished your mom and let her know he couldn't get along without her. Maybe you never heard your mother complain because she was a good mother. Or maybe she didn't have anything to complain about because the instant the bedroom door closed, your dad let her know he loved her and needed her as something other than a cook and bottle washer."

"I do need you, Joy." His voice cracked. He reached out slowly to stroke my cheek as if he was afraid I'd pull away. I didn't.

"I need you every day," he said. "I've never looked at another woman since the day I met you. I don't make suggestions or off-color remarks like some of the jerks at work. You're the only woman ever on my mind."

My heart melted as I looked into the eyes of the Scott I fell in love with. The gentle, loving Scott who made me feel like the most beautiful woman in the world. But if there had ever been a time to get real with what I wanted from my husband, it was now.

"You can say the words until you turn blue, Scott, but I need you to show me. I need to see the passion in your eyes. I need to feel it on my skin. I need you to burn for me."

His jaw worked for a moment before he could make any words come out. "I never knew that stuff mattered to you."

I growled deep in my throat. "Trust me, it matters. I'm a woman first. Always a woman first."

He brought his face to mine. There was no missing the tears in his eyes. He blinked, and a tear slid down his cheek. "I failed you, Joy. I failed both of us."

I shook my head, and our faces moved in unison. "Life's too short to live with past regrets. I don't want to waste another minute of our life together."

"Neither do I. Show me what I can do to make it up to you."

I encircled him with my left arm and closed my fist in his hair. "You're a big boy, Scott. I'm sure you'll think of something."

He smiled. His gaze deepened. "I love you, Joy, and I need you. Always as a woman first."

"That's all I need to hear."

He put his hand on my face and stroked my cheek with his thumb. I couldn't remember the last time we shared a moment of such tenderness. I missed my husband. I missed the intimacy of our early years together. I hadn't realized how much until this moment. I wanted to say something, to put into words how much he meant to me and how much I regretted the distance that had grown between us. I could tell by the look in his eyes he already knew and felt the same. Tears pooled in my eyes. He rested his nose against my cheek.

"I love you, Joy-bell," he whispered so softly I almost didn't hear. "I don't know how I could've gone on without you."

I turned my face to his. "I'm glad you don't have to."

Our lips met. A soft groan sounded in Scott's throat as the kiss deepened. Familiar footfalls sounded in the doorway. Mom cleared her throat. Dylan grunted in exaggerated revulsion.

"You people are disgusting."

Chapter 24

I stayed home Sunday morning while Scott and the boys went to church with Chris and Valerie, Garrett and Peyton. Mom usually attended her church in Loveland, but joined the others this morning after coming by to check on me. She had been surprisingly compassionate and loving since my encounter with Brian. I had half expected her to blame me for getting shot. Instead, she was understanding and gentle. For the first time in my life I felt loved and accepted by my mother. It was nice. I tried not to question how long it would last.

I spent the morning on the couch in sweat pants, watching TV evangelists while I waited for my family to get home from church. Those guys had gotten a bad rap over previous decades. There were some really good ones on, and I enjoyed the smorgasbord of teaching themes and techniques between frequent medicated naps. Someone had cleaned my blood off the front door and out of the hallway while I was in the hospital. The police had removed the bullet from the door, and a guy was coming Tuesday to replace it. I didn't tell Scott, but I almost wanted the door to stay the way it was, bullet hole, tissue, and all. It was tangible proof I could handle anything. Better than that, I didn't need to. God had been with me when Brian's bullet missed my neck and spinal column by inches. A shoulder wound was uncomfortable and limiting, but at least I could walk and feed myself.

Just before one o'clock the kitchen door opened and Aidan's shriek of "Mommy!" startled me out of another nap.

Scott appeared in the doorway behind him, two Boston Market bags in hand. "Easy, buddy. Mommy's still sick."

We still hadn't told Aidan what really happened over the weekend. We probably wouldn't until he was much older. He had liked Gunner/Brian, and I didn't want to do or say anything that would make him afraid of people. He screeched to a halt two paces in front of me and studied my bandaged shoulder. "When are you going to be better, Mommy?"

I pulled him into a careful hug with my left arm. "I'm getting better every day, Lima Bean."

"But it will be weeks before she can play with you on the floor or do all the work she's always done around here." Scott arched his eyebrows pointedly at me.

My heart warmed at the concern on his face. He had taken a family medical leave from work to stay home with me. He wanted to make sure I didn't try to put away toys or run the sweeper or wash a dish. I wasn't allowed to lift more than five pounds on my left side and nothing at all on my right until I went back to the doctor. Scott had even spent last night on the couch for fear of jostling me or making me uncomfortable in bed. I missed him beside me, but I hadn't slept so well in years. I was pretty sure the drugs had something to do with it.

Noise from the kitchen drew Aidan out of my arms. Scott raised the bags in his hands. "Dinner is served, my lady. May I escort you to the dining room?"

My heart filled again. I wondered if I would have ever realized how much I loved my husband and family if Brian Russell hadn't entered our lives. Scott looked like he was thinking the same thing. He shifted both bags to one hand and put an arm around my waist as we walked together through the kitchen and into the dining room.

Mom saw me first. She came over and put her hands on my cheeks and pulled my face to hers. "You're looking better already, Joy. Doesn't she look better, everyone?"

Accent sounded around the room. "Thanks, Mom." I returned her kiss and sat down at the table in my usual spot. It felt strange to sit and watch while someone else set the table, poured drinks, and made sure Aidan and Peyton washed their hands before they took their seats. Strange but nice. The special treatment wouldn't last so I planned to enjoy it as long it did. After I was cleared for active duty, I knew life would return to normal soon enough.

Valerie leaned around me on my left side and set a chocolate cake on the table. "I know you like these," she whispered conspiratorially.

Unexpected tears stung my eyes. I didn't remember telling her Boston Market's chocolate cakes were a favorite guilty pleasure I seldom indulged in. I looked across the table at Scott. Perhaps he told her. He returned my gaze with a blank expression. He probably didn't even know. Valerie must've noticed the way I devoured one at her house.

"You must've been reading my mind this morning," I told her.

She nudged my good arm with her elbow. "They're my favorite too."

"Then we'll share."

"You should probably share with everyone, Joy," Mom said from her side of the table. "Just a slice of that thing has more calories than the rest of the meal."

So much for enjoying my guilty pleasure. It was almost a relief to see things going back to normal so quickly.

Valerie patted my hand sympathetically before taking a seat next to Chris. Scott's lips tilted upward. I smiled back. Somehow Mom's words had lost their sting. She was right. I needed to lose some weight. Brian had proven that when he dropped me on Dorothea's stairs. But it would be by my terms.

My sister-in-law had done something nice for me, and I was going to enjoy a wedge of cake regardless of the calorie count.

Aidan and Peyton dominated the dinner conversation. The adults had been so distracted the last few days, the kids had been pretty much left to their own devices. I didn't know about Peyton, but it was going to take some creative parenting to get Aidan back into a routine. I was glad Scott would be here to handle it.

The Boston Market containers contained little more than crumbs when Dylan set down his fork. "Mom, Dad, I've been thinking."

"Uh oh."

"Watch out."

"Here we go."

He kept his eyes on me while he waited for the teasing to abate. "I think I might like to spend the summer with Uncle Chris and Aunt Valerie."

"And do what?" I asked gently though I pretty much knew what he would say.

He took a deep breath as if he'd been holding in the announcement for some time. "I really liked working in his office the other day. I know I sort of acted like a jerk, but if they'll let me," he looked anxiously at Chris, "I'd love an opportunity for the internship…if it's still available."

Next to me Scott exhaled in relief.

"I'm sure we can work something out," Chris said.

"In the fall, I want to register at the University of Cincinnati as a fulltime student."

It took all of us a moment to regain our balance, me longest of all.

"For now I think I'll register undeclared, but I'd like to take a variety of classes. You know, to see what sticks."

I wanted to go around the table and kiss him, but I was too unsteady from shock and muscle relaxers. Scott rose out of his chair to slap Dylan's shoulder. I gave everyone else time to congratulate him before I spoke up. "Sounds great, baby. Your dad and I will be happy to go over brochures with you and help you see what's available."

"Thanks, Mom."

He gave me a smile that hadn't been directed at me since he was in preschool. It was love, mixed with trust, kinship, and respect. I could get used to it. Even Aidan and Peyton remained quiet while Dylan and I looked at each other, a million words unspoken but the distance shortening between us nonetheless.

Mom set down her fork with a solid clink against a china plate. "I must say it's about time you took some initiative, Dylan. I'm glad to see you're not as much like your mother as I thought."

Dylan's smile faded.

She turned to me. "This might be the push you need, Joy. With Aidan getting older and Dylan leaving the nest, you might be inspired to think about doing something with your own life."

Scott straightened in his chair, ready to jump to my defense. A few weeks ago it's exactly what I would've wanted him to do. Now I was totally capable of defending myself, though in this case I didn't have anything to defend myself against.

"This is my last year with Aidan before he starts kindergarten. Maybe I'll go back to school or look for a job after that. Or maybe I won't. All I know for sure is I'm going to spend the next year putting puzzles together and learning colors and shapes with my preschooler and living vicariously through my college bound son."

Aidan pumped his fists in the air. "Yay, Mommy."

Mom stiffened. "I thought you were going to enroll him in that pre-K program at your church and finally do something for yourself."

"I *am* doing this for myself. I want to be selfish with my little guy a while longer."

"If you're sure that's what you want, Joy," Scott put in. "If you want to go back to school, we'll figure out a way to make it happen."

I shook my head. "I don't want to go back to school, at least not now. College will always be there if I want it. The boys won't."

Mom exhaled. "I don't know why you're being so stubborn, Joy. You heard Scott. If it's the money I'm sure I can request a few more hours at work." She sighed and cast her gaze around the table. "It won't be the first time I've sacrificed to make things easier on you."

My patience thinned. I didn't want to go back to the same feelings of inadequacy and contention. I had been sheltered in a cocoon of peace that surpassed understanding since the moment I realized God was the only one who could help me and Dorothea get away from Brian. I wasn't willing to let it go.

"Mom, I'm not asking you to sacrifice anything. My life might not be the ideal situation for everyone, but it's my life, and I love it. Isn't that what you always wanted for me?"

For a moment my mother was at a loss for words. She looked at Scott for reinforcements, and then Chris and Valerie, but they offered none.

Finally she looked back at me. "All I've ever wanted is for you to be happy." I think she really meant it.

I reached over and covered her hand with my left. "I am happy, Mom. Don't worry. Aidan and I are going to have a wonderful year. Maybe we'll learn a second language. Or design a rocket ship."

Aidan whooped in delight.

Everyone laughed.

"Or we'll make mud pies and get dirty and spend every day at the park."

He whooped even louder. The doorbell rang at the front of the house. Instinctively I prepared to rise. Scott shook his head and put his hands on either side of his plate. Dylan beat him out of the chair.

"I got it," he said on his way out of the room.

"I was just trying to help," Mom told all of us.

I wondered if she had been controlling me for so long she didn't know how to be truly helpful. I didn't say that. It might take some time, but she would get used to the redefined Joy who stood up for what she wanted instead of taking the path of least resistance. Mom and everyone else would see I was capable of independent thought and not worried if everyone liked me or was happy with me.

"I appreciate it, Mom," I said honestly, "but I know what I'm doing. For the first time in my life, I know what I want and I'm going to make sure I get it."

"Good for you," Valerie said with gusto.

I smiled at her. It looked like the two of us could actually become friends. I'd been so busy comparing myself to her tiny waist and perfect hair, I'd never noticed she could be warm and funny and considerate. If I really wanted to redefine myself, it was time I put my feelings of inadequacy toward her behind me.

I wiped my mouth on my napkin and pushed back in my chair. I was amazed at how unsteady I still was. Scott hurried to help me up. With one hand on my shoulder and the other under my elbow, he leaned in and whispered. "I'm proud of you, Joy-bell."

His warm breath tickled my skin. "I'm proud of me too," I whispered back.

"Dorothea's here," Dylan said from the doorway.

Dorothea followed Dylan into the room. "I didn't mean to interrupt your dinner. I just wanted to get a peek at Joy before I went home." She looked at me. "I know you're not up to visitors yet."

She didn't know how ready for visitors I was. "We're just finishing up. Would you like some dessert? Valerie brought me a chocolate cake from Boston Market." I smiled warmly at my sister-in-law.

Dorothea put her hand on her stomach. "I couldn't eat another bite. Marge Kepinstall took me to lunch. All she talked about was what a hero you are. Besides, I wouldn't dream of infringing on your favorite dessert."

She knew me as well as I knew her. I circled the table and kissed her cheek. "I'm so glad to have you back."

She squeezed my left elbow. "It looks to me like you did fine without me."

"Maybe so, but I never want to be in that position again." I took her arm and steered her toward the family room.

"Is there anything I can get you ladies?" Scott asked as he began to clear the dishes.

Dorothea shook her head. I smiled gratefully. "No, thanks. We're fine for now."

Dorothea went to the family room ahead of me and plumped some pillows on the corner of the sofa for me to lean on. I sat down gingerly. She lifted my feet and adjusted them on the ottoman. When I was situated and angled toward the other end of the couch, she sat down and smiled knowingly.

"It looks like your nurse has a crush on you."

I smiled as heat rushed to my cheeks. "He's been very sweet through this whole thing."

She sniffed. "It's about time. I haven't seen you two look at each other that way since, well, since as long as I've known you."

My blush deepened. "Before...before Brian I sometimes wondered if Scott would notice if I was gone. I know he loves me. I just needed to know he needed me too."

She cocked a thin, white eyebrow. "Now you know?"

"Oh, yeah." I leaned forward and straightened my sweat pants around my ankles so I wouldn't have to look at her. It felt strange to admit something so intimate to Dorothea or even to myself. My relationship with Scott had become so chaste over the years, even before Aidan was born. I could only hope our new passion and appreciation for each other would last beyond his initial shock over my possible death.

Dorothea, wise as she was, read through my discomfort. "Passion doesn't have to fade from a marriage. It can last as long as you're breathing if both parties are willing to work at it."

"Is that experience talking?"

She didn't blush or break eye contact. "I never was one to kiss and tell. Just take my word as a more experienced woman in the Lord. Abraham and Sarah started their family when they were nearly a hundred. Abraham had many more children after Sarah died. Don't tell me there wasn't a little passion going on there. As long as you and Scott are alive you'll have each other. Don't let kids or work or stress of keeping the bills paid come between the joy God created for a husband and wife to share. It's what makes all that other stuff worth doing."

I covered a giggle with my hand. She was right of course. She always was.

I leaned forward and grasped her hand with my left one. Using my left hand was becoming more instinctive, but it was still awkward and unnatural to have my right arm immobilized at my side. "I missed you so much over the last three weeks. I didn't realize how much I've come to depend on you. I felt like part of me was missing while you were in that basement."

She tilted her head. "The worst part about it was knowing how much you'd worry."

How much like Dorothea to worry about me when she was the one in danger. "How did you figure out Brian wasn't the real Gunnar."

"Probably the same way you did. He didn't know things Gunnar should've known. His mom, I mean Cathy, had sent a few pictures of Gunnar in elementary school. Every time I mentioned bringing them out, Brian changed the subject. I didn't think anything of it at first, but that coupled with the other little things he said and did, I knew he wasn't my nephew."

"Is that when he put you in the basement?"

"He said he couldn't have me in the way while he was searching for the rest of the collection. So he came up with that story about me going on a cruise." She grinned and patted my hand. "I knew you would be the only one to realize something was wrong. After the first few days Brian let me go upstairs at night to take care of myself. I tried to leave little clues for you in case you got inside the house. Things he wouldn't notice but you might."

"Like putting my picture in Aidan's frame on your fridge."

She laughed. "I know how much you hate that picture. If it didn't jump out at you, nothing would."

"You are so clever."

"Not always. At first I was selfish. I spent the first week praying Brian wouldn't kill me. I knew he had done something to Gunnar. He couldn't have come here without first making sure the real Gunnar didn't show up. I prayed a natural disaster would force rescue workers to evacuate the neighborhood. Anything to make someone search the house. After a while I began to pray for Brian. He needed the Lord in the worst way. After Kimberly came I prayed for her too."

I shifted one of the sofa cushions under my right arm. Sitting was the most comfortable position, but it didn't take long for the pressure on my shoulder to make my arm feel like a hundred-pound weight. Dorothea watched closely to make sure I didn't need anything before going on.

"I knew it was illogical for Brian to keep me alive, especially after he admitted what he'd done to Gunnar. Not only did I know what he was capable of, I had become a liability. The night Kimberly disappeared…" A shiver twitched her shoulders, and she wrapped her arms around herself. "About an hour after I heard her storm out of the house, I heard the Crown Vic start up in the driveway. Brian was gone most of the night. When he got back he parked the car in the garage and never drove it again. I didn't ask what happened to Kimberly. In my heart I knew, but I didn't have it in me to hear him admit it."

We sat quietly for a few moments thinking about Kimberly and Brian and what could've happened to us if things had worked out differently.

With my left hand I adjusted my right arm on the pillow. "I was hiding on the porch that night. It was dumb I know, but I thought if I got some concrete evidence I could make someone do something to find you."

Dorothea's face tightened. "I hate to think you put yourself in danger like that for my sake."

I laughed and gestured at the bandage encasing my right shoulder. "Lurking on your porch listening to what could've turned out to be a lovers' quarrel seems like small potatoes after everything else."

She smiled in return. "I suppose. Just don't ever do it again." She patted her white hair into place. "I don't believe God was responsible for bringing Brian here to hold me hostage and ransack my house, but he used it to accomplish quite a lot. Most importantly, I got to witness to Brian for three weeks. I'm so thankful he didn't die when you bashed him on the head with that dumbbell. God was working on him the whole time. He just didn't know it. Now that he's not trying to get rich on the work of other people, he'll have plenty of time to consider everything I told him."

I hugged my right arm against me as I angled my body toward her. "You amaze me, Dorothea."

"No, dear, God is amazing. Without him, I would've been scared to death. I understand now how confinement can drive a person out of her mind. For the most part, it wasn't so bad. Brian had some serious issues in his life, but he was always gentle with me. The danger was great, but I felt peace the moment I put the situation in God's hands and stopped praying for my own safety. I knew he would do a work. Even if I died, I wanted to make sure he got the glory in the outcome by witnessing to Brian. He needed to know someone cared about him. I don't know if he ever had that."

Tears pricked my eyelids. I thought of when Brian threatened Aidan after following us to the park. I had never been so scared or angry in my life. Even now knowing he was safely behind bars, it rankled me how he used my baby to manipulate me. I shouldn't hate him either. Jesus would expect me to extend the same gentle love and forgiveness to Brian that

God had shown me. I didn't know what Brian had faced in his life. Still, I was angry he used Aidan to get to me; that he told me how he planned to get rid of Dorothea and me; that he killed Kimberly and pushed her car into the river; that he murdered Gunnar Westlake who didn't know how to keep his mouth shut.

I tightened my grip on my arm as a jolt of pain shot through my shoulder. Scott would be in any minute with my next dose of painkillers. He had kept an eye on the clock since the doctor released me yesterday and made sure everything was done exactly as prescribed.

My throat tightened. "When Brian put his arm around Aidan that day on the picnic table or when he threatened you and me with that gun, I sure didn't care whether or not he'd been hugged enough as a kid. He held our fate in his hands. How could you have cared more about his spiritual well being than your own life?"

Dorothea's once vibrant blue eyes had faded to a dull gray over the years. They sparkled with love and patience as she gazed at me. "I didn't want him to kill me, but if he did I already knew where I was going. I was terrified for him for where he would go if something didn't happen. But it did."

"What happened?" Impatience laced my voice. I wanted to go lie down. I didn't want to sit here and listen to how misunderstood Brian must've been to shoot me in order to get at Dorothea's baseball collection.

"You happened, Joy. You rescued both of us. If not for you, he might've killed me and then been killed in a shootout with police. You saved him physically and spiritually."

I stopped kneading my arm, the pain momentarily forgotten. I was happy to save my own hide with nothing worse than a sore shoulder and my sons' respect. Was it possible God had used me for a much greater work?

"I just wanted to get out of there alive."

Dorothea chuckled and leaned forward to pat my knee. "You've never given yourself enough credit. You're stronger than you think. You were strong enough to see through Brian's ruse and you were strong enough to stand up to him."

I thought of Red-Face who had run into my car. The whole accident seemed to have happened to someone else. I wondered how I'd react today if someone slammed into my car and tried to pin the blame on me. I hoped I would be patient and gracious and not fault finding. Hopefully I would rest in knowing God was in control, and if things didn't work out exactly the way I wanted, I'd be okay nonetheless.

It wasn't the accident that changed me. Or the month without Dorothea to lean on. Or even getting shot by a man who had already killed two people. It was learning to completely trust in and rely on God for every aspect of my life. It had taken me thirty-nine years to grasp it. I wasn't on my own. In my weakness I was made strong through him. Not by my own devices or standing up for myself, but knowing God was in my corner, whether fighting with an insurance company for my rights as a consumer or defending myself against a madman.

I was never alone.

I didn't really feel any stronger than I had last month, but a lot had changed since then. A month ago I worried more about how people would react if I stood up for myself than if I was being treated fairly. What skewed logic. Trying to keep a hundred balls in the air had kept me from being who I was—the woman God designed me to be. I was no longer the mouse who strove to remain in the shadows. I had something to say, something worth contributing, and I would make it known when I knew I was right.

I looked at Dorothea. "I wasn't strong enough to accomplish anything on my own."

Her smile widened. She scooted closer until she was perched on the edge of the couch beside me. She clasped my good hand between hers. "It takes a strong, wise woman to accept that."

"A Proverbs Thirty-One woman?"

"Exactly." She rested a cool hand on my face and kissed my cheek. "I'm proud of you, Joy. I'm proud to call you my friend."

My vision blurred as tears pooled in my eyes. No one had ever told me that before. Over Dorothea's shoulder, Scott stepped into my line of vision with a vial of pills and a glass of water. He watched for a moment before backing out of sight.

Dorothea and I sniffed noisily and dabbed at our eyes. She reached across the coffee table to pluck a handful of tissues out of a box. We smiled at each other as we blew our noses and pulled ourselves back together.

I glanced toward the kitchen to make sure Scott wasn't lurking in the doorway, then leaned toward her and lowered my voice. "Whatever happened to the baseball collection? Brian said it was worth millions." I wasn't much of a sports fan and hadn't even known the Dodgers were originally from Brooklyn. But even I was intrigued by a baseball card worth a quarter of a million dollars.

Dorothea chuckled. "The collection wasn't as big as Gunnar led Brian to believe. I don't know if Gunnar exaggerated its worth or if Stephen had exaggerated it to him."

I nodded thoughtfully. None of it really mattered now. The collection had torn a family apart and filled everyone involved with bitterness, regret, and greed. Gunnar, Kimberly, and even Brian had paid the ultimate price.

"Most of the cards are worth less than ten dollars apiece," Dorothea explained. "Now that limited edition Jackie Robinson rookie card is worth a hefty sum, though I haven't done any research on it in years." She leaned back and waved one hand in the air. "Don't even get me started on the autographed 1955 World Series baseball."

I groaned. "Brian didn't get his hands on it, did he?"

She shook her head. "He knew better than to put his fingerprints on anything. Not only to avoid getting caught but also to keep the pieces in mint condition. He treated that collection gentler than most people treat a newborn baby. The police found everything packed in bubble wrap in a suitcase in my bedroom."

I knew it was gauche to ask, but I had to know. "What are you going to do with the collection? You know, when you're gone? Gunnar told Brian you probably planned to leave everything to a museum."

She laughed. "I might. I thought about sending a few things to Albert's alma mater. He would've liked that. I also thought of giving something to Dylan and Aidan. They're like the grandsons I never had."

I gasped. "Oh, no, don't do that. Aidan would lose the ball in the gutter and Dylan would sell the cards for gas money."

She laughed harder. "I wasn't going to do it tomorrow. It's just a thought. For someday."

I exhaled. "I'm so relieved. I couldn't take the pressure of having something that valuable in the house. Knowing me, I'd end up using the Declaration of Independence as a coaster."

Dorothea wagged her finger at me. "No more derogatory talk, Joy. You're a lion, remember?"

It wasn't the first time she told me that. But I was a lot closer to believing it than I had been three weeks ago. I was still a long way from the perfect example of a Proverbs Thirty-One woman I wanted to be, but I was no longer intimidated by another woman's dress size. Nor was I the mom who turned a blind eye when she saw her child behaving recklessly.

If I wanted to take that final step and live a life truly pleasing to God, I needed to forgive Brian. Anger and bitterness would destroy any chance I had at peace and contentment. Gunnar's grandfather had proven that. Instead of nursing the anger toward his father for giving the baseball collection to Albert and poisoning Gunnar's mind, he could've enjoyed a close, loving relationship with his brother. The last three weeks could have been avoided and Gunnar might still be alive.

Maybe Dorothea was right, and God had used me to help Brian come to an understanding of his love and redemptive power. The biggest shock of all was how God used Brian to redefine me. Forgiving him wouldn't be easy. The mother in me still wanted to scratch his eyes out for threatening my baby. But the Proverbs Thirty-One woman I strove to become would make forgiveness possible.

Before Brian Russell and the Brooklyn Dodgers, I would've hidden under the covers, mired in fear and resentment. Now I was anxious to see how the new Joy would react to whatever curveball life threw at her next.

The End

Don't go yet. If you enjoyed **Joy Redefined,** please take a moment to let others know what you think.

Consider leaving a review on Amazon, Good Reads, your personal blog, or any other site that accepts reviews. Follow me on FaceBook and Twitter. Join my mailing list at www.teresaslack.com to stay up to date on upcoming books, enter contests, or just to stay in touch.

I love hearing from readers so drop a line anytime.
teresa@teresaslack.com.

About the Author

Teresa Slack enjoys reading, writing, and sticking her nose into other people's business. Naturally, writing fiction was the perfect career choice for her. Her first novel, *Streams of Mercy*, won the Bay Area Independent Publishers' Association award for Best First Novel. *Evidence of Grace*, the third in her Jenna's Creek Series, debuted at #18 nationwide according to Christian Retailing Magazine. Her down-to-earth characters and realistic dialog have endeared her to readers and reviewers alike.

Teresa and her husband share their southern Ohio home with two rescue dogs. Besides several home improvement projects demanding attention, she runs a Scentsy business and is a field representative for the U.S. Department of Commerce. She is also crazy busy at work on her next novel.

Learn more about Teresa and her books at her website www.teresaslack.com or follow her on her Facebook author page. Like all writers, she loves hearing from readers. You can contact her at teresa@teresaslack.com. Find more of Teresa's books on her Amazon author page.

Made in the USA
Coppell, TX
19 August 2024

36207711R00177